Praise for

C.E. MURPHY

and The Walker Papers series:

Urban Shaman
"A swift pace, a good mystery, a likeable protagonist,
magic, danger—*Urban Shaman* has them in spades."
—Jim Butcher, bestselling author of The Dresden Files series

Thunderbird Falls
"Fans of Jim Butcher's Dresden Files novels and the works
of urban fantasists Charles de Lint and Tanya Huff should
enjoy this fantasy/mystery's cosmic elements. A good choice."
—*Library Journal*

Coyote Dreams
"Tightly written and paced, [*Coyote Dreams*] has a
compelling, interesting protagonist, whose struggles and
successes will captivate new and old readers alike."
—*RT Book Reviews*

Walking Dead
"Murphy's fourth Walker Papers offering is another gripping,
well-written tale of what must be the world's most reluctant—
and stubborn—shaman."
—*RT Book Reviews*

Demon Hunts
"Murphy carefully crafts her scenes and I felt every gust of wind
through the crispy frosted trees.... I am heartily looking forward
to further volumes."
—*The Discriminating Fangirl*

C.E. MURPHY

SPIRIT DANCES

BOOK SIX: THE WALKER PAPERS

LUNA™
www.LUNA-Books.com

LUNA™

Recycling programs
for this product may
not exist in your area.

SPIRIT DANCES

ISBN-13: 978-0-373-80325-5

www.LUNA-Books.com

Printed in U.S.A.

This one is for Matrice,
who has been waiting for it for a long, long time :)

CHAPTER ONE

FRIDAY, MARCH 17, 8:34 A.M.

"Walker, Holliday, you're up. Homicide in Ballard, probably domestic violence. Be there yesterday." A set of sedan keys flew across the room at my head. I caught them painlessly, only because I'd just come in the door and hadn't yet taken my gloves off. The guy who'd thrown them at me—our lieutenant, Braxton, who was decent, hardworking, and who never impinged on my consciousness for a single moment beyond those I spent following his direct commands—jerked his jaw at the door, indicating we should already be gone. I did a quick dance of shedding my coat, shrugging on my duty weapon—an item which, like Braxton, lay outside my realm of active awareness except when I was actually at work—and pulling the coat back on before my partner made it to the door.

Because my desk was three steps from the door, I got

there first, and that meant I won: I got to drive. After nine months of that game, I wasn't sure why we bothered, because neither of us pretended Billy was the better driver. Not that he was a bad driver, mind you. It's just that it was the only class at the academy I'd been too proud to come in anything but first.

He caught up to me and muttered, "I hate domestic cases," as we headed out the door.

"I know." Nobody liked them, which was part of why Billy and I were up on this one. Braxton tried to rotate the DV cases through the whole Homicide team, because under the best of circumstances, they were emotionally messy, and under the worst—which was more usual—cops ended up the bad guys no matter what they did. "Could be worse. At least a murder means there won't be an outraged spouse trying to beat us off because her partner didn't really do anything wrong."

"Walker, are you seriously telling me murder is preferable to a live victim who doesn't want to press charges?"

"That wasn't what I meant." It was, however, kind of what I'd said. No wonder I let Billy do most of the talking at crime scenes. We drove over to Ballard while Dispatch offered a few more details on the homicide we were approaching. There was a pattern of abuse in the family, instigated by the wife, one Patricia "Patty" Raleigh, against whom the city had twice pressed charges. She'd done anger management courses and then a short stint in jail. We weren't sure yet if it was herself or her husband, Nathan, or possibly both, who was the victim: one of their children had run out of the house, bloody and screaming hysterically about Mommy and Daddy being dead. The neighbor had called it in.

Billy left his coffee untouched as the information came in,

muscle in his jaw bulging like flexible stone. "I *hate* domestic cases."

"I know." There was nothing else to say. I pulled up along the curb in front of the Raleighs' ranch-style home a few minutes later, and we got out of the car. It wasn't a wealthy part of the city, the houses mostly from the fifties and sixties. They tended to look careworn, with sagging fences, older tricycles and swing sets in small front yards. A few houses stood out as having been renovated: fresh paint, new roofs, lawns trim and shipshape even though winter was only just letting go its grip.

The Raleighs' house wasn't one of those. I glanced over it, then met the eyes of a broad-boned black woman standing in the next yard over. She had two kids with her, both white, both huddled against her strong form. Her hands were on their chests, over their hearts: protective, like a mama bear. She was probably the neighbor who'd called in the 273D, and the kids were probably Nathan and Patty Raleigh's. I nodded to her once and she nodded back, then retreated to her front porch, taking the kids with her. She'd been letting us know where they were, and now planned to stay out of the way until we needed them and her. Most people intimately involved with a murder weren't that clearheaded. I chalked it up to equal likelihoods that she was involved or that she was very sensible, and followed Billy up the driveway to the house.

He paused at the door, an eyebrow lifted at me. I gave him a nod much like I'd just given the neighbor, then let the Sight filter over my normal vision.

Truth was, though normal investigative homicides like this one made up the bulk of our work, Billy and I weren't partnered because we were good at solving run-of-the-mill cases. We were partners because he saw dead people and

I was a shaman. A healer, basically, though I had a wider range of talents than that. Together we made up Seattle's one and only paranormal detective team, and even on a mundane case, there was no reason to let our esoteric skills go to waste.

The world viewed with the Sight was something of a wonder to behold. Everything shone with purpose, rich aura colors making light of the most ordinary objects. Newly budding leaves on trees thrummed with brilliant blue-green threads that would become bluer as they grew, until they were vibrant with life pouring through them. Houses, buildings and fences tended to radiate a resolute green, a pride in protecting the things they held. Everything, living or inanimate, had purpose, and I could See that purpose when I looked with shamanic eyes.

I could also See people's auras, even through walls, which was unusually handy in clearing a house for entry. There was nothing living inside the Raleighs' house, though a bright orange shimmer said a housecat was probably in the backyard hunting early-season bugs. A crawl space beneath the house would've been a better choice for the cat: plastic tarp down there kept the earth warm and I could See the squirms of potato bugs and other such small things doing whatever it was bugs did. The attic was quieter than that, not so much as a squirrel hiding out. I nodded to give Billy the all-clear.

He knocked anyway, as was polite, and introduced us loudly before trying the doorknob. It turned, to neither of our surprise: if the kids had come running out, they weren't very likely to have stopped and locked the door behind them. And an inSightful all-clear or not, we both went in like we were entering hostile territory, because God forbid I should be wrong and we should fail to follow protocol.

Our boss—Morrison, the precinct captain, not Baxter-the-forgettable—would rip us apart if we did.

Nathan Raleigh was just inside the door, a late, macabre addition to an otherwise low-key, attractive living room. He hadn't been dead all that long. His color was still fading, but there was a remarkable amount of blood soaking into the pale blue carpet. Billy and I exchanged glances, then Billy tipped his head to the left, indicating he'd check out the room through the next doorway, barely two steps away. I nodded and edged forward just far enough to keep an eye on him. There was a short hallway in front of us, down which I guessed were bedrooms, which I couldn't let go uncovered while he checked out the open-plan kitchen and second living room to our left.

He said, "Clear," after a few seconds. "Doorway to my right."

"One to my left here, too." We knocked our respective doors open, winding up on opposite ends of a T-shaped bathroom, guns pointed at each other. Billy crooked a faint grin, then stepped into the top of the T, putting himself exactly opposite me.

A short brunette woman came through the door behind him, a nail-spiked baseball bat already descending toward his skull.

I shot her.

CHAPTER TWO

Time slowed down in crises, for me. I wasn't sure it was possible to drop into actual bullet-time, like in *The Matrix*, but I swore I saw the bullet's spin and the percussion blast as it slammed into Patricia Raleigh's right shoulder. Blood misted out. She screamed. The bat's downward momentum was knocked far enough askew to no longer threaten Billy. He hit the deck anyway, flipping on his back to bring his weapon up defensively, finger still on the trigger-guard.

Mine was still squeezing the trigger. My throat hurt, though I couldn't remember yelling. I knew I should have. *Drop your weapon!* or *Police!* or something like that. Maybe I'd said both. In protocol terms, it mattered. It mattered very much. In real-world terms, it mattered a lot less: my partner had been under attack, and shouting was never going to stop the bat from bashing into him. One shot, a good one, had been enough. Good thing, too. I'd never shot another human being before. I wasn't sure I could do it again, even for a double-tap to make certain Billy would remain safe.

Patty Raleigh staggered a few steps backward and fell over.

My belly erupted with pain, diamond claws digging in and hauling my insides apart as the core of my magic went to war with what I'd just done. I dropped my gun and limped forward, one arm curled over my stomach. I paused next to Billy, who hadn't yet moved, cords standing out in his neck and breath coming hard. He jerked his gaze to me, then nodded, one sharp movement to say he was okay. Nausea that I interpreted as relief swept through the pain in my gut, and I kicked Patty Raleigh's baseball bat—it was already bloodied, the nail thick with matter I didn't want to examine—farther away before kneeling at her side.

There was no exit wound spilling blood onto her pale blue carpet, which meant the bullet had lodged in her right clavicle. A very good shot, then, because the impact and lodgment would have knocked her farther off balance than a clear shot through the muscle would have. In terms of preventing a nail from taking up residence in Billy's head, I couldn't have done better without killing her.

Which I hadn't. She was still breathing, though the inhalations were shallow and shocky, and her eyes were glazed with pain. The wound technically wasn't life-threatening, but that made less difference than people thought, with shooting victims. Shock or sepsis did them in. The human body was not meant to stop small metal objects traveling at 850 feet per second, and tended to react poorly. Patty Raleigh might very well die with me kneeling beside her.

Of course, I could prevent that from happening. Or at least, I could in theory prevent it. My stomach was still a mass of twisting pain, every bit of magic I'd ever commanded turning black and red with its own kind of septic shock. My fingers were too thick to bend, my hands frozen and stiff. I put one on Raleigh's shoulder and applied pressure, disquieted at the heat of her blood. She gurgled, more disturbing than a scream, and I thought if anything should unlock the healing magic I carried within me, it should be that sound.

Nothing happened, not a rush of instantaneous healing, not even the far more familiar layered vehicle body work that I'd used as my healing imagery for most of a year. I was no more use than any ordinary person, putting pressure on a bleeding wound. "Billy."

He started talking as I said his name, calling in the shooting, requesting an ambulance, requesting backup: all the things I'd been going to ask him to do. Intellectually I knew he was on the ball, that it had been barely ten seconds since Patricia Raleigh had swung the bat at his head, but I felt encased in ice, like everything was still happening at a glacial pace. Shock, just like Raleigh was in.

Billy said, "Don't move," to me, and went to clear the rest of the house. I should have thought of that. I should have thought of a lot, except I couldn't think of what else I might have done. Patty hadn't been in the house—hadn't been on the property—when I'd examined it psychically. Either that or she could batten down her aura like nobody I'd ever met, but I really didn't think so.

There was an open sliding glass door beside us, making up the back wall of the living room. She'd clearly come through it, but where she'd been before that, I had no idea. The cat I'd Seen was still pouncing around the backyard, intent on capturing a moth.

"Clear." Billy came back from the bedrooms and crouched beside me, face grim with concern. "You okay, Walker?"

"Yes. No. I can't heal her."

To my utter surprise, he touched my right cheek. I had a scar there, thin and mostly invisible, a remnant and reminder of the day my shamanic powers had exploded to life. "You couldn't heal this, either. Some things aren't meant to be fixed."

"But I did this." My belly cramped again and the words came out tiny and painful.

"Maybe that's why you can't undo it. The paramedics will be here in a few minutes." He was silent a few seconds, then put his hand on my shoulder, squeezing. "You saved my life."

I wanted to make a joke. Just a small one, something about *I had to or your wife would kill me,* but I couldn't. I couldn't at all. I only nodded, a jerky little motion like he'd given me a minute earlier. He offered a heartbreaking smile in return, like he understood exactly what I couldn't say. "Keep pressure on that wound until the ambulance arrives."

It was a very sensible order. It made me feel like I was accomplishing something, when we both knew the truth was I couldn't have moved if I'd wanted to. If I'd had to, yeah, probably. But short of somebody else coming out of the woodwork to kill Billy, no, I was stuck there on my knees next to Patricia Raleigh for the interim. I nodded again, and Billy went to the front door to await an onslaught of cops, paramedics, forensic examiners and, inevitably, Michael Morrison, captain of the Seattle Police Department's North Precinct, and our boss.

I was sitting on the front steps, holding gun and badge loosely in my hands, when he came up the driveway. Any cop involved in a shooting had an automatic three-day suspension, so Morrison didn't have to ask: I just handed the weapon and badge over. Patty Raleigh's blood was under my fingernails, and Morrison noticed it as he accepted them. He checked the chamber and magazine—I'd already unloaded it—then tucked the gun into an empty holster under his suit jacket before asking, "What happened?"

I knew I should probably stand up and make a brisk report, but instead I stayed seated and outlined the incident in as few words as possible, mostly staring at Morrison's belt while I did so. "Paramedics took Raleigh away about three minutes ago. She'll probably live. Billy's, uh. He's inside, heading up the investigation on Nathan Raleigh. He thought it was better if I…"

Morrison nodded, only partially visible from my viewpoint angle. Then he sat down beside me, wooden porch creaking with his weight. "So what happened?"

I looked sideways at him. He wasn't looking at me, gaze focused on the fence or the street beyond it, but he didn't have to be looking my way for me to feel the weight of his concern or his determination to get an answer. I put my hands over my face, realized they smelled like blood, and dropped them again to stare at the street just like Morrison was doing. "I couldn't heal her. I couldn't…"

"I've seen you use shields to protect people. Why didn't you stop her that way? Put one up around Holliday?"

Christ. Morrison, who liked magic even less than I did, would still be a better practitioner than I was. "I didn't think of it. This wasn't a paranormal case. It was a domestic homicide. I don't usually bring the whole shooting match to the day job. She was there, she had a weapon, I had a weapon, I shot her. And now my gut feels like I ate a box of fishhooks and the healing won't respond. And if I was anybody else you wouldn't be wondering why I used my Glock .40 instead of magic."

"That's true. But you're not anybody else." Morrison

exhaled, and I dropped my head again, though I kept my fingers laced together in front of my knees, not wanting to breathe in the scent of blood a second time. He was right. I wasn't certain he was unconditionally right, but the power within me had always put forth some pretty clear ideas on what I should and shouldn't do. The wrenching pain in my stomach and the lack of response from the magic both told me flat-out I'd chosen poorly.

"I'm supposed to be on a warrior's path, you know that?" I asked the stairs beneath my feet. Morrison *didn't* know, because I'd never discussed it with him. I didn't discuss it with many people, much less the boss with whom I had, until quite recently, had a distinctly antagonistic relationship. "That's what I was told right when all this started. That I was a healer on a warrior's path. That I was going to have to fight to make things right. But there's no memo. There's no handbook saying 'these are the circumstances you get to fight in.' Instead what happens is something like today. Or back with the goddamned zombies. God, I hate zombies. Anyway, I always find out the hard way that I can't use the magic offensively or it craps out on me. Now it turns out if I use ordinary real-world physical force on ordinary real-world people, I get bit in the ass for that, too. I know you don't think I'm the greatest cop in the world, but I followed protocol. I did the right thing in police terms to protect my partner. Didn't I?"

My voice got small as I recognized there were probably a million people it'd be better to say this to than Morrison. Unlucky for him, he was the one who'd asked what had happened, and unlike the psychologist I knew I'd have to talk to later, he was aware of and believed in—however reluctantly—the occult side of my life.

"There'll be an investigation before I can properly answer

that, Walker," he said with unusual gentleness. I put my face in my hands again after all, holding my breath to avoid the smell of blood, and startled when he touched my shoulder. "But yes, it sounds like you did." His voice went wry. "And no one else will be asking why you didn't use a magic shield instead of a gun. I just wondered."

"I don't know if I'm ever going to think of the magic first, Morrison. Most cases don't need it. I'm…" I trailed off with no real idea of what I wanted to say, and Morrison got to his feet.

"You're officially suspended from duty pending an investigation into this shooting, Walker. A minimum of three days. Thanks for not making that difficult. You have an appointment with the psychologist at one. Get somebody to bring you back to the precinct building and get cleaned up. I want to see you when you're done talking with her."

I whispered, "Yes, sir," and went to do as I was told.

Being suspended from duty for three days almost certainly meant "go home once you're cleaned up," but although I only lived a few miles from the precinct building, back-and-forthing seemed like a waste of time. I had clothes at work—the blue polyester pants and button-down shirt that were ubiquitous to police officers everywhere—so I showered, put them on and went back to my desk in Homicide. There was paperwork to do, not just for the morning: there was *always* paperwork to catch up on. It was a damned sight better to work than sit at home and brood. One of the other detectives came by to offer me a green armband, which was his way of offering sympathy for the morning's incident without making a fuss about it. I put the armband on, glad not to have gotten pinched, and spent the next three hours writing reports, filling out forms and trying hard not to think about Patricia Raleigh's glassy stare and short, shallow breaths. Mostly it worked, except when I had to write the actual incident report, and then I sat there a long time, wondering why I hadn't responded the way Morrison suggested I should have.

Well, no. Not really wondering. I'd gone to the police academy, and though there'd been three solid years of working for the department as a mechanic before I became a cop, at the end of the day, I'd been trained to react the way I had. A couple of times during the academy I'd awakened from dreams I didn't remember, kneeling in the middle of my bed in a firing position. That kind of training became hardwiring, and nothing I'd done in the past fifteen months had driven magic-using responses that deep into my brain. There was, as far as I knew, no such thing as shamanic boot camp, much as I could use it.

Knives prickled at my gut again, suggesting that I really *could* use a shamanic boot camp, or something else that forced me to react with magic first and brute force later. Either that or it was sheer nervousness, as it was a few minutes to one and I had an appointment with a shrink. I abandoned my desk and went upstairs to her office, heart hammering and hands cold for the second time that day. I'd met the psychologist, talked with her a few times, but never officially, and for some reason it was terrifying.

She took one look at my expression when I came in and said, "Don't worry, everybody feels that way the first time. I promise it won't hurt a bit. Louise Caldwell, not that you don't know that." She offered a hand, I shook it, and we both sat down as she asked, "How're you doing?"

"Been better." A shrink probably expected a deeper, more profound answer than that. I held my breath, sought something more profound and came up with the same thing again, this time as a shaky laugh on an exhalation: "Yeah. Been better."

"Good," she said crisply. "You'd be surprised how many people walk through that door after shooting someone and say they're just fine. Did you have a choice?"

I blinked, taken aback at the no-nonsense approach. I thought psychologists were supposed to pussyfoot around things. Not that Dr. Caldwell looked like the pussyfooting sort: she was in her late forties, gray streaks at her temples probably indicative of carefully dyed hair, and dressed in a well-tailored suit that gave an impression of seriousness. I cleared my throat, wondered if that came across as hesitating and shook my head. "I really don't think so. There was no warning. Detective Holliday stepped into the bathroom and she was behind him, already swinging the bat. If I hadn't reacted immediately he would be badly injured, maybe dead."

"And how do you feel about that?"

"I'd sure as hell rather have shot her than have Billy be in the hospital! Especially since she's not dead." I cleared my throat again, pretty certain that was entirely the wrong thing to say, but faint humor flickered across Dr. Caldwell's face.

"That's a comparatively healthy attitude, Detective. It's easy, in a bad situation, to accept only blame instead of seeing the other potential side of the scenario. As you say, she isn't dead. Was that a deliberate choice?"

"No. It was just the clearest shot I had, her right shoulder. Billy dropped, but I didn't double-tap. That…that was deliberate. Kind of. I don't know if I could've shot a second time." I looked away from her, focusing on one of half a dozen framed certificates on the wall, and much more quietly said, "I could have if she'd kept coming. I would have. I don't think I knew that until right now."

My stomach twisted again, glass shards jabbing at me, but somehow the knowledge made me feel better in a completely screwed-up way. Police officers almost never had to shoot anyone in the line of duty even once, much less twice, but I was darkly certain I could do it again if I had to. I didn't want to, but there was probably something wrong with somebody who *wanted* to go around shooting people. I relaxed a little and Caldwell saw it, but apparently it was okay. She kept me there for over an hour, asking questions that eventually had me weary to the bone, but I walked out feeling like I hadn't completely fucked up, either at the scene that morning or there in her office. I had no idea what she would tell Morrison, but I was too tired to worry about it.

I went by his office as instructed, but he wasn't there. I dropped off my incident report, then went back upstairs to Homicide to collect my coat. At some point "suspended from duty" had to mean "go home," and I was emotionally wrung out enough to decide that point was now. Morrison could kill me for disobeying the come-see-me order later, after I'd napped. Coat in hand, I waved a short goodbye to the rest of the team and headed for the door.

It cracked open before I got there, revealing a sliver of a woman in her fifties. She had an exceedingly mild blue gaze and short hair that had at one time been blond, but had since gone dirty yellow. She was dressed eclectically in a long skirt, a wool overcoat with a reflective vest over it and combat boots. There was a sparkly green shamrock pinned to the vest. On someone else, the whole outfit could've been deliberate eccentricity. On her it looked like the Army-Navy surplus store.

I fumbled to make sure my own green armband was in

place as I tugged the door all the way open. "Oh, hi, sorry, come on in. I'm Detective Walker. Can I help you?"

"Detective Joanne Walker?"

I looked over my shoulder like I expected another Detective Joanne Walker to have appeared, then shook myself and looked back. "That's me. Can I help you?"

A smile rushed across her face and took ten years off her age. "My name is Rita Wagner. You saved my life."

CHAPTER THREE

There was nothing like a statement of that nature to take one's mind off the problems at hand, especially when the problem at hand was nearly the polar opposite. My brain dropped out of the slightly shocky slow motion it had been lingering in all day and surged into its more usual mouthy overdrive.

I had done a variety of remarkable things over the past year. Many of them had involved saving peoples' lives, although most of the time they had looked more like shutting down Seattle's power, rearranging the Lake Washington landscape, or wrestling monsters of differing sizes and shapes. In the handful of cases where I'd actively saved someone, I usually knew what they looked like.

I'd never seen this woman before in my life. I was searching for a nice way to say that when she continued, "You probably don't remember. Officer Ray Campbell told me it was you, though, who got the ambulance there in time to sa—"

She kept going, but I said, "Oh! You're the troll lady!" over her, and only too late realized how awful that sounded. I didn't mean it badly. It was just that she'd gotten in trouble down by the Fremont Troll, one of Seattle's more charming landmarks, and I'd never learned her name. I'd only saved her life. I'd been three miles away at the top of the Space Needle, looking for something else entirely, when I'd Seen a flare of rage and violence in Seattle's city-wide aura. Because of that, the cops had gotten there before aggravated assault turned to murder in the third degree.

She was still smiling. "I am. I'm the troll lady. I know it's been months, Detective Walker, but I wanted to thank you. I—"

Feeling a little desperate, like I'd become a bad host by way of not recognizing the troll lady, I blurted, "Would you like to sit down?" with too much emphasis on the last two words. I sounded like something dire would happen if she didn't. A wince crawled over my whole body, caving my shoulders, and I tried for a more modulated tone: "Or go for coffee or something? I mean, it's great to meet you, but the department's not very comfortable, we could take a few minutes to talk, we—" I wished someone would come along and stuff a sock in my mouth.

Instead Rita gave me another astonishing smile. It really did take years off her face, and I wondered if she was a hard forty-something instead of the fifties I'd originally pegged her as. "If you have time, I'd like to have coffee. You don't know me, but I feel like I owe you something. At least a cup of coffee."

I said, "You don't," under my breath, but it didn't matter to either of us whether she legitimately owed me something or not. I was grateful as hell to get hit in the face with evidence of having done *well*, and even if I hadn't been, I also wasn't callous enough to say "Just doing my job." Even if that was true, when you'd saved someone's life, regardless of the madcap fashion, there was an element to it that ran deeper than just doing the job. Humans were like that. We needed connections and stories to make sense of the world, and Rita Wagner had become part of my story. "There's a terrific coffee shop up the block."

"The Missing O? I saw it, but I thought it was a doughnut shop."

I tugged my coat on, hiding the green armband. "It is, but it has good coffee, too, and we call it a coffee shop as to not perpetuate the stereotype of cops and doughnuts." My indulgence in the stereotype, now that I thought about it, was probably responsible for five or so pounds that had crept up on me the last few months. I made a note to buy vegetables, even though I knew they'd end up melting into brown slime in my fridge's fruit bin, and held the door for Rita. We escaped the precinct building a minute later, me holding the door for her again. "Not to be rude, but why now?"

"Because I didn't think you'd like me very much straight off," she said forthrightly. I did a classic double-take, the second glance offering me a glimpse at her aura as the Sight washed on without my conscious command. That, as much as her mood-altering arrival, was a relief: the soured magic inside me wasn't so intent on punishing me for my misdeeds that I couldn't use the Sight. Rita's colors were mostly brown, earthy and steady, with prickles of yellow poking through. The prickles were nervousness: she was afraid I'd judge her. Or maybe that I'd judge who she'd been three months ago.

It clearly wasn't necessary. She was doing a fine job of bringing down judgment on herself. I said, "Why not?" with genuine curiosity, though I already had a pretty good idea of the answer.

"I was a drunk living rough and fighting over booze and drugs. I smelled like beer and piss and figured I'd die soon and nobody would care."

I said, "Someone always cares," very softly, though I was sadly aware it wasn't quite true. Still, Rita gave me a quick look that turned into another one of her de-aging smiles. For someone who'd been living on the brink of extinction only a few months earlier, she sure seemed to smile a lot.

Then again, maybe she had reason. "I wouldn't have agreed with you, the day I got stabbed. I'd have said nobody ever cares. I had blood leaking through my fingers. I could see it freezing on the ice. I knew I was dying, Detective Walker, and I figured that made me one less problem in the world."

We reached The Missing O as she said that, leaving a nice dramatic moment to pick up from once we'd ordered coffee and doughnuts. Or, more accurately, a hot chocolate with mint for me, pumpkin-spiced tea for her and frosting-covered cinnamon doughnuts called pershings, which were as big as my head, for both of us. Mindful of being in polite company, which was to say someone who didn't put up with me daily, I tried very hard not to lick the frosting off my pershing like a six-year-old while Rita picked up her story again.

"I still have dreams about the ambulance. All the sirens and lights. I was bleeding a lot and it all seemed loud and bright and I got the idea it was God sending angels to say 'Not this one, not yet.'" She picked up her tea, hiding behind it as she gave me a wary, hopeful look. "Does that sound crazy?"

Thoughtful as always, I said, "Yes," then made a face. "Sorry. I've heard much crazier things." I'd *done* much crazier things, but I didn't want to get into that. "They say God works in mysterious ways. Ambulances and cops aren't even all that mysterious, when you get right down to it."

Her eyebrows, which were almost nonexistent, twitched up. "Do you believe in God?"

Man. There was a question I didn't want to contemplate, much less give an answer to. I exhaled noisily into my hot chocolate and stared at my doughnut for a while. "Not by nature, no. But there's a lot more out there than is dreamt of in my philosophy. I know that for a fact." Because fifteen months ago I hadn't believed in magic at all, and these days I was a regular practitioner. Which was something else I wasn't about to lay out for Rita Wagner.

"Me either. Not by nature. If I believed in God at all, it was to have someone to blame. But Officer Campbell said you'd called in the attack before you even got there, and that sounds a lot like a miracle to me. I thought if somebody's putting out a miracle for me then maybe I'd better get my shit together. The hospital got me into an AA program and I'm doing volunteer work at a shelter." She finally put her tea down, though she kept her hands wrapped around the cup. Her fingers were thin and sallow, like they'd been frostbitten. "So I thought now was a good time to see you. I thought now you could be glad you saved me."

Hot chocolate went down the wrong way and I coughed. "I was pretty glad before." My boss and partner had been gladder. I'd been too fixated on the thing I'd been trying, and failing, to do, to be sufficiently impressed with myself for saving someone from halfway across the city. Yet another data point Rita Wagner probably didn't need to know. I chewed my lower lip, not wanting to be condescending. "You didn't have to do all this to make a good impression, but I'm glad you did. You're kind of amazing, Rita. Maybe I saved your life, but you're the one turning it around. That's huge. You should be proud. I am. Is it okay if I say that?"

Pleasure swept her face, like I'd given her some kind of benediction she'd been hoping for. "It's okay."

It struck me that Rita was a very lonely woman, and that I might be the only person to whom she could hold herself accountable. I had issues of my own galore, even overlooking the shooting. The idea that I could be someone else's lifeline back into society would be laughable, if it weren't also so sad. "Well, then, I'm proud of you. Where do you volunteer?"

"At Solid Ground, downtown. At their new soup kitchen off Pioneer Square, mostly, but that's the other reason I wanted to visit you now. They just did one of their fundraising drives and had a lot of people with money at their headquarters last week. The volunteers got prizes drawn out of a hat, and I, well, I can't use mine, so I thought…I thought I could say thank you by giving it to you." She dug into the pocket of her wool overcoat and came out with a small brown envelope which she pushed across the table to me. "They're tickets. To a dance performance. Native American dancers, they're on tour. I didn't know it before I saw you, but you're Indian, aren't you? Maybe you'll like it."

My gaze ping-ponged between the envelope and Rita, astonishment at the gift warring with astonishment at what she said. "My dad's Cherokee, yeah. Hardly anybody sees that in me. My coloring's all wrong." I had Dad's black hair, but I'd gotten sunburnable pale skin and green eyes from my Irish mother, and people rarely saw past that to notice my bone structure. In black and white, I looked Indian. In color, I looked Irish. "Um. God, Rita. I'm not sure I can accept these. I mean, like, legally, ethically, all of that. I had to make the lady who runs my favorite Chinese restaurant stop giving me free food when I became a cop…"

"Take them." She patted the envelope, then pulled her hands away. "I really can't use them, percussion makes me crazy. If you can't use them yourself, you probably know more people who could than I do." She made a small gesture at herself and added, "Most of the people I know wouldn't pass the dress code."

I smiled. "You're assuming I've got something nicer to wear than what I've got on." I did, but even my polyester pants were probably more suitable to an evening out than Rita's blaze-yellow safety jacket. On the other hand, this was the Pacific Northwest. I doubted they'd throw her out if she turned up in it. I picked up the tickets and tapped them against the table, then nodded and tucked them in my coat pocket. I was sure Morrison wouldn't approve, but I didn't want to insult the woman. I'd go back to the office and skulk around until he showed up so I could ask him what to do about them, out of Rita's sight and hearing. For the moment I said, "Thank you. It's not at all necessary, you know that, right? But thank you."

"I know. But I can't use them, and it made an excuse to meet you."

She had a smile to break my heart. I wondered what her story was, and couldn't think of a way to ask without seeming rude. We chatted a few minutes longer, then at the same time glanced toward the clock on the O's back wall and said, "I'm sorry, but I've got to get back."

I grinned, and Rita added, "The shelter starts serving dinner at four and I help cook, so I need to catch a bus back downtown. I hope you go to the concert, Detective. And thank you for letting me meet with you."

I shook my head. "Thanks for coming up. We don't usually get visitors who are just coming to say hi. Usually something terrible's happened. It's nice to see something wonderful happening instead." Especially after today, but that was yet another thing she didn't need to know. We got up and I figured if I was going back to the office, I might as well return bearing gifts. I ordered Morrison what the menu called a St. Patrick's Day Latte, and examined the doughnut cabinet, which had an array of mint- to pine-green frosted doughnuts lined up by hue.

The drink that came back was swamp-green and decidedly nasty-looking. Rita gave it, then the doughnut cabinet, a considering look, then smiled at me. "I'll go catch my bus while you decide if you're brave enough to bring someone that horrid-looking drink or make people break a bunch of Lenten promises with those doughnuts. It was nice to meet you, Detective Walker."

"I think I'll do both." I ordered one of each shade of doughnut and waved goodbye at Rita at the same time. "It was nice to meet you, too. Visit again sometime, okay?" She nodded on her way out the door, and a couple minutes later we waved again as I hurried past the bus stop back to the precinct building.

Billy had returned by the time I got back and took the latte with a suspicious sniff. I'd meant it for Morrison, but Billy's grimace after taking a sip made me just as glad he'd swiped it instead. The rest of the Homicide detectives swarmed the doughnut box like a pack of wolves, and I retreated to Morrison's office, ticket envelope held between my fingers like it might bite.

He was concentrating on paperwork, which gave me a

moment to stare at the top of his head and get my nerve up. I usually thought of him as silvering, but looking at the top of his head made it clear he was really just silver. He wasn't that old, not yet forty. I wondered when he'd started going gray. Not that it mattered. It looked good on him, playing into the whole aging-superhero look that I thought of as being his thing.

I rattled myself and tapped on his door. Morrison glanced up, curiosity sliding across his face. "You look nervous, Walker. Caldwell said the interview went well. What's wrong?"

"You said to come by, and besides, I have a ques…" My knees buckled a little as my brain caught up to what he'd said. I caught myself on the door frame. "She said that?"

Morrison elevated an eyebrow. "Did you think otherwise?"

"Morrison, I've never shot…" I closed the door behind me and sat down, probably signaling to everyone in the open office area outside that I was in trouble again, but for once I didn't care, possibly because for once I wasn't actually in trouble. "I've never shot anyone before," I said quietly. "I've never spent any significant time talking to a shrink. I had no idea if it went badly or well."

"I've talked to Holliday and Caldwell. They're both working up their reports, and I saw you already dropped yours off. It was a shit situation, Detective, and from what I'm seeing so far you handled it as well as you could've."

"Even…" I waved a hand, encompassing the whole magical aspect of my skill set which I'd utterly failed to use.

"As you said, if it was anyone else, I wouldn't even have asked. I shouldn't have asked you. You did what I'd expect any detective to do when her partner was in danger. The suspension is still in effect," he warned me. "I can't do anything about that."

"No, I know, it's fine. It's standard procedure. I just..." The last word came out as a shuddering breath and I pinched the bridge of my nose, trying not to let stinging tears overwhelm me. My hands smelled like maple frosting and cinnamon now, a vast improvement over the pre-shower scent of blood. "Sorry. I'm a little up and down. I just, I feel like I made the right choices, but it helps to hear you say that, sir. Thank you. And if there's anything else I need to do or not do while the incident is being looked into..."

"Just keep your nose clean. You *can* manage that for three days, right?"

I groaned and pushed the envelope across his desk at him. "I don't know. Tell me if this qualifies. The woman whose life I saved down at the Fremont Troll in December just gave me these."

Morrison shook the tickets free of the envelope before eyeing me. "Dance concert tickets?"

"She won them at a..." It didn't matter. "She gave them to me as a way of saying thank you. I told her she didn't have to, but she insisted and I didn't want to insult her and I didn't know if it was like an ethical breach to take them so, well, I just thought I should take them and then come ask you—"

"Ask what?" Morrison said in amazement, interrupting my breathless explanation. "If I wanted to go with you?"

"—er." For an excruciatingly long moment that was all I could think to say. Long enough that Morrison figured out that wasn't at all what I'd meant to ask, and began to look uncomfortable. I followed up my initial witty "er" with a salvo of, "Uh," then rubbed my nose ferociously. "Actually I'd been going to ask if it was an ethical breach or if it was okay for me to take them. But now that you mention it, um, there's only two tickets so I can't invite Billy and Melinda along, and Gary's out of town, so if it's okay for me to accept them, um, well. Would you…*like* to go with me?"

Someone with a modicum of cool wouldn't have put all the emphasis on *like*. Sadly, I was not that person. The way I asked it sounded as if the idea that Morrison might want to go out with me was only slightly less unlikely than, say, the idea that a Hollywood producer might walk into the precinct building and randomly choose me to be the next twenty-million-dollar star.

For a few seconds I waited for a Hollywood producer to walk into the room, but it didn't happen. Instead Morrison glanced at the tickets again, then shrugged. "I don't have anything planned for tonight, and God knows you probably need some kind of distraction. Just log the tickets as a gift, and if the woman ever needs anything else from you make sure every second of your interactions are observed."

"Yes, sir." He could've been suggesting I take a long walk off a short pier, for all I was comprehending. I took the tickets back, got up, made it to the door, and said, "Er," for the second time in our conversation. "Should I pick you up…?"

There was no chance on earth he would agree. My car was a 1969 Mustang named Petite who clocked over a hundred and ninety miles an hour. His was a nameless 2003 Toyota Avalon with the highest safety rating in its class. Ne'er the twain should meet.

Morrison's expression, almost without changing, suggested the idea was so outrageous it stretched all the way to funny. "I don't think so, Walker."

"Well, then, we'll have to meet there, because I have my

pride." And my smarts. Petite would never forgive me for tarting around with an Avalon. She knew these things.

Minute laugh lines crinkled around Morrison's blue eyes. "Fair enough. I'll see you at a quarter to eight, then. Go home and get some rest."

CHAPTER FOUR

I scurried back up to Homicide, where, fortunately, all the doughnuts had already been eaten. I'd have gone on a panic-inspired binge if they hadn't been. Instead I seized Billy's arm and hauled him off to the broom closet which doubled as a crash pad for cops whose shifts had gone on too long.

He came along willingly enough, though he did say, "Do I need to tell Melinda you're dragging me off to bed?" as I banged the closet door open and propelled him inside.

"Please don't. She may be little, but she be fierce, and she'd kick my ass. Billy, something has gone terribly wrong. Somebody gave me concert tickets and now I've got a…a… like a *date* with Morrison!"

My partner was a steady soul. A good man. The sort, in fact, who could walk away from nearly getting a nail through the skull and still remain a bastion of calm. I was sure he, too, had seen Dr. Caldwell this afternoon, but there was nothing in his demeanor which suggested he'd had a bad day. That's how glued-together he was.

So I hardly expected him to fall into a fit of what could only be called giggles, even if men who stood well over six feet tall were not normally prone to giggling. Offended, I stared at him, which upgraded his giggles to whoops. He staggered back, sat on the army-corners bed and leaned against the far wall while gales of laughter shook his body. It took over a minute for him to catch his breath, and I thought perhaps he was just a leeeettle more on edge about the morning's events than he'd been letting on. Still, it was with genuine merriment that he said, "Sorry, Joanie, it's just that when something's gone wrong around you it usually runs to the apocalyptic. The captain having a date, even with you, probably isn't a sign of the end times. Besides, isn't it about time?"

My head heated up. I hated to think what color my cheeks were. "It's not that kind of date!"

"Of course it is." Billy wiped his eyes, looking as happy as I'd ever seen him. "For one thing, if you didn't think it was, you wouldn't be having a meltdown."

"Billy, he's my boss! Our boss!" Which, while true, had hardly stopped me from slowly falling for the man. I really didn't know when it had happened.

Just because I didn't know when it had happened, however, didn't mean every single person I knew hadn't noticed it happening. In fact, they'd all clued in ages before I did, which was its own kind of humiliating. I sank down on the bed beside Billy and mumbled, "It was his stupid idea," into my hands.

Billy patted my shoulder and did a credible job of not sounding too interested in the details. "Really? Morrison asked you out?"

"Well, sort of!" I knew he was going to go home and gleefully tell Melinda everything, but I explained the awful scene in Morrison's office anyway.

Billy manfully didn't start giggling again. "He likes you, you know."

"I drive him insane."

"Which doesn't negate the point. Look, Walker." Billy knocked his shoulder against mine. "Just go and have a good time. A date is not the end of the world."

"It is if I don't have anything to wear!" Oh, God. I was turning into a stereotypical female before my very own eyes.

Billy choked on another laugh. "Call Phoebe. She likes dressing you."

I opened my mouth to argue, then slumped. My friend Phoebe was a fencing teacher by vocation, but a fashionista in her heart of hearts. Tall, generally slender me was her idea of a perfect model. She loved dressing me up. Moreover, she had vastly better taste in clothes and style than I did, and I had the entire remainder of the afternoon, thanks to the suspension of duty. There was no chance she couldn't make me presentable. "Okay, but I'm blaming you if this is a disaster."

"It won't be a disaster."

That was our cue to leave the broom closet, but I only nodded moodily and sat there, slouched, for a minute before nerving myself up to say, "So how're you doing?" in a much more subdued tone.

Billy pushed out a huge breath of air and said, "Okay," after a while. "You?"

I bobbed my head around in a noncommittal *okay* of my own. "I haven't heard how she is, yet."

"Stable. She's going to be fine. You did good, Joanie. The

neighbor—not the one with the kids—said he thought she'd been hiding in their doghouse."

"Big dog."

"German shepherd."

That was big enough, all right. "How'd she get into the yard?"

"Hole in the fence. The kids use it to go back and forth to play."

I said, "Shit," and put my face in my hands. "I should've looked beyond the Raleigh property. I'm sorry, Billy."

"We weren't supposed to be checking out anybody else's property. You did fine. You saved my life."

This time I managed the tiny joke I'd been reaching for earlier: "Had to. Who else on the force is going to put up with my bizarre life?"

He knocked his shoulder against mine again, a familiar and comforting action. "Nobody, that's who. Don't think I don't know it."

I wobbled from the impact. "Don't think I don't." I had, for most of the four years we'd known each other, given him endless hell about his belief in the paranormal, right up until the paranormal came and bit me on the ass. Since then he'd put up with my shenanigans, held his tongue time and again and generally been as stalwart a companion as a girl could ask for. *Nobody* would have treated me as well as he did, past, present or future. I didn't deserve him, but I was grateful as hell to have him. "You call Mel yet?"

"No. Morrison's sent me home for the afternoon, soon as I get my report in. I thought it'd be better to talk to her face-to-face. She can't panic about me being dead if I'm standing right there."

"As long as the news isn't reporting a North Precinct cop

involved in a shooting incident yet, that's probably a good idea."

Billy looked pained and stood up. "I better check on that. You heading out?"

"Yeah. To let Phoebe dress me, I guess."

My partner grinned. "Get a photo. 'Cause I promise, it won't be a disaster."

FRIDAY, MARCH 17, 7:53 P.M.

It wasn't a disaster.

Phoebe had slicked my short hair back in that wet look that either really works or really doesn't. To my surprise, it worked: without any bits of hair to soften them, my cheekbones looked sculpted. Then she'd applied just enough makeup to smooth my skin and emphasize my eyes, so I almost didn't look like I was wearing makeup, a trick I'd never myself learned. At my insistence, she'd left my eclectic jewelry—ivory coyote earrings, a silver choker necklace and a copper bracelet—alone.

The jewelry, though, was the only decision I could pretend was my own. I wouldn't have dared put me into a forest-green velvet sheath that bared my broad shoulders and made my waist look improbably small. Also, any dress I would have chosen would've come to my ankles, whereas this one stopped somewhere just beyond fingertip-length. My legs were long to begin with. A dress that quit that far above my feet, coupled with three-inch strappy gold heels, made them go on forever. Every time I caught a glimpse of myself in a mirror, I didn't know who I was, which made me accept the possibility that I was smokin' hot. I owed Phoebe one.

The advantage to being a smidge under six feet tall in

bare feet was that if I wore three-inch heels, there was almost no one I couldn't see over. Beautifully dressed theater-goers milled around me and I stared over their heads, watching the front doors. In another two minutes I was leaving. The insurance I'd taken out on my nerves to make myself leave the apartment in my fancy new dress didn't cover being stood up. It wasn't a scenario I'd even considered.

Anticipated humiliation was getting my heart rate up when Morrison walked in. I'd never seen him in a tux. In fact, of all the people I interacted with regularly, the only one I'd seen in a tux was Billy's wife Melinda. She'd been nine months pregnant and cute in a penguinlike way.

I had, therefore, kind of forgotten that men tended to be more devastating than cute in a tuxedo. Particularly if they looked comfortable in one, which Morrison did. It got a whole James Bond thing going, like he was slightly ruffled because he'd stopped to casually beat up forty-seven bad guys on his way to meet the girl.

Maybe that's why he was late.

He saw me from across the room, which would have sounded a lot more romantic if I didn't tower over everyone around me. We nodded at each other and I let him come to me, based on me being much closer to the theater doors than he was. It took him a minute to get to me, during which time I watched a couple dozen admiring women, and at least two equally admiring men, shift slightly so they could get a better look as he passed. I gave myself two points for having the best-looking date at the theater. Then I gave *him* two points for having a none-too-shabby date himself, when some of those lingering glances followed his trajectory and came to land, with hints of bitterness or approval, on me.

He had a shamrock pinned to his lapel. I touched it with

a fingertip. "I think that's cheating. You're supposed to wear green, not be nominally adorned by it."

"Are you going to pinch me?"

"Would I get fired?"

Morrison laughed aloud, which I didn't think I'd ever heard him do before. While I gaped, he offered me his elbow. "Don't risk it. You clean up good, Walker."

"You're not half bad yourself, sir." I tucked my hand into his elbow and, unable to resist, added, "Except unusually short."

"You didn't warn me you were wearing platform heels."

"If I was wearing platform heels your nose would be in my clea—" I cleared my throat, and Morrison, God bless him, slid a glance at the half-mentioned décolletage. We were exactly the same height, he and I, and in police-issue shoes neither of us ever had the height advantage. Back when we were still pissing in each other's cereal for the crime of existing, I'd been known to wear extra-stompy thick-soled boots for the sheer glee of looking down on him. In retrospect, which I was only applying right now at this very moment, it had never seemed to bother him at all. "Right. Rented tux?"

"Will it damage your perception of me if I say I own it?" Morrison guided me to the theater doors, where I handed over the tickets, and then he walked me down the long aisle as though he had a great deal of practice at it. I, who wore heels seldomly, clung to him like an ingénue and couldn't answer the question until he had me safely seated.

Then I couldn't answer it anyway, because I was too busy gazing around the theater. We were twelve rows from center stage, just where the seating's rake started to pick up speed. "Holy crap, these seats are fabulous. I'm going to have to go down to Solid Ground and thank Rita again. Wow."

Morrison agreed, "Not bad," and settled down to glance through the program, which gave me a few seconds to examine him surreptitiously. I always thought he looked like an aging superhero with his silvering hair and blue eyes and strong build, but in the tux, man, there was no *aging* about him. He just looked like a superhero. Not that most of them wore tuxedos, but that wasn't the point. When he glanced at me, an eyebrow elevated—I wasn't all that surreptitious, apparently—I blurted, "It doesn't. Damage my perception of you. Owning a tux, I mean. You probably do this kind of thing all the time. Isn't a lot of being a captain political?"

Morrison looked at me long enough that I began to feel like maybe my scattering of freckles had turned green to match the dress. All he said, though, was, "Enough to warrant a tuxedo, yes." Then he smiled, which was about as accustomed an expression as his laugh earlier had been. It looked good on him. It looked very good on him. Brightened up his blue eyes and made him seem younger than his silvering hair suggested he was. "And you? What about the dress? I didn't know your legs were that long, Walker."

That was patently untrue. I had worn a much shorter skirt to the Halloween party I'd thrown, and Morrison had definitely seen me that night. He'd even danced with me. I opened my mouth to say that, and for once realized ahead of time that it was a completely inappropriate response to what amounted to a compliment from my boss. I managed to say, "Thanks," without strangling on my tongue, then brushed my palm over the velvet's nape. "Ha. No. I mean, it's not rented, but it's a very expensive dress to hang in the back of my closet for the rest of my life. If I'm lucky, Phoebe will get married or something before I'm too old to wear it so it'll get taken out a second time." God, I was talking and I couldn't shut up. I seized the program from Morrison, willing to start gnawing on it to give my mouth something else to do.

"I never really thought that was fair. Men rent tuxedos, but women have to buy their formal wear. It's like haircuts. Your hair isn't that much longer than mine, but I bet you pay three times as much to get it cut."

"Actually I go to a barber who cuts it for seven-fifty." I grinned as Morrison shot me a look comprised equal parts of astonishment and impressed-ness. "What? I've been going to him since college. I'm not going to pay fifty dollars for a haircut, and if he screws up, which he never has, hair's not like a leg. It grows back."

"So it does." He took the program back from me—at least I was only bending it, not chewing on it—and flipped through it without really looking. "Know anything about this group?"

"Just what I read on their website. Native American group on tour, doing a kind of ghost dance. Supposed to be pretty uplifting."

"You, ah…" Morrison, who had been doing so well at the casual conversation thing I'd mostly forgotten to be an idiot, lost his cool with a cautious glance toward me.

All of a sudden I wondered how much of how he was acting was just that—an act—to give me a comparatively stable evening after a bad day. It was a depressing thought, and I seized on his failure to finish a sentence a little desperately, just to keep the conversation going. "Me ah what?"

"Is the ghost dance something you're familiar with?"

Half a dozen answers, ranging from amused to annoyed, vied for a chance to answer that. I went with dry academia, mostly because I didn't think Morrison expected it. "The ghost dance was invented in the late 1880s by a spiritual leader who'd had a vision. It caught on and spread around the western U.S. for a while. It's supposed to help assure worldly happiness and make the time until you see your dearly departed again seem less awful."

Morrison's eyes widened in respect, at which point I couldn't keep a straight face anymore. "Sorry. I only know any of this because they had an article about it on their website this afternoon. It's not automagic shamanistic mojo knowledge."

"Automagic?"

"Matic. Automatic. *Anyway*," I said a little too loudly, particularly in view of the fact that the lights were dimming and everybody was settling into their seats and into silence to await the performance. A few people looked around at me and I covered my face with one hand, mumbling, "Anyway, it's just research, nothing strange," into my palm.

Morrison murmured, "Just as well," and pulled my hand down so I was watching when the lights slammed up and movement exploded across the stage.

A woman garbed in gold literally flew on. Her costume trailed glittering feathers from the arms, her body arched forward like a bird facing the wind. There were no wires, though the height and length of her leap said there had to be: I couldn't imagine how anyone might have thrown her so far. She was caught by two men who appeared from the wings at the last possible moment, eliciting a gasp from the audience. With no recovery time at all, they flung her skyward again, back across the stage, and the theater's silence was filled with an eagle's call.

Every hair on my body stood up and I shuddered violently, thrown viscerally into memory. She was the thunderbird, the giant golden eagle, enemy of the serpent and an archetypical character of Native American mythology. I had, months ago, been briefly claimed by a thunderbird.

This woman's dance, her freedom of spirit and her raw un-adulterated strength, her utter confidence in herself and in the men—four, now—who threw her across the stage and captured her safely again, embodied the power and certainty the mythical beast had imbued me with.

There was no music, even as the dance progressed, only the eagle's cry and a sometimes lonely howl of wind that matched her fall or rise as her partners gave her wings. A fifth man came onstage, sinuous, winding, dangerous. Panic struck me through the heart, knowing what would come next. They fought, the thunderbird and the serpent, and in the end died together, tangled in eternity. I was on the edge of my seat by then, fingers digging into the seat-back in front of me, and when the drums began for the next piece, I was lost.

None of the dances were entirely traditional Native American. They all incorporated Western dance styles, throws and leaps and lifts mixed with atonal harmonies and storytelling hands, but it resonated. The drums themselves could have carried me to another world—I had one myself, which had been given to me with the express purpose of doing just that—but the dancers brought it to another level, generating so much energy I could feel it buzzing against my skin. I kept my vision resolutely in this world. I could easily have watched their auras, watched the auditorium fill with the power they were dancing up, but I wanted to see *them*, to revel in the beauty of humanity in motion. I could get tickets to another performance and watch them on a mystical level then, if I wanted to.

A wonderful formality came over them as they began the last dance. They came out of the wings in costumes unlike any they'd worn yet, five of them painted and dressed as totem poles, with another five in black and the final five wearing ferocious animal face paint and wigs. Bear, raven, coyote, rabbit, whale, dancing and weaving together with foot-stomping excitement. My heart raced like I was up there myself, putting everything I had into the performance as I watched them dance the story of a single man who came into the spirit world and learned the ways of the beasts. The rabbit taught him speed, the bear, strength. The coyote taught him cleverness and the raven taught him joy, and the smiling whale oversaw wisdom. He took it all into himself, and the totems grew taller, the masked dancers astride the shoulders of their black-clad partners, and the totems in front of them to make the illusion of height and continuity. Energy poured from them, virtually lighting the theater even without the benefit of my second Sight turned on.

Then the solitary dancer went to each of the totems, and was blessed by them, taking on their aspect. I couldn't explain how he did it, but he *became* the bear when the bear totem touched his head: he filled with strength and size and danced a bear dance across the stage, catching salmon and eating berries and slumbering through winter before the raven touched him, and he became a creature of sky and scavenging and sledding on snow. He—*they*—were astonishing, transforming with each touch, and in doing so giving honor to the world that man had come from, and so often ignored. My chest ached with breathless tears, with admiration for their skill and with joy for the strength they offered to the audience. It seemed impossible that anyone should watch their performance and be unmoved.

And I was right, because as the lights came down, the audience surged to its feet, shouting, clapping, whistling, stomping their feet. Everyone around me except Morrison and myself, because he caught my shoulder as I started to stand, and kept me in my seat with an urgently whispered, "*Walker!*"

Bewildered, I turned to him with a protest forming, but he caught my wrist and yanked my hand up, putting it in my line of vision.

Putting a clearly defined coyote's paw in my line of vision.

CHAPTER FIVE

My yelp was drowned beneath the cheering and applause from those around us. Just as well: it sounded suspiciously like a coyote's cry. I yanked my hand from Morrison's grip to press it against my throat.

It *felt* like my hand. It felt perfectly normal, aside from the residual power of the dance still playing my skin. Morrison, wearing the most stricken expression I'd ever seen, shrugged out of his tuxedo jacket and draped it around my shoulders, hiding my entire torso. Hiding my *paws*. I thrust a foot out to stare at it, but my legs were unaltered. Just ordinary human feet in expensive sandals.

I wasn't one who typically cared for being manhandled, but I was just as glad when Morrison caught my elbow and levered me to my feet and down the aisle, muttering apologies to the still-applauding patrons upon whose toes we trod. My shoes, the cause of so much caution earlier, didn't stymie me at all now that I needed to run for the doors. Here I'd always thought women in the movies who ran in their heels were just managing a lucky take. Turned out it could be done, if necessary.

To my dismay, the ushers held the theater doors open behind us. In terms of fire code that was no doubt the right thing to do, but in terms of getting me away from the roiling energy the dancers had called up, it was no good at all. I whispered, "Out, out, out, get me out of the building, just get me out," like it was a mantra to keep me safe, and Morrison did so, hustling me ahead of the breaking-up crowd.

The crisp March night air knocked away the sensation of power crawling over my skin. I sagged, willing to stop right there, but Morrison tugged me farther down the street, well away from the smokers who filed out after us. Half a block from the theater he sat me down on a short wall and crouched in front of me, working hard to watch my eyes instead of my hands. "You all right, Walker?"

I shivered my hands out from inside his jacket. They still felt normal, but they were tawny gold and fur-ruffed, pads where my palms belonged and black claws where I was meant to have fingernails. All the times I'd changed shape when scrambling to my garden—into the private center part of me that reflected my soul—I'd known my psychic shape had changed, but it had always felt the same. I'd also known it was only my psychic self changing, not my physical form.

This was definitely physical. And of all the people in the world to lose control in front of, I'd chosen my boss. I had half a dozen friends who would take it in stride, but no, I had to go all magic-freaky on the one guy who was about as enthusiastic about my esoteric skills as I'd once been.

The paws were wavering, my fingers starting to show through as fur faded. It wasn't me undoing the magic; in fact, given how hard I was focusing on the horrible fact that I was *turning into a dog*, it was a miracle the magic was letting loose at all. But I was outside the dancers' sphere of influence, away from the power of their dance and reverting back to normal. There was no pain or discomfort, just a gradual slip back to normality, though when my fingers had returned, I still had the distinct, uncomfortable feeling that it would only take a moment's concentration to bring the paws back.

My skin didn't tingle with the dancers' energy anymore, but the core of magic inside me felt replenished. Or, if not replenished, at least a whole lot more willing to play ball than it had been since that morning. It felt like my reserves had been topped up and were bursting the dam, ready for use and impatient for me to do so.

Morrison's shoulders dropped about four inches when my ordinary hands peeked out from his jacket. He closed his eyes for a full five seconds, breathing carefully through his nostrils, then looked at me again. "What the hell was that?"

I laughed, a high trill of unhappy sound, and pulled the jacket up around my head to hide in it. It smelled good, like Morrison. Just a hint of old-fashioned cologne, nothing trendy or high-priced. I breathed it in for a few moments, trying to regain my equilibrium and trying not to think about Morrison or his cologne being aspects which could allow me to regain it. After what seemed like forever, but probably wasn't, I whispered, "Coyote's been telling me all along that shapeshifting was something I could do in the real world."

"Sha..." Something about the way Morrison said half a syllable tidily filled in everything that might have followed it. It went something like this: "Shapeshifting? Are you insane, Walker? People don't shapeshift!" followed hard by *except she was just shifting shape in front of me, and I'm not stupid enough to disbelieve that after everything I've seen her do the last year*, all of which I heard clearly enough that I actually said, "You're not stupid at all," in response, and made myself meet his gaze.

For a man who'd just hauled his date out of the theater because she was changing form, he looked remarkably calm. Slightly amused, even, though he said, "Thanks," with perfect solemnity. "What happened in there?"

"Couldn't you feel it? The energy they were putting out?"

He shook his head, though his mouth said, "Sure, performers do that. I've never seen anybody…"

"Get hairy?" I volunteered weakly. His lips twitched and a tremulous smile of my own shook some of my nerves loose. "It was more than just a performance, boss. They were channeling real power. They were…making magic." I'd never thought about where the magic came from, not clearly, but I'd experienced similar rushes of power on much smaller scales. My drum could fill me up that way, but never until I overflowed so strongly that it started manifesting in physical changes. The dancers had created something new and strong that hadn't been there before, something powerful enough to affect me. "You really didn't feel anything? Nothing like…like your skin was going to come flying apart? You must have. Everybody did. The way the audience came to its feet…"

"I saw a hell of a performance, Walker. The kind that makes you want to cheer, sure, but something bigger happened to you, or we'd all be running around howling by now."

I blinked at him, then laughed. "You'd make a pretty

werewolf, boss. With your silver hair and blue eyes? The girl wolves would be, I don't know, whatever girl wolves do. Panting after you." Morrison snorted, and I didn't want to tell him "panting after you" was a damned sight better than suggesting they'd be sniffing around his hindquarters, which had been the first thing that came to mind.

Somehow, though, his pragmatism made me feel better. I got to my feet and he straightened out of his crouch, looking like he wasn't sure if he should offer support again. "I'm okay. Boss, somebody in there, the choreographer, one of the dancers, maybe a bunch of them, but somebody in there is like me. That dance, the last one, the shapeshifter's dance… that had intent in it. I don't know if it was just the storytelling or if they've got something else going on in there, but they were working so much power with so much discipline that it affected me. I've got to talk to them." I'd started walking back to the theater without noticing. Morrison caught up and touched my arm, slowing me enough to notice his expression of concern.

"Are you sure that's a good idea?"

"Not even slightly." I wrapped my arms around myself, hugging Morrison's jacket to me, and stopped where I was, still a good distance from the theater. I watched it, not my boss, while I spoke. "But I can't stand not knowing what happened, or how or why, and at least when I go back in there I'll be a little more prepared. And if I go right now, without thinking about any of this too hard, I don't have to admit that I'm completely horrified and embarrassed that I lost control of my stupid magic and started *changing into a dog* in front of you."

Morrison, unexpectedly, said, "Coyotes aren't dogs," and I laughed out loud. He said, "What? They're not!" and I laughed again.

"I know, but Coyote says that all the time. I never expected to hear you say it. I'll have to tell him you said it." Coyote was my mentor, another shaman whom I'd thought for years was actually a spirit, because I saw him most often as a golden-eyed coyote. I never tired of referring to him as a dog, mostly because it annoyed him so much. He was also potentially a whole lot more than just a mentor, and it occurred to me he might not like Morrison treading on his *I'm-not-a-dog* territory.

A frown appeared between Morrison's eyebrows, making me think maybe he didn't like being compared to Coyote in any way, either. I wondered if men made everybody's lives complicated or if I was just unusually incompetent in that field. All he said, though, was, "Just tell me if we need to get out of there, all right, Walker?"

I nodded. "I will, but you might be more likely to notice than I am. I didn't feel myself changing."

"I'll keep an eye on you." Morrison headed toward the theater, only turning back when he realized I wasn't following. "Walker?"

"Why aren't you freaking out?" God, of all the graceful questions I could've asked. I put a palm to my forehead, searching for a better way to phrase it, but Morrison chuckled.

"I've run out of freak, Walker. When it comes to you and Holliday, there's no barometer. Every time I think I've seen or heard the strangest thing you could possibly come up with, you trump it. Besides, if somebody else in there had noticed what was happening, you'd have been in a world of trouble. I don't care how weird you get. You're one of my officers. I'm not going to let you down, not if I can help it."

In other words, if anybody under his command had

suddenly started turning into a coyote, he'd have hustled them out of public view and worried about the details later. I wasn't getting preferential treatment. That sort of made me feel better, but only sort of.

Mostly what it did was remind me what a decent person my boss was. He'd gone out of his way for me more than once, even when we were barely on speaking terms. I shouldn't be surprised that he could handle a little something like me shapeshifting, but I was. I fumbled around for a way to express that, and finally settled on a wholly inadequate, "Thank you."

Morrison crooked a smile. "Come on, Walker. The show's about to start again."

I didn't enjoy the opening of the second act nearly as much. Not because it wasn't as good, but because I was concentrating so hard on not getting lost in the power the dancers generated that I couldn't get lost in the stories they told, either. Morrison leaned over at one point and whispered, "Relax," but that was easy for him to say. He wasn't in any danger of sucking up so much magic he would start changing shape. I wondered if I'd have been so vulnerable if it hadn't already been an emotionally traumatizing day.

Not that it mattered. After a while, it became clear I wasn't going to slide down that slippery path again. Where the first part had begun with the thunderbird and climaxed with the shapeshifter's dance, the second opened with a piece that felt more familiar to me. I'd done spirit quests a-plenty over the past year, and the dancers called up the wonder of drifting in darkness as power animals came to examine, consider and eventually to choose. I half expected the audience to start exclaiming over their own spirit guides appearing, and even stole a glance at Morrison to see if he had been granted a vision by the dancers' skill.

He was watching me, not the stage. I muttered, "I'm fine," and turned my attention back to the show.

Their second dance tread more territory I recognized. The lights went hard red and yellow, making the stage a rough approximation of the Lower World, a place inhabited by demons and gods. One of the dancers became lost in that world, only to be found by the newly-spirit-guided lead from the previous dance. By the end of the third piece I knew where they were going, because I'd walked the path myself. The first act had followed a shaman's journey as a shapeshifter, something totally outside my own experience. The second, though, was unquestionably the healer's path. I was sure the final piece would be the ghost dance, and I knew exactly what to expect of it.

A shaman could, in theory, affect a full-blown healing with the force of his will alone. It required belief on the part of the one being healed, as well, but extraordinary things could happen if both parties were utterly confident in the outcome. I'd only experienced it on a minor level myself, though I knew the power to heal completely lay within me.

I was willing to bet it lay within the dancers, too. Not exactly as I experienced it, maybe, because my magic was largely internal, and they were unquestionably creating something external. My magic wasn't something that caught others up in it, not the way a dance performance did. I couldn't imagine a better way to draw people into the necessary mindset for healing to succeed than with a completely captivating dance. It didn't have to be active belief—fully healing unconscious people was much easier than healing someone who was awake—but the dances could lower defenses, make people susceptible to a healing power they might not even realize existed.

All of a sudden I understood the glowing reviews they'd received all around the country. Everyone, from the man on the street to the most jaded critic, had mentioned feeling lighter, happier, healthier, when they'd left the show. I'd read no reports of miraculous recoveries from terrible illnesses, but that made threefold sense: first, someone that sick might well not be at a dance performance, and second, even if they were, the chances of associating recovery with a theatrical show were slim to none. Third, while I had very little doubt the dancers could affect healing, dissipating it over hundreds of audience members might weaken it enough that no single individual would benefit one hundred percent from the magic.

Never mind that I didn't believe that last at all. Those who were most captivated would probably benefit the most strongly. It wasn't impossible that a terminally ill patient caught up in the ghost dance would be healed, while the people around her, too concerned for her health to entirely focus on the dance, would only feel a brief lifting of their worry.

Entranced by the thought, I closed my eyes against the dancers themselves and opened my senses to the audience around me. I'd never tried this before. Generally speaking, the idea of opening myself up to the pain, exhaustion and illness of hundreds of people at once wasn't high on my list of things that sounded like fun. On the other hand, doing it in the midst of a performance was probably as good a time as any I could try: most people would be thinking about it instead of focusing on their aches and weariness, which had to lighten the burden a little. I hoped.

Viewed through the Sight, the dancers on stage nearly

overwhelmed their audience. People generally had two dominant colors to their auras, but at the moment the dancers each blazed with singular hues. That was a mark of focus, of giving everything they had to the moment, and it was wonderful to behold. I'd never seen so much energy focused together, vibrant shades of many colors giving and taking, aware of each other and building to create a whole out of their many pieces. I had, a few times, asked my friends to lend me strength to fight with. Their best efforts looked paltry compared to the dancers'.

I shivered and turned my face away from the stage. Eyes closed or not, I could still See them too clearly to gauge the audience unless I directed my unseeing gaze elsewhere.

Onto Morrison, in this case. I saw a red streak of concern leap in the rich blue and purple that was his usual aura, and put a hand on his arm in reassurance. Surprise spiked through him, then was tamped down so solidly it made me smile. I was glad he was there: he was a gauge to judge everyone else against. I knew what his colors should look like, even when he was intent on something.

He also gave me something familiar to focus on until I could disengage the dancers' radiating presence from the audience. It was harder than I expected: they wanted to be the center of attention. They were, in fact, giving being the center of attention everything they had, and there was a feedback loop going on: they wanted attention, the audience was providing it, I got sucked into what the audience was watching....

I actually had to open my eyes and blink furiously at Morrison before I could disconnect myself from the loop. His eyebrows wrinkled and I said, "Keep looking at me," which made his eyebrows convert to question-arches, but he did as I asked. I closed my eyes again, safe in his gaze, and that time was able to slip beyond the dancers' pull to properly see the audience.

They were, by and large, healthy people. A head cold here, a migraine there, the latter exacerbated by the drums, but the woman was determined to stay for the whole show, someone with a broken arm, a sprained ankle…minor discomforts, in the scheme of things. Only a dozen or so had darker shadows riding their auras. Some of them were grieving and unable to push it away for the space of an evening's performance. Others were ill: cancers making black spots in auras or chemotherapy leaving irradiated stains. One woman almost certainly wouldn't know yet that there was a spot in her breast which glowed an unhealthy pink to my Sight, like the awareness campaign had colored my perception of the illness itself. I didn't care what else happened: I would find her after the show and if I couldn't heal her myself, I would tell her to go to a doctor. She'd think I was insane, but that didn't matter as long as she went.

I let the Sight go, not exactly reluctantly. Looking into humanity's illnesses wasn't enjoyable, but I'd be able to look at them again when the dancers were done and see if any difference had been made. I was certain that if I caught their power at its apex and directed it, I could make a world of difference to the genuinely sick people in the room. But I had no idea if the dancers had a specific manner of releasing the magic they were creating, assuming they even knew they were doing it. If they did, I couldn't risk screwing it up by taking over. If they didn't, there would almost certainly be enough residual power during the curtain call that I could shape it without damaging the dancers.

Morrison was still watching me. I shook my head, whispered, "I'm okay. This one's about healing, not transformation," and settled down, much more relaxed, to watch the performance. They moved from one dance to another, until the last piece, their ghost dance, began on a barely backlit stage.

They'd foregone traditional costuming throughout almost the whole program, and the ghost dance was no exception. The men and women who rose up were ethereal, garbed in gray and white. Only the lead dancer wore red and black and yellow, making her lively and vibrant amongst the ghosts. They each told their stories, tales of life and happiness and sorrow and death, and in doing so gave her the strength to live her own life with grace and charity.

More than that, though, viewed with the Sight, they were preparing her, and themselves, for the dance's final moments. Energy coiled inside each of the dancers, ready to be released. I leaned forward with my breath held, waiting for the climactic finale and the vast outpouring of healing power I anticipated.

It happened so quickly I lost what breath I held. A surge hit the lead dancer, magic so blended it was incandescent white. She spun to face the audience a final time, arms spread in an open embrace so crisp I could see the design behind it, the intention to throw all that strength and beauty out to the audience.

Instead the magic sucked upward out of her body in a bleak whirlpool, and she collapsed on the stage in silence.

CHAPTER SIX

The audience gasped, not sure whether they'd seen something deliberate or tragic. I popped to my feet, wanting to rush the stage, and Morrison followed my lead.

Everybody else took it as the surge into a standing ovation, and people came to their feet all around us, cheering and shouting and applauding. Panic flared across the stage, the dancers at a loss until one of the men stepped forward to collect the woman who'd fallen. Her boneless form in his arms, he turned to the audience and led a troupe-wide curtain call. Fixed smiles looked like rictuses to me, but I could almost hear the axiom driving them: *the show must go on*. The audience was still going wild when they withdrew, and I knew they wouldn't return for a second bow.

"What's going on, Walker?" Morrison's voice was pitched below the exuberant audience's catcalls.

I flinched, becoming aware I was straining forward like

I'd start climbing over seats and people to reach the stage. In fact, the only thing stopping me was Morrison's viselike grip on my elbow, which I only noticed belatedly, despite the fact that once I noticed, I realized it was cutting off circulation. "Remember what happened to Billy in July? How he went to sleep because something was draining the life force out of him?"

Poor Morrison gritted his teeth and nodded. I'd explained it all at the time, but there wasn't much in the way of actual physical evidence for things like that. He believed me, but he didn't like it.

"Something like that just happened to her, except she'd gathered up all the focused power the dancers were creating. That kind of drain might have killed her, Morrison. I have to get up there!" And there was no way to do it. The aisles were already full in the way theaters always managed the moment a performance ended, even when the audience was going nuts with applause. I was sure it violated some law of physics.

Morrison gave me one brief, searching look, then, as far as I could tell, employed some kind of secret law-enforcement signal code that I wasn't yet privy to. Within seconds we were in the aisle, Morrison with his badge out as he politely but firmly created a path to the stage. Rubberneckers realizing something was wrong started to clog up the aisle, but somehow Morrison kept being right between me and them, full of professional apology as he got people out of my way. I wanted to kiss the man.

We reached the stage and he did a two-step that landed him behind me. I went to vault up, not sure my dress would survive it, and to my astonishment, Morrison caught my waist and simply dead-lifted me up.

I weighed in at about one sixty-five, which was by no

means the featherweight division. I also had very long legs, made longer still by my goddamned high heels. I wouldn't have thought anybody could lift me four feet straight into the air so smoothly I barely knew what was happening until my feet hit the stage. I stumbled out of pure amazement, and Morrison, who vaulted up after me, offered a briefly steadying hand before we both ran for backstage.

The whole cast was gathered around the fallen woman. Their auras were painful with worry, shooting spikes that made my head hurt. Every one of them looked drained physically, emotionally and spiritually, which made sense. Not only had they danced their hearts out, but the power they'd been offering to their lead dancer had gotten sucked out in a way it was never meant to be taken. I was surprised they were still all on their feet, metaphorically speaking.

A few of them glanced up as Morrison and I came through the wings. They were obviously expecting someone. Paramedics, maybe. Morrison said, "Police," at the same time I said, "I'm a healer."

For maybe the first time in my life, nobody looked any more surprised at the one statement than the other. In fact, a couple of them just got out of my way, clearing a path to the dancer's side. Morrison walked away as I knelt next to her, and I half heard him talking to stagehands, asking them to set up a barrier and refuse all nonofficial personnel access to the backstage area.

The dancer wasn't breathing. I'd known that on some level, right from the moment she'd collapsed. There were signs of fresh bruising on her chest, like they'd failed at CPR. "What's her name?"

Someone said, "Naomi Allison."

I whispered, "C'mon, Naomi," put my hand over her heart, and went searching for her soul.

★ ★ ★

Like the breath from her body, it was gone. Not almost-gone, not hanging on in hopes of rescue, but somewhere beyond the veil of death. There was no hint of life to her body, no aura clinging to her skin, no spark buried somewhere deep inside. If life essence was something that could be held in a pool, it was like someone had reached in and with one giant handful, emptied every drop. I had a whole shiny range of esoteric powers, but seeing ghosts didn't rank among them. I was pretty certain if Billy were here, he'd already be talking to Naomi's crossed-over self.

I'd never brought anyone back from the dead before. I'd managed to bring people back from mostly dead a couple of times, but not from genuinely, full-stop dead. I wasn't actually sure it was possible.

From the outside—which was to say, from anyone who hadn't been watching with my second Sight's point of view—I thought her death must look like a heart attack. There was no other even vaguely feasible explanation for it. Of course, with my hand over her heart and my magic opened up, I could tell that there was no damage at all to her heart muscle. Nor were there any brain clots or embolisms or other physical symptoms that might explain a phenomenally fit woman in her early thirties suddenly dropping dead.

On the other hand, there was nothing physically wrong with her, except the part where she was dead. If I could manage to catch her soul before it slipped away entirely, maybe I could bind them back together. Unfortunately, since I couldn't see or communicate with ghosts, that really only left me one place to go.

I called it the Dead Zone, and the first time I'd gone there chasing a wayward soul, I'd very nearly gotten myself and someone I loved killed. But I was a little better prepared these days. It didn't take much to let myself slide free of my body, not with the amount of power I'd taken in from the dancers. Not so long ago, that would have bothered me. I liked being connected to the world. The idea that I could slip into a black empty place just a finger-length smaller than infinity would have scared the crap out of me. Tonight, though, I was glad I didn't have to push myself through rituals to make it work. If Naomi Allison had any chance for life, she needed me to be as quick as I possibly could be.

The Dead Zone really was impossibly, hideously large. I always felt like it presented itself that way semi-consciously, as if to make me aware of just how tiny I was. A speck of insignificance on an endless black plain: that was me in the Dead Zone.

I took a breath of cold still air and called, "Raven, guide me?" into the Dead Zone's infinite curve.

For a few moments silence greeted me, and I wondered if I hadn't left enough shiny food out for my spirit guide lately. He had a weakness for Pop-Tarts—a weakness I shared, in fact, although I liked the fakey white frosting and he liked the flimsy tinfoil wrappers. I'd gotten much, much better about leaving him treats and generally trying to be appreciative since he'd hauled my ass out of a scary spiritual snowstorm, but I still probably wasn't the world's most grateful shaman.

His wings cut across the silence of the Dead Zone like the air was frozen, a *whish-whish* of sound that settled calmness around my heart. He *plonked* onto my shoulder and stuck his beak in my hair, pulling it, and I turned my face to grin into his feathery chest. "Hey, Raven. Thank you. I'm looking for a dead woman. A dancer. Naomi Allison. She…understood magic," I said after a moment's consideration. "Can you help me find her? You're a lot cleverer at navigating the dead places than I am."

Raven let go a caw that sounded ridiculously proud, and beat his wings in the air. Or against my head, more accurately, but I wasn't going to complain, because as he did so, the Dead Zone changed.

I'd been flattering the bird outrageously, but I wasn't lying. He walked a line between the living and the dead that I could never do without his help and guidance. Through his eyes, the Dead Zone became manageable: still terribly large, but traversable. Rivers appeared, some with boats full of the dead drifting down them, others broad and wide with ferrymen poling coin-eyed corpses across. Grim reapers, ranging in form from beautiful, gentle creatures to the scythe-bearing hooded thing of nightmares, led ghosts across the realm, bringing them from their mortal lives to something beyond. The Dead Zone was a transitory place, somewhere people lingered only briefly.

And I, as a living thing, had no business there. The dead and their masters could be drawn to the living, and when they were, they tended to want to consume it. Without Raven's presence, I was alarmingly vulnerable. With it, I merely wanted to get out of there as fast as I could. I said, "Naomi Allison," aloud, and waited to see if reverberations touched any single soul in particular.

I couldn't see it, if they did. Raven, though, gave an excited *quark* and dug his claws into my shoulder, wings smacking my head to urge me forward. He didn't weigh very much, but his wingspan was more than two feet across, and he hit hard. I made a feeble sound of protest, but broke into a run. There wasn't much point in asking for his help and then sulking when he smacked me around so I'd notice it.

I didn't think of the Dead Zone as having any features

like hills or plains, but we crested a hill and I skidded to a stop looking down on a ghost dance somewhat more literal than the one at the theater. This one, for example, was being performed by actual ghosts.

And Naomi Allison was at its heart. She wasn't dancing, only standing as she had been in the last moments of the theatrical performance, like she was waiting to take in all the power the others were building for her. Their dance was silent, with neither song nor drums, but somehow I could still hear both of those things in the small bones of my ears. Noiseless chanting grew in strength, reverberating around the Dead Zone and warning that my time was growing short.

I let out a yell and slid down the hill, disrupting ghosts that were barely more than mist on my skin, raising hairs against a chill. They dissipated into nothingness as I brushed by, but others—or maybe the same ones, hell if I could tell—appeared and continued the dance. There was a different sort of feel to the Dead Zone dance. It lacked the real world's vibrancy and sense of life, reaching beyond it to attain acceptance that had an urgency all of its own.

I recognized the difference only a few steps from Naomi's side, and knew then that I was already too late.

The soundless music stopped in a shout. Naomi's smile was brief, breathless, incandescent: all the things it should have been in the last moment of her dance at the theater. Power rushed her, but not the healing magic her troupe had built. This was the last push to take her over to the other side.

And like that, she was gone.

I gasped, a hard sound that hurt my throat, and to my horror, the dancers turned to me. Made me the centerpiece of their dance, the recipient of their next push. The raven on my shoulder flapped his wings like a mad thing, as if he could fly us both out of there.

Which he probably could, actually. He'd done it before. But given that I was in full agreement with him as to the importance of skedaddling, I thought this time I could do us both a favor and use my nice long legs to run like hell.

I ran all the way out of the Dead Zone, and awakened slumped over Naomi Allison's unmoving body.

The worst part was watching hope fade from everyone's eyes as I looked up. Some of them were already crying. Others had been hanging on until I shook my head, and emptiness filled their faces. I said, "I'm sorry. She was already gone," very quietly, and at more or less the same time people in the background began shouting about paramedics and please get out of the way and emergency action.

I got up awkwardly. My knees were bright red from kneeling on the floor, and though I didn't think I'd been there very long, my feet had gone to sleep. I opened a thread of healing power within myself, trying to encourage blood flow to return, then had to clench a hand in the nearby curtain to keep myself from doing a dance of *oh, God, ow, my feet are waking up ow, ow, ow.*

One of the paramedics frowned at me, which was question enough. He wanted to know what a theater patron was doing backstage bending over the dead woman. He obviously hoped I was a doctor.

I said, "Police." His expression cleared and he turned his full attention to Naomi, shooing the dancers back to give his coworkers room to do their jobs. I watched bleakly, hoping for a miracle I was quite certain wouldn't manifest.

"Walker?" Morrison appeared at my side and I had the weary impulse to bury my face in his shoulder. Maybe there was some universe out there where I was five foot six and that would've been charming, but as it was, I'd have to stoop. Even if it weren't professionally inappropriate, it would just look wrong.

"They'll have to call it heart failure," I said softly. Very softly, because I didn't want anyone else to overhear me. "I don't know what else they can call it. But she was murdered, Captain. I'm sure of it. And I'm probably the only cop in the city who might have a chance at figuring out by whom."

"What about Holliday?"

My partner, after all, was the one who saw ghosts. Murdered ghosts, which would make Naomi Allison a prime target for him to talk to, if she hadn't already scurried off to the Great Beyond. I shook my head. "He's good with violent deaths. This was close enough to natural I don't think her soul even considered sticking around. I'm sure he'll be able to help, but…"

Morrison sounded like he'd rather be shouting. "Murder is never close to natural, Walker."

"Tell that to King George." I sighed as Morrison's ears turned red, sure sign he was working hard not to yell. "George the Third of England may have been poisoned with arsenic so slowly over so many years it looked like a natural descent into madness and death. His spirit wouldn't have known to hang around hoping to be avenged any more than Naomi Allison's might've."

"How do you know this, Walker?"

I wasn't sure if it was exasperation or incredulity in Morrison's voice. "How do I know about King George or how do I know ab—"

"About King George!"

"I don't know, Morrison. I read it somewhere. Saw it on the Discovery Channel. Something. The point is—"

"The point is you tried to help Naomi." A third person interrupted, the man from the troupe who'd carried Naomi's body offstage. He was, at a glance, more Native American than me, with coppery skin tones and dark brown eyes. He was also wound as tightly as anyone I'd ever seen, exacting enormous control over his emotions. I wanted to hug him, just to offer him a release, but I doubted he'd appreciate the effort right then. He was probably doing his best to hold himself together for the troupe. "Thank you for that. I'm Jim Littlefoot."

I couldn't help it. I looked at his feet. He made a sound that said everybody did that, and offered his hand as I looked back up. "Naomi's older sister Rebecca and I founded this troupe a few years ago. She's the one holding Naomi now. You said you were a healer."

"Not much of one today," I said unhappily. "I'm so sorry, Mr. Littlefoot. She was gone before I could do anything."

"She was gone before you got to her," Littlefoot said very steadily. "We all felt it, Ms....?"

"W-w-wah, Walk. Er." I knew my last name. I really did. It was just that the one on my birth certificate and the one I used in day-to-day life weren't the same. I had, over the past decade, chosen to use the former about six times, and I was in no way prepared for the impulse to use it now. "Uh. Walker. Detective Joanne Walker. This is, uh. This is my boss, Captain Michael Morrison of the Seattle Police Department." I gestured to Morrison, who stared at me so hard I thought my hair might light on fire. He knew the other name, the one I'd inherited from my Cherokee father, and he clearly recognized I'd just had the impulse to use it. I was going to get grilled later for that. Well, fair enough. I kind of wanted to grill myself. Maybe with a nice teriyaki sauce.

Standing eight feet from a dead woman while talking to

someone who'd been closer to her was not the time or place to notice a growing hunger in my tummy. Jim Littlefoot shook Morrison's hand, but turned his attention back to me. "What kind of training do you have?"

"Shamanic. Your first act nearly turned me into a coyote." Wow. I hadn't meant to say that, either. I hastily withdrew into myself for a moment, imagining my greening garden, then reinforcing the shimmering silver-blue shields that kept it safe from outside intruders. With no offense meant to Mr. Littlefoot, people who made me blurt details about a magic I preferred to keep quiet could be highly dangerous. I'd found that out the hard way. It wasn't a road I wanted to go down again.

A mixture of curiosity and apology came into Littlefoot's eyes. "It's meant to prepare the audience for a transformative experience in the second act, not literally change people. I'm sorry."

"I know. It wasn't your fault. It's just the amount of po…" My brain caught up to what he was saying. "So it's deliberate. I mean, it had to be, with the amount of power you were generating, with the focus, but—but you do know what you're doing. What you're creating."

A fleeting smile crossed his face. "We do. We spent nearly two years perfecting these pieces, getting the right dancers, before we took it on the road. Even one cynic among the troupe can destroy the synergy. It hasn't been an easy program to develop."

"How long have you been touring?"

"Since last September. We wrap up in May in Chicago." Littlefoot cast a glance over his shoulder, then looked back at me with his mouth a thin unhappy line. "Or that had been the plan. I don't know what we'll do now."

"Since September." Dismay coiled through me, cool and loathsome. "So this attack could have be—"

Littlefoot interrupted, "*Attack?*" and paled, like he hadn't thought through all the possibilities behind Naomi's death.

I said, "I'm sorry," and turned to my boss. "This could have been months in the planning, Captain. Can we get the list of credit-card purchases for the tickets to tonight's show? The theater was packed, there must've been five hundred people here, but it's a place to start investigating."

"Walker." Morrison drew me back a step, though it wasn't really an attempt to take me out of Jim Littlefoot's hearing range. "You already said they're not going to find anything to provoke a murder investigation. She'll be autopsied, I'm sure, but—"

"Are you really going to tell me not to investigate this, boss?" I took a breath, steadying myself. "Do you really think I'll listen if you do? Because I—I need to, Captain."

Morrison's expression softened just slightly. I sort of felt like I'd thrown a low blow, given the circumstances of the day, but I was willing to take any bend I could get.

"Hey." One of the paramedics lifted his voice, clearly not talking to us, but garnering our attention anyway. I was just as glad: backstage at the theater probably wasn't the place to argue with Morrison over what my duties as one of Seattle's only paranormal police detectives entailed. Then the paramedic uttered seven little words that invalidated my concerns about being allowed to investigate.

"Hey," he said, "don't you think this looks weird?"

CHAPTER SEVEN

There were puncture wounds over Naomi Allison's heart. Five of them in an arc of about two hundred and forty degrees, like somebody had sunk extremely pointy fingernails into her flesh. They got worse as we watched, deepening until her chest started to cave in.

Morrison drew breath to speak and I snapped a hand up, fingers rigid, to silence him. To my astonishment, it worked, though I'd probably pay the price later. But I had a good idea of what he'd been going to say—something along the lines of "No signs of murder, Walker?"—and I was a lot more interested in watching Naomi's degradation than I was in being scolded.

Besides, I'd been right. When I'd said there were no obvious signs of foul play, there hadn't been. That, however, had been a whole two minutes earlier, and lots could change in two minutes. I'd gone from being a mechanic to a shaman in that time. Stranger things could happen. Around me, they usually did.

"It's a physical manifestation of the power drain. Somebody sucked the energy out of her so fast it's taken a couple minutes for the corporeal damage to catch up. But I bet dollars to doughnuts there's somebody out there whose visualization on this is ripping her heart out." I put my fingertips over the wounds, which were now deep enough to start bending around the heart. There was very little blood, given the depth and the fact that I could see torn arteries. Postmortem injuries were like that. No heartbeat to pump the blood, so the best it could do on its own was ooze and pool.

Jim Littlefoot said, "*Why?*", the paramedic said, "What the hell are you talking about?" and Morrison, in a low, dangerous voice I'd become accustomed to, said, "Walker..." all at more or less the same time. I ignored the latter two and shook my head at Littlefoot.

"It's not personal, if that's what you're asking. It's the power you're generating. Someone wants it, and they're using the idea of the heart as the soul's center to focus their desire. They weren't after Naomi. This would have happened to whoever was the lead dancer tonight." It was so clear to me I could almost See it, though the Sight itself wasn't offering much. I was a day late and a dollar short: if I'd chased the black whirlpool of magic when it had fled Naomi's body, I might have followed it back to the perpetrator.

But it hadn't even occurred to me. My only thought had been getting on stage and trying to heal the fallen dancer. I was hell on wheels at second-guessing myself, but for once I wasn't convinced I'd made the wrong decision. Nobody, not even Coyote, had suggested it was within my power to split my focus in two completely different directions, physically attending to a healing while spiritually charging off for a fight. I'd made my choice. I would have to live with it, even if Naomi Allison hadn't.

"Can you tell who's responsible?" Littlefoot's voice, like Morrison's, was low, but not with warning or anger. With despair, and I had no good answer for him.

"I'd be looking for someone overflowing with power, but anybody in the theater—" I broke off. If the ghost dance had worked properly, if Naomi had been permitted to release the magic into the audience, then everyone would be glowy and happy, but she hadn't. Only the spirit thief would be boiling over now, assuming he was in the theater at all. I looked at Morrison, who shook his head, but turned and left the backstage with purposeful strides. It was almost certainly far too late already to corral the audience so I could look them over, but he was going to try. I thought of the woman with the lump in her breast and a wave of sick concern broke over me, even though it was so far out of my control that worrying about it was ludicrous.

That was probably why it bothered me. Easier to focus on the details or the impossible than what was right in front of me. Hell, I'd spent half the day doing that deliberately. I said, "Stop anybody you can at this point, okay? I'll take a look at them, and if we can get the credit card sales, well, at least it's someth…" to Morrison's retreating back, and "Oh. Oh, God, gross," to the dead woman in front of me.

Naomi's heart shuddered, sharp tooth marks tearing flesh, and an entire bite disappeared as we watched. Then another, then a third, and the heart was gone, gulped away. I pressed the back of my hand to my mouth, gagging. The paramedic didn't fare so well, and lurched a few feet away to empty his stomach. Naomi convulsed once more, then went still. Littlefoot turned an unblinking gaze on me, tears draining down his cheeks. All I could do was whisper, "I'm sorry. It's over now."

That much, at least, I was sure of. The bodily attack had finished catching up to the magical, as if time had slid slightly out of sync. I didn't think that was it, not really. It was just that the psychic attack was so virulent it had taken Naomi's life before the physical could have its turn. At least there'd been no agony, this way. It had been over the moment power whirlpooled out of her.

Littlefoot nodded, lips tight. "Can you find what did this?"

"Yeah. I'll find it, and I'll stop it." I had no idea how, but I was pretty confident I could. "Your people all look exhausted, Jim. They won't want to, but make sure they eat, okay? What happened to them is a lot more than coming down after a show. All that energy they were supposed to throw out to the audience should have come back to them in a way, and instead it's been stolen. Even if your friend hadn't died, they'd be a lot more drained than usual. A drum circle wouldn't hurt, something to replenish them a little. In fact, I'll come back later to lead one, if you want."

I had no idea who I was, making an offer like that. The Joanne Walker of fifteen months ago wouldn't have thought of it, much less genuinely meant it. Littlefoot made a motion of agreement, but asked, "Later?" in a way that put a lot more questions into the word than seemed possible.

"I need to check whatever's left of the audience, just in case the killer is here. If he's not, I want to take a look over the city and see if I can find a flare where there's too much power. And I have to figure out what did this, if I can. I haven't seen anything quite like it before."

Littlefoot started to speak, then let it go in a rush of breath. The second try worked better: "We'll gather a drum circle. Don't feel obliged to come back. I think you have enough to do already."

I got to my feet, touching his shoulder as I did so. It was rock solid, dancer-trained strength knotted into tension. I gathered a pulse of healing power, magic warm and comforting in my belly before I released it into Littlefoot. Experience said he should relax, at least a modicum; that the influx of strength and calm would help even if he wasn't aware it had arrived. I might as well have been trying to heal a rock, for all the difference it made in his anxiety levels. That didn't actually bode so well for me helping out in a drum circle, so although I meant it when I said, "It's not an obligation," the feeling of obligation lessened some.

He nodded and I stepped back, finally giving him and ultimately his people the space they were going to need. "If any of you know anything about shielding, that would be best. Keep what you do internal, just for the troupe. You usually only do one performance a day, right? So if whoever's behind this has been watching you, he's probably not going to be looking for a second hit right away, but there's no sense in offering him an easy target." Not when I had every intention of offering up a much harder target.

Me.

Morrison had done a hell of a job corralling the audience, given the late start he'd had. There were probably three hundred people still in the lobby, and security guards at the doors chitchatting politely with men and women who didn't seem too terribly eager to escape, anyway. Human nature, I guessed; they probably wanted to be among the first to know what had happened, all the better to gossip about in the morning.

Lots and lots of them turned my way when I came out

of the theater, their auras spiking with curiosity. With the weight of their interest, I realized that between my height, the form-fitting green dress and the fact I'd run up on stage seconds after Naomi collapsed, I was probably pretty recognizable. Sneaking out a side door or up to the mezzanine floor to peek at the crowd might've been smarter, but smart wasn't so much my stock in trade.

Not mostly, anyway. I was smart enough to not say "She's dead," which was sort of my first impulse. Even when people started asking, I kept my mouth shut and just looked over them, grateful that the strappy heels meant I could see virtually everybody.

Nobody had the mark of a killer. Auras were rife with nosy interest and concern, with boredom, with amorous intentions and chilly brush-offs, but no one was burgeoning with the kind of energy the killer had stolen. I sighed, singled Morrison out of the crowd—he was at one of the doors, badge on display as he smiled at a redhead at least ten years older than he was—and made my way through the gathering to his side. "Can I talk to you privately, boss?"

The redhead's expression flashed from a downright sulk at my interruption all the way to smug delight as I finished with the word *boss*. She actually tucked a card into his lapel as he backsided the door open and gestured me through. I couldn't help stealing another look at her as Morrison followed me, and my big mouth said, "You like redheads, huh?" without consulting me on the topic first.

Morrison looked back at her, too, then at me. "What makes you say that?"

"Oh, Barbara Bragg was a redhead, and now her. I don't know. It doesn't matter." Rita Wagner had asked if I believed in God. I thought a kind God would probably strike me dead right then just to save me from myself. Since nobody did, I chalked one up in the "not so much" column, and tried to shrug off the conversation causally.

Morrison was amenable enough to shrugging it off, though he said, "Maybe redheads like me," before a considerably more relevant, and much more Morrison-like, "What happened after I left?"

"Whatever attacked Naomi ate her heart." I was horrified at how steadily that came out.

Morrison's eyes popped. "What is it with you and bodies getting eaten lately, Walker? Is it another wendigo?"

"No." I had plenty more to say than just a categorical denial, but it struck me again that Morrison had been bizarrely normal all day. Normal like a normal person, not normal like my boss, which was a much more antagonistic kind of normal than normal-normal was. I knew why: he was going easy on me because of the shooting, which meant he really didn't think I'd screwed up. I was glad of that, but he was shooting so straight I thought maybe inadvertently asking him on a date hadn't been a mistake after all. I didn't know what it meant if it wasn't a mistake.

And it didn't matter very much right then. Morrison's expression descended toward its more-usual exasperation the longer I didn't answer the question. I spewed a more detailed answer, hoping to get the more genial Morrison back as a reward. "The wendigo was eating souls, but I was able to track Naomi's into the Dead Zone. Whatever attacked her was just after the energy she'd collected. It's a completely different M.O."

"And the heart?"

"The wendigo wasn't after viscera. It was chewing the external flesh, trying to re-establish a body for itself. No, this is different, Morrison. I'm sure the heart was the focal point for whatever magic was used to strip Naomi of all that

energy." I put a fist over my own heart. "It's what we per-
ceive as the center of our emotions. I mean, we say we mean
things from the heart, we suffer heartache, we pledge our
hearts, we wear our hearts on our sleeves. The only other
organ we assign as much importance to is the brain, except
brain-dead bodies can be kept alive if the heart continues
pumping and not the other way around. The heart is our
core, the perfect and obvious point to attack if you're trying
to collect the emotional and spiritual power of an individual.
If I was going to try something like that—"

"*Which you wouldn't.*"

I broke off, gaping. "No, because I'm not *insane*. I mean, I
couldn't, this is black magic, it's sorcery, not shamanism, I'd
be—I mean, Jesus Christ, Morrison, of course not! What the
hell?"

His nostrils flared and words came through pinched lips:
"You have a track record of doing incredibly stupid things in
an attempt to figure out who or what your adversary is. Re-
verse engineering something like this sounds right up your
alley."

Righteous indignation bubbled up and spilled over into
splutters. Splutters only, because he was right. It did sound
like exactly the kind of moronic thing I'd try.

This did not seem like a good time to explain my plan
had actually been more along the lines of throwing down
a big shiny gauntlet of my own power in an attempt to get
the killer's attention, even though in comparison to Morrison's fears, it seemed very mild and practical. Instead I collected my splutters into words. "Even if I wanted to, *which I
don't*, I think my magic would cut out on me. It has definite
opinions about what I'm allowed to do with it. I mean, it
went flat this morning, and that whole scenario was a hundred percent mundane, no paranormal activity involved. I'm

pretty sure eating people's hearts, even with the best of intentions, is right out."

Morrison harrumphed, apparently satisfied, and I tried to gather my derailed thoughts. "If I was going to try something like that, *which I'm not*, I would use representational magic. Like voodoo, where you use a doll to—right, you know what voodoo is. Only instead of a doll I'd use a candy heart, or something. I'd devour it—would you stop looking at me like that?"

"I was wrong," Morrison said in a deadly tone. "I thought I was all out of freak, but listening to one of my detectives discussing devouring hearts while dressed to kill pushes the limits. Skip to the end game, Walker. I can't take much more of this."

Probably the "dressed to kill" bit wasn't supposed to make me grin, so I tried to keep it to a tiny smile, and looked somewhere else so meeting Morrison's eyes wouldn't loosen the expression into full-blown idiocy. I could be such a girl sometimes that I wanted to kick myself. Fortunately there were several dozen people still outside the theater, hanging around muttering quietly and eyeing the lobby in hopes of someone coming out with answers. They gave me something to focus on while I gave Morrison his end game. "Eating the representational heart would give me the physical and emotional target to draw down the power. Once the power drain was complete, destroying the actual heart would sever any link between myself and the body. There's nothing left, no representational evidence, no physical evidence, no psychic residue. Excuse me. I have to go cop a feel on a pretty woman."

Morrison said, "You what?" in the sort of resigned tone that indicated he'd never keep up with my inconstant ways, and stayed where he was while I hurried across the theater patio.

The cancer-infected woman I'd noticed in the theater was tall, maybe five foot nine, but she wore flats, so I towered over her as I tapped her shoulder. She turned from her friends, an eyebrow arched curiously, and looked me up and down. I did the same, because the word *statuesque* could have been coined just for her. Valkyries of yore wanted to look like this woman: broad-shouldered, generously endowed, long legs and a mass of genuinely golden hair that I didn't think came out of a bottle. Her eyes were brown, which surprised me: I almost expected them to be as yellow as her hair. If she'd had a hint of a tan, the snug goldenrod dress she wore would have made her look like a giant banana, but she was so fair-skinned I couldn't even find any freckles. She was about thirty-five, and aside from that touch of malignant pink in her breast, literally glowed with health. I wished everybody—including myself—had her level of fitness, and said, a bit rashly, "Hi. Do you believe in magic?"

"I don't know about magic, but if you're about to ask me on a date, I'll believe in miracles," she offered.

Apparently she had the confidence necessary for the bright-colored dress, too, and for a moment I genuinely regretted my limited palate of sexual preferences. "I'm sorry. I wish I was. Instead I'm going to say something really, really weird, and I hope you'll believe me."

She arched an eyebrow, looked over her shoulder at her friends, then faced me again, arms folded under her breasts. It was closed-off body language, but she contradicted it by putting her weight on one leg, hip cocked out and the other foot angled sideways to indicate a degree of willingness to listen. I had clearly been a detective too long, if I was studying her body language that carefully, but she took my mind off it by using her language-language, too: "If this is the 'you should be a model' speech, I've heard it before."

"It's much weirder than that. I'd like to hold your hands for a minute or two."

Her other eyebrow skyrocketed up to match the first. "Are you sure you're not asking me out?"

"Sadly, yes. I'd rather explain afterward, if that's okay."

She *oofed* as one of her friends elbowed her in the ribs and made a ribald comment, but she put her hands out. I took them, but she made like it was all her idea, grasping mine firmly. Her hands were rough, as if she worked with chemicals or just did fifty pull-ups on an iron bar every day. "You work out?"

"Enough to get noticed, I guess." A glow of pleasure erupted from her, turning her dominant-yellow aura as brilliant a goldenrod as her dress, and putting her in exactly the kind of mental place I wanted her in. Overlooking the morning's mess-up, I'd been able to heal people with a drawn-out vehicle analogy for most of the past year, aligning aliments to my mechanic's trade knowledge. More recently, though, I'd stepped it up a notch, and could affect a healing pretty much instantaneously. It helped enormously, though, if my patient was receptive. Joyful and full of self-confidence was just about as positive and receptive a mental space as I could ask for.

She said something I didn't hear as my attention went internal. My power leaped to life, no longer reluctant as it had been that morning. It felt like it was making up for lost time, or more likely, making up for the choice I'd made that morning. I didn't exactly feel guilty, but I did feel like it would take a lot of healing people before I balanced out gunning one down.

Silver and blue magic, topped up and bubbling over from

the energy the dancers had put out, was eager to go where I focused it. I'd never had a target like this one: no more than a handful of cells, lethal pink, unwelcome but unstoppable in the host body.

Habit lingered. It was easy to think of those few sick cells as tiny rust spots that needed sanding, polishing and repainting so they wouldn't spread to the body around them. The real difference to me was not going through those steps. Once the analogy popped into mind, the work was done between one thought and the next.

What I didn't expect was the staggering whirl of magic that surged toward the deadly pink cells, obliterating them. But it didn't stop there. Time tunneled forward like a bad 3-D effect, showing me much paler pink cells, like ghosts of futures yet to come. Those cells multiplied, became blotches, became lumps, became masses, metastasizing and spreading. Healing magic charged headlong into the future-that-could-be, tearing sickness apart and leaving healthy flesh in its wake. It ran all the way through the cycle of disease, destroying it not just now, but all its potential in the future. I caught a glimpse of a double helix, of an off-shoot ladder rung that didn't belong, and felt my magic gather itself, preparing to fix that, too.

Panic spurted through me and I clawed the magic back. It hesitated, still focused on that genetic anomaly, then rolled back into me, so drained I could barely feel its presence. Time wound backward, landing me back into the here and now, where my knees buckled. The woman's grip on my hands kept me upright, but she let go, obviously feeling the flux of power. "What the—what'd you do?"

"Removed some rust." My throat was dry. I coughed and tried again, but shivers wracked me so hard I could hardly focus on the woman before me. Her aura was no longer marred by the scant touch of unhealthy pink, but even my grip on the Sight faded as I reached feebly for something to lean on. She was the only thing available, and to my relief she put her hand out again, strong fingers banding around my arm.

"Are you all right?" Her voice was pitched high with concern.

I managed a nod. The cancer hadn't spread, but the amount of magic bent to finding and destroying those sick cells offered a warning: potentially terminal illness, even if it hadn't come anywhere near actually terminal, was *not* something to mess with lightly. I had the ugly feeling I could have easily killed myself with that unconsidered effort. Walking blithely through cancer wards and laying on hands was clearly not going to be an option.

"What'd you do?" she asked again, this time more mystified than alarmed. "I feel like champagne. Bubbly inside."

"Do me a favor." I sounded like I'd drunk a cupful of sand. "Go to the doctor. Get a mammogram. Just to be sure."

She went white, long rangy lines going rigid. "You don't think...?"

"No." Not anymore, but that didn't seem like a useful thing to say. The image of the distorted double helix popped up again and I crushed my eyes shut, wishing I'd dared try shaving that wrongness away. There were at least two good reasons not to have: one, I didn't know what the long-term ramifications for her genetics would be if I had, and two, I thought I was lucky to not already be dead. Rewriting DNA was not in the game plan. "Just go to the doctor to be sure, okay? Please? Get one of those genetic tests, if you can, to see if you've got a predilection for the disease."

She relaxed incrementally at the reassurance, then frowned again. "I will. But what did you do? Who are you?"

"I'm a healer." It sounded absurd, but I was too tired to come up with something clever. No healing I'd done had ever wiped me out so badly. I was going to have to talk to Coyote about tempering the magic so I didn't kill myself while doing my duties. "I'm a healer, and I think you'll be okay now, but go to a doctor anyway. Please?"

"A healer." Befuddlement darkened her eyes and she caught my arm. "Really? That—it sounds like bullshit, but I feel...people like you exist? For real?"

I breathed a tiny laugh. "For real. But you'll go to a doctor anyway, right? Please?"

"I will." She didn't let go of my arm, though, expression searching mine. "But I'd like to see you again, too. Just to be sure. Would that be okay?"

God. It was considerably more bizarre to have someone believe me than not. I smiled, wishing I was more comfortable with being someone's hero, and nodded. "My name's Joanne Walker. I work for the Seattle Police Department, so I'm not hard to find. Give me a call sometime, if you want. That would be fine. But, um, don't noise this around, okay? Faith healing isn't exactly on my résumé."

She finally let me go, glancing at her own hands in embarrassment. "Right, no, of course I won't. And I will call. Sorry. I didn't mean to be so pushy. I just never felt anything like that before, and now you say I had cancer and it's gone and—" She broke off, took a deep breath, and repeated, "Sorry. Sorry, Miss Walker. I'll call you." She glanced in the direction I'd been trying to go, toward Morrison, and tilted her head curiously. I sort of shrugged, and she got a small, crooked smile. "Nice."

It was an assessment I couldn't argue with. I smiled a bit

in return, nodded and wobbled back to the theater building where I could lean on a wall.

Morrison joined me, breath drawn to ask a question, but I shook my head. Something was nosing at my exhausted magic, like a dog that had found something interestingly stinky to explore. It was a new sensation, and it withdrew as I reached inside myself to scrape together enough power to create shields. Withdrew, nosed the shields themselves, then disappeared entirely, leaving behind only a fading sense of inquisitiveness and a faint but familiar tugging in my belly, fishhooks pulling me toward some kind of encounter.

Every part of me wanted that sensation to be nothing more than my imagination. Failing that, I liked the idea of it being a good guy recently come to Seattle and just discovering there were other people of power hanging out in town. There'd been no sense of malice or danger from the feeling, just interest.

Nothing in the past fifteen months, though, had given me any reason to believe the happy fluffy bunny scenario. I was dead sure that I'd gotten the killer's attention.

"Talk to me, Walker. You look like a ghost." Morrison ducked his head so he could catch my gaze and bring it up, which was surprising enough that it worked.

For a second, anyway. The pedantic part of me then couldn't help looking over myself, wondering if I really did look like a ghost. Not really: they tended to be more transparent and monochromatic than I was, though I had to give Morrison the nod for my color being off. "Sorry. That woman had breast cancer. Healing it wiped me out."

"You can…" Morrison sounded like he was about to swallow his tongue. "You can do that?"

"Apparently. I'm also thinking it's not the best idea I've ever had, not unless I want to kill myself. There's probably a better way, maybe if I set up a healing circle, a drum…" I trailed off, letting the building hold me up as I looked toward the theater inside. "Like what they were doing.

Creating a controlled center of power. I'll work it out later. Long-term project."

One side of Morrison's mouth curled up. "You've changed."

I blinked back toward him. "Really?" It was a stupid question. I knew he was right. Still, having him come out and say it warranted a slightly incredulous response.

My stupidity didn't seem to bother him, as he simply nodded instead of calling me out on it. "You're a lot more confident."

"I was always confident." About cars.

For some reason I didn't have to say the last two words aloud. Morrison managed to hear them anyway, or at least I hoped that was what he was responding to as the rest of his mouth joined the smile. "No, Walker. You were arrogant. You probably still are, but confidence sits better. I think even three months ago you wouldn't have been standing here telling me flat-out this thing wasn't a wendigo or that you could heal terminal illnesses but thought you needed a focal point. The whole thing would have embarrassed you."

Now the corner of *my* mouth turned up. "And it would've pissed you off. Sir."

"My mother likes to say 'a body can get used to anything, even being hanged, as the Irishman said.'"

I laughed, then became more solemn. "Oh, great. I don't know, Morrison. I've screwed up so much. So many people've gotten hurt. I had to get over myself. And…"

His eyebrow twitched upward and I found myself at a loss. I'd been going to say "Coyote coming back really helped," which was true, but which was also suddenly something I really didn't want to say to Morrison. Not when we were getting along so well. So what came out of my mouth was unexpected, if heartfelt: "And you helped. No matter how much you didn't like it, you took this talent of mine in stride way before I did. It's been a year now, you know? Since the banshee? A year almost to the day. And you were the one who pulled me onto that case, because you accepted I had a potentially useful skill set whether you understood it or not. So I owe you a lot, boss. Thanks."

"You're welcome." There was a momentary pause while we were both uncomfortable with all of that before Morrison got another very slight smile, this one sly. "Or were you just saying all that to soften me up for something I'm not going to like?"

I groaned. "No, not on purpose, but now that you mention it, I'm pretty sure I got the killer's attention when I healed that woman."

Morrison's good humor drained away, leaving him to study me as though I was some kind of new and especially nasty stain on his shoe. "Take a walk with me, Detective."

That couldn't be good. I fell into step with him, arms wrapped around myself. Sleeveless velvet sheath dresses were very sexy, but not at all warm, and I'd left my coat in Petite for dramatic effect. Women weren't too bright sometimes. We got a little distance from the theater before Morrison said, "You remember you're suspended from duty, right?"

"The theater's not in our jurisdiction anyway. It all works out," I said flippantly. "It's not like either thing is going to stop me from investigating."

He glowered at me, but it was a resigned sort of glower. "I know. Walker, what do you mean, you got his attention? From what you've said, from what I've seen, you've been throwing power around Seattle for the last year like Jackson Pollock threw paint, and this guy only just now notices you? Explain that to me."

We hadn't gotten more than fifty feet away from the

theater, but I stopped to goggle at my boss. Never mind women not being too bright. *I* clearly wasn't too bright. There was no need to damn my entire gender just because I was a moron. I tented my hands over my nose and mouth, stared at Morrison over my fingertips and finally said, "I can't. Not unless it's someone brand-new to the Pacific Northwest, but if it is, I don't know why he'd choose here to make his attack. I'd want to work from comfortable territory, myself."

"The date?"

"I don't think International Everybody Is Irish Day carries any kind of mystical *kaboom*. If it was the equinox, may…" I looked skyward. It was a gorgeous clear night, with a few determined stars glittering past the city lights and the moon's glow. I said a few choice swear words under my breath, then, aloud, said, "It's not the date. It's the damned moon."

Morrison looked up, too. "Full moon? What, it's a werewolf?"

I glared at him, equilibrium further restored by familiar irritation. "I don't think there's any such thing. No, it's all about dates and phases of the moon with me. Twelfth night, spring equinox, summer solstice, Halloween, wint—"

"Fourth of July?"

I hunched my shoulders guiltily, having skipped that one on purpose. "I don't think that one has any mystical relevance. I'm pretty sure it was completely my fault, just backlash from the solstice. Backlash from the whole first half of last year. It just reached critical mass in early July. The point is I'm betting this is tied up with the full moon, whatever it is. It's not as perfect as last year, when the moon lined up with the equinox, but the dancers were still rehearsing then. Even if my guy's been watching them that long, they wouldn't have been ready to…harvest." I wished to hell another word had come to mind.

From Morrison's expression, so did he. It took several long seconds for him to get over it, but eventually he said, "Can you backtrack the guy?" in a tone prepared for disappointment.

Unfortunately, it was the right preparation. "Not from here. I'm a lousy tracker, Morrison. I'm still relying on getting up high and taking a look around the city for anything that looks wrong."

Morrison turned his wrist over, looking at his watch, then dug into his lapel to retrieve and activate his cell phone as he headed for the parking lot. "Seattle Center's closed, but I'll call ahead and have security let us in."

"Us?" I ran after him, trying not to gape, and caught his arm to haul him away from the Avalon. "No way. I get to drive. First, you always drive, and second, my coat's in Petite and I'm freezing."

"Walker, your vehicle is a death trap."

"Petite saved my life in a race with the Wild Hunt. I'd like to see your puny fiberglass Avalon do that." Toyota Avalons weren't fiberglass. They had full steel bodies, just like my Boss 302 did, but I was willing to bet Morrison didn't know that. Either way, I was driving my own damned car to the Seattle Center, with or without Morrison in it.

I wasn't about to admit aloud that I kinda hoped it was with. Petite was accustomed to my long legs climbing in and out of her, but she'd never had a tuxedo-clad man in her soft black leather interior. I thought they'd look good together, and wanted an eyeful of that particular candy.

Instead I got an eyeful of Morrison grinding his teeth. "Do you expect to be outracing the Wild Hunt this evening, Walker?"

"That's not the point." I reached Petite—I'd tucked her into as protected a corner as I could find in the lot, since I trusted no one and nothing with my baby's handcrafted purple paint job—and turned back to my boss, one eyebrow elevated in either challenge or expectation, depending on how he wanted to interpret it.

He said, "I'll meet you there," and left me to climb into Petite all by my lonesome.

A dour security guard at the Seattle Center examined Morrison's credentials and my lack of them—I'd handed them over to Morrison that morning, and for some reason he wasn't carrying them around with him—and gave us a look that said *yeah,* sure *you're on police business,* but he keyed the elevator on and sent us up to the Space Needle's rotating floor without any vocal commentary.

Seattle at night from the darkened restaurant was spectacular. Bridges and their reflections stretched across the water, and streets busy with cars glittered with motion. Six hundred feet in the air was much too far away for sound to carry, especially through the heavy glass windows, so the changing lights and roadways had an unusual serenity to them. And that was just with my normal vision.

I wouldn't have said so aloud, but I was relieved I could trigger the Sight. I wasn't as bone-exhausted as I'd been in the moments after healing the blonde woman, but I didn't feel all that bright and perky, either. I hadn't been sure I'd be able to See anything at all, after that over-exuberant display.

With the Sight triggered, Seattle took on gorgeous overtones, brilliant streaks of red marking human life along the highways, which were themselves black dead strips across the earth, unnatural with their engineered curves and straight lines. Off to the east, the university poured out the whole spectrum, many of the colors reaching both deep and high, as if scholarship had taken root and reached for the stars.

That was the healthy living layer of the city. Beneath it, or beside it, or maybe even occupying the same space, I couldn't exactly tell, was Seattle's darker side. I'd only learned to see it recently, and I didn't like looking at it at all. But I knew better, by now, than to ignore it. There were markers all over of things that had gone wrong: murders, car crashes, suicides, fights. The dance theater was a new bleak mark on the cityscape tonight, and I thought if there was a modicum of fairness in the world, there would also be some kind of nasty streak leading directly from the theater back to our killer's lair.

There wasn't, of course. The image of Naomi's heart being eaten rose again, putting a new thought in my mind: that all the power she'd briefly harbored had also been eaten in one great gulp, effectively hidden from view until it—to put it less than delicately—passed out the other end.

"Ew." I wrinkled my nose and glanced down, taking in the quiet Seattle Center grounds below me. The icky image faded, leaving me to think that the security guard's skepticism wasn't that far off the mark. Sneaking up here could fall under a seriously romantic gesture, if things were just a little different between me and my boss.

But despite a handful of moments in which I'd regretted it, they weren't different. Morrison had brought me up here to study the city on an esoteric level, not to admire the view. Last time he'd made a gesture that big, it had been an offer to drum me into a shamanic trance, something so far out of his comfort zone that I was still astonished he'd made it. I wasn't the only one who'd changed, though I didn't know that he'd appreciate the observation.

He came up behind me—I didn't know what he'd been patrolling the restaurant for, but he'd made a full round of it while I'd just gone straight to a window—and said, "So what do you see?"

"Nothing wrong, yet. Nothing that looks like a power surge. Do you want to see?" I dragged my attention from the far-below grounds and turned to Morrison, half afraid and half hoping he'd say yes.

His eyebrows furrowed, physical manifestation of emotion that was equally visible in his aura: a jolt of red went through his usually purple-and-blue colors, but was tamped by a swirl of pale yellow, irritation just slightly outgunned by curiosity. "Do I want to see what?"

"Seattle's colors." I slipped my heels off and lost my height advantage plus some, since Morrison was still wearing shoes. Being shorter than he was felt vulnerable, and it took active willpower to not put my shoes back on, or at least stand on my toes. Icy palpitations rushed over me, more than just the floor beneath my bare feet being cold. My heartbeat was jackrabbit fast and my stomach full of sloshy discomfort, none of which had happened last time I made this offer. "I tried this with Billy once and it worked. I can lend somebody the Sight for a minute or two, if you want to see how I see."

Morrison looked at my feet. "Do you have to be barefoot for it to work?"

"No, but you have to stand on my feet and that would hurt like hell, on heels. Take your shoes off, for that matter. I'm not having shod feet standing on my bare ones."

Curiosity won out, though Morrison shot a glance toward the elevator as he toed his shoes off. "If that guard comes up to check on us…"

I grinned. "Yeah, I know. But wait, it gets worse. Have

you ever had anybody older than about six try to stand on your feet?"

"I taught a girlfriend to waltz in college. She stood on my feet."

"You can waltz?"

"Can't you?"

"Morrison, some days I'm lucky to be able to walk. Okay, put your feet on mine. No, really stand on them. Don't worry, Billy must've outweighed you by fifty pounds when we did this." I wrapped my arm around Morrison's ribs and hauled him right up against me. He emitted a sound I could only define as an undignified squeak, and I grinned again, this time from about a centimeter away from his face. Laughing at him—at us—made it easier to not think about being pressed up against my boss in what could only be considered an intimate manner. Laughing also made it slightly easier to ignore the scent of Old Spice, which, antithesis of trendy or not, really did smell good. It made me want to put my nose in his neck and inhale, which would almost certainly be ill-advised.

That was not the path I needed my thoughts to be going down. I gave myself a mental shake. "This is the 'worse' part. How hard did you have to hang on to your girlfriend to keep her on your feet?"

Morrison made another sound, this one more of a grunt and therefore slightly more dignified, and put his arms around my waist. "She was a lot smaller than you are."

"I'm sure she was smaller than you are, too. Look over my shoulder." Unreasonably piqued by the comment, I slapped my hand on top of Morrison's head with a little more force than absolutely necessary. "I bind what I hold and share the Sight of old."

It was a marginally better couplet than the humiliating

gibberish I'd spouted when I'd tried this with Billy. Morrison still slid an arched-eyebrow look at me, which meant I got to watch from up close and personal as gold filtered through his blue eyes, sure sign that magical vision was kicking in.

He reared his head back, enough of a retreat that my stomach soured with hurt disappointment. I loosened my grip, but he tightened his in turn, so I was stuck there, clinging to him. There were circumstances under which this would seem ideal. Somehow this wasn't turning out to be one of them. Heat crawled up my cheeks and I reminded myself, not for the first time, that I should make a habit of thinking before speaking. If I'd thought about it I'd have never, ever offered to give my boss a glimpse of the world the way I could see it.

Morrison adjusted his weight and balance again, reversing his retreat without ever taking his gaze off mine, and wet his lips before saying, very softly, "Your eyes are gold."

"So are yours."

Whatever he'd expected me to say, that apparently wasn't it. The heart-pounding intimacy of being wrapped around each other couldn't stand up to Morrison abruptly crossing his eyes, like he'd be able to see them if he only tried hard enough.

I laughed out loud and turned his head slightly, so he was looking over my shoulder again. "Check out the window, boss. You're supposed to be seeing what I see."

He murmured, "Subtle silver and blue," next to my ear. He'd shaved today—I'd only seen him stubbly once in the four years I'd known him—but eighteen hours after the fact, I felt sandpaper brushing my cheek. It gave my heart a little twist and made me want, again, to put my nose in his neck.

I was saved only by him adding, "Is that what you see when you look at people?"

"What? No. What?" God, I was a stunning conversationalist. Even if people with bodies mashed up against one another weren't typically expected to have profound conversations—after all, they were probably either in a subway or a bedroom, if they were as pressed close as Morrison and I were—monosyllabic inanities were still on the disappointing end of witty repertoire. Fortunately after a second or two my brain caught up to what he was probably actually asking. "That's just me. My aura. It's usually silver and blue. You're purple and blue. Billy's fuchsia and orange."

"Really? I'm purple? I thought you would be. Like that car of yours."

My mouth, unwisely, said, "Maybe that's magic's way of saying we're *simpatico*," and Morrison, much more wisely, released me and stepped back.

I looked down and to the side, suddenly brimming with self-loathing at a potency level usually reserved for teenagers. If the floor opened up and dropped me six hundred feet to the Seattle Center grounds, that would almost be sufficient punishment for the humiliation of saying something so incredibly stupid and desperate and stupid. And desperate. *I'd* closed the damned door on a potential relationship with Morrison months ago. The niggling detail that at least one of us had put a foot in that door to keep it from slamming shut was not supposed to bear any relevance to my life.

It might have borne a lot less relevance if I wasn't half-sure it was Morrison's foot in the door. He'd asked me to dance at the Halloween party. He'd gotten huffy and territorial when Coyote came back. He'd even come to get me on New Year's Eve, thus pretty much ensuring he and I would be ringing in the new year together, whether or not anybody else was around.

None of which overruled the fact that he was my boss, but all of which, put together like that, set fire to my humiliation and turned it into good old-fashioned crankiness. Okay, fine, I'd put us in a bit of a compromising position there, but if we were doing some kind of stupid song and dance around a not-relationship, it wasn't fair that he made small advancing movements and then staged full-scale withdrawals when I said something imprudent but hopeful.

Genuinely pissed off, I snatched up my sandals and glared at my boss. "I'm going to check out the other side of the city. I'll call you tomorrow if I've found anything."

Morrison's expression shut down, betraying a whole lot as it did so. I wasn't sure he knew what he'd done wrong, but I was even less sure he *didn't* know. I caught a hint of *I deserved that* and a pinch of *I'm your boss, how dare you* and some disappointment and some resignation, all of which transformed into a mask as stony as my own before he said, "I'll tell security you'll be out shortly," and stalked to the elevator.

I waited until the doors dinged shut before pitching a shoe after him as hard as I could.

CHAPTER NINE

Emotional turmoil probably wasn't the best mental state to hunt bad guys in, but I stomped around the empty restaurant anyway, widdershins to its rotation, and stopped where I could see the northern half of the city. Everything blazed with too much light, like my temper offered the Sight extra oomph. That would've been great, if it just zoomed in on one particular shining spot, but no, instead it had to make everything more brilliant and vital. The actual places of power I knew about, like Thunderbird Falls on Lake Washington, were glorious, white magic reaching for the sky like welder's arcs.

The phrase *white magic* caught my attention and broke my own temper tantrum. The power dancing over the waterfall was literally white, fed daily by the goodwill and positive energy of those people who were drawn to a place where magic had happened. They had chosen to make the new falls a place of companionship, if not exactly worship. The visible-to-me result of so many Magic Seattleites offering up a bit of who they were to keep the place refreshed and invigorated was a magic made of so many people and colors and auras that it became white, a culmination of all colors.

I'd never thought about it before, but the correlation between white equaling good magic and black equaling bad magic suddenly seemed pretty fricking obvious. It didn't even strike me as much of a values judgment. It was just that bad magic tended to be detractive—like, oh, say, *eating somebody's heart out*—where good tended to be additive. In the light spectrum you generally ended up with either black or white if you did enough of either of those things.

Well, in theory, anyway. My vaguely recalled artistic attempts at finger painting as a child suggested if you kept adding one color to another what you really got was nasty brown-gray muck, but that was of absolutely no help here and now. Besides, auras blended better than acrylics.

Minor turn-of-phrase epiphanies aside, the Sight-bright city wasn't showing me much of what I hoped to see. I was disappointed, but a small calm spot inside me suggested I wasn't surprised. If I'd been planning a major power-grab, I'd have created some kind of haven where my newly stolen magic wasn't the moral equivalent of a neon arrow flashing to say *BAD GUY LOCATED HERE!* It wouldn't be a null spot, either, because that would be just as obvious. It would look, in essence, like the rest of the city: streaked with life and activity, but not so much or so little as to stand out.

I probably should have thought of that before dragging Morrison up to the Space Needle in the middle of the night. Not that I was about to apologize. I went back to the elevator and collected my shoe, keeping an idle eye on the view while I waited for the doors to open. It appeared I was right about getting up high to have a look around not being sufficient as a tracking method. Well, I lived and I learned. Though more accurately I got stabbed, beaten up, rolled over, hung out to dry and learned, but at least I was learning.

And if the view-from-above approach hadn't worked, then I could be grateful that for once, I actually knew what tactic to try next. Shoes dangling from my fingertips, I headed back home to wake Coyote from a sound sleep.

SATURDAY, MARCH 18, 1:58 A.M.

In an ideal world, that would have meant climbing into bed and putting my cold feet on him. On the other hand, in that ideal world I would've had no reason to accidentally take Morrison on a date. *Ideal,* it seemed, had many strange and unexplored convolutions. Either way, instead of climbing into bed, I changed into sweats and a T-shirt, got my drum and tucked a blanket against my apartment's front door to cut down on the draft. I hadn't eaten in hours, so I was as prepared as I could be to settle down on the living-room floor to thump a quiet fingertip beat against the drum's painted surface.

Fifteen months ago, mostly I'd moved from one realm to another by dint of getting hit on the head, or from pure exhaustion loosening me from my body and sending me somewhere else. I'd gotten better at it, and could largely step from the Middle World—day to day reality—into shamanic trances that let me travel to a wide variety of different planes at whim.

My whim was evidently not on call tonight. Half-formed images kept flitting through my mind: Patricia Raleigh's snarl as she'd swung the baseball bat, Naomi's heart being gobbled up, Raleigh's shock when the bullet impacted her shoulder, the blonde woman's cancer stretching forward into her future, Raleigh lying wide-eyed and shallow-breathed on the floor, and more vividly than any of those, Morrison's eyes filtering gold.

Morrison cropped up a lot, in fact, not just memories from the evening, but from the years we'd known each other, all the way back to him mistaking Petite for a Corvette. That was what had gotten us off on the wrong foot—I simply could not understand how any red-blooded American male could make that mistake, and had said so, loudly, pointedly, and mockingly, shortly before discovering he was the newly appointed Captain of Seattle Police's North Precinct. *Oops, sorry* didn't cover it at that juncture, and we'd spent most of the past four years on the wrong foot.

Which had ended up with me throwing a shoe at him tonight. There was probably cosmic justice in that, but I neither appreciated nor admired its irony. Mostly I wished I could just let the idea of him go, so I could get into the garden that was the center of my soul and talk to Coyote. My apartment had gotten chilly and gray around me, features fading into a nothingness that Morrison wandered through time and again, usually in the suits he wore to work, but occasionally—enticingly—in shirtsleeves or flannel, the latter of which I'd never seen him in. Not in the real world, at least. Just in his own soul's garden, where bits of hidden personality leaked through even the firmest of reserve.

Coyote, behind me, said, "It's three in the morning. Could you spare me the dream-wrought fantasies about someone who isn't me?"

I yelped, Morrison disappeared and the dreamscape suddenly became recognizable in its featureless nothingness. I'd been here before, in a space between dreams, though not for a long time. "I'm *asleep?*"

"Evidently." Coyote always sounded much more dry and sour as a coyote than he did as a man, so I wasn't surprised, when I spun around, to find him sitting there, tongue lolling and his feet placed with catlike mathematical precision, all tight and tidy.

"I haven't fallen asleep on a psychic journey in months. God, am I regressing?" I prodded at the dreamscape mentally, trying to push myself from sleep into the half-conscious wakefulness of a trance. The quiet gray nothing swirled around me, making halfhearted attempts at forming images, then fell away again, uninterested.

Coyote frowned, an expression that had a lot to do with what would be his eyebrows if dogs had eyebrows, and not so much to do with his long grinning mouth. "You're not regressing. You're exhausted. Your aura's almost flat. What've you been doing, Jo?"

"Making new exciting mistakes."

"Normally I'd say that was better than repeating the old ones, but I'm not so sure, if this is what it does to you." The nothingness around us shifted as Coyote spoke, drawing away from the realm of dreams into a desert landscape. A hard white sun glared out of an equally hard blue sky, and the earth beneath me warmed to uncomfortably hot. Red rock formations cropped up, offering some degree of shade, and for a moment Coyote disappeared into the heart of his garden, hidden and protected by it.

Then he came over the stone ridges, no longer the eponymous coyote, but a jeans-clad shirtless man with skin colored brick-red and shining black hair that fell unbound past his hips. His eyes, like his coyote form's, were gold, though I knew in real life both his eyes and skin were softer in shade.

Here in the garden of his soul, though, he saw himself as the shamanistic leader he'd been trained as, super-saturated by life.

He walked right up to me, concern still furrowing his eyebrows as it had when he was a coyote, crouched and put a hand over my heart. I'd have slapped anybody else for being fresh, but there was nothing sexual about the gesture at all. Especially when, a moment later, a burst of desert-dune and blue magic swept through me, replenishing some of the energy I'd lost.

If I hadn't already been sitting, I'd have dropped to the earth with gratitude. As it was I tilted sideways. Coyote caught my shoulder, propping me, then tipped my chin up so he could frown at me more directly. "What happened?"

"Well, first I shot someone. Then there was the dance concert that almost turned me into a coyote, then a psychic murder at the end of the concert drained every ounce of deliberately-awakened power from the dancers, and then I healed somebody with really early-stage breast cancer and saw something screwy in her genetic code and almost fixed it, so I think maybe that was, like, accidentally almost re-writing it to remove the predilection her family has toward the disease." That sounded like quite enough. I didn't think I needed to mention offering Morrison the Sight.

Coyote paled, which was quite an event for a man of his red-brick complexion. He sat down with a *thump*, sand dusting up to coat his thighs, and for a long few moments had nothing to say. I couldn't recall that happening before, and marked two points on the *Joanne has made some truly heinous mistakes today* scoreboard.

He finally said, "You shot someone," in a way that suggested he was only groping for a place to start, rather than it necessarily being the most important topic at hand. I almost felt guilty for bringing it up, but since it had kind of gotten my day off on the wrong foot, and was showing no signs of ceasing to prey at my thoughts, I couldn't really imagine having not mentioned it.

"She attacked Billy," was all I said, though. There wasn't much else to say, not when I'd do the whole thing over again in a heartbeat, if I had to.

To my astonishment, Coyote, who had extremely pointed opinions about what I should be doing with my gifts, paled even further and said, "Is he okay?" Not *is* she *okay,* which is what I'd expected, but is *he* okay. I hadn't known Billy would rank higher in Coyote's hierarchy of concerns than somebody that a nominal healer had shot at.

"Yeah, he's...he's fine. She missed, she...I was faster. And she's okay, too. In the hospital. Shattered clavicle, but she'll be fine. I couldn't heal her. The power went flat."

"You said your magic's responsive to your needs, even when you don't want it to be. That it has opinions. If your need was an act of violence I'm not surprised it wouldn't respond. Jo," Coyote said carefully, "shamans aren't supposed to hurt people."

"And cops aren't supposed to let their partners get a nail through the skull." I thought it was a pretty inarguable defense.

Coyote stared at me a moment, then closed his eyes, shrugged all over and nodded. I had the impression a lot went unsaid in the context of that shrug, but I couldn't read it, and what he said next was clearly not a direct follow-up to his thoughts: "Cancer?"

He said it in much the same tone as *you shot someone?,* like he was really still just trying to find a place to start. I judged it for an opening salvo and remained silent, which let him say, "Cancer is dangerous, Joanne. As healers we're

supposed to show the body a path to health, but the healing strength itself has to mostly come from within the patient. You could—" He swallowed, pulled his hand over
his mouth, looked away, and looked back. "You could kill
yourself, healing cancer with your magic alone. I know the
last spirit quest gave you the focus to effect an instantaneous
healing, and you have astonishing raw strength, but…"

"Yeah. I kind of figured that out when I almost fainted. It
was like time tunneled forward and I was healing all the potential damage. How do I…" I tilted my head back, wishing
I had something nice and hard behind me to thunk it on,
like a rock. Beating my skull against stone seemed like the
only way anything was ever going to sink in. "I've mostly
only healed small things, Yote. Things I can use my own
power for. I didn't even know I didn't know how to use
someone else's strength to help them heal themselves."

"Jo, you've never done a proper shamanic healing in a
sweat lodge or healing circle. The setting is important to
creating the right mental space for the healer as well as the
healed. Don't you remember *anything* I taught you?"

Feebly, I said, "I thought she was in the right headspace,"
but the question was a depressingly legitimate one. I did
remember. Hell, after the antics I'd gone through to access
the memories of his teachings from back when I'd been
a teen, I'd *better* remember. Much of my bad attitude and
mucked-up view of the world was my own fault, in a way
that blithely disregarded the usual linear development of
time. But I remembered discussing healing circles and the
mental transport created by sweat lodges, how those things
readied a human mind for the extraordinary. I'd just never
applied them in my own roughshod shamanic practices.

In fact, I had the sudden sinking feeling that I'd been ar-
rogantly assuming the rules didn't apply to me. *Other* people

had to build sweat lodges and use healing circles, but *I* could just go larking off doing what I wanted, because Grandfather Sky had seen fit to pump me full of extra-special magic mojo.

Coyote'd told me early on I was a new soul, mixed up fresh. The advantage to that was I had no baggage from previous incarnations, and could focus all my strength and power going forward. The disadvantage was I had no baggage from previous incarnations, and got to make great huge rutting mistakes that a more-experienced lizard brain might warn me about ahead of time.

I said, "Okay," very quietly. "No more healing, especially big stuff, without the right preparations."

Coyote's shoulders dropped so far I half thought he was going to slide right out of his man shape and into dog form. He lifted his eyes to give me a sharp look and I smiled a little. "I know. Coyotes aren't dogs."

Instead of scolding, he said, "Tell me about the shapeshifting."

"It was completely involuntary." I outlined the dances and the collected power I'd felt, and somehow accidentally left out the detail that Morrison had been my date and he was the one who'd noticed me changing. "As soon as I got away from the theater I started reverting, but I could feel the potential still under my skin." I rubbed my hands, remembering it even now, and in absolute, utter denial of what I'd experienced, whined, "People can't *shapeshift,* Coyote."

"Of course they can, although you're so ungodly stubborn about it I might have believed you couldn't. What's your newest spirit animal, Joanne?" Coyote sounded tired, which made me feel guilty for whining, and my answer was subdued.

"A rattlesnake. You know that."

"And what do rattlesnakes do?"

"They bite things. All right, all right, sorry. Mine's a symbol of healing. And he gave me super reflexes in the Lower World, at least. Snakelike reflexes. *Whssht, whssht.*" I made a couple of karate chops, mimicking my snake-granted speed, and subsided at Coyote's heartfelt sigh.

"What else, Jo?"

"Um. They shed their skins? Symbol of renewal and all that?"

"Symbol of change."

I opened my mouth, shut it again, then said, "Oh," in a smaller voice. "Like shapechanging, maybe?"

Coyote said, "She can be taught," to the hard blue sky, which was probably kinder than I deserved. "I should be there for this, Jo. To teach you this in person. Shapechanging can be dangerous."

Everything was dangerous. I just barely restrained myself from the snarky comment, reforming it into something slightly more constructive: "Like healing cancer dangerous or different dangerous?"

"Different. Overdrawing the healing power could kill you. Shapeshifting magic can make you forget who and what you are."

That was twice in a row he'd subdued me with a look or a handful of words. I hunched my shoulders. "Like the wendigo?"

"No, the worst thing about wendigos is they remember, in some part, what they were. Uncontrolled shifting can just turn you into an animal for good. You got lucky tonight. Look, if I leave right now I can probably catch a six o'clock flight and be up there by noon. Can you promise not to do anything stupid before noon?"

What I really wanted to do between now and noon was

sleep. I rubbed my eyes, which reminded me that in the waking world I hadn't taken my contacts out before falling asleep, which meant my eyelids would be glued together when I actually woke up. I wondered if a little healing magic could lube up my eyeballs, a thought that had never occurred to me before, but I was fairly certain the magic would place a failure to remove contacts under the heading of *my own dumb damned fault* and be mysteriously unavailable to ease the discomfort. "I can probably manage not to do anything stupid before noon, but…is there anything you can just teach me now?"

Coyote went quiet. Not a good quiet, but the kind that worked its way through a lot of silent guesses and unspoken commentary and arrived at a conclusion it didn't like. "You don't want me to come up. Who'd you say your date this evening was?"

"I didn't even say I had a date."

"So it wasn't Gary."

"Gary's in California for the weekend. Something about old army buddies and a pool of green beer. I didn't want the details." Actually I was dying for the details, but my septuagenarian buddy had sparkled his eyes at me, mimed zipping his lips, and jet-set off to San Diego for three days. My only consolation was imagining his profound disappointment at missing me learning to shapeshift.

"Morrison, then."

"Cyrano, I didn't even say I had a date!"

Bitter triumph flashed in Coyote's eyes. I dropped my head into my hands. My mentor's real name was Cyrano, but I'd spent most of our relationship thinking he was a spirit animal, the very coyote I usually saw him as. Consequently, even after learning he was a more or less ordinary human with a more or less ordinary name, I called him

Coyote. Except, as he'd all-too-sagely noticed, when I was upset with him. "All right, fine, yes, I had a date, and it was with Morrison, and if you want to know so much he's the one who noticed I was shapeshifting and got me out of the theater before I turned into a *dog* in front of everybody!"

"Coyotes aren't dogs!"

"That's what he said!"

I'd been right. That wasn't a piece of our banter Coyote wanted to share with Morrison. He looked about five years old and utterly betrayed for a couple of seconds, then popped into his coyote shape so fast I was left with the afterimage of a man shadowing the beast.

"Shapeshifting," he said through a mouthful of very pointy teeth, "is about control, and knowing yourself, and giving yourself up completely to the magic. It requires incredible focus if you don't want to lose yourself, which is why it's most safely done within the confines of a power circle, even when you're as good at it as I am. The rattlesnake will help you make the shift and retain your sense of self, so call on him any time you even think about changing shape. *Never* make the change unless you're alone or with someone you trust with your life, because you'll be incredibly vulnerable in the moments of transition.

"It doesn't hurt unless you fight it. It's a flow from one state of being to another. Until you have absolute control over the skill, it's possible for someone else to force you into the change, either deliberately or accidentally, so you'd better keep your shields at full strength, if you even remember how to do that." He snapped his teeth on the last word sharply enough that the sound reverberated against hot stone.

I whispered, "I never said I didn't want you to come up," but I was talking to a dreamscape.

CHAPTER TEN

SATURDAY, MARCH 18, 6:32 A.M.

No decent person would show up on a friend's doorstep at six in the morning. Not even if they were reasonably certain that the friends, who had a four-and-a-half-month-old baby, would be awake. That was why I'd sat in Petite for half an hour on the street by my partner's house, growing steadily chillier because the idle on a 1969 Mustang was at best a dull roar. I didn't dare leave her on for warmth and risk annoying the neighborhood.

Billy, who had refused days off after his near-death experience—better to get back on the horse, he said—had to be at work at eight-thirty like I normally would be, so even sans the newborn he was likely to be up by six-thirty or seven. I still hadn't talked myself into going and knocking, though, when their front door opened and his berobed wife appeared to crook a finger and tilt her head in obvious invitation. I slunk out of Petite feeling silly for not having wanted to bother them.

She whisper-called, "Close the gate behind you," and I made sure to, securing myself inside a white picket fence that enveloped a large yard littered with mostly-melted snowmen. I picked a hat up from one of them and brought it to Melinda like an early-morning apology, and she laughed quietly.

"Robert won't forgive you for rescuing this. He thinks he's too cool to wear a winter hat now."

"I thought he must have hit that age when I saw it on the snowman right before Christmas. How're you doing?"

Melinda crushed me in a hug, which took some doing, as I was taller, broader and stronger than she was. Still, I grunted, and after a long rib-squeezing moment, she said, "Thank you," into my chest. "Thank you, Joanne."

My whole head got stuffy with the threat of tears, and I snuffled as I squished her back just as hard. "You're welcome. How's Billy?"

"Fine. He was antsy last night, but that's no surprise. We spent a lot of time trying not to think about what might have happened."

Which almost certainly meant they'd talked about nothing else once the kids were put to bed, and that they'd said, again and again, "But it turned out okay," and probably held on to each other harder than usual. I gave Melinda another tight hug and whispered the fortunately-true platitude myself: "It turned out okay."

Mel nodded and finally let me go, backing farther into the house. Her eyes were bright, cheeks flushed, but high emotion looked good on her. Most things did, honestly: Melinda Holliday was most of a foot shorter than me, had enviable hourglass curves that even a bulky terry-cloth robe couldn't hide, and her vivid Hispanic coloring made her film-star radiant even in predawn light after what had probably been a very long night. I was pretty happy with my tall build, but if I ever needed to trade in for another shape entirely, I wanted to look like Melinda.

"How about you? Are you okay?" She invited me in and I got rid of my clompy boots right inside the door, hoping not to wake any of the kids. Melinda gave an approving nod that made me feel warm and fuzzy inside, and I murmured, "I'm doing okay, all things considered. It's been a long day."

Melinda arched a concerned eyebrow. "It's six-thirty in the morning. It's a new day."

"I might have forgotten to get any sleep."

"Oh, Joanne." Melinda pointed toward the kitchen. "Billy's in there with Caroline and a pot of coffee."

"You are an angel among women." I followed Mel down the hall into a kitchen that still looked brand-new, seven months after being rebuilt. There were no scars on the walls from the monster that had nearly broken their house apart, and the whole room—the whole house, really—had a warm and comforting ambience. I had no earthly use for a sprawling suburban home, but I never once visited the Hollidays without wishing I lived in a place like theirs.

Melinda picked up the coffeepot and waved it in my direction, her eyebrows elevated. I desperately wanted a cup, but I shook my head as I sat down at the kitchen table across from Billy and Caroline. The latter was happily sucking down a bottle of milk, big brown eyes focused on her daddy, and Billy gave me a quick smile before returning his own besotted gaze to the baby girl. Melinda put the coffeepot down and her hands on her hips. "Lurking in the driveway at six in the morning and now refusing coffee. Did your date with Michael go that badly?"

Although I knew Morrison's given name was Michael—James Michael, in fact; I'd seen it on his driver's license—I'd never gotten used to the fact that Melinda actually called him by it. At work he was Morrison, Captain, Sir or Boss, and it continued to seem peculiar that someone would call him by any other appellation. I inhaled, searching for an appropriately cheeky response, but what came out was an all-too-honest, "You have no idea."

"Oh dear." Melinda sat down and Billy went so far as to drag his attention from Caroline to me.

I sat there for a moment, hands folded on the scarred table surface—five kids left a lot of stories on the battered wood—and finally, inanely, said, "Actually the date part wasn't so bad. Even after the murder."

My hosts made spluttering noises as I described the evening, up to and including Coyote's snit fit, before pulling my glasses off to clean them—I'd finally taken my contacts out when I woke up—as I transferred a helpless look to Melinda. "So I spent the last few hours reading about shamanic shapeshifting on the Net and in some of my books and then I came here. I was hoping I could use your sanctuary to give this a try under controlled circumstances. It's the only way I can think to have some idea of how to stop it accidentally happening again."

Billy cast his gaze skyward. "Sure, she gets suspended from duty and gets to spend the morning learning to shapeshift while I have to go to work and miss all the fun. Where's the justice in that?"

I grinned. "You sound like Gary. He's going to pop a vein when he gets back from California. I was under strict instructions to not do anything exciting without him."

"I'm calling him," Billy threatened.

"And interrupting his weekend with beer and the boys? I don't think so. I'll try to do anything interesting in the next hour, before you have to leave, okay?" I got up, and Melinda nodded me toward the kitchen door, stopping to kiss Billy on her way by.

His attempt at pique failed, and he smiled at his wife. "You two be careful."

"We will be. Come on, Joanne. Come downstairs."

Six months earlier I hadn't even known Melinda Holliday had a sanctuary in the daylight basement of their rambling home. I'd barely even known that Melinda, like Billy, had long-established ties to the world of weird which I'd only recently entered. Even now I still wasn't entirely certain what Melinda *was*, in Magic Seattle terms. An adept of some kind, and not a shaman like myself or a medium like Billy, but she wouldn't even go so far as to call herself a witch. She'd said she was just a wise woman, when I'd asked her about it, and while I couldn't argue, I also had the feeling that title barely scratched the surface.

Her sanctuary was a simple room filled with candles and pillows, its concrete floor and spackled ceiling painted with matching power circles. Magic brought to life within those circles was fully contained, as safe as it could be, and with Coyote's tetchy warning still echoing in my mind, I was all for playing safely.

I prodded the edge of the circle, feeling no residual power. Melinda hadn't called up magic any time recently. I caught her watching me with an expression of amusement and folded my hands back, embarrassed. "Sorry. I should've asked. May I enter?"

Her eyebrows elevated. "Of course, but what do you want from me here, Joanne?"

I stepped inside the power circle, pausing to nod in each of the cardinal directions before answering. "I know I've awakened it before, but I'd like you to do it this time, with a keep-things-in intent. If I lose my mind to a coyote shape I'd rather not be able to escape and chew anybody up."

"Do you think that's likely?"

"I sure as hell hope not." I sat in the middle of the circle, cross-legged, and Melinda made a pile of cushions to settle down on, just close enough that she could reach forward and touch the painted lines on the floor. At the last moment, I triggered the Sight, curious to see what her active magic looked like.

Buttercup-yellow flickered around her, a sunshine color that went hand in hand with her personal warmth. The painted circle came alight, flickering up to meet its match on the ceiling. I watched the power dance, as mesmerized by it as I would be by any fire. Calm seeped around me, a gentle cushion protecting me from the world. I wanted to bask in it, to catch up on the sleep I'd missed in this quiet reserved space.

That, however, wasn't in the cards, though I indulged for a few minutes, absorbing some of the tranquility. Relaxed and content seemed like a good way to start a shapeshifting attempt.

I'd felt nothing untoward when the dancers had triggered my transformation, and Coyote had said the process shouldn't hurt. That was well and good, but I needed to be aware in a way that I clearly hadn't been the night before, and so from a pleasant centered place I murmured, "Rattler, can you guide me?"

Scales slithered across concrete, a rasping sound that wore

away at my calm. I'd spent years in North Carolina, where that sound—the soft *whish* of a snake's movement, not necessarily over concrete—meant stand still and pray. A decade and more later, that instinct was still well in place, even if I'd called up the rattlesnake deliberately. He coiled around me from behind, wrapping into my lap before lifting his snaky head until his eyes were level with mine.

Like my raven, within the power circle he was made of glowing lines of magic, solid but also not quite there. We would have to move to another plane for him to take on a less ephemeral shape, but I was pretty certain I needed his guidance in the Middle World. Shapeshifting in the Lower or Upper Worlds, or even in my garden, was a spiritual matter. I was looking at physical transformation, entirely within the world my body belonged to.

Apparently I'd been sitting and thinking too long: the snake's darting tongue tasted my nose, which was sufficiently odd to make me smile. I offered a rub along his jaw, and he leaned into it like a cat with no purr.

"I understand your gifts are threefold, Rattler. I'm supposed to learn how to shapeshift today, if I can. Will you help?"

He tasted my nose again, then tilted farther forward, neck bending until his forehead touched mine. A splash of light obliterated my vision. I blinked it clear, but the rattler was no longer in my lap.

I could feel him inside me, though, coiled up in my mind. A wonderful itchy sensation came over me, so intense I wriggled with it. My skin, and within my mind, the snake's skin, started wrinkling away in the simplest, most basic, most instinctive transformation a reptile could offer. Beneath the shedding layer, I felt slick and damp, easing the passage from one skin to another. My impulse to help tear away the changing skin was stymied by a sudden lack of arms, startling enough that I flinched forward, breaking free of the old skin and rearing up in my new.

The sanctuary looked odd. I could still See the power circle, but its vivid colors had faded to a grayscale aurora, of absolutely no interest. The walls, however, glowed interestingly: I could see—not with a capital S—hot water pipes and heating vents in them, and even the warmth of electricity zipping from one place to another. There were no dangerous hot spots, but it all gave off an ambient warmth.

Melinda herself was much brighter, a human-shaped blob of heat. She was on her feet, pressed against the comparatively cool wall, and she swallowed twice before whispering, *"Joanne?"*

I didn't quite hear the question. I saw its shape on her lips, and felt it tremble over my skin, peculiar enough to make me look at myself. Look and look and look and *look* at myself, in fact, because I was a rattlesnake at least fifteen feet long and as big around as my thigh typically was. I could tell, because my clothes had all sort of slithered down around me and my copper bracelet was lying on the floor with my glasses. My shirt had plenty of room, but I was nicely fitted into one pants leg without much room to spare.

I snapped my head around, searching for my socks, and rattled one off the tip of my tail. I spent a few seconds trying to count the number of rattles before giving it up as a bad job. There were a lot. That was all that mattered. I also took a look around for a Joanne-shaped shed skin somewhere in the circle, and was incredibly, incredibly glad to not find one. The gross factor there would've been off the scale.

I swung my head back around, trying to focus on Melinda with something besides the heat vision. I could see relatively well—not that I needed to in hunting terms, with the infrared kicked in—but I felt my eyeballs flexing in a completely unnatural way as I worked on examining my friend. She looked tiny and appetizing, not that I had any intention of making her an appetizer. Still, I had to be a good three times her length, and rattlesnakes of normal size would take down and eat a rabbit, given the opportunity.

That was not a good direction for my thoughts to be wandering in. I looked at myself again, astonished at how easy shifting had been, and wondered if my rattler guide's template had made it simple or if I could do something totally different, like a coyote, with equal ease.

Of course, I would make a very large coyote, just as I made a very large snake, unless I learned how to transfer some of my mass into a waiting zone. But then, I'd never seen Coyote in his coyote form in real life. It was entirely possible he was a human-weight coyote, which would be downright mythological in its own right. I flashed on Big Coyote, the archetype trickster I'd met once or twice, and tried to put a size to him. Since I'd mostly met him when I was at a tremendous disadvantage, my general impression was that he was Bigger Than God, which, if a measly little shaman-turned-coyote was a massive human-size beast, made sense.

On the other hand, it kind of suggested that if I shifted into a bear, I'd probably better choose a black bear instead of a grizzly. My hundred-and-sixty-five-pound self would make a pretty pathetic-looking brown bear. I was going to have to look up animals in my weight class so I had some idea of what species I'd be relatively normal as.

Oh, what my life had come to, that such a thought even crossed my mind. I laughed—hissed, more accurately—and turned to the silent waiting rattler in my mind. "How do I—aghglt!"

Snakes were not meant to talk in human languages. I *kakked* and hissed and spat the handful of words I tried, then sank down in a giant puddle of embarrassed snake and hid my nose in my coils.

Snaky laughter buzzed through my skull. *Sssilly ssshaman. Ssspeak inssside.*

My "Easy for you to say" came out another series of choking hisses and coughs, and I hid my face farther into my coils. They were nice raspy coils, warm with the heat of Melinda's sanctuary, and I was just as happy to stay there being humiliated by an inability to talk out loud. Plaintively, silently, I asked, *How do I change back?*

Ssshed thisss ssskin, too, of courssse. The ssshaman liesss within.

Of course I did, or I'd have probably tried eating Melinda by now. I tried pressing my eyes shut, but having no eyelids made that tricky. *Okay. Before I do, is it always going to be this easy?*

My rattler made a sound of amusement. *Nothing is easssy with you, Sssiobhán Walkingssstick. Today, in this moment you are frightened of missstakes, and are unusually ressseptive. Perhaps confidensse from this transssition will carry over. Perhaps in the future you will fight it. I cannot sssay. Time isss not mine to travel in sssuch a way.*

"I gueack—" *I guess I'll just have to try, then. Thank you, Rattler. This has been...very interesting.*

He made another sound of amusement and didn't disappear, but went quiet inside my mind, clearly waiting to see if I could get back to human shape on my own. Well, not on my own: he was right there to help, as he would presumably always be. I concentrated on the idea of molting again, as the drone of Melinda's voice bumped over my skin a second time. I couldn't *hear* her properly—rattlesnakes apparently didn't have ears—and hastened my shedding process so I would catch what she had to say.

"—othes. Oh, dear. Too late." The last words were muffled behind Melinda's hands, which did nothing to hide the laughter in them.

Nor did I require any kind of translation, as I was lying constricted in my own clothing. Both my arms were inside my shirt, which wasn't so bad. They were also both inside my bra, which was not meant to be stretched around another dozen inches of width. I wasn't entirely certain the bra hadn't come unfastened and that I wasn't entangled in straps, but I couldn't quite tell. Either way, the upper half of my body had nothing on my lower half's troubles, as both my legs were stuffed into one leg of my jeans. The fabric should have, by all rights, exploded. Instead it had stretched to its three-percent-spandex-maximum, and the seams were strained to bursting. The other leg of the jeans flopped to one side like an empty sausage skin. I was afraid to wonder what had happened to my panties. My feet were bare and rapidly going numb from lack of circulation.

I said, "Help?" in a very small voice, and Melinda collapsed on the floor, weak with laughter. I wanted to be annoyed, but my predicament shot straight past irritation into the absurd, and I, too, began to giggle.

Giggling while bound up in denim and underwires had to be one of the least comfortable things I'd ever done, which only made it funnier. I struggled to free an arm so I could wipe my eyes, and succeeded mostly in rolling myself over. My pants leg gave up any hope of molecular cohesion and tore with a sound unfortunately similar to passing an enormous amount of gas.

Melinda's shriek of laughter covered the denim's last gasps. I kicked myself free of the shredded fabric, discovering in the process that the elastic on my panties hadn't been nearly so stubborn as the jeans and had already given up the ghost. I crunched up to sitting and wormed a hand up to wipe my eyes. Melinda threw a pillow at me. "Cover yourself, woman! You're indecent!"

I threw the pillow back, but it bounced off the keep-things-in circle. "What'm I going to do! I don't have any extra clothes with me! And I loved this shirt, well, I guess the shirt's okay..." I got myself free of it and shook off the remainders of my poor bra, which would never cup another breast in its life. "Apparently shapeshifting is to be done naked."

"Did I hear somebody say naked?" Billy came down the stairs and I shrieked like a teenager, scrambling to yank my shirt back on.

"Stop! Stop! Don't come down! Don't come in here, anyway! I'm naked! My clothes are ruined!" I surged for the pillow, clutching it modestly as Billy appeared in the sanctuary door and peered at me.

"I've seen naked women before, Walker. What happened?"

"You haven't seen *me* naked!" I dragged my ruined jeans toward me, not that there was any hope at all of resurrecting them, and repeated, "Shapeshifting is apparently a skyclad kind of activity."

Billy said, "She said skyclad," to Melinda in a voice of pure amazement. "I think that's the official last nail in the coffin on her skepticism. Where'd you even hear that?"

"I read it in one of the magic books. Would you please get me some sweatpants or something? I can't leave your house like this!"

"Oh, so you're done and ready to go now?"

"Well, not right now, I'm naked!" At some point I was

pretty certain I'd start to be embarrassed, but my sense of ridiculous was too well defined just yet. Then Billy's expression, which had gotten more serious, sank in, and I frowned. "What's wrong?"

"Nothing to do with you, except it is. That woman from yesterday, Rita Wagner, just called in to report a murder downtown."

CHAPTER ELEVEN

SATURDAY, MARCH 18, 8:48 A.M.

I was suspended from duty, but downtown wasn't our juris-diction anyway. Furthermore, Rita had specifically asked for me, so I figured on some level that worked out, and tagged along with Billy. I was still self-conscious walking into the Pioneer Square crime scene, though: I knew I didn't belong, and plenty of people there were entirely capable of handling a murder investigation.

It was, however, just slightly possible that my self-consciousness was less centered on whether I belonged there, and more concerned with the unusual detail that I was wear-ing a miniskirt.

It was not a miniskirt on Melinda Holliday. On her, it was a cute fitted black knit skirt that hugged curvaceous hips and followed the slim line of her thighs down to just above her knees. It looked equally terrific with either knee-high boots or heels, and made a potent reminder that Billy's wife was a bombshell.

But she was a bombshell who stood nine or ten inches shorter than me, and at least half of that difference was in the leg. The knit fabric ensured the skirt fit me as snugly—and attractively, even if I said so myself—as it did Melinda, but its only acquaintance with my knees was passing over them on the hem's way to its final resting place halfway up my thigh. It wasn't precisely the ideal outfit for a self-respecting police detective to show up to a crime scene in. Especially since my bra had exploded during the course of my transformation, a detail which I fully intended to keep well under cover. My jacket was zipped to my collarbones, hiding not only excess jiggle but the fact that my sweater didn't match the skirt.

It could do nothing about my stompy boots not matching the skirt, either, but I was trying to convince myself the boots were some kind of awesome Goth statement about fashion in the modern era.

I didn't buy it, and, at a glance, neither did the two detectives, the patrol officer, or the incoming forensics team. For a moment I wished I'd borrowed some of Billy's clothes instead, but they were as much too big on me as Mel's skirt was too small, so it was either the Charlie Chaplin look or legs from here to Sunday. In retrospect, though, clownishly large clothes might have been warmer. I'd have to keep that in mind for next time I destroyed my outfit by shapeshifting while wearing it.

"Our witness is this way," one of the detectives said grumpily. He was middling height and slim, with brown hair worn in a classic cut that could have come from any era from Victorian to present-day. It gave him a bit of age and gravitas, even if his bad mood hadn't already. "She doesn't want to talk to anybody unless you're here. What are you, her lawyer?"

Derailed from calculating the odds that I'd ruin half my wardrobe by slipping from one form to another, I followed him, mumbling an explanation: "I saved her life a few months ago. She'd been on the street, so she probably just wants a familiar face, somebody she has a little reason to trust. Believe me, Detective…"

"Monroe."

"Monroe, I don't want to take over your case. It's your jurisdiction, your territory. Only thing I'm here to do is facilitate the interview." Damn. Miniskirt or not, I sounded like a professional.

And miniskirt or not, apparently Monroe thought so, too. He glanced back at me, expression thawing noticeably. "That's good to hear. So what's with the outfit? Working undercover?"

God. I should've worn Billy's clothes after all, if I looked like a pro in Mel's skirt. "I tore the seams out of my pants this morning and this was the only thing I had to wear. If it doesn't warm up soon I'm gonna make a break for the Market and buy some pants."

Monroe gave me a very brief smile. "Don't get pants. Get some of those leggings to wear under the skirt. It'll warm *my* day up, anyway."

There was probably a better response than "Aheh," but I couldn't think of it. Fortunately Monroe led me into a café about twenty yards from the cordoned-off crime scene— I hadn't even gotten a look at the body, though Billy was down by the yellow tape, presumably doing his ghost thing—and pointed me at Rita Wagner. She was shrunk into a corner, sallow fingers wrapped around a cardboard coffee mug.

I sat down across from her, a spike of sympathy piercing me. I'd had a long night, but I had healing magic to shore me up. Rita, whose morning had apparently started with a murder, but who lacked my talent, looked small and fragile and hard-used again, like she had in the first moments we'd met. "Hey, Rita. You doing okay?"

She lifted her gaze, film of despondency clearing from her eyes as she recognized me. "Detective Walker. I didn't think you'd come. I didn't do it."

I blinked, first at her, then at Monroe, who hadn't yet sat down. He shrugged his eyebrows and gestured to the third chair at the table, questioning. I raised a finger to ask him to hold off and turned my attention back to Rita. "This is Detective Monroe, who's going to actually be handling this case. It's way out of my jurisdiction, so the best I can do is be here while you tell us what you saw. You mind if he sits down?"

She glanced up at him, shook her head and looked back at her coffee cup as Monroe pulled the chair out, turned it backward, and sat. I downwardly revised my estimation of his age to something closer to my own, especially since upon inspection, there were no gray threads in his brown hair, then focused on Rita, who started talking like she'd been waiting on my cue. What she said, though, had nothing to do with the case: "Was the show good?"

Her expression was so quietly hopeful I didn't have the heart to tell her what had transpired the night before.

Not that it would be useful to do so during a witness interview, anyway, so I said, "It was unbelievable," which I thought covered both the amazing performance and the dreadful aftermath in sufficiently enthusiastic yet noncommittal terms.

I got a hint of her youthening smile as a reward for my discretion, though her gaze went straight back to the coffee. "I helped close up the Solid Ground soup kitchen last night. It's open late because there are so many homeless down here, so it was after midnight when I left. I stayed nearby—"

"Where?" Monroe was taking notes, and his interruption—though I'd have asked the same thing—was unwelcome. Rita glanced at me nervously and I nodded, encouraging her. She didn't look encouraged, which made it Monroe's turn to eye me, in a get-her-talking manner.

"I'm guessing you stayed somewhere you're not supposed to." At Rita's nod, I opened a palm, brushing away her concern. "We're looking at a murder investigation here, Rita. Nobody's interested in busting you for an illegal flop-spot. You or anybody else who's using the place, for that matter. Okay?"

Her gaze shifted between us, guilty. "We—I—stay in the Underground a lot recently. Outside the tourist area, so they don't have any reason to run us out."

I nodded, having expected that. Seattle, like half the big cities in America, had burned down once upon a time. When they rebuilt, they'd moved street level between ten and thirty feet higher to help cut down on flooding and backed-up toilets. The old city disappeared under the new, until by the early twentieth century, the only people in the Underground were people like Rita today: homeless, criminals, or both. Parts of it had been reclaimed and made into a tour—I'd gone on it—but there was a lot more Underground than there was safe territory to explore. I personally had no clue how to access the less-safe areas from the outside, but then, I'd never had reason to search for a comparatively safe, warm place to hide from the elements or the law. There were five or ten thousand homeless people in Seattle. It was a safe bet that a fair chunk of them knew a lot about surviving beneath the city, even if I didn't.

Rita watched Monroe and me both carefully, waiting to see if we were going to condemn her or her fellows. When neither of us spoke, she exhaled quietly and went on. "So we're nearby, but not close enough to hear anything. I just know he wasn't there last night when I left the kitchen, and he was when I went out this morning. I turned him over. I had to, to see if he was dead. I shouldn't have done that, should I? It means my fingerprints will be on him and I'd be easy to throw in jail. But there was blood everywhere, so I had to see. And then I saw I called you. I didn't know what else to do."

Her aura was agitated, earthy colors rubbing against each other like static-furred cats, but there was no deception streaking through it. She was just afraid, as I would probably be in her position. "You did the right thing, Rita. Did you know him?"

"His name was Lynn. He was a Vietnam vet, and I don't know how he ended up on the street. He hardly ever drank, and he liked blues music. He used to hang out at Holy Cow Records in the Market. They might know more about him. I just know he was a nice man. I always thought he could've made it, if somebody'd just given him a hand."

"Any enemies you knew about?"

Rita gave me a look purely the opposite of her youthening smile. It turned her into a bitter old crone, so full of anger at the world that even her aura darkened with it, deep crimson spilling through otherwise gentle shades. "Anybody can be your enemy when you're living rough, Detective Walker. Even your best friend, if you've got booze or smokes or food he wants. People liked Lynn, but that doesn't have to mean anything."

"Anyone you know with a violent enough temper to have done this?" Monroe put in. Rita gave him the same look she'd given me, though she shook her head.

"You'll laugh, but we try to police ourselves in the Underground. It's warm and safe down there, and we keep watch at night. We're trying to get by," she said fiercely. I squelched the urge to pat her arm in reassurance, and she went on, focus bright and angry on Monroe. "Nobody down there could've done this. I'm not even sure anything human could have done it."

She didn't look at me when she said that, but my stomach lurched anyway. All of a sudden I didn't know if she'd asked for me because she wanted someone she trusted on her side, or if she had a deeper understanding of just how I'd saved her life a few months earlier. More important, I also realized I had no idea how the vic—Lynn—had died. It was a lousy time to ask, but the question was on my lips when Monroe said, "Then why'd you call it in as a murder?"

Rita had a whole repertoire of scathing looks. "Because there's blood everywhere, but no paw prints, and if a dog was hungry or desperate enough to attack a man, wouldn't it have done more than rip his throat out?"

I swallowed a squeak. Ripped-out throats were a new exciting kind of violent death for me, and I was torn between terrible urges. One: run home and hide under the bed. Two, and much stronger: run outside and see if Billy had found a ghost to talk to. I pushed my chair back, preparing to do that, but Monroe fixed me in place with a glare worthy of the Mighty Morrison, and turned his next question on Rita: "Can you describe what you saw when you approached?"

She put her face into her hands and sighed, words muffled

behind her palms. "The sun was just coming up, not high enough to be daylight yet, just lightening. There wasn't anybody else around right then. That's unusual. There are usually joggers out that early." She lifted her head to show lines drawing deeper around her eyes and mouth. "Do you think one of them saw something and decided not to get involved? I can tell you what some of the regular ones look like. Homeless people see more than you think."

Monroe actually looked pleased. "That would be very helpful. I'll get our sketch artist to come talk to you. Go on."

"I don't sleep a lot, so I was up early to go help the kitchen get started. Saturdays are busy. I saw him at the corner, just lying on the sidewalk facing the wall. I thought he'd fallen asleep there, and that he was lucky it was one of us and not a cop who'd seen him first, so I went to wake him up. When I got closer I saw the sidewalk was wet around him, but it hadn't rained, nothing else was wet. It just looked dark, not red, until I got closer. And then I saw, and I rolled him over, and he was dead. He looked terrified. Death isn't supposed to come on you like that. You're supposed to be able to just close your eyes and slip away." She sounded like she wanted to believe it and knew better. She *should* have known better: she'd almost died violently not so very long ago.

"What else?" Monroe wasn't pushy, but he wasn't going to let her be distracted, either. I'd been in that position myself, finding ways to draw details out of a witness happier to dwell on something else.

Rita folded her hands around her coffee cup again. "He was already cold. The blood was thick on the sidewalk. I tried not to step in it. I didn't try to take his pulse or anything. I just ran for the pay phone. I left bloody footprints and that's what made me think of the paw prints. That's why I said it was a murder. And that's why I asked for you, Detective Walker. I thought you'd believe me."

I was not about to screw up somebody else's murder investigation by assuring Rita that I did believe her, even though I did. "I'm glad to be able to help, Rita. Look, I need to go talk to my partner, if that's all right with you two."

"Not a problem." Monroe stood up and gave Rita an acceptably genuine smile. "Thanks for your help, Ms. Wagner. If you want to stay here another few minutes I'll get you another cup of coffee and send an artist to talk to you about the regular Saturday morning joggers."

Rita looked into her cup and shook her head. "I'm okay."

"All right. Sit tight, I'll get the artist in here right away." Monroe left. I, who'd instigated the little party's breakup, went and got myself and Billy giant cups of coffee, and got Rita one and a pastry, too, despite her refusal.

And, despite that refusal, she took both. I sat down again, curiosity prodding me to ask, "Is our relationship the only reason you asked for me?"

She gave me a funny smile. "Relationship?"

I made a face, feeling silly. "Cop talk. It's one of those words that carries a lot of weight in civilian terms but is easier than finding more delicate ones on the force. Acquaintance, if you like."

"I thought you'd believe me," she repeated, then made a long, silent observation of her pastry before finally adding, "and I think it'll take a miracle to find Lynn's murderer. You're the miracle that saved me."

A sad soft place opened up in my heart. "Why do you think it'll take a miracle?"

"Because he's nobody, Detective. He's just like me. I'm sure that other detective will make some effort. But we're just a bunch of vagrants. Someone with money or family will get killed soon and nobody will care very much that Lynn's case goes cold. Except maybe you. You cared enough to save me."

This was not the right time to protest saving her had been a complete accident. It wasn't the right time to protest much of everything, except a gentle, "This isn't my jurisdiction, Rita. I'm not supposed to work cases downtown."

"Will that stop you?"

The woman had my number. A sigh, resoundingly heartfelt, escaped me. "Probably not. Look, I'll ask Detective Monroe to keep me in the loop on the case, okay? Because you're right. If this doesn't get cleared up really fast, it probably won't at all. That's how murders are anyway, but the circumstances here aren't favorable. If it slips off Monroe's radar, I promise I'll pick it up. Okay?"

She smiled and the soft place in my heart took an arrow through it. It was easy to look through people, especially street people, to pretend they didn't exist at all. But confronted with Rita Wagner's youthful smile, I couldn't do that. I didn't even want to. Somebody had granted me a phenomenal cosmic power set. In my good moments I thought I could save Seattle, maybe even the world. In the more realistic ones, what mattered, what really *mattered*, was that I could just maybe save one person. Nobody could save everyone, but I could help individuals, and that, when I got right down to it, was a hell of a thing. "I can find you at the soup kitchen if I need you?"

"If I'm not there someone can find me."

"All right." I stood up again, collecting Billy's coffee as Monroe escorted the sketch artist in. "Take care of yourself, Rita."

"You too, Detective."

I left the coffee shop feeling like I'd made the world a slightly better place.

CHAPTER TWELVE

The feeling lasted all the way back to the crime scene. Billy accepted his coffee with a grimace instead of a thanks, which didn't bode well. I barely got a look at the body before he herded me across the street, where we had a semblance of privacy. "Not much to tell," he informed me grimly. "The victim's name is Lynn Schumacher, but that's just about all he remembers. I don't think the medical examiner has pinpointed a time of death yet, but it was more than two hours ago and its violence isn't triggering enough need for retribution that his ghost is hanging on with any strength."

"That probably means his own perception is that it wasn't murder, right?" Mostly the dead passed over to The Other Side, whatever other side you chose to believe in, without much fuss. Violent deaths tended to leave ghosts behind, sometimes because the spirits were simply so shocked they didn't know they were dead. Other times they knew very well they were dead and were in search of some kind of vengeance. Experience indicated those were not nice ghosts to deal with. More often, though—from what Billy said— ghosts lay between those two extremes: they had some idea what had happened, and were hoping to impart a little information or be satisfied that someone sought justice on their behalf.

Billy nodded and I sighed into my coffee cup, blowing amaretto-scented steam into the street. It was good for Lynn that he wasn't traumatized by having his throat ripped out, but not terribly useful for us. "Does he have any information at all?"

"Not much more than we can glean ourselves. Dog attack of some kind. He thought it had yellow eyes."

I crossed my eyes as if to see them, much like Morrison had done the night before and with about as much success. I wasn't calling on the Sight right now anyway, so they wouldn't be gold, but I wondered what color they'd been when I shapeshifted. Coyote's were always gold in his coyote form, but then, coyote eyes *were* gold. I dug my cell phone out of my coat pocket and tapped in Billy's home number. "Dogs, domesticated dogs, don't have gold eyes very often, do they?"

"Not the ones I see. Of course, the ones I see don't rip people's throats out very often, either." We exchanged dirty looks, and Billy added, "Seattle's got coyotes, though. I never heard of anybody seeing any downtown, but it was a rough winter."

"I don't think coyotes rip people's throats out very often, either, for that matter. I don't think they usually att—hey, Melinda? This is Joanne. Don't worry, everything's fine, I just have a weird question. What color were my eyes when I shifted?"

Melinda Holliday could take anything in stride. She barely missed a beat before saying, "Yellow, which I didn't even think about until you asked. Snake eyes are black. Why?"

"Just a data point. Maybe a totally useless one, but I wanted to know. Thanks."

She said, "Sure," and hung up, leaving me to bump my phone against my lips until I remembered I had a much tastier coffee to sip. "I was saying, coyotes usually won't attack adult humans, either, unless they're cornered."

"Well," Billy said dryly, and gestured to where Lynn Schumacher's body had been found. "Technically that's a corner."

I whacked his shoulder and he grinned. "Why'd you ask Mel about your eyes?"

"Because I'm paranoid that everything I come in contact with anymore is supernatural." I was only half kidding, and Billy gave me a sympathetic smirk. A little more seriously, I said, "Because Rita said there are no paw prints around the body, even though there's blood everywhere. A dog could have gotten really lucky, maybe, but since I just shapeshifted for the first time last night I'm wondering if other people at the dance concert could've been similarly affected. Maybe it's 'I have a hammer so everything is a nail' syndrome, but I did have Morrison there to pull me back. What if somebody else went through a metamorphosis and just panicked?"

"You *are* getting paranoid," Billy said, but somehow it sounded like a compliment. "You think that's a possibility?"

"I think it's as likely as a coyote or mad dog attacking somebody off Pioneer Square." I had to be quiet for a minute after that, just to stand there and appreciate how topsy-turvy my world had gone in the past fifteen months. Then my phrasing caught up with me. "It's an animal attack, so the

M.E. will check for rabies, right? Maybe I really am paranoid and it's just a mad dog."

"Maybe. Are you going to proceed as if it is?"

"You mean am I going to proceed on this case which
isn't in my jurisdiction and may have nothing to do with
the paranormal and so can't possibly be justified to my
ill-tempered boss who has already, and with good reason,
suspended me from duty, much less some other precinct's
captain?" I finished my coffee, threw the cup away and
shrugged. "Yes, I am, and no, I'm not going to assume it's
rabies, not until the M.E. says as much. I wonder if I can get
Reynolds to nab a copy of the autopsy report."

"Paranoid and devious," Billy said with admiration.
"We'll make a detective of you yet."

"Not if I get busted for treading in other peoples' territory
when I'm not supposed to be working at all." I finally triggered the Sight as I spoke, looking for...

Well, I didn't really know what I was looking for. Signs of
magic having been done, or some helpful flash in a pan that
suggested some other poor sap had gotten hit with the same
theater whammy I had. Coyote'd said changing without
intent was dangerous. I'd gotten lucky, but if someone else
hadn't, I might be able to help them get back to normal.

Except there wasn't any lingering trace of magic in the
square. The West Precinct's squad was doing its job with
focused efficiency, auras touching and blending so they
became a single creature with many parts, all bent on the
same ends. Lynn Schumacher was the quiet point at the
center of their work, but I couldn't see ghosts at all, and he
had no residual marks of power left on him. "I'm starting to
think most magic just doesn't track well. Unless there's some
kind of significant ritual or major physical upset, it's there
and then it's just gone, poof."

"Can't be. Every action has an equal and opposite reaction."

I was about to argue that magic by definition wasn't physics, then remembered the backlash of my powers reawakening and silenced my own protests. "So I'm just a lousy tracker."

"Nobody's perfect. The good news is that old-fashioned police work gets the job done, too, Walker. This could just be a wild dog."

"Yeah." But Naomi Allison's death hadn't been, and I was the only person who had any chance at all of solving that. "All right. I'll ask Doctor Reynolds to try to get a copy of the autopsy report and until then I'll assume this is a perfectly ordinary wild dog killing in downtown Seattle. In the meantime—"

"Detective Walker?" Rita Wagner, looking less haggard than she had earlier, appeared at my elbow. "Detective, I thought of something that might not be important...."

"About Lynn?"

"No. Just about the Underground." She gave Billy a cautious look, but went on, apparently trusting that if neither Monroe nor I had busted her for camping out in the lost parts of Seattle, Billy wasn't likely to, either. "Or about the people who stay there, I guess. Some of them have disappeared."

A mixture of sorrow and resignation filled my chest. "I hate to say it, Rita, but..."

"I know. We're vagrants. We disappear, we move on, we end up like Lynn. But the population down there is pretty steady. Like I said, we keep an eye out for each other."

I'd already promised the woman I wouldn't dismiss her or her concerns, so I nodded, determined to at least hear her out. She smiled, but it faded fast. "Even when we do take off, it's not usually in clumps. Maybe two or even three, but it's five, Detective Walker."

"All from the Underground? How recently?"

"I've been staying there lately, so I wouldn't know about anywhere else. In the last ten days or so, though. One every couple days. It's too many."

"But no murders? Nothing like what happened to Lynn?"

Rita shook her head and I puffed my cheeks. "That's something, I guess. All right. I'll try to look into it, Rita. Missing persons aren't my department."

"I know. I just thought maybe I should mention it."

"Mention it to Detective Monroe, too. Just to cover my ass, so he can't say I'm hiding anything from him, okay?"

She gave an unenthusiastic nod and went to shadow the crime scene's edge, clearly waiting to be worthy of notice. Billy watched her, his mouth twisted with uncertainty. "Somebody like that could get more attention from this one incident than she's had for years. I hope she's not making things up to stay in the spotlight."

I didn't want Rita to be lying, but my partner had a point. "I'll come back down here tonight, on my own time, to ask around about missing people."

"And right now?"

"Right now I'd really like to go home and put some pants on."

Unfortunately for me, I actually *had* tagged along with Billy instead of driving Petite downtown, in order to make my presence at the scene slightly more acceptable. Women in miniskirts climbing out of purple classic Mustangs were not likely to be taken seriously at a crime scene. So he brought me back to the precinct building, where I followed him upstairs to Homicide in hopes of bumming a ride back to the Hollidays' house from somebody going off-shift.

Jim Littlefoot was waiting for me when I got there. I had a brief vision of myself: cropped hair a mess from the hat I'd been wearing, winter-weight police jacket unzipped to show my sweater hanging over the silly knit skirt and my bare legs poking out until heavy boots enveloped my ankles. It wasn't, overall, a particularly flattering picture.

It was still a hell of a lot better than Littlefoot looked. I knew I hadn't slept, but he obviously hadn't, either, and his dancer's stamina did nothing to alleviate the bags under his eyes. I almost yawned, looking at him, and did make my eyes water by fighting the yawn off. "Mr. Littlefoot. I didn't expect to see you. This is my partner, Detective Billy Holliday." I gestured to Billy and got out of the way so they could shake hands.

They spent about five seconds trying not to do the obvious: Billy struggling not to look at Littlefoot's feet, and Littlefoot fighting the urge to ask if this was live or Memorex. Nobody much cared that it had been Ella Fitzgerald on that recording. She and Billie Holiday were contemporaries, and that was close enough.

When they'd both manned up, gotten past impulses and shaken hands, I offered Littlefoot a seat, took my own and said, "What can I do for you?"

"You can come to tonight's performance." Littlefoot pushed a pair of theater tickets across the desk toward me. Billy's eyebrows rose with interest, and he pulled a chair over from nearby, thumping down to listen in. Littlefoot glanced at him, then turned his attention back to me. "The troupe decided this morning that the only way to honor Naomi's memory was to continue the show."

"You have someone who can…" I didn't want to say *take her place*, because that sounded needlessly callous. "Who can dance the part? You said it had been hard to find the right people for the troupe."

"Two understudies. You can't go on a tour this long without a more-than-full complement. The understudies are as much a part of us as the primary dancers. And they understand the risk they're taking."

It took *me* a minute to catch up to the risk, and then I straightened in my chair. "This isn't just about the show must go on, is it? You're hoping to draw another attack." It was exactly the kind of thing I would do. I had a disconcerting moment of heart-lifting admiration combined with gut-clenching fear, and wondered if that's what people around me felt when I charged off on some particularly stupid campaign against evil. I didn't dare look at Billy for fear of finding just exactly that expression of accusation on his face.

"Only if you'll help us," Littlefoot said, therefore showing far more wisdom than I was ever inclined to. "You said last night you'd been unable to track the attack after the fact. What if you were prepared for it?"

"I might be able to, then." After today—after the wendigo, after a whole series of failures to track or recognize bad guys when I thought I should be able to—I wasn't going to make any promises. "What I can almost certainly do is protect you all from the attack. It's psychic, which means I should be able to shield you from it."

Relief shadowed Littlefoot's dark eyes. "We all understand the concept of shielding, but the ghost dance—the entire program—is about sharing, not shielding. I'm not sure we could change our intent fast enough, even after last night, to protect Winona. Naomi's replacement," he said to my brief incomprehension, though he and I both winced at the choice of word. "Naomi's understudy."

I nodded, then had to say it, just to be sure: "You realize this is a completely insane risk you're taking here, right?"

A smile flickered across his face. "Not if I'm right about trusting you. I have to get back to the theater, Detective. You're welcome to join us as early as you like. The tickets are a formality, in case you want to be in the audience, but I don't know what you'll need to do."

"I'll be there early enough to meet everyone. That'll make shielding them easier."

"Good. Thank you." Littlefoot stood and so did I, with Billy, who'd remained suspiciously silent, coming to his feet a moment later. We shook hands with Littlefoot and as he left, I reached for the tickets he'd put on my desk.

Billy snatched them up. "Bet Mel and I can find a babysitter for tonight."

I took them out of his hand. "I have to go tell Morrison about this."

He took them back. "It's Saturday. He's not in. Call him."

Thwarted, I shrugged my coat off and rooted around for my cell phone, dialing Morrison's number. I had finally learned how to save numbers in the damned thing, but still feared the atrophying of my brain if I didn't make myself memorize and dial phone numbers.

On the other hand, Morrison's slightly impatient, "What do you want, Walker?" made me think phones as a whole were overrated, never mind their anti-atrophy potential.

Resentful, I said, "I said I'd let you know if I had anything interesting. Jim Littlefoot just gave me two tickets for tonight's dance performance. I thought maybe it qualified."

"What time?"

I took the tickets back from Billy and checked the performance time. "Same time. Eight o'clock."

"Fine. I'll be there." Morrison hung up.

I stared at my phone. "I do not understand that man."

"What'd he do?" Billy lunged for the tickets and I made a clucking noise of disapproval as I held them out of the way.

"He says he'll be there. You'd better call the theater if you want to bring Mel tonight."

"Oh, Mel gets trumped by Morrison? She'll get a kick out of that." Billy got his own cell phone out, looking pleased.

I snorted. "No, you get trumped by Morrison. Melinda can have the other free ticket."

My partner gave me a credible look of heartfelt betrayal, at which I laughed. "Don't worry. Maybe he'll be just as disappointed as you are to find you're his date for the evening. Why's he even coming?"

Billy's expression slid from heartfelt betrayal to sly knowledgability. I didn't kick him, but it took so much restraint not to that I had to stomp out of Homicide and down to the locker rooms, where instead of finding a change of clothes—I'd already used my spare set this week—I found a sink so I could splash water over my face and a mirror to glare into.

I was bad at relationships. I was bad at reading between lines, at figuring out what people really meant if they didn't actually say it, and at being charming or flirty or whatever it was, exactly, that women were supposed to do to attract men. My skill sets lay along the lines of taking apart car engines, drinking grown men under the table and—more recently—solving esoteric murders. I was therefore equipped to deal with men who liked those things, not off-limits police captains who got equal parts protective and pissy about me. I wished the affair with my coworker Thor hadn't ended so abruptly, or that Coyote actually lived in Seattle. The facts that I apparently hadn't really trusted Thor and that I'd refused to go with Coyote to Arizona were completely beside the point. At least I knew how to relate to them. With Morrison it was just one run of bewildering incidents after another.

I said, "You could talk to him about it, you know," to the mirror, and the faintly scarred woman reflected in it looked intensively skeptical. I sighed, backed up until the end of a locker room bench caught me in the knees and sat with my face in my hands. A nap would probably restore my equilibrium, but I didn't see one in my immediate future, so hiding in the locker room was as good as it would get.

Inevitably, of course, the door swung open and someone came in. There were actually comparatively few female officers in the precinct—in the whole Seattle Police Department, for that matter—but there was some kind of law of averages which said if you needed a minute to breathe, that was when a parade would march by.

In this case it wasn't a parade. It was a friend of mine, Jennifer Gonzalez, who worked upstairs in Missing Persons. She passed by the lockers aisles at the far end of the room, visible only in reflection, then backed up. "Joanne? Are you all right?"

"Just tired."

Evidently I wasn't convincing, because she came down the aisle and sat behind me, hunched forward so I could see bits of her image in the mirrors. I half expected her to rub my back, simply because she always shook hands with somebody when they came into the room, so being greeted without some kind of physical contact was unusual. "You haven't dropped by lately."

"Missing Persons gives me the creeps."

"And yet you work Homicide. So what's wrong?"

Jenn, like everybody else I had a passing acquaintance with at work, had long since recognized Morrison and I had some kind of Not A Thing going on. I was reasonably certain it was a topic of gossip that managed to stay mostly out of earshot, but once in a while I'd said something about Morrison and gotten a resounding, "Ah," in response, the sort of "Ah" that said, "Well, everything I suspected has now been confirmed." Jenn had used that kind of "Ah" on me. So it would be perfectly reasonable for me to tell the truth, and have a nice little vent about totally failing to understand men in general and that man in specific.

So of course I said, "Is it even possible to file missing persons reports on the homeless? I mean, does it do any good at all?" instead.

Jenn's reflection turned its head to arch an eyebrow at me. She'd gotten glasses recently, and I thought they made her look saucy, since she was a little too strong of jaw to be quite cute. "Not much," she said after a moment. "The handful of homeless actually reported as missing tend to turn up again as homicides or suicides. But the population's itinerant and even though Seattle's winters are mild—or they used to be—there are plenty of people who head south and never come back. Do you need me to look somebody up?"

"Maybe tomorrow." I frowned. "No, wait. It's Saturday. What're you doing in?"

"I forgot my gym bag here last night." Jenn got up, patting my back after all. "If you're fretting over the guy who gave you the earrings, stop fretting and go for it. Life is short."

Oh, yes, I was so very sneaky I'd slid that right under her radar, all right. I touched the coyotes dangling from my earlobes, then looked over my shoulder at her. "What if I'm fretting about somebody else?"

She got that "Ah" look in her eyes and smiled. "Then wear a different pair of earrings next time you see him."

And for some reason, that made perfect sense.

CHAPTER THIRTEEN

Jenn gave me a ride back to Petite, and I drove myself home with the vague intention of getting some sleep. But for the second time that day, the mirror arrested me when I went into the bathroom. I wasn't accustomed to noticing myself so often: mostly my vision of me was a quick glance to make sure my hair wasn't actually frightening, and then I went out the door. But I kept seeing the sliver of a scar on my right cheekbone. Someone had opened my face with a butterfly knife the day I became a shaman, and the injury had preferred not to be completely healed. The scar was a subtle reminder that I'd left my old life behind.

So were the pieces of jewelry I'd slowly taken to wearing over the past year. My mother's silver choker necklace, embedded with traditional Irish symbols, and the copper bracelet with pictographic animals rushing its circumference that had been a gift, years ago, from my father. Even Coyote's earrings, not just the dangling ivory coyotes themselves, but the stylized gold ear wraps, one a snake and one a raven, which my short hair could never hide. They were all outward signs of the path I was walking, things that not so long ago I'd refused to wear because I so fervently disliked where they were pointing me.

Oh, how the mighty had fallen. I turned the shower on and stood there staring at myself until steam clogged my view, then stripped off my clothes and climbed in to sit in the bottom of the tub. Moody introspectiveness was not a headspace I wanted to fall asleep with, and showers were wondrous for either clearing my mind or waking me up. Either would do just fine.

Patty Raleigh's pale, shocky expression planted itself behind my eyelids as soon as I got under the water. I made a fist and hit the tub, not hard, but muttered, "Okay, fine. I'll go see her when I'm done showering. Subtle much?" to my brain.

Astonishingly the image faded, though it was replaced with Naomi Allison's collapsing form. This time I smacked my temple, exasperated. Taking a shower did not constitute avoiding responsibilities. I knew that, but my brain was apparently eager to keep me on point, which would have been more helpful if I could instantaneously step it up in the magical tracking department. Short of miraculous improvements in that regard, I wasn't sure what else I could do. Maybe try to contact Coyote again and ask for more guidance in the shapeshifting realm, but my mentor was clearly unhappy with me. Besides, if my experiment with the rattlesnake was any indicator, I didn't really need Coyote's help. I just wanted his reassurance.

I flashed on the idea of the rattlesnake as a hunter, wondering if the fascinating heat-sensing ability could be turned to a magic-sensing skill. That was something Coyote probably *could* help me with, if he was so inclined. I just didn't figure he was inclined.

"You really do have the most peculiar mental processes," he said mildly. I surged backward with a yelp, scraped my back on the tub faucet and howled a mix of genuine pain and utter indignity as my mentor cocked a pointy ear at me. "How was your shapeshifting lesson?"

I folded a washcloth behind my back to daub at the scrape, then peered at the cloth miserably, convinced by the shock of pain that I'd find gushing blood. Disappointingly, there was just a bit of dead skin. "I know I'm not asleep this time. What are you doing here? I'm in the shower! And what is it, you can read my mind? How come I can't read yours? It's not fair."

"It's not like I haven't seen you in the shower before, Jo."

That was true enough to make me blush, although the first several times he'd seen me in the shower it had been just like this, with him a spirit-guide coyote and me in some kind of uncontrolled trance. Which shouldn't be happening, at this stage in my shamanic career.

"You're right. It shouldn't be. The odd thing is your shields are up, which they never were back at the beginning. They're just very weak. What have you been doing?"

"Nothing. Reading auras, that's it. Shapeshifting this morning, but that was really easy. Rattler helped, and it didn't feel like it took a lot." I couldn't see the scrape on my back no matter how hard I twisted. Sullen, I laid a paint job touch-up image over it, and the pain faded. "*Can* you read my mind?"

"When your shields are this weak, yes." Coyote paused, then did a doggy shrug. "All right, most of the time, for that matter. I've known you a long time, Joanne."

I curled my lip and hunched forward, arms wrapped around my shins as water beat a rhythm down my back. "I've known you just as long. How come I can't read your mind?"

"Maybe you want me to read yours."

That seemed deeply unlikely, a thought which made Coyote quirk a challenging eyebrow. I muttered, "Oh, shut up," and put my head on my knees. Coyote wasn't really there, for all that I felt entirely awake. He'd be soaking wet by now if he was, which image cheered me enough to say, "I've been wrung out since the healing last night. Maybe it's screwing with my shields and my…dimension-hopping abilities."

"Planes. They're planes of existence, not different dimensions. I shudder at the thought of you hopping dimensions."

A rush of lives I'd chosen not to lead, shown to me by the granddaughter of a god, swept through my memory. "What's the difference between a dimension and a timeline? No, never mind, it doesn't matter. What are you doing here? I thought you were…" *Pissed at me,* was how that sentence ended, but I kept the thought stuffed behind my eyes, where hopefully Coyote wouldn't hear it.

I was pretty sure he didn't, but on the other hand, it didn't take much imagination to figure out what I'd been going to say. He said, "I was, but it occurred to me I was being a dick," and the timbre of his voice changed as he spoke.

I looked up, pink-cheeked again because I expected, and got, the handsome brick-red man instead of the coyote form. "You came to me for advice and help, and got a temper tantrum in return. I'm sorry about that."

I mumbled, "It's okay," because it was hard to stay angry at someone who insisted on recognizing and apologizing for his wrongdoings. That was probably a lesson I should take note of. "I wanted to ask you if shamans have a predilection for a specific shape, if they're changing form. Because I started turning into a coyote last night when I was taken off guard, but this morning I didn't even think about choosing a shape. I just slipped into Rattler's skin. Metaphorically speaking."

"You should have chosen a shape." For once the chiding was barely that, more just a worried reminder. "Shifting with a spirit animal's guidance is much less dangerous, but you should always have a firm idea of what animal you want to become before you begin. If you'd tried without Rattler's presence you might have become anything."

"Like a coyote."

"Or a flounder, which probably would have drowned in the air before you figured out how to get back to your own form. This isn't to be done lightly, Joanne."

The possibility or the dangers of becoming a flounder had not occurred to me. I blinked at Coyote, who, despite his solemn warning, smiled. "Okay, a flounder was unlikely. We do tend to unconsciously gravitate toward animals we're fond of or have some kind of link to."

"Like I have with coyotes, because of you," I said hopefully.

His smile got a little bigger, then faded a bit. "That's very flattering. But you see the risk?"

"Yeah. I'll keep a specific animal in mind in the future. Okay. I had another idea this morning, a—" I took a breath, stopped myself, and said, quietly, "I'm glad you popped into the shower, Coyote. I had questions, but I was afraid you'd be too pissed to answer if I called. So thanks."

He wrinkled his nose, an expression that worked better on his long-faced coyote form. "Some shamanic mentor I am, if I leave you afraid to try contacting me."

"Emotions," I said in the understatement of the year, "complicate things. Okay, so my other question was this: is it possible to track magic when shapeshifted? Can it be scented, if that's the right word? The whole process of changing from one form to another, I mean, part of the reason you do that is to access other abilities, right? Better hearing, faster running, whatever. And it's pure magic. It can't be done in the normal world. So it seems like there must be aspects of the shift that would help me to track or hunt magic itself, just through attunement…"

I trailed off because Coyote was looking at me like my nose had expanded to three times its usual size. I peeked at it surreptitiously just to be sure, then arched my eyebrows at him.

"I never thought to try." My mentor, the source of much, if not all, of my shamanic wisdom, sounded dumbfounded. That was not how this was supposed to work. He was supposed to be the repository of all knowledge and clever thoughts, whereas I was supposed to be at the back of the class, scrambling to catch up.

Then again, fighting the wendigo had, bit by bit, shown me that Coyote was as limited in his own ways as I was in mine. We weren't following the same destiny, no matter how much I wanted to fall in step behind someone who understood what he was doing. I'd been told very early on that while I was a shaman and part of my duties were to heal, ultimately my path was that of a warrior. Coyote was the gentler soul, and unquestionably a healer. I *wanted* him to have the answers, but in all honesty, there was very little reason a healer would need to think in terms of tracking and hunting.

Which didn't put a damper on his enthusiasm now that the idea had been introduced. He was bright-eyed, and, despite being in human form, darned near bushy-tailed as he leaned forward to speak rapidly. "It's a brilliant idea, Joanne. I have no idea if it would work, but it's certainly worth pursuing. I should have flown up there after all. This is something you'd need two shamans to safely explore the possibilities, one to track and one to be tracked. I can catch a flight tonight—"

Beneath his excitement, I said, "Two adepts."

Coyote broke off with a squint. "Two what?"

I exhaled, regretting having to burst his balloon. "You said two shamans. It doesn't need two shamans, it needs two magic-users. Billy's friend Sonata called them—us—adepts. Coyote, if you want to come up, that's great, but I can't wait for you. I've got to start the hunt tonight, before anybody else gets hurt."

"You don't even know if it'll work, Jo. This isn't something you should field-test before trying it in controlled conditions."

I quirked a sad smile. "I've been field-testing all along, Yote. This is how I work. I won't say it's ideal, but I haven't quite killed myself yet, and I don't have a lot of time to spare right now. I can try tracing Billy's talent as an experiment before the big production number, but I've only got a few hours before it's all going to hit the fan."

"Detective Holliday is a medium, isn't he? It's a passive magic, Jo. It depends on external forces reaching out to him. It's not the best way to test this."

"I don't do much of anything the best way. It'll be fine." I reached out to take his hand, wondering how I'd become the one offering reassurance.

He caught my hand and squeezed, golden eyes still worried. "Joanne, I want to be there for this."

"I wish you were." I wished a lot of things, but they all

kept coming back around to the awareness that I would say no, when he'd half asked me to join him in Arizona. He couldn't stay, I couldn't go. We'd both known it, and we'd both left an opening for later, for the chance that I might not say no a second time. "You wouldn't be happy here, would you," I said very softly. "In the city, instead of out there in the desert and smaller towns."

He gave a stiff, tiny shrug. "Coyotes are better off in the wild."

So it would have to be me. I'd be the one leaving my life behind, if he asked again. He wasn't going to be coming north to try his hand at being a city shaman. It wasn't that I couldn't, or even that I wouldn't: I'd loved the desert when my father and I had driven through the southwest when I was a kid. It was just...

Well, it wasn't *fair*, which was childish and inane, but it was also sort of the crux of the matter. If I was willing to consider giving up my life and moving a thousand miles to be with somebody, I wanted him to be willing to consider the same. Poorly acquainted as I was with relationships, I wasn't quite bad enough to generally think of them as power-balancing scenarios. In this case, though, the balance of power struck me as out of whack. Figuratively, because if we went to the literal on that particular topic, it had become clear it was out of whack in my favor.

And maybe that meant I should be willing to bend further, but instead it made me just a little more rigid. I couldn't help the amount of magical potential I'd been granted. Making allowances for that talent with regards to someone else's within the context of a romance looked to me like a surefire recipe for long-term resentment and misery. I was pretty sure normal people faced this kind of problem over career trajectories or having children, but I'd left normal far enough behind that I didn't have a problem with where I landed on the Richter scale of bizarre.

I had a lot more problem with watching slow understanding come into Coyote's golden gaze as he recognized where my thoughts were going. He said, "We need to talk," cautiously, and I shook my head.

"I'm not sure we do, Yote. And even if we do, now isn't a good time. I've got to get to the theater and make sure nobody gets killed tonight. I'll check in with you later to let you know I'm all right." I squeezed his hand and let go, but at least Coyote smiled.

"That sure of yourself, are you?"

To my surprise, I grinned back. "Know what? Yes, by God, I am."

He gave me a broad wink and disappeared as the shower water turned cold. I got out, and, watching myself in the mirror, removed the dangling coyote earrings.

CHAPTER FOURTEEN

SATURDAY, MARCH 18, 11:28 A.M.

Patricia Raleigh was out of the ICU and under police guard, which struck me as somewhere between reasonable and comical. People with shot-up collarbones didn't strike me as especially likely to make a break for it. On the other hand, it would be a deeply humiliating mark against the police department if she did, and succeeded, and so a couple of my coworkers were slouching around outside her room, looking very, very bored. One of them, a guy I knew mostly as his nickname, Flathead—he had a very round skull—gave me a cautious wave when I came down the hall. "Aren't you on administrative leave, Walker? Y'know, for…?" He jerked a thumb toward the room behind him, and I nodded.

"I thought I'd come by and see how she was doing. Are you allowed to let me in?"

"You really want me to?"

"Sixty-four thousand dollar question, that." I didn't know the other officer, whose military haircut and posture suggested he was just out of the academy. I stuck my hand out with an introductory, "Joanne Walker."

"Dale Aldred. Look, I gotta ask, what's it like to shoot somebody?"

That was possibly the crassest thing I'd ever been asked. Flathead thought so, too, hissing a warning breath, but it was too late. Aldred, who apparently lacked the socializing factor which might've told him he was on thin ice, didn't even blink. That was not a quality I wanted to see in a cop, not that I had any say in the matter.

What I could and did say was, "It sucks," in a cold enough voice that it got through to him. Worry furrowed his eyebrows, and Flathead, whose real name I could not remember, muttered, "Tell you what, go ahead and pop in for a minute if you want. She's probably sleeping, they're keeping her under pretty heavy sedation, but go ahead."

I thanked him, tapped on the door to be polite and slipped in to the sound of Flathead smacking Aldred with a meaty fist. Aldred said, "Ow," petulantly, and the door closed on his whined, "What'd I do wrong? Don't you want to know?"

Raleigh had a private room. I wondered if her insurance covered that, or if suspected murderers were automatically spared roommates, which was probably the wrong-way-round way to look at it. Either way, she was alone in the middle of the room, sunk into her bed, with tubes running in and out of her. She looked small and pathetic, and I waited for the surge of sympathy and the impulse to heal that would normally accompany seeing somebody in that condition.

I had none. Regret, yeah, but only at a comparatively shallow level. I wished I hadn't had to shoot her, but mostly that meant I wished she hadn't been so stupid as to attack a police officer.

Anger flared, burning up regret and turning my hands to fists. I was *angry* that she'd put me into that situation. Which wasn't fair, since I was a cop and therefore the decision to potentially enter that kind of scenario was mine, but fair didn't come into play any more than it did with regards to Coyote. The bottom line was Patricia Raleigh had broken all the rules of polite society and forced my hand in a way no reasonable person would do.

A bright knot of magic twisted in my gut, harsh reminder that the power, at least, didn't approve of shooting people. I snarled, "Jesus Christ, neither do I," to my own belly as quietly as I could, but this once my talent was not taking the right-of-way. I'd told Morrison and I'd told Caldwell, and now I told *it*: I'd been doing my job, and letting her brain Billy had not been an option. Healer or not, the whole shamanic power set could go stuff itself if it didn't like this particular choice I'd made.

It pulsed sullenly, reminding me of Aldred. Teeth gritted, I granted one concession, and skulked to Raleigh's side. I could heal her—not all the way, because I was in no mood to offer inexplicable medical miracles—but at least ease some of the discomfort she had to be in. Therein lay the middle ground between warrior and shaman, I figured. Not a full-on healing, but some basic body work, putting the frame back together with the raw unfinished solders which would eventually provide the basis for detail work. The visualization was easy. I'd done things like it a dozen times.

There was no power behind the imagery at all. No surge of silver-blue magic, no eager rush to fix the things that were wrong. I huffed, shook myself and reached for the healing talent again, this time more focused on it than the idea of *how* to heal my patient.

It was there, responding, awake, a soft core of possibility. It ran through me willingly enough, clearing away vestigial sleepiness, but it simply stopped at my fingertips. No extension into Patty Raleigh, no exploration to understand what was broken, no healing burst to right what was wrong. It felt as though I had stiff bandages wrapped around me, refusing to let anything out.

I said, "Shit," very quietly, and triggered the Sight.

The "bandages" were shields, sucked up so close to my skin I couldn't tell where one ended and the other began. Coyote had been giving me grief for over a year about the poor quality of my shields. He would have to admire these ones, though he wouldn't for a moment admire the reasons behind them. I shimmered with my own magic, containing myself so tightly that not a drop of healing power was about to escape me.

The *magic,* having gotten over the previous morning's shock of me shooting someone, was willing to ante up. *I,* however, was manifestly not. I didn't think Patricia Raleigh deserved the easy way out. She had attacked my partner and very probably killed her husband, and I apparently felt she'd earned every licking she was going to take, including a bullet through the collarbone.

Not even I could pretend that kind of judgment call was a positive development for somebody whose job was to heal.

Except it wasn't my job. It was my calling, maybe. My duty. But it wasn't my job. My job was as a homicide detective for Seattle's North Precinct, and nowhere in its description did it say anything about playing heroic healer to the bad guys.

I slipped out again, thanked Flathead for letting me visit, and left Patricia Raleigh in exactly the same state I'd found her in.

Since I was visiting hospitals anyway, I headed over to the King County Medical Examiner's Office, which wasn't actually a hospital, but that was the sort of technical detail people could lose friends over. The point was, it was where Nathan Raleigh, Naomi Allison and Lynn Schumacher's bodies were all to be found. Chances that the M.E. I knew best, Sandra Reynolds, would have worked on any of them, much less all of them, were slim, but there was an equally slim chance she might be willing to share office gossip with me. I wished I knew her well enough to come bearing a gift, but I had no idea what kind of coffee she drank or snacks she preferred.

I went into the offices reaching for my badge, and ended up at the front desk patting my chest and feeling like an idiot while the girl behind it watched me curiously. Resigned, I said, "I'm with the police, but I'm on suspended duty, sorry," and turned for the door.

"The Raleigh shooting, right?" the girl asked. "Doctor Reynolds mentioned she knew you, when the story broke last night. Is there something I can help with?"

Evidently there were benefits to being infamous. I turned again and came to lean on the desk. "I was hoping to talk to Dr. Reynolds about—well, two things. First I wanted to know if they've examined the baseball bat Patty Raleigh attacked my partner with to see if it was the murder weapon, and then there was a dog attack downtown this morning I wanted to ask about."

"I'm totally not supposed to tell you anything like this, but I got to observe part of the autopsy," the girl said cheerfully. "If it wasn't the murder weapon, then that poor guy got bashed in the head with a different baseball bat with a nail driven through it. They sent it to Forensics already to look for fingerprints and test the blood to match it against Mr. Raleigh's, but I don't think you're going to have any problem going back on duty, Detective Walker. They'll clear you for sure."

It hadn't occurred to me I might be asking because I was worried about returning to duty, but it was an excellent reason. Mostly I was backwardly justifying not healing Patricia Raleigh, though even if she hadn't killed her husband, taking a swing at my partner was all the justification I needed. I cleared my throat. "Thanks. I don't suppose you know anything about—"

"The homeless guy? No, sorry. How come you're looking into that? I thought you worked North Precinct."

"He was a friend of a friend. Look, I know you're not supposed to, but is there any chance you can let me know—or if you could get Dr. Reynolds to let me know—if there was any sign of rabies in the saliva from the attacking dog?"

The girl, who was probably really about my own age and not a girl at all, gave me a dour look. "It'll be on the news tonight either way. If it's rabid they're going to tell people to watch out for it, if it's not they'll tell people not to worry. I'd worry anyway. Did you see what it did to that poor guy?"

I hadn't, and so shook my head, which was apparently the response she wanted. "It was awful. It just about bit his head off. I've never seen a dog big enough to do that. Jeez, listen to me. It's probably a good thing they won't have me doing the news report, huh? Anyway, is there anything else I can help you with, Detective?"

"Sure," I said, because what the hell, she was chatty and

it never hurt to ask. "Did that dancer, Naomi Allison, come in last night? Have they done any work on her yet?"

"Oh, she got priority because she's not local and her troupe's supposed to leave Monday morning. The boss came in to look her over, it was so weird. But that's all I know. They said it looked like her heart got ripped out or eaten or something. What is this, a horror movie? Like those zombies at Halloween. We keep a *shotgun* in the morgue now. Can you imagine?"

Creepy-crawlies crept up my spine. I hadn't thought about what a morgue would be like during Seattle's brief but extremely unpleasant flirtation with the walking dead. Probably not worse than the graveyard, but still bad enough to give me the heebie-jeebies. I was not good with the undead. "Actually, yes. I'm surprised you remember that." People tended not to, or more specifically, to attach some kind of mundane explanation to the utterly impossible. It was a sanity-saving measure.

My new friend evidently wasn't overly concerned with how her sanity was perceived by others. "Kind of hard to forget when the fridge doors burst open and people you were just examining come crawling out. Everybody who was here went nuts trying to fight them. The boss chopped one of them up with a *scalpel*. Do you know how long that takes? I had a bonecutter, it worked better. But we don't talk about it very much because who would believe us?" She gave me a suddenly suspicious look, like I'd deliberately drawn her out and would now mock her. I raised my hands and shook my head.

"Most people wouldn't. I'm glad everybody here was okay." I hesitated. "Everybody was okay, right?"

"Yeah." She shivered, threw it off and launched in another direction: "Anyway, so the big boss looked at the dancer and you could see him thinking, everybody thinking, that it was something as freaky as the zombies, but who was gonna say that out loud? I don't think they're going to release her body before her troupe leaves. It's too weird. They're going to keep looking for *why* her heart's gone. I hope they find some kind of acid attack or something. That would at least make sense."

I crooked an unhappy smile. People by and large didn't want to believe in magic, but there were at least a few of them out there who didn't have inherent magic, and who still hunted things that went bump. This girl seemed like she could be one of them. I wondered what she'd say to that, but I'd learned my lesson: telling the truth just made people think I was crazy. Even somebody who'd fought zombies was probably unlikely to accept the truth. I'd had to, but I was sort of in a league of my own, and I'd gotten to where it all more or less made sense. "Unlike zombies."

"Totally. So I wish I could be more help, but that's all I know. And, um, Detective Walker? You won't tell anybody I told you all that, right?"

"My lips are sealed. Thanks." I went back out into the afternoon feeling more lighthearted, if no more illuminated about the status of any of the cases I was unofficially involved with.

Daylight made my eyes hurt, a shiny reminder that I hadn't slept since the previous morning. I slumped in Petite's driver seat, trying to think of anything at all I could do which would be useful on any of the cases, and woke up seventy minutes later when my cell phone blared its obnoxious ringtone through the car.

"Somebody called in for you," my buddy Bruce from work informed my panicked grunt of a hello. "Said it was personal, so I thought I'd check to see if I should put it through. Her name's Tia Carley."

"Never heard of her," I said tiredly. "Okay, put her through. Thanks, Bruce."

"No problem." The phone beeped twice, and then a woman's vaguely familiar voice came over the line: "Miss Walker? Detective Walker, I should say?"

"Yeah." Nobody called me *miss*, which triggered recognition. "Ms. Carley? From the dance concert?"

"That's right!" Delight swept her voice. "I was afraid you wouldn't remember me."

"Did you know your name means 'Aunt Carley'? Uh. I mean, I mean. Yeah. I remember who you are. I'm sorry, I just woke up." I sat up, one hand knotted around the steering wheel, and blinked furiously at the world beyond Petite's hood until my brain started to function a little better. "What can I do for you, Ms. Carley? Have you seen a doctor?" That seemed well-nigh impossible, since I'd only told her to the night before.

"Maybe let me buy you a cup of coffee, since I woke you up. And no, no, I haven't, I can't until Monday at the soonest, but I hoped you might not mind telling me a little more about what you did."

I slumped deeper in Petite's seat. "You can't go to a doctor and tell them what I did, Ms. Carley. They'd never believe you."

"Oh, I know. I want to know for myself. I don't want to harass you, but I'd like to hear a little about what you do."

"You're not a reporter, are you, Ms. Carley?" I already had one reporter on my case, though that one had bitten off enough of my world to actually back away a bit. I didn't need someone who wouldn't.

"Please, call me Tia, and yes, I did know what my name

means. My nieces call me Auntie Chuck, because *Carley* is derived from *Charles*. My family's not normal," she said cheerfully. "But I'm not a reporter, just someone who believes there's more to this world than is dreamt of in most philosophies. Could I buy you a coffee, Detective?"

Gary had quoted that line the morning we'd met, and I'd used it on Rita Wagner just yesterday. At least, I thought it had been yesterday. Either way, its use disposed me more kindly toward Tia Carley. I breathed, "What the hell, I could use the caffeine," and more clearly, said, "Yeah, okay, sure. Where can I meet you?"

"I'm downtown right now. At the Elliott Bay Bookstore, maybe?"

Just a few blocks from where Lynn Schumacher had died. I rubbed my eyes, nodded even though she couldn't see me, said, "I'll be there in thirty minutes," and made it downtown in twenty.

Tia Carley was waiting for me, a newspaper pinned to the table she'd staked out by a cup of black coffee and a muffin that looked suspiciously bran-y. No wonder she had such a terrific physique. I waved hello and went to order the largest latte they had available, and eyed the sweets cabinet, trying to remember when I'd last eaten something that wasn't a doughnut-based life-form. Tia appeared at my elbow, paid for my coffee and said, "The lemon muffins are especially good."

"Which is why you're eating something wholesome and poppy-seeded, right?" I ordered a lemon muffin anyway, and a prepackaged turkey sandwich for dessert. Food in hand, we retreated to Tia's table and I took a couple fortifying slurps of coffee before saying, "People don't usually want to know about what I can do."

"How many of them have just been told they've been

healed from early-stage breast cancer?" Tia kept her voice low, which I appreciated. "I don't even know if I said thank you. Is it something you can teach someone to do?"

I shook my head. "You're welcome. And I'm not sure, honestly. I have an aptitude for it."

Disappointment flashed through her eyes, but she contained it in an instant. "It seems like something that should be taught, if it can be. Can I ask, though——? You wear glasses. And you have a scar."

I touched the scar on my right cheek, then automatically pushed my glasses up. "Not everything wants to be healed. Some things are in the genetic code, I guess, or have emotional importance that outweighs the need to be physically perfect." I sounded very mature and wise.

Tia, however, looked skeptical. "If I had something wired into my genetics, I'd want to be able to control it."

I remembered the odd spur in her DNA, and bit my tongue on saying "You do." It took a moment to find something *else* to say, but fortunately I had coffee, a muffin and a sandwich to occupy my mouth with. I alternated between the first two while I ripped the sandwich packaging open. Turkey and limp lettuce exploded over the table, and I sat there a moment, chipmunk-cheeked with muffin and gazing in dismay at the mess I'd made. "Sometimes," I said around the mouthful, "screwing with things that don't want to be screwed with has an effect kind of like that. Especially where magic's concerned."

Tia didn't look like she believed me for a second, but she put the sandwich back together with a grin. "Still, it must be amazing to know you can control your own body that way. I do yoga, but it's not the same at all, is it?"

"I couldn't do a yoga stretch if you paid me, so I don't know. Mostly, though, it's not really about controlling what my body can or can't do. It's trying to help others whose bodies or spirits are failing them somehow." I sounded so much like I knew what I was talking about that I started to think I'd been replaced by Folgers Crystals. "I know there are local classes in shamanism, which is the basic practice I'm starting from. You could look into those, I guess, to see if you have any skill for it yourself."

"How long does that take?"

I ducked my head and chuckled. "I don't know. I started studying when I was about thirteen." Nevermind that my studies had lasted about fifteen months and then had gone on violent, determined hiatus for more than a decade. The idea that she wanted a time frame suggested she probably wasn't all that well suited to pursuing a healer's path, but I didn't figure it was my business to say so.

"Oh." She looked dismayed, but then smiled. "I suppose I should get started, in that case. At least by taking some classes. What's it like, healing people? Changing them that way?"

"Scary. Wonderful, when it works. Exhausting. It's not something I would have chosen, but I'm getting better at it." I bit off that last confession, wishing I hadn't made it. People, even curious polite people I'd healed recently, probably didn't need to know about my doubts. Or maybe that was exactly what she needed to know. "Worth it," I finally said, more quietly. "It's hard, but it's worth it."

Tia gave me a broad, excited smile. "Then that's all I need to know. Thank you, Miss—Detective—Walker. Joanne. May I call you Joanne?" I nodded and her smile got that little bit much bigger. "I feel like I've been looking for a path for a long time. Maybe you've helped me find it."

I smiled back, but worry sank a pit into my stomach. Whatever my talents were, I was certain nobody should be looking to me as any kind of guidance counselor. We chatted a while longer before I made my escape, wishing I'd never agreed to meet her.

CHAPTER FIFTEEN

SATURDAY, MARCH 18, 6:22 P.M.

The girly part of me I rarely acknowledged existed wanted to find something as knockout gorgeous as the velvet green dress I'd worn the night before. The practical mechanic part of me won out, and I turned up at the theater in black jeans and a dark blue nubbly sweater.

Jim Littlefoot gave my glasses a curious glance as he let me in through a side door. I wanted to explain that shamanic magic didn't have the same coverage as LASIK—which would have been the clever thing to say to Tia Carley, had I thought of it—but he said, "If you don't mind taking your shoes off," as a pragmatic introductory sally that didn't invite explanations about magic. I followed him down a hall and into the wings, then stopped at the duct-taped-down edge of a black rubber mat stage floor to do as he asked.

The scent of makeup and sweat was strong under blazing stage lights. The house lights were on, too, making the whole theater a beacon of brightness very unlike the night before. Dancers not yet in costume were running through a half-assed rehearsal, doing none of the incredible throws or lifts they'd done during the performance. Even that much came to a halt as I followed Littlefoot onstage.

Their grief was palpable, though a glimpse at their auras also showed the emotion locked behind high thick walls. Saving it, I guessed, for the show, just as they saved the high-energy lifts and tremendous leaps. I was abruptly glad I'd be watching from the wings and not actually part of the audience at whom their pent-up bereavement would be directed.

Littlefoot took center stage, me at his side, and raised his voice. Not that he needed to draw attention: everybody was already watching us—me—mostly with more gratitude and less resentment than I'd expected. I had, after all, failed their friend the night before.

On the other hand, I'd at least tried, and maybe that made a difference. Littlefoot introduced me, saying, "Most of you saw her last night. She may be able to track Naomi's murderer at the climax of the ghost dance. She *will* be able to shield us all, so that no one else will be hurt."

Part of me winced, prepared for a wave of skepticism from the dancers. Instead there were a handful of nods, and a general sense of reasonable acceptance. I'd never been in the presence of so many people who took the concept of psychic shielding so easily, not even when I'd briefly tangled with a coven. It was sort of heartening.

A tiny redhead stepped forward, unfolding one arm from its tight wrap around her ribs to wave her hand like she sought permission to speak. She didn't wait for it, though, just said, "I'm Winona, Naomi's understudy. First, I wanted to say thank you for trying to help last night. I don't think we even knew what had happened, but you were already up here."

"I'm sorry I wasn't able to do more."

Winona nodded, but she obviously wasn't looking for an apology. "I just want to know: if you're going to be shielding us, does that mean the ghost dance is going to lose its power?"

I went a little slack-jawed, seeing her point instantly but not certain of how to deal with it. The whole purpose of the dance was to share energy with the audience. If I had them shielded well enough to keep our bad guy from draining all that built-up power, then it was essentially going to rebound on the dancers, not be released into the waiting crowd. After a rather long moment, I said, "Crap," which got an unexpected low chuckle from the dancers.

Even Winona offered a small smile. "That was kind of what we thought. I guess the other question is, do you think you can track whoever did this if they don't get to steal any of the ghost dance power?"

That, I'd thought of, and shook my head before she finished asking. "I'm going to have to let some of it leak through to make an...appetizer. I can—and will—snap the shield up at pretty much the last second, so there's no warning to keep him away, but I think some of it's going to have to go to feeding the killer just so I can get a bead on him. I'm hoping cutting the power off so abruptly will hurt him enough to leave a scar I can follow." A scar, a scent, a track; whatever I wanted to call it, I hoped like hell my magic-tracking hypothesis held some water. But Winona had made me consider the audience, too, which shed light on another possibility. "If it hurts enough I think he'll retreat. If he backs off fast enough, I might be able to drop the shields and release the energy into the audience within a minute or two. It might be diluted, but…"

The proposal was met with dropped shoulders and sighs of relief, a whole flood of tension releasing from the thirty or so troupe members. Jim Littlefoot said, "That would be very much appreciated," in a tone which suggested words didn't begin to cover it. "In many ways tonight's dance will be our tribute to Naomi. The idea of losing that energy, even to trap her killer, is…"

"Dismaying," I supplied, and he nodded. I said, "I'll do my best," and hoped it would be enough.

I spent the next hour meeting the troupe as individuals, mostly shaking hands, exchanging names and expressing condolences. I wasn't certain it was necessary. I'd shielded people I didn't know even that well, in the past. I was, however, sure it wouldn't hurt, and that weighed more heavily than the question of absolute necessity. Naomi's sister Rebecca hugged me, which I didn't expect, and I felt her utter exhaustion in the embrace. I wasn't exactly at the top of my game myself, but the magic inside me couldn't let that go unanswered. I sent a pulse of gentle power through her, hoping to renew her energy a little, the way I'd done time and again with weary or injured people around me.

She drew back, dark eyes startled, and gave me a fragile smile. "Save it for the shields, please. Dancing will help me."

I said, "Dancing will help everyone," and didn't mean just the troupe. Her smile strengthened and she retreated with what I imagined was a touch more lightness in her step. Moments later they brought the lights down, leaving me alone on a dim stage. I was glad I'd thought to wear dark clothes:

they'd help me hide in the wings, where I retreated to put my shoes on and spend a few minutes collecting the dancers' nervous preshow energy behind shields and releasing it again, as practice.

It was more tiring than I expected. I moved farther back and sat down next to the fly ropes, where I was pretty sure I'd be out of the way. None of the previous night's performance had relied on wires, just muscle. My *own* muscles felt watery, like mental exertion was manifesting itself in my body, and Coyote's warning about the healing I'd performed the night before came back to me. Watching auras didn't take much, but even something as comparatively low-key as raising and lowering shields was enough to slow me down.

Lucky for me, then, that I had a whole troupe of performers whose entire purpose in dancing was to create psychic energy. I knew, this time, what their focus was, so it wasn't going to take me by surprise the way it had in the previous concert. I could fill up on some of the first half's outpouring of strength, and turn it around to keep these men and women safe.

Assuming, anyway, that I didn't accidentally turn into a flounder while they danced. I stayed where I was, listening to the sounds of the theater preparing to come to life, until I heard the house doors open. Morrison was probably out there somewhere waiting for me, possibly along with Billy and Melinda. I got up and dusted my bottom, then slipped out the same side door Littlefoot had brought me in through, making sure to prop it open with a stone so I could get back in.

All three of them were indeed waiting in the lobby, Morrison glancing at his watch impatiently as I skulked up. He wasn't as formally attired as the night before, which was a relief and a disappointment all in one, but he still looked sharp in a three-piece suit. Melinda was in a form-fitting black satin gown that made me wonder how I'd ever thought I looked curvy in my green dress. Billy, rather to my surprise, was in a zoot suit of bright blue cotton. He and Mel looked like they'd stepped directly out of the early forties, but since Billy's idea of formal wear was usually identical to Melinda's, the outfit made my eyebrows crawl up my forehead. "That's a new look."

He brushed his knuckles over his shirt—white silk, to contrast with the suit's brilliance—with a hint of self-consciousness. "Something changed after Halloween. She'll always be a part of me, but…"

I steepled my fingers over my mouth, a tight smile half-hidden behind them as my nose and eyes prickled with sentiment. Billy's older sister Caroline had died when he was eight and she was eleven, but their bond had been deep enough to keep her spirit nearby—within him, really—for decades. Once I'd learned that, I'd stopped imagining his cross-dressing quirk was in retaliation against his parents for his unfortunate name, and started understanding that it was at least in part an homage to the sister who'd died as a little girl. Eventually I'd gotten a good look at Billy in his own garden, his perception of himself at a soul-deep level, and I'd understood even more. It wasn't just an homage. Caroline was part of him, a slightly feminizing factor in a big lunk of a man. The garden Billy dressed more like my partner had been doing lately: softer shirts and well-cut suits, masculine but not butch. And given the opportunity to dress up, he apparently hadn't lost any of his outrageousness, just redirected it a little now that Caroline's spirit had finally moved on. I whispered, "I think she'd approve," from behind my compressed fingers, and Billy looked unusually pleased.

Melinda tucked her arm through Billy's. "So what do you

need from us tonight, Joanie? Bill impressed upon me that this wasn't just a date."

"Hopefully it will be, but there might be something you can do, Billy. If things go wrong—is it possible to stop a soul from crossing over? Can you distract a ghost?"

Morrison put a hand over his face, which I thought was out-of-proportion funny, and my shoulders shook with silent giggles as Billy's mouth twisted. "You should have invited Sonata, if that's what you need. I might be able to, but I'm not in her weight class."

We all paused to take a look at him, since Billy was out of all our weight classes, and the idea of five-foot-six, hundred-and-thirty-pound, sixty-year-old Sonata Smith throwing down with him and winning was ludicrous. Billy rolled his eyes. "You know what I mean."

"Yeah, but the image. Anyway, at the very end of the last dance I'll throw a shield up—Mel, can you see that?"

"Try," she suggested, and I slipped one up around first Morrison, then Billy, then finally myself. Melinda's eyes glimmered gold, not nearly the depth of change mine underwent, and she nodded. "Faintly, but yes."

"I can make it more visible if I have to, but I'd rather not." I released all the physical shields and went back to my explanation. "It should cut the killer off at the knees, but just in case it doesn't, I think I should be able to bring the lead dancer's spirit back to her body as long as she doesn't just cross right over. I was too late last night with Naomi, but a distraction…"

Billy shook his head. "You should have called Sonny. I'm good with lingering ghosts, but calling someone back is—" He broke off, mouth tight.

"Yeah, I know, out of your weight class. On the other hand, I've been a student of the 'argue for your limitations and sure enough, they're yours' school for the last year, so I feel justified in saying—"

"Suck it up and try?" Melinda asked archly, when I stopped abruptly.

I cleared my throat. "Something like that, yeah. I guess I don't feel all that justified in saying it after all."

To my relief, Billy grinned. "Good thing we found a babysitter tonight, then, so Mel could put words in your mouth."

"Why," Morrison said to me, "did you invite me?"

My mouth said, "I didn't. You invited yourself," which was perfectly true, but I wished like hell Melinda had put some other words in it. It didn't make a damned bit of difference that I wasn't wearing the coyote earrings, not if I was going to be a hundred percent stupid at the first opportunity. And besides, Morrison probably hadn't noticed the earrings, so there was no point to any of it anyway.

I dropped my head, pushed my glasses up and pinched the bridge of my nose. I wanted to count to ten so I could trust myself to speak, but Morrison's scent and body heat were already retreating, so I only got to about one and a half before looking up again. My boss had fallen back three steps in the time it took me to do that, and his expression was full-on Police Captain, all professionalism and no emotion. I wanted to cry.

"Actually," I said as much precision as I could muster, "I was hoping you would watch the show from backstage with me. You're the only person I know who consistently brings me back to myself if something goes wrong."

I wasn't looking at the Hollidays. I didn't dare look at them, especially when Melinda gave a tiny pleased squeak, like I'd said something revelatory. I kept my gaze on Morrison, whose gaze thawed marginally, but not enough to suggest I'd genuinely redeemed myself. I said, "Please," very quietly, and after a moment he nodded.

My shoulders dropped about six inches. "Thank you. I've got a side door propped open so we can get backstage. We should probably go. The show starts in a few minutes. Enjoy it," I said to Billy and Melinda, and Mel veritably sparkled her eyes at me as they went one way and Morrison and I went another. I kicked the stone out of the side door and closed it behind us, warned Jim Littlefoot that Morrison would be backstage with me and showed Morrison my hiding place next to the fly ropes, where we were well out of the way and surrounded by darkness.

He waited until the performance began and there was no chance at all of, "Bring you back to yourself?" being overheard before he spoke.

"You saved my life at least once." My shoulders hunched again, rock solid with tension, and I kept my gaze locked on the stage. "The morning I found Cassandra Tucker in the locker room, I went chasing after her spirit, and I couldn't get back to my body. Phoebe kept trying to wake me up—yelling at me, shaking me—but she couldn't. You, though. You just put your hand on my shoulder and I woke up. Right before a monster ate me. It's happened a couple other times, too, besides last night."

My poor boss was magnificently silent a moment. "And you didn't think to mention this?"

"It was awkward."

Morrison snorted laughter. "Unlike the rest of our interactions."

I said, "You're a very confusing man," under my breath, and did my best to focus on the dance performance after that.

Its impact was lessened by dint of being on the sidelines

rather than in the audience. A few things—the thunderbird's entrance, flying across the stage as she did, for example—were even more dramatic, because she came straight at us. But mostly, I couldn't see the structure of the dances building to the shapeshifting climax, and that helped me retain a degree of control. The dancers still buzzed with, and built, enormous energy, but it was directed outward, not into the wings, so instead of being body-slammed by it, I could just siphon off dregs.

The atonal music, the drums, the heat of stage lights—impressive even from the wings—made my skin tingle, lifting me out of myself in a gentle, reverent way. I was held to my body by threads, a double-existence I'd only experienced a few times before. It had never been so comfortable, or filled my chest with so much delight. For the first time I could remember, I was *happy* to hold myself in two planes of existence. I was aware of my body, of the heat and the smell of makeup and sweat, of my sweater's soft nub and the rougher cotton denim of my jeans. My feet felt heavy in their bulky shoes, and I found the idea that they anchored me amusing. As long as I kept my shoes on, the dancers couldn't take me away.

But the detached from my body watched them with a shaman's eyes. I Saw the creatures they made themselves into instead of the human forms throwing themselves across the stage. Their auras were extraordinary: even tinged with grief—or possibly because they were saturated with it—they leaped high and wide, a metaphysical echo and prediction of what the dances themselves did and would do. It took effort not to join them, spiritually if not physically, but my presence would mar the patterns of light and power they built. I felt magnificent, much better than I had since the healing the night before. This was what Coyote had tried to impress upon me, about ritual and drum circles and sweat lodges: power combined and shared and focused was much more effective than anything I could draw on by myself. Passion like this could be drained, of course, but it also renewed itself by its very nature. The fact that the dance troupe had lost a member less than twenty-four hours earlier, and were still able to waken and share depths of magic from within themselves, was existential proof of that.

Morrison touched my shoulder very lightly. I turned toward him, pleased I retained sufficient bodily awareness to do so even when floating just outside of myself, drawn to the dancers. He tapped a finger beside his eye, indicating—indicating what, I wasn't sure. That my eyes were gold, probably, but that was practically standard operating procedure now.

Oh. No. He was asking if *he* could see what I Saw, a revelation which came like a heady thunderbolt. God, we'd changed, both of us. Maybe we'd even changed since last night, given that it didn't seem likely the man I'd thrown a shoe at would be asking for a repetition of the performance leading to the shoe-throwing.

On the other hand, I couldn't see me from the outside—well, actually, I could if I wanted to, but looking at Morrison was more interesting—and I suspected I was sort of flushed and joyous and possibly like everything was going to be right with the world. If I was standing next to someone who looked like I felt, I'd want in on some of that happy juice, too, and Morrison knew I could share if I felt like it.

I didn't bother with the silly rhyme, this time. I just tugged him close, his feet on mine, and put my hand on top of his head as I whispered some of that replenished power out of myself and into my boss.

Right then, the first act ended. A tremendous surge of

shifting magic flooded from the dancers, hitting me in the spine and crashing through me in waves. It was intensely, exotically erotic, and I ducked my head against Morrison's shoulder, trying to keep my breathless laugh silent.

I got a nose full of fur. I jerked back, sneezed and came face-to-face with an armful of silver-furred, blue-eyed, deeply bewildered wolf.

CHAPTER SIXTEEN

As a rule, wolves, like coyotes, were not human-size. Then again, as a rule, wolves were not found in the wings of a Seattle theater, much less wearing a three-piece suit and standing on somebody's feet with their front paws sliding frantically around that somebody's waist.

I grabbed two fists full of suit jacket at the nominal shoulders, trying to catch enough fur to keep my boss from falling down. Trying to catch enough to keep him from tearing off into the audience, for that matter, but the combination of clothes and fur made for a poor grip. On the other hand, neither of us wanted him to be standing upright, so we sank to the floor together, nose to nose as the dancers poured off stage.

Bewilderment faded from Morrison's blue eyes, panic replacing it. He jerked violently when the first dancer gasped upon seeing him, and reared back as more of them by turns jolted and pushed to a stop. I didn't even need an animal's senses to catch the fear and confusion in their scents: it was pungent, pouring off sweating bodies and from heaving lungs.

In face of all that, two fists full of suit-covered fur were not enough to keep a hundred and ninety pounds of wolf in place. His claws scrabbled on the floor—no soft rubber mat here, just black-painted pine—and I was hauled under him, gathering a whole host of splinters in my backside as he lurched toward the rear of the backstage area. I swallowed a gurgle of pain and held on, determined not to make this worse by allowing my boss to run amok on four legs through the streets of Seattle. My brain was already shrieking *your fault your fault this is your fault!* and miserably, there was no doubt about that at all. Morrison had the magical aptitude of a horseradish.

This was not a condemnation. It was simply the way of things, and it was probably part of why he could ground me so fast. He was absolutely, solidly connected to the ordinary world. Or he had been, until last night's unfortunate thought that he'd make a very pretty wolf had met up with me working a bit of magic on him tonight while two dozen dancers poured out a river's worth of power meant entirely to soften an audience up for a transformative experience.

God, I was an idiot.

Morrison gave a truly magnificent surge which almost shook me loose. I snatched at his haunches as they passed over me and managed to de-pants him, which presented me with a much more up-close-and-personal encounter of canine genitals than I'd ever hoped to have. I said "Aaghg," and hauled myself over his ribs, trying to crawl up his bony, furry spine. It gave me a glimpse of our location—the stage's absolute darkest, farthest-back corner, with nowhere in particular to go, for which I was grateful. There was a door only a few yards away, but it was closed and I didn't think Morrison was quite up to knobs just then.

The entire dance troupe was crowded as far away from me and Morrison as they could get without spilling back onto the stage. Not one of them had made a sound, though several had stuffed knuckles into their mouths to accomplish such silence. I perversely admired the training that ranked "shut the hell up backstage" above "OH MY GOD THERE'S A WOLF BACK HERE!" and tried to keep my grunts quiet as I got some leverage, flung myself forward and wrapped my arms around Morrison's neck.

It wasn't a particularly natural direction of attack on a wolf, and I had no idea how much of Morrison was in control. Enough that he hadn't bitten my face off in the first seconds after transformation, but the panicked retreat to a defensible corner seemed pretty lupine to me. So did the snarling, snapping, writhing attempt to chew my arms off once I got a neck lock on him. I'd put sleeper holds on people before. I'd never tried it on a dog.

Somewhere very far at the back of my mind, I whispered *wolves aren't dogs,* and that part of me produced a shrill giggle as I folded one elbow around Morrison's neck and grabbed that wrist with my opposite hand. Humans tapped out or went unconscious from a well-applied carotid restraint within about ten seconds. Canines, it turned out, were a whole hell of a lot less obliging.

Morrison slithered backward and to the side, not quite escaping my grasp only because I was pretty much sitting on top of him when he started. I slid to the side, still trying to keep a grip around his throat, but his neck-to-head ratio was all off, from a chokehold perspective: thick neck, stream-lined skull, certainly compared to a human. Furthermore, humans usually required some degree of training to get out of a sleeper hold, either by learning early on to duck the chin so a lock couldn't be made, or—more usefully, after the fact—by doing something like slamming their heel into their attacker's instep, which could easily hurt enough to make an assailant loosen his grip.

Wolves, I discovered, just naturally went for a *let me try to disembowel you with my hind feet* attack. My bowels were, thank God, not quite in his line of fire, but my thigh was. Denim shredded under his claws and I shrieked like a little girl, letting go so my quadriceps weren't also shredded.

Morrison leaped out of reach, careening down the length of the backstage with his tie flying over one shoulder and his suit jacket flapping wildly along his back. I was a *moron*. I should have grabbed the *tie*. This piece of information now solidly in mind, I took off after him without considering the futility of a two-legged creature trying to catch a four-legged one. The stage scrim rippled wildly as we bolted alongside it. I hoped the curtains were closed so what audience remained in the theater during intermission wouldn't see the artistic, shadowy rendition of Woman Chasing Wolf across the stage.

Two legs versus four or not, I caught up to my panicked, shapeshifted boss because there were no open doors at the far end of the stage, either. He backed into a corner, snarling, and I dropped down low, hands spread wide to make myself as unthreatening an object as I could. Morrison lowered himself to the ground, his own front paws spread wide and his haunches raised, similar to my own position. Except on him, it looked familiar. I'd seen wolves do that on documentaries, and I was reasonably certain it was prelude to a dramatic last stand.

I said, "Shit," out loud and fell over, throat and belly

exposed in my very best attempt to project canine body language.

On the positive side, he didn't rip my throat out. On the somewhat less positive side, a stagehand flung one of the backstage doors open. Morrison tore through it—knocking the stagehand to the floor in the process—and disappeared down the bright-lit hallway that led to the dressing rooms. I gave up on any pretense of backstage silence and bellowed, "Close the doors! Close all the doors!" as I got my feet under me and ran helter-skelter after my four-legged boss.

The hall behind the stage was mostly concrete, with an ordinary door directly opposite the one I'd burst through, a thankfully closed giant corrugated steel door at the far end, and a sharp turn just beyond that. I spasmed with indecision, then yanked the door across from me open to take a look at what lay beyond.

A warehouse-size room with set pieces, costumes, marked-off rehearsal areas and another enormous corrugated steel door—this one open to the world—spread out in front of me. I slammed my small door shut, breathlessly confident that Morrison's only escape route lay that way, and that he currently lacked the skills to open the round-knobbed egress. I pelted up the hall and rounded the corner, increasingly certain he'd come that way when I discovered the adjoining hall to be lined with dancers pressed against the walls and all staring in the direction I was running.

A door slammed somewhere in front of me and my stomach turned leaden with fear. I skidded around another corner, and there, fifteen feet ahead of me, was a set of double doors with broad press-bar handles. The same doors, in fact, that I'd propped open earlier so that Morrison and I could slip into the theater's backstage areas without disturbing anyone. And like in all public buildings, for fire code reasons, the doors swung outward, making them easy for almost anyone to open.

I crashed through them at top speed, but the last I saw of my boss was a streak of silver and a flapping tie disappearing into a nearby patch of trees.

I wish I could say I swung right into action, but in fact I just stood there for what seemed like an awfully long time, staring after Morrison. Disasters of every magnitude ran through my mind: Morrison getting hit by a car. Morrison getting shot by some redneck. Morrison escaping the city and living out his life howling at the moon. I wondered how long wolves lived, anyway. Morrison starving to death because what the hell did he know about hunting in wolf form, not that instinctive lupine behavior appeared out of his grasp. Coyote had said a forced or unexpected shift made it easy, even likely, that you'd get lost in the animal. I had to assume Morrison's frenetic fleeing was pure panicked wolf, not the basically unruffleable man who'd become a precinct captain at the tender age of thirty-five.

The doors opened behind me and Jim Littlefoot, cautiously, said, "Detective Walker?"

"There's a six-foot-three man in the audience wearing a bright blue zoot suit. He's with a Hispanic woman a foot shorter than he is, wearing a black satin fitted Veronica Lake-style gown. I need you to get them, please." I didn't sound like me. I sounded like my head had been hollowed out and then refilled with worry so profound all it left was a scary degree of calm.

Littlefoot hesitated audibly, then exhaled an agreement. The door closed, but didn't latch. I reached for my cell phone, rediscovering in the process that the right leg of my jeans was shredded. Welts had risen on my thigh, for that matter, big thick red strips which probably should have torn into muscle. I'd been lucky, or Morrison hadn't really been trying to hurt me, or the magic within me had dealt with a more grievous injury while I wasn't even paying attention. All three seemed equally possible.

I dialed Dispatch while my mind made all those little observations, and gave my name and badge number when the operator answered. I still sounded like someone else as I said, "I need Animal Control and the citywide police force to be on the lookout for a giant silver wolf in the West Seattle golf course area. It is absolutely fucking critical that the animal not be shot. Tranqs are all right, but mostly if it's sighted and can be corralled, I need to be notified immediately."

A long, long silence met my demand before the dispatch operator finally said, "Just how big of a wolf are we talking about?"

"Huge. Twice the size of a normal wolf. Silver fur, blue eyes. It may be wearing a suit jacket."

The operator started giggling. I couldn't blame him, although I also wanted to kill him. I waited for his laughter to die down, which happened very abruptly after about twenty seconds when he said, "911 just had a call about a gigantic wolf in that area."

"Tell the 911 crew that the animal isn't dangerous unless it's engaged and that everybody should leave it the hell alone. That Animal Control is on its way. Get the message on the radio, on the news, whatever it takes to get the word out. Did the call say anything about a suit jacket?" I'd begun walking as I talked, still mechanical, and I broke through a tangled thicket of branches as I asked the question.

Maybe, *maybe*, if I'd kept running, I'd have caught Morrison, because he'd taken a moment there in the brush to scrape the tie and coat off. I took the tie, particularly, as a positive sign: a paw print on the neck suggested he'd worked a foot between throat and tie to loosen it, which had to require some vestigial form of human thought. The coat and shirt's seams were torn, savage tooth marks ripping at cloth, but tellingly, the collars were hooked on a brambly branch. It looked like he'd managed to back out of them, much like he'd squirmed free of me. I picked up the coat in a fist and buried my face in it, inhaling Morrison's cologne and a distinctly more animalistic scent. Not quite dog; not quite anything I'd ever smelled before. Wolf, or maybe just shapeshifter. I didn't know. "Forget the suit jacket. Just a silver wolf, about a hundred and ninety pounds. That's about twice the size of your average wolf. Tell people to stay away and that it's not dangerous unless provoked."

I hoped to God that was true. The dispatch guy agreed to do as I said, probably more because of incoming 911 calls than any confidence in my sanity, and I left the copse with a fistful of Morrison's clothes.

Billy, Melinda and Jim Littlefoot were waiting for me beside the theater. I said, "I've fucked up beyond all possible belief," still very calmly as I approached them, but from the Hollidays' expressions, Littlefoot had already come to, and shared with them, a reasonably accurate conclusion of the scenario.

All Billy said was, "What do you want us to do?"

"Call Sonata. Get her to contact anybody in Seattle who knows anything about shapeshifting or tracking and tell them they're looking for a man who's been shapeshifted into a wolf."

Melinda, clearly feeling she was on dangerous ground, said, "There's a name for that, Joanne...."

I closed my eyes and turned my face skyward, like I could find strength or answers from the motion. Barely twenty-four hours earlier, I'd told Morrison that there was no such thing as a werewolf. "I shapeshifted into a rattlesnake this morning, Melinda. Am I a weresnake?"

"Of course not. That was—"

I reversed my gaze and pinned her with it. "Then Morrison's not a goddamned werewolf. Werewolves are monsters controlled by phases of the moon, and I don't want anybody getting the idea this should be solved with a silver bullet. Morrison's been inadvertently shapeshifted and that needs to be made clear to anyone who might be able to help." There was a cold place inside me, so angry at myself that it wouldn't let much of anything else through. Drill sergeants were friendlier than I was coming across as. But if there was one thing in my favor, it was that the hard cold place could evidently *plan*, which wasn't normally my strong suit. I was much better at rushing in where angels feared to tread.

Billy had his phone out as he asked, "What're you going to do?"

I pointed toward the theater, hating myself for my response and knowing I'd hate myself just as much for any other. "I'm going to go back in there and make sure nobody dies tonight, just like I said I would."

Billy obviously didn't like that answer any more than I did. He folded up his phone and stepped toward me, voice dropping. "Joanne, this is Morrison we're talking about. You can't…"

"I can't what? I can't trust he's going to have to be smart enough not to get hit by a car? I can't let him run amok through Seattle while I lark off doing something else? Billy, there are a couple dozen people you and Sonata know who can maybe help find Morrison and, if not change him back, at least get him somewhere safe until I can get there and try to help. But as far as I know I'm the *only* person in Seattle who has a chance of protecting the troupe and getting a bead on whomever attacked them last night. I'm sorry, partner, but I don't see a choice here!"

Billy, thunderously, said, "You've changed," and opened his phone again to make the calls.

I rolled my jaw and looked at Melinda, whose expression was less condemning than her husband's. I was grateful, though the cold, scared place inside me knew that in the end it didn't matter. Littlefoot, hanging back a few feet, looked a whole lot more appreciative than I deserved. As far as I was concerned, there was nothing noble or sacrificing about the choice I was making. For once I knew I was right, no matter how much being right sucked. "Mel, I'm going to need you and Billy to go ahead with your part like I asked earlier. If nothing goes wrong—" which seemed pretty flipping unlikely at this juncture "—Billy can leave right after the curtain call to go help look for Morrison, if that's what he wants."

"And I can't?" she asked with the faintest trace of humor.

I wished I had some of that humor to spare, but it hit me like a flat iron. "That's not what I meant."

She put her hand on my arm. "I know, Joanne. It's all right. Michael will be fine."

Possibly, but as I watched them retreat to the theater, Billy's shoulders knotted with angry tension, I wondered if he and I ever would be again.

CHAPTER SEVENTEEN

I did not enjoy the second half of the performance one little bit at all. I'd wrapped shields around myself until I could barely breathe, just so I wouldn't be a scar of angry frustration on the psychic plane, but my heart rate spiked every time I remembered Morrison, which was constantly. After twenty frustrating minutes, I started a deep breathing practice, which was as close as I got to meditation. It almost certainly wouldn't hurt my long-term prospects to get much closer than that to meditation, but for the moment, it had to be enough. Once I got my heartbeat slowed down, the music helped, drums drawing me into a different state of mind whether I wanted them to or not. And to be fair, I did. I just also wanted to be in two places at once, which I didn't think even the limits of my talent would provide for.

Winona looked very small and fragile out there on the stage, centerpiece of power that she was. That actually helped, too: she was a smaller person than Naomi had been, and her physical delicacy made her seem that much more vulnerable. It drove home both just how open to disaster, and how extraordinarily brave, she was. I focused on her, and by the time the last dance began, I'd reached the same semi-detached state I'd been in during the first act. I tingled with magic, filled up by the drums and the dancers. I glanced at my hands, unsurprised that my skin held a familiar translucence that showed silver and blue power running through my veins like blood. I didn't glow: it wasn't something anyone who didn't have the Sight could see. In fact, my shields were so solid that even to a Sighted person, my accumulating power shouldn't be more than the faintest blip on the radar. But to my own eyes, I was alight, and the potential for disrupting a dark magic felt good.

I wanted very badly to pry and prod at the theater, to see if I could edge the killer out of the shadows. If he was there, if he was watching, waiting for the moment to pounce on the troupe's outpouring of power, then he almost certainly would have some kind of psychic presence. As flush with energy as I was, I thought I should sense it if I went looking.

Except every time I'd tried something like that it had been an abject failure. This was not the right place to run yet another disastrous experiment, particularly when the dancers were doing exactly what was necessary to draw him out. Even more particularly when me doing anything untoward, psychically speaking, could very well warn him off and make the whole evening a wash. I knew that. I *knew* it, but knowing didn't make waiting any easier.

I crept forward to just outside the line of sight in the wings without fully realizing I'd moved. The final dance was in its last minutes, and my heart, already strained, ached with the power the dancers were accumulating. I felt it from the audience as well as the dancers themselves, something I hadn't noticed the night before. I'd thought it was just the dancers, but there was already a huge wash of positive feedback radiating from the audience, edge-of-the-seat involvement in the dance preparing for an explosive climax.

The sexual connotation there didn't escape me, and I had just enough time to wonder if that was part of what the killer was after before the dance ended and my attention went in a million different directions at once.

I'd created nets and shields with other peoples' offered energy before. The magic's strength had varied accordingly to whether they'd been adepts themselves, and to some degree on my own skill. I had never, though, had the opportunity to direct the magnitude of power the dancers had deliberately collected and were now releasing. It rode outward, incandescent white to the Sight, and all I had to do was turn its leading edge solid by adding my own talent, my own vision of an impenetrable silvery shield, to their outpouring.

Hunter-moon orange slammed into that leading edge with killing intensity, and shattered with a purely animal yelp of pain.

Triumph shot through me, as hot and white as the dancers' magic. I held the shield: that was easy, easy, *easy*, with the power flooding from the stage, and I spared a glance for Winona and the others. They were radiant with hope and fear, still waiting to see if the attack would come. Waiting to see if they might yet mourn their friend in the best way they knew how, by giving everything they had to an audience prepared to accept anything. The window was so narrow, the moment between cutting down their attacker and still permitting their power to make a difference, and the killer's fractured magic was still whimpering with pain against my own.

Then it retreated. There was no sensation of conscious decision, just an instinctive flight from something larger and stronger. I couldn't tell how much time had passed: everything was stretched and clear and slow to me, but I thought the rebound was almost instantaneous, that the pause between pain and withdrawal was merely my own unhurried sense of time allowing me to see—and See—what was happening.

I bet it all on that being true, and let the ghost dance magic flood the audience.

Part of me felt them surge to their feet, felt the wall of roaring approval as power in itself, crashing back into the dancers, assuring them that they'd succeeded. That same part of me felt something within Winona and Littlefoot and all the others *break*, not in a bad way. Just the sudden painful release of emotion they'd both used and bottled up, an abrupt permission for tears, even as they held their places on stage, chests heaving, muscles trembling, holding their final poses until such a time as the audience's cheers began to wane.

From the slow-time place I was in, that dwindling seemed unlikely to ever come. That was okay, so long as my injured opponent didn't come slinking back to try for another feeding. I didn't think he would: the hunter-moon colors were still in retreat, though not yet out of view. All I had to do was follow them.

As if they'd heard me, they winked out, a shield dragged into place. I snapped my teeth, as animalistic a response as the killer's yelps and whimpers, and whispered *Rattler?* inside my head.

He was there, waiting, all sibilant interest, as if I'd already prepped to call on him. Maybe I had: the drums and the dances were powerful things, and after more than a year of shamanic practice, my hind brain was well-trained to associate drumming with transition. Grateful, I said *thank you for coming so quickly. I need your hunting skills and your shapeshifting guidance. Will you share them with me?*

I'd never thought snakes, by nature, looked pleased, but the glowing white-line spirit animal in my mind looked pretty damned pleased. *I shift. I ssstrike. I heal. It is rare, shaman, that sssomeone thinks to ssseek my hunting ssskillsss. I shall ssshare what I can.*

He was getting better at his S's, at least the SH-ones. I grinned, oddly delighted by that, then repeated, *thank you. I need another shape this time, not a snake. Four legs for swiftness, and a keen nose for hunting.* Oh, God. I was doing the bizarre phraseology that seemed to overtake people when they started dealing with magic. I didn't know if there was some kind of ritual or formula in speaking affectedly, but it seemed to be pervasive, and I hated it, even when I did it. Maybe especially when I did it.

Rattler, however, managed to look increasingly amused, and bobbed his head once in a remarkable approximation of a human nod. I built a very clear mental picture of what I wanted to become, then whispered, "Crap!" out loud and started scrambling out of my clothes.

I got the sweater and underlying T-shirt off, at least, before power welled up around me and changed what I was forever.

A snake's view of the world was hot and cold, alien enough to my warm mammalian mind that the morning's transformation had merely been *different*, not lacking or improved in any manner. A hunting mammal, though, with hyper-acute senses…that was something else. That was the difference between seeing the world and Seeing it: I had always feared getting lost in the shamanic view of my surrounds. Suddenly, with my hearing and scenting opening up in extraordinary ways, I knew just how limited my human perception of the world really was. Part of me, in those very first seconds, knew I would never want to go back to being fully human. That I would lose something when I did, and the anticipation of that loss filled me with regret in a way leaving the Sight behind never did.

Coyote senses: eyesight much sharper than I'd expected, with the slightest movement becoming of great interest to me. Scents were incredibly strong—I could smell Morrison, both as a man and a transformed wolf, even through the dancers and the audience and the dust/makeup/heat of the theater. I could pick out Billy and Melinda from the crowd, and I'd never known I had any particular sense of what they smelled like. There was so much noise I almost couldn't hear anything, though the slightest twitch of my ears—which had to be enormous, given that I was pretty sure I was a hundred-and-sixty-five-pound coyote—honed in on tiny abstractions of sound that I'd never have caught as a human. The near-silent creak of fly ropes, a cough from the audience audible beneath the roaring applause and a swallowed squeak of astonishment from one of the dancers whose gaze strayed my way.

I didn't think more than ten seconds had passed since the dance ended. No more than five seconds since I'd transformed, but even so, I was already losing time. I was also already panting. I didn't know what my body temperature was, but backstage was warm enough without wearing a fur coat.

The obvious answer was to leave the backstage. I backed up—awkward as hell when I was still tangled in my pants—and kicked the jeans off to leave them behind. God had not intended a coyote to open round-knobbed doors any more than he'd intended wolves to, but I had an advantage over Morrison in that I'd retained my intellect.

Stainless steel polished by thousands of human hands twisting it open had the most ungodly salty flavor I'd ever encountered. I gagged on my very long tongue, trying to spit it out, and was incredibly grateful for the bar handles on the outside doors so I didn't have to taste *that* again.

Outside, Morrison's scent was bright and clear, wind playing with it but in no danger of reducing it to a faintness I couldn't follow. My gut seized up, impulse at war with promises. I could find him. I could find him *quickly*, reducing the danger he'd be hurt or killed—assuming he hadn't been already, and I had to assume that. I wanted to so badly I could taste it in great gulps that washed away the doorhandle flavor. I'd gotten him into the mess he was currently in. I should be the one to get him out.

Teeth bared, anger directed entirely at myself, I deliberately turned out of the wind and whispered another plea to Rattler: *Can you show me how to See? I hunt a hidden magic and a shaman's eyes are not enough to flush it out.* I was doing it again, the weird semi-ritualistic speech patterns. On the other hand, Rattler exuded a sense of approval from somewhere behind my frontal lobes, so maybe stilted language wasn't such a bad idea. *I'm shifted,* I whispered, *magic personified. I'm a coyote, predator personified. Teach me to hunt magic, Rattler. I need your guidance.*

Triggering the Sight, even in shifted form, wasn't difficult, but nor was it quite normal, even for the Sight. In my own full-color vision, I saw the animistic world as a deepening of the physical world around me. Auras lit up from within, typically, each object proclaiming its own particular duty by whatever color it shone with. My coyote-sharp eye-sight didn't have the color range the human vision spectrum did, but I lost none of the brilliance I was accustomed to Seeing. It just…moved. Moved deeper into my brain, where it resided as information separate from but related to the physical world. It looked as though someone had painted the entire landscape in light, the way it could be done with long camera exposures, and then set the entire image inside my head where it could be consulted at need without interfering with my real-world coyote vision.

I was pretty certain that was entirely Rattler's doing, not my own. It lingered a moment, letting me get used to it, before fading. For a disorienting moment I caught a glimpse of the warm/cold world the rattlesnake saw, entirely at odds with my still-mammalian brain's expectations. Then even Rattler's view transmogrified, and the overlay of heat sens-ing made sudden vivid sense.

Warm-blooded creatures left heat trails where they moved. They didn't last for long, but to a rattlesnake, the difference between a few seconds' visible heat trail and the lack thereof could mean the difference between dinner or going hungry. Similarly, with ordinary Sight, the whole world lit up, but with Rattler's pared-down heat sight, only the left-behind trails of old magic glowed. To me, hunting magic, the difference was between finding a killer and let-ting one go.

Or finding Morrison and letting him go. His trail, like his scent, was clear. Both would fade, possibly before I could get back to this starting point and follow him to wherever he'd gone. But there was a better chance of tracing his phys-ical scent later than there was of chasing the hunter-moon orange blaze that even now retreated from the theater. The killer had crept up on it, shielded but questing: he had to be open and aware of the dancers in order to time his attack perfectly, so couldn't hide himself as well as I'd done. All I'd had to do, after all, was watch: an advantage to working from the inside.

And all I had to do now was follow him. I snarled at the wind, at the scent that promised I could find my wayward boss, and turned away from it. The killer's fading streak of color, the mark left from his shielded approach and retreat, wasn't something I could put my nose down and follow. It was somewhere between my mind and my Sight, and it didn't tidily use city streets to get between points A and B. It went as the crow flew—a stupid phrase for anyone who'd ever seen a crow fly to use, since they hopped and flitted and winged their way all over the place, rather than going in the straight line implied by the colloquialism, which tangent made me wonder how much of it was me and how much of it was the irritated musings of a coyote which had tried to hunt crow, *none of which was important right then*. I hauled my brain back on track and trotted through the parking lot, focused on a halfway point between the real world and the Sight which allowed me to follow a killer's trail. My nose and ears, not especially useful in this particular tracking attempt, informed me that patrons were beginning to leave the theater, a piece of information I took in stride until a woman started screaming bloody murder.

Like everybody else, I jumped about four feet into the air—well, no, not like everybody else, because I actually *did* jump four feet into the air, possibly more, which I hadn't known was in a coyote's repertoire—and came down with my heart racing as I looked around for whatever the hell had inspired her shrieking.

A fist-size stone caught me in the ribs, and a scared, angry male bellowed, "G'wan, get out! Get out of here!" at me as he scooped up another rock. From the flower beds, no less. That wasn't fair. I yelped as the second stone hit home, then fled, tail tucked between my legs, for the self-same copse Morrison had retreated to. Apparently there was at least one disadvantage to retaining human intellect in a shapeshifted body: completely forgetting that everyone would see a gigantic, potentially dangerous wild animal. Following the killer's trail was going to be harder than I thought, but for reasons I hadn't even considered.

Grumpy and with brambles sticking to my fur, I crept out of the trees on my belly, keeping to the shadows. In human form, I could bend light around me to make myself almost invisible, but I was reluctant to try layering magic like that outside of a controlled environment. Coyote would be proud of me. And coyotes, small-c, were decent at skulking and dodging, so I skulked and dodged until I was in a pool of dimness between two streetlights. Theater traffic hadn't started pouring out yet, so the road was relatively empty. The nearest traffic light was red, a couple vehicles idling at it, and the headlights approaching the traffic light had a fair distance to travel. I took a good hard look both ways and bolted across the street.

A semi truck blew through the red light and caught me in the teeth of its grill.

CHAPTER EIGHTEEN

Truly astonishing pain erupted in my left hip and thigh bone. In my whole left side, in fact, though it radiated from the hip joint. The world went white with agony and gravity briefly lost its hold on me. That was bad, because eventually it was going to demand its due, and I already hurt more than I could remember ever hurting in the past. I'd been impaled repeatedly, but somehow in comparison that seemed localized, whereas pain was now ricocheting down through my feet and up along my ribs into my arm. I thought there must be streamers of red flowing from my toes and fingertips. Not blood, just a visible arc of pain, like a manga comic book character might show.

Rattler hissed, *Apologies, Sssiobhán Walkingssstick,* and my world went away in new and exciting ways.

Everything twisted: the earth, my bones, my memories. The latter enveloped me, a comforting cushion to take me far from the deep wrenching dreadfulness that was *now.*

Then, I was a kid barely big enough to see out the window of my father's big old boat of a Cadillac. Vast trees with leaves so rich in shade they shimmered blue-green reached over the road, making a canopy for us to drive through. *Later* I would associate stretches of road like that with Anne Shirley's White Way of Delight, but *then* I was too small, and only enamored of the colors and how sunlight filtered through them. My father was talking, something I didn't remember him doing all that often, and since time had rearranged to give me the opportunity, I paid attention.

"…almost home. Your grandmother will be glad to see you. Do you remember her, Joanie?"

I shook my head. Grandmothers were an abstract concept, just like mothers were: mine had deposited me with Dad when I was six months old, and I hadn't seen her again until I was twenty-six. I'd spent the intervening years resenting her for dumping me with a father who had no apparent interest in me, though this was a revelatory and completely unremembered moment. Joanne Walker of the present day had no memory at all of a grandmother, nor of visiting North Carolina until I was a teen. Now that he said it, though, I recognized the roads and trees my small self was being driven down: we were, in fact, almost to Qualla Boundary, the Cherokee land trust where I'd gone to high school.

"Well, she remembers you. Thinks I'm terrible for keeping you away. Am I terrible, Joanie?"

"Nuh-*uh!*" I leaned out of my seat belt to stretch way across the car's bench seat and pat Dad's thigh. "Drandma's *wrong!*"

Dad grinned at me, flash of white teeth in a warm brown

face, and time slid forward a ways, landing me in a kitchen I
recognized from my teen years.

The woman in it, though, was completely unfamiliar. She
wore bell-bottom jeans over rough bare feet, and a square-
cut cotton tunic with an embroidered slash at the collar. It
reminded me of commercially-made shirts intended to look
handmade, except it somehow seemed authentic, like she,
or someone, actually *had* made it. She was tall and strong-
featured, with a beaky nose like my own. Her black hair
was barely threaded with white, and her brown eyes were
extremely serious.

So serious, in fact, that they couldn't be taken seriously,
especially when I'd just watched her plate up a bunch of
cookies and knew she was holding them behind her back.
"Which hand?"

I pronounced, "Bof!" with a three-year-old's utter confidence. The woman—presumably my grandmother, though
she didn't really look old enough to be a grandmother—
laughed and turned around, revealing she was indeed holding the cookie plate in both hands. I nabbed two and stuffed
both of them into my mouth, giving myself strained chip-
munk cheeks.

My father, somewhere behind me, said, "Joanne," in a
mildly chiding tone, but it was too late: spitting them out
would be infinitely more disgusting than slowly mashing my
way through them. I mumbled, "Sowwy," and "Thank you"
when I'd cleared my mouth enough to do so, and amends
were made.

Grandmother said, "You're welcome," and gave me two
more cookies, which I gnashed into happily. The now-me,
the adult, saw the whole thing as a distraction from Grandmother's gentle, "You should settle here, Joe," addressed to

my father in an obviously trying-not-to-be-pushy manner. "I'd love to have her near."

Dad stepped in for a couple cookies himself, nodding as he did so. "I've been thinking about it. The mountains are a good place to grow up."

"And there's…" Again, the adult-me heard a significant pause there: Grandmother had no intention of finishing the sentence, but every confidence Dad knew what she meant.

And he did, though he stopped any chance she might continue with a wave of one of his absconded-with cookies. "Not now, Ma. Maybe later."

Acceptance flickered through her dark eyes, and time bounced forward again. A matter of hours, maybe: certainly not more than days. Dad held my hand, his voice terribly neutral as we looked at the mangled wreck of a blue 1957 Pontiac Star Chief. That was what he was telling me, what kind of car it was, and, "I remember when your grand-mother bought it. I was five. My father and I used to work on it together. You wouldn't remember him, Joanie. He died a long time before you were born. I think she'd like it if I put this old beast back together, but I can't, sweetheart. Not right now." Then he picked me up and hugged me, and although as an adult I remembered none of the rest of it, I did remember that hug as the only time I ever saw my father cry.

We left Qualla Boundary in the Cadillac a few days later, and I didn't see the place again for ten years, when I de-manded he cast off his wanderlust and settle down in one location long enough for me to go to high school. Dad had looked at me like he'd never seen me before. We hadn't been getting along for a couple years at that point, and I'd always thought that expression was borne of him being uncertain of how he'd ended up with a kid at all, much less one with opinions and demands.

Now, faced with the idea that he'd almost done just that—settled down to raise me in one place and had instead lost his mother to a horrible car crash—put a whole new spin on that expression. Maybe we could have settled anywhere, but maybe Qualla Boundary was the only place he'd ever thought of as home. Maybe facing that place again without his family there was a little harder than angry-at-the-world teenage Joanne Walker had ever considered.

There was a lot I hadn't considered. Things I would have to take a look at, assuming I survived being hit by a semi.

Memory warped away, as if I'd reminded it I didn't belong *then*. Pain flooded back, no longer just setting my left side afire, but blazing through my entire body. My bones were jerking, reforming, shaping themselves in new dreadful ways, and I heard Rattler's sibilant apology again. I wanted to say it was okay, except I wasn't at all sure it was. There were afterimages in my mind, shucked snakeskins built from thin strips of light, my own broken form flailing in anti-gravity, a coyote fur lying bedraggled on the ground. Every one of the images wrenched my whole body, yanking things in and out of alignment, changing the shape of my spine, my bones, my skin.

Coyote, my Coyote, my golden-eyed mentor, appeared in the midst of all the chaos, human form bristling with fear just the way his coyote shape might do. "Joanne? *Siobhán?* What's happened?"

I wailed, "You said it's not supposed to hurt!" as I writhed again, leaving yet another snakeskin behind. Everyone was calling me by my real name, the one on my birth certificate, rather than the use-name I'd carried most of my life. Siobhán Grainne MacNamarra Walkingstick, the Irish-

Cherokee disaster bestowed upon me by my mother, who had given no thought to how an American might view *Siob-hán Grainne*. Even I'd been half convinced my own name was pronounced Seeobawn Grainy until Mother confirmed the correct way of saying it, Shevaun Grania. But since she hadn't raised me, Dad had taken one look at the whole mess and dubbed me Joanne. I'd started using Walker instead of Walkingstick the day I graduated high school, cutting all ties with who I used to be.

Or maybe not quite all. The shamanic heritage I'd boxed off and forgotten about had burst through eventually, and was right now stripping me to my skin, to the muscle, to the very bone, and rebuilding me from the inside out. I'd shapeshifted twice, and it *wasn't supposed to* hurt!

"You're not shifting," Coyote whispered, though that was manifestly untrue. Even he sounded like he wasn't sure of what he was saying. "Joanne, what *happened*?"

Rattler's apology hissed through me a third time as my back arched like a chest-burster was about to, well, burst out of my chest. I screamed this time, something I didn't think I'd been doing, but there was nowhere else for the pain to go. One more snakeskin fell away, and the white-hot agony drained from my vision so I could see the real world again.

So I was fully aware that the final twist of earth/body/memory was gravity calling me home. I smashed into asphalt and bounced down the street to the scent of burning rubber. Metal shrieked somewhere very close and voices rose above it in fear and dismay. I kept rolling after I'd stopped bouncing, and finally came to a stop as a bruised, huddled mass on the roadway.

I hurt everywhere. Not the explosive pain from the impact, but like I'd been thrown forty feet and bounced off the street a few times. People survived that all the time in the movies, but I never thought they should. I wasn't entirely certain I *had*. The toes of my right foot twitched involuntarily, and I was grateful even though it made every muscle even distantly attached to my toes hurt. I twitched my fingers experimentally, and that worked, too, although it hurt all the way to my spine. Big girl that I was, I whimpered instead of actually screaming.

The rattlesnake coiled in front of me, looking unusually mortal and real, and bent his blunt head down to tickle my face with his tongue. It did tickle, which made me flinch, which made me hurt. I did my big-girl whimper again, and the snake, against all laws of snaky nature that I knew about, slithered to my feet, then uncurled himself against me, following every body curve he could get to. I was a pretty small ball for someone nearly six feet tall, and he was unusually large; after a few seconds I was almost entirely wrapped in cool, sympathetic snake. *Ssiobhán Walkingstick,* he said inside my head. *Thiss wass not meant to happen thiss way, and I am sssorry.*

He shuddered—*I* shuddered—and the physical became metaphysical, Rattler melting deep into my skin.

Most of the pain vanished, or retreated so far as to become inconsequential by comparison. I cried out, a weak little startled sound mostly of relief, then dragged in a deep breath and let go a much gustier howl. A barbaric yawp, to steal a phrase. It was undignified and angry and pain-ridden and an announcement that against all odds, I was still alive.

And in the midst of that yell it came to me, quite clearly: Siobhán Grainne MacNamarra Walkingstick had only just now been born.

On the upside, despite needing glasses which were no longer on my face, I had better vision than your average newborn. The first thing I saw when I lifted my head was the semi's bed swung across half the intersection, its head-lights glaring down on me. The second thing was that the arm supporting me was bare, which made me crane my neck, wincing, to take a look at myself.

I was quite, quite naked. Quite human, and quite naked, with road rash in places I didn't even know I had places. I closed my eyes and very carefully put my forehead against my forearm, resting there a moment while my muscles screeched protest at being used, and then took a second look at myself.

Still naked. Well, yes, of course: I'd shed my clothes in the theater whilst changing into a coyote. Clearly I hadn't considered the full ramifications of that decision, although even if I had, they would not ultimately have led to the con-clusion I would shortly be lying starkers in a city street while a panicked truck driver thundered toward me. I was going to have to reassure him, which at that very moment seemed a task well beyond my capabilities.

The poor guy dropped to his knees a few feet away and skidded over asphalt on sheer momentum, tearing up his jeans in his bid to not run me over a second time. He was huge in a manner which suggested he both ate way too much truck-stop food and that he spent all his off time at a gym turning grease into fat-lined muscle. He was the Kobe beef of truck drivers, except I had the vague idea Kobe beef involved massages rather than exercising.

Mr. Kobe Beef had a high tenor voice which had no busi-ness coming from a body that size, and it said "Ohmygodoh-mygod IswearIseenadog abigfuckingdog Ididn'tmeantohitit JesusChristitcouldn'thavebeenadog Ihityou youmustbedead areyoudead pleasedon'tbedead ohJesusohGodohJesusGod" until I croaked, "I'm not dead yet," and waited for Monty Python to finish the rest of the scene.

Monty Python were disobliging, and did not appear. Other people were starting to: theater-goers, the people from the cars that had been at the traffic light, and in the very far distance, sirens. I couldn't quite determine which branch of public safety they belonged to—cops or fire department or paramedics—and a thin wave of regret mentioned that my coyote hearing would have picked them out clearly.

"Miss," Kobe Beef said in a tone somewhere between reverent and befuddled, "you're *naked*."

Ah, yes. I was not dead, and therefore it was more important that I was naked than it was that he'd just run a red light and knocked somebody forty feet down the road. Such was human nature. I said, "Yes, I am," after a few moments. "I don't suppose you have a coat I can borrow?"

Kobe lumbered to his feet and rushed back to his truck at a pretty good clip, for such a big guy. I sat up very cautiously. Tiny pointy stones poked me in the ass, adding insult to the road-rash injuries I'd already taken. I was covered in black smears and road burn, the former of which manifestly refused to disappear under my insistent shamanic imagery of a car wash. Sullen and aching, I dragged every last ounce of reluctant power to the fore and succeeded in giving myself a new paint job that removed the road rash before Kobe Beef returned with an enormous flannel-lined jacket that smelled like French fries. He draped it over my shoulders and I shivered hard, surprised at how cold I'd gotten without noticing. "Thank you."

"You're welcome. Did I, ImeanIguessIdidIhadtohavebut did I hit you, miss? I was drivingtoodamnedfast I'msorry

it'slateI'mtired justtryingtogethome Ididn'tnoticethelight you
should be *dead*—!'"

I stared over his head toward the traffic lights. There were
cameras on all four crossbars above each street, making it
almost certain that the whole wreck had been filmed. Everything, including my transformation from coyote to woman.
For a moment, I longed for a world in which magic wasn't
something that could be caught on camera, but I knew from
personal experience that it could be. Somebody—probably
my periodic nemesis, news reporter Laurie Corvallis—could
make a big stinking story out of this.

Except Laurie wouldn't. Not after what had happened
with the wendigo. Maybe I could get her to tread on a
few toes and make sure nobody else turned it into a story,
either. Or maybe I could get somebody in traffic control to
accidentally wipe a magnet over tonight's traffic tapes, or
whatever the modern equivalent thereof was. That would be
better all around.

"I'm not dead." Interrupting Kobe's squeaking, alarmed
rant felt better than it probably should. "Obviously you
didn't hit me. I'd be dead if you had."

His jaw flapped, but there was a certain infallible logic
to my statement, and relief started creeping across his thick
features. "I'm probably just some crazy woman," I went on.
"Out crossing the street naked in the middle of the night.
Probably your truck's impact against…" I looked around,
trying to find something the truck had actually hit, and settled on the median strip. "…against the median had enough
concussive effect to knock me off my feet and down the road
a bit."

"That…must've been what happened…" Kobe's forehead
sank into deep wrinkles, and I almost felt sorry for him.

Almost. Not quite sorry enough to go try to straighten

out the witnesses' stories, for example. My largesse ended with climbing stiffly to my feet—the paint job that cleared my rash up hadn't dealt with the pain of muscles abused by bouncing down the street—and patting Kobe's shoulder. "If you ever drive tired or above the speed limit again, God Himself is going to come down on you like a load of bricks. Trust me. I have connections."

I left him there looking like I'd put a gypsy curse on him, and not feeling one little bit bad about it as I limped down the street. I was exhausted, but I was alive, and that was good. I suspected I'd been through some kind of rebirthing, that Rattler's frantic scraping off of my old skins to reveal new, fresh, healed ones had probably done something profound, and that once I understood fully what had happened, I would have my feet under myself a whole lot more solidly. That was also good. By all rights, I should be happy.

But I had by now lost any hope of tracking the hunter-orange killer, and that was not good at all.

CHAPTER NINETEEN

Under anybody's definition of normal circumstances, a six-foot-tall woman walking barefoot down a city street wearing only a smelly lightweight coat would attract an impossible amount of attention. Moreso when she was leaving the scene of a wreck while more or less everyone else was running toward it.

It being me, though, I turned one of my oldest tricks to my advantage. Typically bending light around me to render myself essentially invisible was pretty easy. It took a little concentration, a little envisioning light waves just sort of washing on by without bouncing off me with any real enthusiasm.

Walking down the street and keeping myself relatively unseen was one of the hardest things I'd ever done. It took a quite literally staggering amount of concentration. I kept weaving around, sometimes bouncing off passersby who had no idea what had hit them.

I wanted specific passersby. I wanted Billy and Melinda, or failing them, Jim Littlefoot, though the Hollidays were by far my first choice. Unfortunately, my phone was back at the theater with my clothes, and I wasn't expecting happenstance to put them in my path. Odds were Billy was already hunting for Morrison, and that Melinda was either helping or on her way home. The passing fancy that I could retake a coyote form and search for Morrison myself struck me.

My knees collapsed at the idea, thigh muscles squealing in protest as they tried to keep me from falling to the sidewalk. They succeeded, just barely, and I lurched to a nearby tree, holding myself up until my legs were trustworthy again. Coyote had said shapeshifting didn't hurt. He hadn't mentioned it left a person completely fricking exhausted. Someday I was going to write that Shaman's Handbook that no one had seen fit to give me. It would be full of useful information like *don't trust snakes in your garden* and *start and end your shapeshifting adventures at home, so you don't lose your clothes and so you can collapse into sleep for twelve hours.* Although now that I thought about it, that first one was a bit Biblical and I was, in retrospect, even dumber than I'd realized. The second part, though, was helpful.

Way back in the recesses of my mind, like I'd summoned him with the power of thought, Coyote said, "Joanne?" in a very quiet worried voice.

"Am I in a trance? How can you even be talking to me? Are you telepathic now?" Startled passersby looked at where I wasn't, and I cleared my throat. Invisible cloaks apparently didn't work on vocal cords. Oops.

"You're using some kind of magic," he said gently. Cautiously. "It puts you in the right mindset to be receptive to someone calling to you from the astral plane. Are you all right, Jo?"

"Mostly." I started toddling down the street again, on the dubious logic that a moving voice coming out of nowhere was less alarming than a stationary one. "I think I'm going to need therapy after this is over, though."

A hint of a smile came into his voice. "Physical therapy?"

My mind went dirty places, just like it was probably supposed to, and I got a little more spring in my step. "Yeah, maybe. No, mental therapy. Something happened, Coyote. Something..." Words failed as I let myself peek, just a little, at the difference I felt within.

It felt like somebody had taken a loofah to my psyche. To my *magic*. Like it had been exfoliated, scrubbed, scraped, pared, polished and finally put away to rest. Like it had shed layer after layer of nasty old snakeskin that had dimmed its potential, and now it was ready to consider what it could actually do.

At the moment, that wasn't much. Newborns weren't often capable of great feats; being born was, after all, hard work, and it took some time to get used to the bright, loud, cold world. Right now the core of my power felt like it was doing exactly that. All the things I'd learned to do over the past year or so were still accessible, but not at full strength, or what I'd come to assume was full strength.

"Something big," I finally said to Coyote. "Something too big to think about right now."

"If it's big you *need* to think about it, Jo—"

"No." I actually held my hand up to stop him, not that he or anybody else could see me right now. "Look, just no, Cyrano. This isn't burying my head in the sand, okay? I'll deal with it. I just can't right now. A nice homeless lady wants me to look into some missing persons, I lost the ghost dance killer's trail and Morrison's been turned into a wolf. I cannot cope with anything else right now."

"Morrison's been what?" Coyote managed a vocal knife's edge balance between horrified and thrilled.

I crossed the street into the theater's parking lot, muttering an explanation that made confused arts patrons look around in search of the body providing the voice, and finished with, "I'll call you back later, okay? I have to get dressed and try to salvage this mess."

"You're naked?" That went a lot more toward thrilled, and I snickered through my weariness.

"Naked but invisible. I'll talk to you later, Cyrano, okay?" Dropping a psychic connection was harder than hanging up a phone, and I got a mental echo of his goodbye for a few seconds before shaking it off and going in search of my clothes.

Billy and Melinda were backstage, the latter with my clothes neatly bundled in her arms. She said, "You dropped these," and handed over my copper bracelet and glasses. I pressed a hand to my throat, astonished to discover my mother's silver necklace hadn't ruptured when I'd shifted form. I was pretty certain my coyote-neck was thicker than my own.

Then again, the necklace hadn't fallen out of place when I'd changed into a snake earlier, either. I was absolutely certain I'd had greater circumference as a rattler than my neck typically did. I slunk into the changing rooms with my clothes, stopping to frown at myself in the mirror when I was dressed.

Cernunnos, Horned God of the Wild Hunt, had recognized the necklace. Had, more importantly, recognized its maker: Nuada of the Silver Hand, who was an elf king or a small god or something of that nature. Not human, and not as powerful as Cernunnos himself, but a silversmith of literally legendary proportions, regardless of his ranking in the esoteric echelon. Even I'd heard of him before Cernunnos mentioned his name, and my repository of magical knowledge was still far more limited than it should be. My mother had bequeathed to me a necklace of great history and possibly enormous power without one word of explanation. I probably shouldn't be surprised that a minor detail like retaining its position around my throat wasn't beyond its capabilities.

Frankly, if I ever got over being surprised by things like that, I would consider myself way too jaded and go sit on a mountaintop and meditate until some of the wonder came back into the world. And *that* was such a far cry from where I'd been a year and a half ago that I left the dressing rooms with far less trepidation than I might have, given that the Hollidays' continuing presence at the theater suggested something had gone wrong.

The dancers were gathered on stage behind the closed curtains. Jubilation and sorrow sparked from them as they embraced each other, obviously still coming down from the high of the performance. Two or three were carrying drums, though they hadn't begun to beat them. A weary selfish part of me wished they would: I got a little buzz from the energy they were still radiating, but I needed a whole lot more than that. Or a good solid night's sleep, which didn't seem likely to be on the agenda.

Winona was at the center of everything, passed from one dancer to another, congratulations and thanks murmured to her with each hug. It looked like they'd been doing the same thing since the curtain came down, but I imagined they

C.E. Murphy

could keep it up a while yet. She'd gone above and beyond the call of duty, and everyone knew it. Whatever had happened to keep Billy and Melinda here, at least I hadn't failed the troupe.

I exhaled, tension sliding free on the breath, though my shoulders sagging reminded me again that my whole body ached. "So what happened?"

Melinda smiled. "You were perfect, that's what. *They* were perfect. I've never seen a performance like that one."

"Me, neither. But so why are you still here?"

"Why are *you?*" Billy demanded. He was still pissed I hadn't gone after Morrison, which was only unfair in that even with my phenomenal cosmic powers, I couldn't be in two places at once.

At least, I didn't think I could be. I gave the shining kernel of new-forged power inside me a prod to see if it agreed. I got back a sensation very like a mother's disapproving look, and barely restrained myself from giggling aloud. Billy's expression darkened and I wiped all laughter from my face, which was less difficult than it might have been. "I got hit by a semi while trying to cross the road. I lost the killer's trail and I have about as much shamanic energy as a...a..." I couldn't think of something with insufficient amounts of power to even finish the sentence, but it didn't matter. Pissed or not, Billy went white and Melinda caught my arm as if assuring herself I was still alive.

"You got hit by a *semi?*"

"I was a coyote, he ran the light, I...look, I'm okay. I'm just a little flat in terms of power reserves. The last day has been like a yo-yo with that."

"You're more than a little flat." Melinda pursed her mouth prissily, looking me over like a side of meat. "I've never seen your aura so low, not since before last January, anyway."

Distracted, I said, "You looked before then?"

Melinda shrugged. "Bill had told me what the little ghost girl said about you. Any time a clairvoyant mentions someone is unusual, I'm interested. So I'd looked, yes."

I remembered the girl in question, Emily Franklin. I'd been a mechanic at the time, not a cop. The only reason I'd encountered her—or hadn't, more accurately, since she was dead—was I'd been out with Billy, trying to hear a hitch in his vehicle's engine, when he got the murder call. Emily, victim of a violent death and a budding clairvoyant, was lingering and had seen me waiting for him. Besides what she'd told Billy about her own murder, she'd mentioned I had no visible past beyond the twenty-six short years of my life. She'd never seen anyone like me.

None of that was something Billy could have told me at the time, some three years ago now. I'd have laughed at him, to say the least. But apparently he'd told Melinda, and I'd had even more people looking out for my eventual arcane awakening than I'd known. Not for the first time, I mumbled, "I don't deserve friends as good as you."

Melinda smiled. "You only say that because you've never seen Bill's expression of smug 'I told her so' when he's spilling the details of your adventures to me."

Billy looked guilty enough to make me chortle tiredly. "You had to be saying it to somebody. You were incredibly restrained with me. Okay. So yeah, I'm flat. I don't think I've got it in me to transform again, and even if I did, I'm not sure I could pick up the trail. It was like a heat trail, fading fast, so I'm back at goddamned square one. So anyway, why *are* you guys still here?"

Whatever humor Billy'd manifested fled. "I was hoping you'd be calling with some kind of information about Morrison. I thought this would be the place to start from."

"That's it?" This time relief, not exhaustion, made my knees buckle. "Nothing went horribly wrong with the dancers?"

Billy wrapped a hand around my elbow, supporting me. "It looks like the only person something's gone wrong with is you."

"Detective Walker's been injured?" Jim Littlefoot appeared like he'd been summoned, worry creasing his forehead. "Are you all right, Detective? Everything went so well on stage…"

"It was nothing to do with you," I promised. Billy's hand around my arm was more helpful than I wanted to admit to. In fact, I kind of wanted to flop over and lean on him, or possibly just to sit down in a lump and stay there until I was about a hundred and twelve. "I wasn't able to track the killer. I'm sorry, Jim."

Disappointment flashed through his dark eyes, replaced almost instantly by resolution. "We have one more performance."

"Ha." I didn't mean to laugh, but the sound popped from my throat. "You people are insane. Insanely brave. Insanely…insane. Tomorrow, I don't know. Maybe tomorrow is good. I'm just so *tired* right now."

Onstage, somebody smacked the heel of his hand against the drum he carried. The vibration rippled through the air and caught me in the belly, a *twang* so deep and profound my knees buckled again. This time, despite already having a grip on me, Billy didn't manage to keep me on my feet. I flumped to the floor, sitting cross-legged and pushing my glasses up so I could cup my face in my hands. A few more drumbeats thumped through me, each one like a physical, palpable hit. I was used to the magic inside me coming alive in response to a drum, but it just took the beats like body blows, shockwaves hitting me from within. I curled down even farther, hands folded behind my head like I could protect myself from the music.

Melinda crouched and put her hand on my shoulder. Worry pulsed through her touch, so strong I didn't need the Sight to know it flowed toward me. I wanted to explain how Rattler had shed my skin a million times, stripping me down physically, emotionally and magically in order to save my life. I wanted to tell her about the peculiar feeling I'd been reborn, and Rattler's apology about how it wasn't supposed to have happened that way, like I'd gone through not just a rebirth, but a premature rebirth. Telling somebody those things seemed important, and Melinda, who had five kids, might just understand.

All I did, though, was whimper, a tiny pulse of sound every time the drum was hit.

Melinda withdrew her hand and stood, her voice calm and quiet above me. "Bill, Mr. Littlefoot, could you bring Joanne onto the stage, please?"

Normal people would have asked why. Normal people would have said *what the hell?* and fussed about it, which was what I wanted to do. Instead the two men shared a few seconds' silence in which I imagined they at least exchanged *what the hell* glances. Then Billy slid his hands into my armpits and uncurled me a little. Jim Littlefoot took my knees, and they carried me onstage and put me back down. They didn't try to rebalance me on my butt: they just tucked me down on my side, and I curled up a little smaller, fetal position.

The troupe, who were not especially loud, got much quieter as I was carried out. The drum stopped, and I could feel everyone's eyes on me, the weight of their gazes. I thought probably they should be offered some sort of explanation as to what one used-up shaman was doing lying center stage shortly after their dance performance.

Melinda, however, was going to have to offer that explanation, because I didn't have a clue. All I knew was that the rubber dance mat was unexpectedly comfortable, and that the stage lights from the wings were warm enough to make my bones start melting. In fact, despite my ventilated jeans, I thought I'd start sweating pretty soon, which would have been a more dismaying prospect if I wasn't distantly aware of the already-pungent scent of dancers. I'd fit right in, smelling up the place.

Three people hit drums at the same time, abrupt enough that despite my weariness, I flinched. Footsteps ran across the stage, quick light sounds that changed to more solid thumps as whoever it was reached the nonpadded wings, paused, then came rushing back to spring across the mat. The next drumbeat came from four instruments, low rumble of quick beats which moved clockwise around me until the dancers and the drumming alike came to a sharp stop. I had a dizzifying vision as if from above, of the four musicians slotting into place on a power wheel, one taking up a position in each cardinal direction. And then I knew why Melinda had put me onstage, and what the troupe themselves instinctively understood.

They were offering me a spirit dance.

CHAPTER TWENTY

The part of me that wasn't beaten down and wasted—I was sure there had to be a part like that buried in there somewhere—thought I should probably sit up and watch, to properly appreciate what was going on around me. The rest of me, however, was completely content to lie huddled in the middle of the stage, listening to drums and footsteps falling into patterns around me.

At first it was just the drummers, sound pulsing in almost visible waves, for all that my eyes were closed. Then someone else joined in, using heavy steps to make a counter-rhythm, one-two-*three*. Within a minute the stage vibrated with the weight of feet matching that pattern, and the high-pitched drums were a fourth beat thrown into the air to make certain the cadence didn't become too comfortable. The sounds sent goose bumps down my spine, then crept in along the big nerves and nudged my exhausted, fragile power.

It didn't so much nudge back as go *splaaaaah!* like a dog rolling over to have its tummy rubbed. Dignity wasn't one of my strong suits, and it was all I could do not to roll over and go *splaaaaah!* myself. Instead I just sank a little farther into the mats, letting drumbeats and dance steps wash over me. The stage lights pounding down were magnificent, their warmth lifting me out of myself to drift on the dance Littlefoot's troupe was offering.

I actually did rise out of myself, the world becoming half-visible through the Sight, like my closed eyes were partially obscuring my vision. That didn't normally happen—usually I could See very clearly whether my physical eyes were open or not—but I appreciated it. Full-blown Sight would've been overwhelming, and I'd kind of had enough of overwhelming for one day.

Watching the dancers, though, was worth the effort. They weren't doing one of their choreographed pieces. They moved in toward me, backed away, dropped in and out, clapped or stomped their feet, and as a whole appeared to dance as the spirit moved them. Their auras flowed together and separated again, always achieving lighter shades when they touched one another, though not once did they reach the blinding white of the ghost dance's final eruption. That dance had been impassioned; this one was gentle.

I was profoundly grateful for the quieter approach. More would have flattened me, not that I could get much flatter either figuratively or literally. Every time the energy they danced up roiled forward to touch me—and it did, even if they didn't themselves—my own magic sighed a little more deeply, as if it was being massaged back into wakefulness.

Admittedly, wakefulness wasn't a place I had any raging

desire to be. Conked out on the dance floor mat sounded pretty good, really. I snorted a near-silent laugh into my forearm, and a remarkably good mimic of the noise echoed within the constraints of my skull. My eyebrows flicked upward, and Raven glided out of the stage lights to flit around me, finally coming to a stop by way of multitudinous hops. He gave another snorting laugh, this time sounding a bit more ravenlike, and cocked his head to give me a good hard look with one bright black eye.

I said, "Up here," because while I retained enough connection to my body to laugh, mostly my consciousness was detached and basking in the light and energy above me.

Raven twisted his head to peer up at me, then cawed in delight and leaped back into the air. He was unusually solid, all gleaming blue-black feathers and massive ruffed throat instead of the outlined white light form I often saw. He winged his way around me, going *ek! ek! ek!* with approval, like floating around outside my own body was an excellent place to be. Probably from his avian perspective, it was. He probably considered humans to be depressingly limited, what with being stuck to the earth all the time. I was starting to get behind that train of thought myself when he stuck his entire head in my belly and said "*Quaaarrk!*" in unmistakable dismay.

I muttered, "It wasn't my *idea*," and he pulled his head out of my stomach to glower and batter me with his wings. It always hurt when he did that, but it seemed like he was putting more oomph into it this time. I smacked back at him with childish displeasure. "Knock it off! Talk to Rattlesnake, if you want to bitch somebody out! He—"

Well. Technically Rattler was at fault for the reduced state of power that Raven evidently found so distressing. On the other hand, I would be a thin red smear across a Seattle street had Rattler not done what he did. "He saved my life," I finished, considerably more graciously than I'd started. "It just about wiped us out. Well, me, anyway. He's probably okay. I mean, it's hard to hurt spirit animals, right?"

Raven, who very rarely spoke—because ravens could talk in the real world, Rattler had said—gave me a distinctly concerned look and *quark*ed again. I said, "Okay, okay," and drifted back down toward my body. Not really into it, but closer to its general vicinity than I'd been. Raven winged down beside me and strode around self-importantly while I whispered, *Rattler?* in the recesses of my mind.

Like Raven, he came out of the light, slithering between dancers' feet as he materialized into something that looked very much like a real-world rattlesnake. There was a thread there, a commonality, it seemed. The more out-of-body I was, the more real my spirit animals were. If I was solidly within myself, they manifested as quick sketches of light and power. I wondered if they saw me similarly when I wasn't inhabiting my flesh.

Rattler crawled over my hip and settled into the warm divot between it and my ribs, then lifted his head to have a look at Raven. They weren't usually in it together: I tended to need one or the other, not both. The once I'd needed both had been in the Lower World, where we'd all been busy enough with our separate tasks to not have any kind of territory wars. Not that I had any idea if spirit animals had territory wars, though it seemed unlikely. The whole point was they each offered a shaman very different skill sets, so in theory there was no toe-treading or reason to argue.

I still had the distinct impression they were arguing. Raven went *klokklokKLOK!* and hopped around, wings and chest puffed with disapproval, while Rattler stuck his long forked tongue out repeatedly, which somehow came across as a two-year-old's behavior instead of a snake's. It wasn't good form to tell outsiders what your spirit animals were, but I suddenly wished the dancers could see my two guides in their private little battle. I wanted to see how they would interpret it, and how it would affect their dance.

Because it wasn't, at the moment. It affected me: even if they were arguing, and over what I had no idea, their dual presence made me feel better in much the same way the dance did. They were part of my energy, maybe even part of my soul at this point. Whatever snapping, biting, hissing disagreement was between them, having them both beside me gave the fragile core of magic within me a boost of strength and confidence.

That affected the dancers. Someone among them—maybe many of them—was profoundly sensitive to energy levels. The stronger I felt, the quicker the drumbeats became, and the more involved the dancers. They were still light-years from the ghost dance, but there was more strength to what they offered, as if they knew I was better able to accept it now. I took a breath deep enough that I felt it even in my semi-disembodied state, and sank a little farther into the dance mats. Rattler slid over my ribs, dislodged by my breathing, and turned his attention from Raven to stick his tongue in my ear, a scolding if I'd ever received one.

Raven took it as triumph, fluffed out all his feathers until he was twice his normal size and sat with a smug *klok!* that reverberated in the small bones of my ears.

One drummer hit a note that echoed the tone and pitch of Raven's call perfectly, and the theater ripped down the middle, folded away and left me in the midst of a harsh white desert.

★ ★ ★

I had been here before.

Past experience didn't make sipping at searing air any easier. It didn't make the unrelenting brilliance of the too-close sun any easier to bear, either. I still didn't want to look at myself for fear I'd see the very bones outlined in my flesh, light so intense it could only burn me away. Tears, precious liquid, drained from my mostly-closed eyes because the light was simply more than could be borne. They ran across my nose and dropped to gleaming white earth, sizzling into nothingness within an instant. I was very nearly as physically miserable as I'd ever been, and that included having gotten hit by a semi less than an hour earlier.

On the other hand, I wasn't dangling upside-down from the only tree in Creation. I could feel its roots under my ribs and thigh, and if I dared open my eyes that much, I knew I'd see its bleached-out spirally bones reaching for the nearby sun and providing no shade at all. I didn't want to look that hard. For the moment, I didn't have a headache so bad it seemed likely to split my skull in half, and wisdom seemed the better part of valor. Instead I peeked through my lashes at the close horizon, and conceded that overall, magic-drained or not, I was in *much* better condition than I'd been the first time I came to this place.

And this time, I wasn't surprised at all when a coyote trotted out of the desert whiteness to greet me.

He was, once again, possibly the most beautiful creature I'd ever seen. Coyotes in general were tawny, good for blending into shrub-infested yellow deserts. This one might blend into a precious metals mine if he tried hard enough. Every strand of fur glittered like they'd been hand-painted in gold and copper and bronze. His eyes were black, not coyote-gold, and stars lay within them, shining pinpoints from all edges of the sky.

He moved like a dream, not convincingly bound to the earth, and brought slightly cooler air with him, the difference between coughing on each breath and being able to swallow it down. When *he* breathed, the air expanded, shimmering like a heat mirage and expanding the pocket of cooler air. I wanted very much for him to lie down next to me so I could pull enough air into my lungs, but I had to settle for him sitting, paws tidily aligned a few centimeters from my nose.

It helped. After a minute or three I pushed up on an elbow, then into a sitting position, and croaked, "Hey, big guy."

This archetype of the Trickster, this primal chaos force of the universe, this prophet and world-maker whom I called Big Coyote, closed his starry eyes in a slow greeting blink, then bashed his head against mine hard enough to give me starry eyes, too.

I had the brief thought that, though I'd never say so out loud, I was becoming rather more fond of spirit animals who actually spoke to me, like Rattler, than of ones who used brute physical force to get their points across. Then the expected ache from Big Coyote's head-butt kicked in, and I didn't think very much at all, just remembered.

Remembered the past thirty-six hours, specifically. Starting with pulling the trigger to bring Patty Raleigh down, and speeding through every moment thereafter both linearly and statically, so I was caught up in a barrage of everything happening *now*. I saw every action I'd taken illuminated by the close white sun, no shadows to hide in, no excuses to be made. Blood misted from Raleigh's shoulder, the most appalling violence I'd ever done to a human being. Morrison shifted, caught up in my magic. Naomi Allison collapsed, too far gone for me to rescue. Rita Wagner asked for help and Tia Carley didn't, but they both offered possible redemption for my failures with Raleigh and Allison alike. The ghost dance killer's trail bled hunter-moon orange and faded away. I walked away from Patricia Raleigh's sleeping form with no regrets. Bare skin shredded as I bounced across the pavement, pain exploding through my bones. Emotion sluiced through me, exhaustive, pulling in a dozen directions at once as Big Coyote sat over me like a curious god, examining each choice I'd made in the last couple days.

I suddenly felt like a grad student defending her thesis. I wasn't absolutely certain I *needed* to defend myself, but there was a distinct on-the-spot sensation about the whole thing. Warily, I said, "I'd do it again."

Memory went still, and Big Coyote cocked his head at me, one ear flicked: *which part?*

"All of it." I rubbed my eyes, knocking some of the mental imagery away. When I dropped my hand again, Big Coyote was predominant, his hard white desert a little duller and easier to look at. "Not shapeshifting Morrison, not if I could help it, but that was an honest mistake and as long as we get him back safe I'm not going to beat myself up over it. I'm tired of that crap. The rest of it, though, you know what? You want to hang me out to dry? Fine. You've got the tree right there."

I gestured without looking, trusting that the hanging tree was indeed still there. Big Coyote's wiry gold eyebrow spot shot upward, and he *did* look at the hanging tree. Thumped his tail once against the ground, then bared his teeth in a wide coyote smile. Very white clean teeth, like he was a rock star who'd had them bleached, not like he was the Platonic ideal of a predator/scavenger. Though I supposed a

Platonic coyote would, in fact, have flawlessly white teeth, since all other coyotes would have to try—and fail—to live up to its perfect image.

By the time I'd run through that entire mental machination, Big Coyote's threatening smile had sort of faltered. Apparently I wasn't supposed to get caught up in the details of impossible perfection when he was trying to intimidate me. Another one for the handbook.

"I am doing my best," I said in a low, level voice. "I've got two worlds I'm trying to balance here. You—*somebody*—put me on this path. Shaman and warrior. They're conflicting interests, big guy. If you don't like how I'm handling it, take away the cosmic powers."

Big Coyote's ears flattened, and I sighed, understanding him perfectly. No wonder half the spirit creatures I'd encountered didn't speak aloud. They didn't have to.

"No," I said to his flat ears. "I don't really want you to, not at this point. I'd miss them, if you want to know the truth. I'd miss being able to help people the way I've learned to, and believe me, a year ago I never thought I'd hear myself say that. Could I live with it? Yeah, I could, because hey, I managed to get through most of my life without being some kind of shamanic superstar. There are things not being a shaman would make a lot easier."

Like my *job*, at least the mundane part of it. Like whatever was going on with Morrison. Like hanging out with people who had once been my friends and who were now just a little scared of me. My life was maybe a lot more interesting now, but it sure as hell wasn't any easier. I'd gotten past resenting that, but I still missed the old sane world I'd been part of. I didn't say any of that out loud, but Big Coyote's ears twitched again, and I thought he'd gotten the message as clearly as I got his own nonverbal communication.

Buoyed, I leaned forward and poked him in the chest. "So if you're not going to take them away, stop standing over me like judge, jury and executioner, because I am *doing my best*."

A glint of satisfaction sparked in Big Coyote's eyes. Fishhooks settled into my belly and yanked hard.

I woke up sitting upright amongst a host of dancers.

I felt better. I felt so much better it wasn't even funny, but it seemed a lot more like feeling good for standing my ground than pure replenished energy. That was improved, too, but it wasn't quite enough to justify the weight having been lifted from my chest. I leaned forward until my forehead almost touched the mat, and smacked the floor in time with the drummers, finally really enjoying the music and rhythm going on around me.

The stage was brightening, my awareness heightened and comforting. Billy and Melinda were in the wings, strong butter-yellow dominating Melinda's aura as relief for my recovery caught her in its grasp. Billy was a bit more stolid, like he was playing a bit of the tough-guy alpha male standing strong beside his worried mate, but the more I added a counterbeat to the music, my palms pattering against the floor, the more vivid his aura became, too. The dancers were responding, too, delight flexing into the energy they extended: they recognized I'd come through some kind of sea change, and were more daring in the energy and wildness of their performance.

Raven, who knew a party when he saw one, hopped around me, *caw*ing and *klok*ing and *quark*ing with pure excitement. He whacked my ribs, my extended hands, my head, my spine, my tailbone, any part of me he could reach as he danced around. It felt like an oddball massage technique, enlivening my very skin with the short sharp impacts. Rattler, a bit more dignified, stayed out of Raven's way but did his own sinuous dance, coiling up against me, stretching away, lifting himself impossibly high onto his tail and dropping back down as if to prove his own remarkable physical prowess. I chortled and sat up, tipping my head back so my throat was long, and let go a high tonal undulation.

It cut through the theater like a shockwave, making me realize no one had made any sound until then, not beyond footsteps and drumbeats. Usually either the dancers or the watchers yipped and called out as they were moved to as expressions of enthusiasm or camaraderie. Even the theater audience had succumbed to the impulse a few times, which made the dancers' silence even more unusual.

But my cry was like permission being granted. Answering calls rolled back at me, lifting me to my feet. One of the men began to sing, finally adding a melody to the drums, and though I was by no means a dancer myself, I spun around, then fell into a three-beat step that brought me around the whole dance circle. I stopped to greet every dancer, following their leads in movement, and when I got to the drummers I bowed, acknowledging them as well as the four-spoked circle they'd built around me. I even danced my way out of the circle, grabbed Billy and Melinda, and hauled them inside until the three of us were a laughing, dancing triangle at the heart of the power circle.

I had no idea how long we danced for. Until my feet were numb from pounding against the floor. Until my hands were red and swollen from clapping, and until Melinda and Billy were pink with exertion. Until the dancers' auras were a whirling, brilliant pool surrounding all of us, and until at some shocking, unspoken command, every single one of us came to a stop at once. Voices, drums, footsteps, even the stage lights all went away, leaving the theater a silent dark sanctuary.

I flung my head back, threw my hands wide, and gasped as power exploded through me.

CHAPTER TWENTY-ONE

It felt—almost sorta kinda—like the moment when I'd invited the entire city of Seattle to hit me with its best shot. Except that had been untempered power, and I'd been a raw newbie, desperate for a surge that would help me knock down a demi-god. This was focused, and all I needed it for was replenishing a magic I'd become accustomed to using. I'd been topped up by drum music before; I knew how it was supposed to go.

Feeling like a bottle of liquid soap had been poured into a fountain was not generally how it went. Bubbles popped through me, toe to skull, palm to palm, and I expected to see them drifting from my fingertips like I'd become a giant Joanne-shaped bubblemaker. It tickled ferociously, but giggling seemed wholly inappropriate, so I breathed through my nose until it became a series of perfectly horrible snorts that were too funny to ignore. The lights came back up as more bubbles erupted in my nose, and I did giggle, then laughed out loud at the smiling, bemused faces around me.

Last time I'd done this—when Seattle had overloaded me—I'd accidentally become an end-times sign for the Navajo Nation. My silver-blue power had changed to colors of the whole rainbow, power strong enough to last all day. I was much more contained now, radiating blue and silver, but not so out of control that I went full-spectrum. That was an enormous relief. Even with Rattler and Raven on my side to help smooth things over—and they'd disappeared with the burst of power, their job here evidently done—I didn't need a second round of explaining to a god that I was merely incompetent, not intentionally dangerous. Happy, even gleeful, I triggered the Sight so I could thoroughly enjoy being punched up to full throttle.

The theater went white as a flash-bang erupted in my vision. I howled, clapping my hands over my eyes, which was about as useful as holding my nose when magic was providing a visual component. I could See through my eyelids and fingers, though the only thing to See was the astonishing whiteness. My head rang with it, which was all new; the Sight had never had a soundtrack before. Not that it was much of a soundtrack, just a high-pitched squeal that could've been the result of leaving a rock concert. Except this was much, much louder, like I'd gone to every rock concert in creation at the same moment, and my skull was vibrating with the aftermath.

So was my skin, for that matter. It felt like someone had run a zillion needles over it, leaving invisible but painful scores. My hands tingled, my cheeks burned, my stomach cramped, all of it making me seem more alive, somehow. *Too* alive: people weren't supposed to feel at this level, not if they wanted to retain their sanity. I wanted to escape myself, leave my overloaded body behind and get somewhere safe.

For most people that was nothing more than a nutty wish. In my case, I slipped free the surly bonds of flesh and rose up into the whiteness. It surrounded me, too harsh to be comforting, and I spun around in search of yet another way to escape.

Hunter-moon orange, violent in its contrast against the brilliance, seared through me. I flung my hands up again, even more uselessly in my disembodied state, and clawed the Sight back, trying to turn it off. It faded reluctantly, leaving behind pinprick tingles and ear-ringing. I rubbed my eyes, trying to erase the flaring white edges of everything I looked at, and finally scraped enough brain cells together to focus on where the orange shard had pierced my vision.

Winona, Naomi's replacement, stood right in front of me, confusion writ large on her delicate features. A sense of the absurd bloomed in me. I'd automatically assumed an outside force attacking the dance troupe. It hadn't even occurred to me to look for a devil within, much less to look at the individual who would gain the most, careerwise, from Naomi's death. Some detective I was.

But then, from a self-castigating perspective, it was a little odd that Morrison hadn't thought of it, either. That left me with three possibilities: either my boss was losing it, the snake within the troupe's grass was running a look-elsewhere spell, or my shamanic instincts were dead on target and it was somebody else entirely. Of those three, the first was the least likely, and I had to admit that given my track record, the third didn't seem all that likely either. I was all light-voiced and hollow as I asked, "Did you kill her?"

Winona paled, a fair trick for someone of her already-porcelain complexion. "Why would you even think that?"

"The killer's aura is hunter-moon orange, and that color just slammed me between the eyes when I looked at you." I triggered the Sight again as I spoke, wanting to see if guilt or horror surged through Winona's colors.

Obliterating white smashed into my head again, sending the bells in my ears to new frenzied pitches and making my skin itch until I wanted to score it off. Orange stabbed through the white, pulses emanating from Winona. I tried to stalk forward with a commanding air and instead staggered in a circle, holding my head as I turned the Sight off yet again and waited for its after-effects to fade. I'd had my vision go on the blink before, a physical warning against the wrong mystic path I was charging down, but I couldn't remember the Sight itself acting up in quite this way. I had no idea what was wrong with it, but I wished it would stop.

When my vision had cleared again, the dancers had moved. Some had stepped closer to Winona, supporting her. Others had fallen back, just as clearly rejecting her, fear greater than friendship. I gritted my teeth and moved toward her. "Tell me what happened, Winona. I can't believe you tried an attack tonight, knowing I was here to shield everyone."

"I don't know what you're talking about!" She backed away from me, her small group of supporters moving with her. "I didn't kill anybody! I would never hurt Naomi. She was my friend!"

"Winona, I can See it. I can See the hunter-orange blazi—"

"Joanne," Melinda said gently, "Winona's aura is emerald-green with touches of red. There's no orange in it at all."

Cold sluiced through me, washing away the anger at my own assumptions and leaving an acidic pit of worry in its place. Even if I knew hundreds of magic users—adepts; I had to remember to use that word, because I liked it—even if I'd known hundreds of adepts, my temperament would almost certainly leave me disinclined to believe most of them when they made a flat statement. I would want to see it myself. That was the nature of a Joanne.

Melinda Holliday was one of the few exceptions I could think of to that rule. If Melinda said it, I believed it, even if my own empirical evidence was to the contrary. I stopped where I was, teeth and fists clenched, eyes closed so I couldn't see Winona and give in on the urge to advance further. I triggered the Sight for a third time, prepared for it to white out the world and set my skin afire, which it did. I turned my head toward Billy and Melinda, because of everyone there I *knew* their aura colors, and after long moments spoke. "Okay. All I can See right now is white, Mel. I can't even See your colors, so okay, if you say Winona's red and green, she's red and green. But something's not right. Orange is cutting through the white, and it's the killer's signature shade."

Melinda, still in the same calm, gentle voice, said, "I don't see it." She wasn't arguing its existence, just making an admission. I exhaled noisily and nodded, then turned back toward Winona, my eyes still closed. A headache was building and I wanted very badly to stop using the Sight, but screwed-up or not, it was providing the only lead I had. I edged forward and extended a fingertip, trying to locate the very heart of the orange blaze. When I was almost touching it, I opened my eyes again.

Winona was holding her breath, my finger an inch from her breastbone. I couldn't see anything out of the ordinary, given she was wearing a thunderbird costume. Long feathers and bright bits of gold adorned her, all of them making a loose flowing outfit that both hid and enhanced her form. "Have you changed anything in your costume lately?"

She clapped a hand against her chest and shook her head. "No. It's Naomi's costume anyway, not mine. I—" Her eyebrows furled and she closed her fingers around the feathers just beneath her hand and just beyond my pointing finger. "Ow. This is supposed to all be soft, not—" She tugged, then came up with a small bone, holding it in her fingertips. "God, what is that, a bird bone?"

Three or four people said, "No," including me. I went on to add, "It's not fragile enough. But maybe I can use it as a tracking device, since it's got the killer's colors," as I reached for it.

Melinda said, "Joanne, I don't think you should touch that," exactly one second too late.

Power sluiced out of me like somebody'd opened a drain on the Mississippi. No: more like somebody had stuck the world's largest straw into the Mississippi and was schlucking it all out in one gigantic gulp. My knees and brain both went wobbly, the former delivering me to the floor with a crash and the latter filling with a static rush that made thinking hard. I'd given blood a couple of times in the past. The feeling of light-headedness from standing up too rapidly after blood had been drawn was not dissimilar to the power drain, only magnitudes less significant.

One fuzzy thought came clear: this was exactly the kind of thing Coyote kept warning me about. If I didn't get out of it intact, he was going to deride me from here to breakfast. Of course, if I didn't get out of it intact, he probably wouldn't be able to, which wasn't exactly reassuring. I fell forward to dig my fingertips into the dance mat and tried to concentrate.

A ball of nausea rolled my stomach as a reward for my efforts. I'd always felt the magic start in my gut, and now it was being sucked out from there, vampire-like. Not that I'd ever heard of a vampire that attacked peoples' stomachs. Which was just as well, because ew.

Somewhere at the back of my mind, a weary little voice suggested that following thoughts like that to their inevitable conclusion was perhaps a result of a static-filled brain, which was in turn the result of having power gulped out of me. It was not, in other words, the kind of focus I needed to shield against the power drain and survive this so Coyote could yell at me for it. I lowered my forehead to the mat and squished my eyes shut, determined to See what was happening.

The Sight exploded blindingly white again, so brilliant that for a moment nothing else mattered: mostly I was interested in figuring out why that was happening. I had control of my magic, these days. Getting pumped up full of spirit dance drumming shouldn't supercharge me to such a degree that the Sight rendered me, well, sightless.

Except all the control I was accustomed to having was shaped around the relatively comfortable Joanne Walker limitations, rather than the new exciting Siobhan Walkingstick potential. I knew from firsthand experience that the problem with mystical potential was once unleashed, it was disinclined to fit back into the tidy little box it originally came in. Rattler had scraped me down to a spark, and the dancers had thrown that spark into an ocean's worth of metaphysical gasoline. I probably shouldn't be surprised when explosions ensued. I *was* surprised, but I probably shouldn't be.

Of course, at the rate power was draining out of me, in a minute I'd be somewhat less than even my usual comfortable level of magical self, and that would be bad. Bad for the troupe, bad for Morrison, bad for me. I gritted my teeth and looked for my shields, uncertain if I'd find them intact or obliterated, and not sure which to expect under the newly-changed circumstances.

Silver-shot blue was there, but weak and unimpressive. Given my overflow of power, I thought it should be like the walls of Jericho, except that was a bad analogy, because they'd come tumbling down. Or maybe that made it a good analogy. Either way I clawed at the magic flowing from me, trying to shape it into shields instead of a river.

I might as well have tried stirring the ocean with a Popsicle stick. It was worse than futile: achieving a degree of focus simply awakened vicious hunter-orange stripes in the whiteness still filling the Sight. They dove into my faltering shields and drained them ever-faster as I poured more strength into them. The bone I'd taken from Winona's costume burned my hand, giving me something physical to fixate on for what felt like the first time in forever, but it wasn't enough. Orange slipped inside the silver-blue of my shields, worming its way deep inside and leaving streaks of pain where it touched me. Agony drove inward and gathered like a storm waiting to break.

And break it did. Or, more accurately, *I* broke, the bones of my skull crumpling with a hideous series of grinding pops. My brain cramped, suddenly no longer fitting inside my head, and someone gave a tiny, desperate gasp of agony. I suspected it was me.

I was getting tired of pain. Sadly, pain was not tired of me. It stretched and wracked me just as violently as Rattler had done less than an hour before. Except Rattler had been frantically trying to put me back together, and this new exciting pain was clearly trying to pull me apart.

No. Not trying to pull me apart. Trying to *reshape* me. Bones cracked, marrow oozing out, and my skin split to expose blood and muscle. Fur burst from joints that crackled and reformed, and panic spurted through me as I concentrated on remaining human.

Derision slammed through the flow of orange power, a belief that to be merely human was pathetically inadequate. My fingernails turned to claws, black and short and shining under the stage lights. A whimsical and very stupid part of me thought it might be interesting to see what shape I was being forced into, and in that instant I lost a huge amount of ground. My hands, my forearms, all the way up to my elbows, cracked and shifted. A canine of some sort, but not the semi-familiar coyote form: the color was wrong. I let myself observe that, then knotted my fingers against the mat, determined that they should *be* fingers, and not paws.

I might as well have wished they were fishes, though with someone's malicious shapeshifting magic running through me, that was probably a dangerous thought. The howl that ripped from my throat was distinctly doglike and ended in a series of panting whimpers. Fear built at the back of my brain, eating away my understanding of what was happening: making me less human and more wild. Another minute and I would no longer know who or what I was supposed to be.

Fresh panic surged through me and caught hold of my magic, finally stopping the terrible outpouring I'd been experiencing. The power woke, suddenly mine to command. It was *not* an offensive weapon: I'd had that beaten into my head in unpleasant ways. But shields were defensive, and staggering amounts of magic were still fluctuating inside me. I solidified my shields and shoved outward, power bursting forth in a shockwave. The killer's magic dispersed over a suddenly enormous surface of outgoing magic, and for the briefest moment my hands were my own again. Triumphant, relieved and terrified all at once, I flung a net, trying to capture my attacker's thinned-out magic.

An impossibly large pulse of magic roared out of me for the second time. A patch of damp bothered the corner of my mouth, drool collecting on the mat. There was too damned much power running through me. I couldn't control its output, nor the equally sudden influx as it returned to full strength, which it did in exhaustively quick cycles, regardless of how much my opponent sucked down. I was starting to feel like an all-night smorgasbord, which was probably just dandy for the guy whose original plan had been intended to suck up as much power from the troupe as possible, but wasn't so great for me. He gathered his hunter-orange power back together while I scrabbled uselessly at the floor, and when the next surge of shapeshifting magic flowed toward me, I had no focus to stop it with.

A clear yellow shield rose up out of nowhere and surrounded me. The killer's attack cut off like it had never happened. Bewildered and exhausted, I wheezed, flipped on my back and stared upward.

Stared, actually, at Melinda Holliday, who stood above me blazing with glorious, inhuman luminescence.

CHAPTER TWENTY-TWO

I had, in my short career as a shaman, run across quite a few non-human beings. Melinda was not one of them. Of that, I was absolutely sure. But the woman standing over me was clearly Melinda, and just as clearly touched by the gods, a phrase I did not use lightly. Her eyes were as gold as mine had ever been in the midst of power throes, and there was a radiance to her I'd never before seen embodied by anyone. Not even Cernunnos, ancient and terrible god of the Hunt, had glowed the way Melinda did. It was as if someone had taken her already generous and gentle spirit and hooked it to a star, until barely-contained grace and power shone through her fragile, mortal skin.

That power was more than enough to trump mine. I could See properly again, Melinda's talent blotting out the whiteness in an effervescent glow. Wisps of color floated round her like she might be lifted into the air by them, their delicate dance mesmerizing until Melinda knelt beside me, concern in her gaze. *Deep* concern, more than a human, even a good friend, could contain. My heart missed a beat and hurt when it started up again, though I had no idea why. I inhaled to risk a question, then jerked my hands upward, making sure they were, in fact, hands.

They were, no trace of shapeshifting left on them. I exhaled all the air in my lungs and let my eyes close with the breath, taking an instant to not care that I didn't understand and to revel in my gratitude for Melinda's interference. Then I opened my eyes again. Melinda was still brilliant, the stage lights far above somehow dull by comparison. There were traces of someone unfamiliar in her features, like someone else was looking out through her eyes. Disconcerted, I turned my head away, glad I hadn't asked that question after all. I wasn't sure I wanted to know who or what was within my friend.

Billy's shoes intruded on my vision, reminding me of the day I'd gotten a sword stuffed through my gut. He had been there then, too, seen from the same angle. He'd been off duty that morning, and wearing a killer pair of high-heeled blue pumps. Tonight they were spats, every bit as theatrical but in a whole different way. I smiled at them, then cautiously offered the smile to the Hollidays.

From their expressions, my smile was more of a horrible grimace than an expression of pleasure. I stopped doing it, and they looked grateful. Melinda, still in the same gentle voice she'd been using for some time now, said, "Are you all right, Joanne?"

I croaked, "Yeah," then swallowed a couple times, trying to loosen my throat. "What just happened?"

"Your energy was being torn apart. I shielded you." Melinda's tone held the slightest hint of reproval, which was a whole lot less than I deserved. Part of me wanted to address that fact.

The other larger, nosier part of me said, "You can do that?" in genuine astonishment.

She said, "I can at the moment," which I suspected also needed addressing, but instead of pursuing it I transferred my gaze to the high stage lights and chose to admire how I was no longer writhing in misery. Melinda had done that somehow, and while curiosity killed the cat, I wasn't going to look a gift horse in the mouth. After a moment I gathered myself enough to say, "Good news is, I think I can safely say we're dealing with a shapeshifter."

Melinda's voice went wary: "And the bad news?"

"He's better at it than I am." There was a terrible scent of burnt feathers in the air. I held my breath as discreetly as I could, looking for the smell's source.

Winona was just beyond the Hollidays, gaping at me. Gaping at my hand, specifically. I lifted it, wondering what was so interesting.

My fingertips were blackened, the charred remains of a tiny bone still clutched in them. I considered that a while, then frowned at Winona. A small round burn mark marred her breastbone, exposed by melted fabric. The feathers adorning her costume were singed, and her expression was stricken, like she was hurt but too shocked to fully realize it. I got to my feet carefully and put my palm over her breastbone, calling up healing power.

Blue-rimmed silver ricocheted out of me, so brilliant the entire troupe gasped. It was *possible* for my magic to have a visual component, but it didn't normally. Then again, it didn't normally make my eyes cross or my knees buckle, either. Billy saved me from collapsing as Winona stepped backward, staring at her own chest before raising her gaze to mine. Her brown eyes were silver-shot, my own residual power coloring them. It faded quickly, but left her glowing with health and strength, no sign of grief or the performance's exertions weakening her.

I, on the other hand, said, "Wooga," and let Billy take more of my weight than a self-sufficient independent woman should rely on a guy to do. My vision tunneled, then righted itself, and I stood up with a whisper of thanks. Only then did Winona say, "What was that?"

"A talisman." I turned the blackened bit of bone in my fingers. "A focal point. Something that belonged to the killer, something he could focus his power through to attack the troupe. He, um. Shouldn't be able to again. Unless it's just a way to make it easier, and given the thrashing he just gave me, that's poss…" I could tell from Winona's expression I should have stopped with "shouldn't be able to." My shoulders slumped. If there was a PR department for shamans, I needed their help. I mumbled, "Nevermind. Obviously when I touched it he used it to focus on attacking me, but now it's burned up and that really should render it powerless."

"You did more than that." Billy had a deeply unfocused expression, like he was looking at something far beyond what normal people could see. Farther beyond than usual, even, since he generally *did* see things normal people couldn't. His voice was unusually light and soft as he said, "Only one person has ever died in this theater, Walker. I can see her now. Do you need to talk to her?"

My stomach lurched, all that fresh new magic suddenly worried. There were a dozen reasons Billy shouldn't be seeing Naomi Allison's ghost. First, though it had been murder, she'd gone so fast she had no idea she'd died brutally. He didn't see ghosts from non-violent deaths. Second, though technically it was within his two-day window for seeing ghosts, I knew very well that Naomi had danced right into the Great Beyond, and Billy had always only ever been able to communicate with the dead who remained on this side of that divide.

Okay, that was only two reasons, but two was close enough to a dozen for my purposes. The point was, it took a medium of much greater psychic stature than Billy commanded to speak with the dead who had shuffled off this mortal coil as thoroughly as Naomi had.

Apparently I wasn't the only one undergoing a surge of power. I doubted very much the troupe had intended to boost my friends, but I'd drawn them into the center of the circle. Even if the dancers had been focused on me, residual energy had left its mark on the Hollidays. Melinda had always insisted she was a blip on the radar, nothing much in terms of adeptitude, and Billy had been comfortable with his talent's limitations as long as I'd known him. I wondered if they were going to have to adapt the way I had—though no doubt much more graciously—and then because I wasn't *that* stupid, I said, "Yeah, I'd like to talk to her if it's possible."

"So," came Jim Littlefoot's emotion-harsh voice, "would we."

I'd only participated in one or two séances in my life. Billy and his bright blue zoot suit would have struck me as an extremely unlikely medium had the first séance-leader I'd met not worn hippie skirts and violent comic-book T-shirts. Much of my life appeared to be a lesson in not judging books by their covers.

The dance troupe apparently already knew not to. None of them looked even slightly suspicious of Billy's ability to bring their friend back across the Great Divide. Then again, if I did nightly what they did, I'd probably be fairly confident in people and their ability to breach other realms, too. In fact, I was getting there.

Sonata Smith, the medium who'd run the séances I'd attended, had been a bit on the mystical gooshy side of things for me. Billy only asked that everyone sit—not verbally, but by patting his palms toward the floor—and let a flicker of appreciation dart over his features as the troupe joined hands without prompting. They'd already made a power circle with their dance. The physical link between their bodies only shored it up, creating—to my eyes, anyway—a visible rippling wall which I very much doubted Naomi would be able to cross, should she be of a mind to.

Melinda and I, like Billy, remained standing. I did it because I was going to have to ask some questions and wanted to be on equal footing, as it were. I suspected Mel was mostly too busy being agog at the depth of Sight she was encountering to think of sitting. Either way, Billy didn't ask us to, only said, "We're ready for you now, Naomi," in the same extraordinarily gentle voice I'd heard him use before, when speaking to lost spirits.

Powerful stage lights did ethereal bodies no favors at all, though at least they also disguised any physical damage her ghost might have shown from her untimely death. But my brief impression of Naomi Allison had been of a vibrant woman full of passion and physical strength. Most of that passion was lost with the amber lights pouring through her, stripping away any color or vitality she might have shown. I had the impulse to run offstage and see if I could find a switch to dim or darken them, so she might seem more real. I didn't, partly because I wasn't sure what would happen if I broke out of the circle, and mostly because I thought it might be even harder for her friends and family if the woman they'd lost became any more real than she was at the moment. I wasn't the world's most sensitive sensitive, but I was getting better.

Naomi was completely focused on Billy. The rest of us might not have existed, and for all I knew, from her perspective, we didn't. She hadn't been pretty: she was too thin and too muscled from dancing, without enough softness to her features, for prettiness. Her intensity on stage had drawn the eye, though, and she showed a similar intensity in how she observed Billy. It made her interesting, even attractive, despite a lack of conventional beauty. And despite being dead, which was the much more disturbing thought.

"I have someone here who'd like to ask you some questions," Billy said to her, "and some others who would like to say goodbye. Is that all right?"

Naomi tilted her head, gaze sweeping the circle, though nothing suggested she took note of any of us. She nodded, though, as she came back to Billy. He gestured me forward, muttering, "Keep it short, Joanie. I've never connected with someone this far gone and I don't know how long she'll stay."

Implicit in the statement was *and these people have a lot more to say to her than you possibly can.* I nodded and stepped right up to his side, hoping proximity to him would help her awareness of me. I even loosened my shields a little, trying to become brighter, in spiritual terms, so I might be easier to see.

It worked: her eyebrows furrowed and she tipped her head again, now watching me, but as if I was as washed-out and difficult to see as she was.

I only had one question, and it caught in my throat. Billy gave me a sharp look. I fell back a step, losing most of Naomi's attention, and shook my head. "Let them say goodbye first. I'm not sure what my question will do to her."

Naomi's sister, Rebecca, whispered, "Thank you," and joined the hands of the two people on either side of her so she could rise without breaking the circle. She came to stand by Billy, face contorted with tears, but Naomi's expression lit up and she extended her hands toward Rebecca. I fell back another couple of steps, not really wanting to eavesdrop on the last words two sisters shared, and kept my eyes mostly averted while a handful of others came to say their good-byes as well. Breathing the air within the circle hurt; it was that full of loss and sorrow. My refreshed power pounded at my temples and in my heart, searching for some way to ease their pain, but they already had their mechanisms. The ghost dance was meant to do just that. They would be fine, in time, perhaps especially because they had this rare oppor-tunity for closure after Naomi's sudden, terrible death.

Gradually—actually rather quickly, but it seemed slow because of the ache in the air—the few who'd come to say a specific goodbye rejoined the circle at large. Others obvi-ously wanted to take their place, say goodbye individually, but Naomi was visibly fading, Billy's grip on her loosening. They began to sing, a Native American song I imagined was a mourning tune from Naomi's tribe. That was how the bulk of them would say goodbye, by overriding their own desires so I would have a chance to ask my question. I joined Billy again, knowing what I owed them and still reluctant: Naomi seemed relatively at peace, and I was afraid what I had to ask would shatter that calm.

On the other hand, I didn't see that I had much choice. The killer's trail had gone cold, and while going out hunting Morrison was a worthy cause for the remainder of the night, it wasn't going to render the dance troupe safe from another attack. "Naomi, can you show me where your killer is?"

Naomi Allison withered, shrieking, and spun skyward to rush out of the theater, every goddamned bit as untrackable as the killer's trail had been.

The circle broke up around us, dismay crowing from every throat as dancers scrambled to their feet in Naomi's wake. Rebecca was in tears, hiccups of "But she was fine, she was okay, she was fine," clearer than most of the other babble. Littlefoot pulled her against his chest, scowling over her head at me. Not blaming me, I didn't think. Just angry and frustrated and probably scared because he didn't understand what had happened.

Neither did I, exactly, except I'd been relatively sure asking about her killer would upset her. I'd hoped she might do something mundane like point in the right direction, or better yet, give me an address, though I'd thought the former more likely. Zipping off into the ether was really no help at all, though it was a little hard to condemn the ghost of a murdered woman for not wanting to consider the means or perpetrator of her death.

"I've got it." Billy sounded as thick as he'd sounded light before, like a sinus headache had suddenly taken up all the space and comfort in his head. "I can see her trail. Almost. Close enough to follow, anyway."

Breath whooshed out of me, and the hubbub fell silent as everyone absorbed that. Rebecca sobbed one more time, a short sharp noise, but this time there was relief in it: maybe Naomi's horrible departure had a purpose. Even I thought that somehow made it better.

I grabbed Billy's hand, said, "Sorry, I'm stealing him," to Mel, and started tugging him toward the door. "Where?

Which way? I can't follow a trail very long and I don't know how long a ghost trail might last. Where do we need to go?"

"Joanne!" Melinda's voice cracked across the stage and I turned back, electricity jittering down my spine. She softened a little, though her voice remained serious: "Be careful."

I gave her a weak smile, nodded and hauled Billy out of the theater. He shook off the deepest part of his malaise as we got outside and cleared his throat. "Keys."

I dug them out of my pocket as I scurried along, and he thrust his hand at me. I frowned at it. "What?"

"Give me your keys. I'm the one seeing ghost trails."

A little bubble of astonishment popped at the very bottom of my soul. It gave rise to lots more, like soda fizzing in a glass. The closer they got to the top, the more they exploded with tiny bursts of outrage instead of astonishment. "You want to drive *Petite?*"

"Everybody wants to drive Petite, Joanne. She's a beautiful car. People who don't drive want to drive her."

"And nobody gets to!" One person. One person besides me had driven my baby since I'd rescued her from a North Carolina barn over a decade earlier, and I'd torn into that person with the unholy vengeance of a thousand paper cuts. I had put blood, sweat and soul into my big purple beauty, and *nobody* got to drive her but me.

Billy, with infinite patience, said, "Don't be an idiot. Give me the keys."

I clutched them against my chest, eyes wide with indignation. "Do you even know how to drive a stick?"

"Walker!"

Sullen, I said, "You sound like Morrison," and tried to hand over the keys. I did. I really tried, but my hand wouldn't uncurl from my chest, nor would my fingers un-clench from around the keychain. "I can't."

"You can't hand over your keys."

They cut into my fingers, I was holding them so hard. It hurt enough that I was starting to want to let go, but my crimped fingers wouldn't loosen. "I really don't think I can. *Nobody* drives Petite, Billy. Nobody but me."

My partner flung his hands into the air—a remarkably melodramatic and impressive act, in his bright blue zoot suit—and stomped around the car. "Morrison is right. Your relationship with your car is pathological, Walker. If we lose this trail because you miss a turn, I will haunt you for the rest of *eternity*. Do you understand me?"

I said, "Yes," in a tiny voice, and even believed him, but it was still me who got in the driver's seat.

Billy alternated between giving directions and cursing me, all the way downtown. I parked Petite at the all-night garage on Pine Street, grumpily aware that I wouldn't get to write off the parking fee because I wasn't officially on a case. Billy stopped swearing once we were safely parked, sat silent a minute or two, then started up again. "I can't see the trail anymore. We need to go south from here."

"I don't know if there's any overnight parking south of here and I'm not leaving Petite on the street." I got out of the car, locked my door, and waited for Billy, cursing all the while, to do the same.

"Is this what it's like when you try to track?"

"Yes."

"No wonder it pisses you off."

"You got us a hell of a lot farther than I have." We headed for street level. "I don't know. Maybe if I shift into a coyote again I could pick up the trail."

"You've been hit by a truck once already tonight. Why

don't we try something else first? We're in the right ballpark. Let's go talk to your friend Rita Wagner. If I were downtown working a major spell, I'd want to be well out of the way. Maybe she'll have some ideas on where."

"Why not the Olivian?" I jerked a thumb northeast, toward the high-rise apartment building a block or two away. "I mean, that'd be plenty out of the way, plus a nice penthouse view. There's no reason to assume a power-stealing madman is hiding in the down-low and dirty parts of town."

"Except it was a homeless guy who was murdered downtown yesterday morning, not a business executive in a high-rise."

"Yesterday?" I looked at my wrist, where I'd taken to wearing my copper bracelet instead of my watch. The bracelet was prettier, but much less good at telling time. But Billy was right: it was probably past midnight, so Lynn Schumacher had died yesterday. "Okay. Yesterday. God. Long day. Okay. You were saying?"

"I was saying, assuming they're connected—"

"And why would we do that?"

"Because you're at the center of it all."

I shut my mouth so hard my ears popped. Billy waited for me to come up with an argument, but all I could manage was a silent, not especially creative litany of bad words.

There was a non-zero probability that he was wrong. It was possible Rita Wagner had come back into my life simply to pass on her gratitude for us saving her life. It was possible someone within her sphere of influence had died horribly out of pure random hideous circumstance, shortly after she re-entered my orbit. And it was possible there was no connection at all between that death's physical location and the generalized area Melinda had been able to point us at for our magic-stealing-murderer's location. It was *possible*.

It was also *possible* that a wendigo had just happened to take up hunting in my neighborhood, or that the right pieces to shatter an ancient, powerful death cauldron had come into play around me coincidentally. It was possible. It just wasn't very damned likely.

"I'm like that woman," I said after a long time. "Angela Lansbury in that TV show. No one in their right mind would be friends with her. No one in their right mind would be in the same *town* as her. No one should ever, ever go to a cocktail party with me. Or on a road trip. Or—"

"So we'll go see Rita." Billy gestured me out of the garage, and I shuffled toward Pioneer Square, wondering how the hell to escape being a danger to my friends and coworkers.

CHAPTER TWENTY-THREE

The soup kitchen was closed by the time we got there—the Pine Street parking garage was a mile away—but a few stragglers were still making their way out the door. Billy caught the door behind one of them and I ducked under his arm into a long pale-floored room that reminded me of a school cafeteria, right down to the narrow brown tables with built-in colored benches. Rita hauled pans from the food service area, showing more strength in her small form than I'd have expected. The door creaked as it shut behind us, and she, along with another half-dozen volunteers, called out variations on, "Sorry, we're closed, come back at seven tomorrow morning!"

My conditioned response was, "We're the police," except I thought that would get entirely the wrong reaction, so I said, "Actually it's Joanne Walker," as if my very name was excuse enough to barge in after hours.

Fortunately I was right. Rita put her pans down with a bang and turned to gape like she'd never expected to see me again. I was equal parts pleased to confound her and guilty that it had taken Billy's reminder to get me back to Rita and her case. Guilt beat pleasure and I mumbled, "Could you use a hand cleaning up?" which made Billy shoot me a look suggesting I would die slowly and painfully, later, for having volunteered.

Rita, though, exchanged glances with another one of the women, then pulled her apron off and came around the counter. "It's okay. You came back. Did you find out anything about Lynn? I think the detective this morning just wants to write it off as a dog attack. I heard on the radio tonight people had seen a wolf. Can you imagine? A wolf? In Seattle? It must've gotten loose from the zoo."

My heart did a sick lunge into my stomach and churned it up. "What else did the radio say?"

"Just to call it in if anybody saw it, that Animal Control and the police were tracking it. They didn't say anything about Lynn. Do you think it was a wolf attack?"

I bit back a bile-filled burp and very carefully didn't look at my partner. "No. The wolf only...got loose...around nine o'clock tonight. Did they say where they'd seen it last?"

"On the West Seattle Bridge, heading for the viaduct."

"The we—what the hell's he—" I broke off, looked at Billy this time and said, "That's northeast of where it was last sighted," as carefully as I could. "Why would he head downtown?"

Billy, aggrieved, demanded, "You're asking me?"

"Well, who else am I supposed to ask?" If I were a sensible shapechanged human, I would slink home and wait for somebody to come rescue me. That would be easier, in theory, for Morrison than it would be for me, as he owned a three-bedroom house with its own small plot of land, whereas I was still renting the fifth-floor apartment I'd moved into my sophomore year of college. At either location, the doors would be a problem, though Morrison might be able to manage the garage door at his house. I really wanted him to be holed up there, gnashing his teeth over the situation I'd gotten him into.

But all of that assumed some level of human intellect and not just a panicked animal running down whatever streets looked least threatening. Not that the Alaskan Way Viaduct, which was also Highway 99, was exactly non-threatening, even at midnight on a Saturday.

I put my head in my hands, trying to press my thoughts back into a more useful order. "One crisis at a time, Joanne. Take it one crisis at a time. All right. Rita." I looked up, and she came to attention like I was a drill sergeant. "My partner here thinks a bunch of unrelated things are actually related. I'm going to go out on a limb and say your missing friends are related, too."

"Why?"

I flexed my jaw, making cords stand out in my throat. "I don't suppose you'd just take it on faith."

Resignation deepened lines around her eyes. She would take it on faith, obviously, but I got the feeling it made her a little bit less of a person, somehow. I said, "Okay," very softly. "It's just usually easier for people to not really pay attention to what's going on around me, but you might be an exception. You know how you said you being alive was a miracle?"

"I said you saving me was a miracle," she corrected. "Me being alive, that's a gift I don't want to screw up."

I couldn't help smiling. I'd screwed up so much myself it was nice to come across somebody else trying not to blow it, too. Kindred spirits, we, not that I'd have ever imagined such a thing. "Ever heard of shamans?"

"Like medicine men, right? Indian medicine men?"

"Native American, yeah, although a lot of cultures had, or have, shamans. Anyway, they're healers. We might call them magic-users."

"And you are one, and that's how you saw me get attacked and called it in before I died?"

My jaw flapped open and Rita shrugged. "What else were you gonna say, with that kind of lead-in? What's the difference between magic and a miracle, Detective?"

Billy came to my rescue while I continued to wave my jaw in the wind: "From the outside, probably not much. From the inside, I don't know that I want to get into the theology of it."

Rita smiled. "I don't think it matters. So there's something magic going on?"

"How is it that everybody else is much calmer about that idea than I've ever been? I mean, doesn't it seem incredibly unlikely? Like, totally preposterous?" My voice rose, and Billy very sensibly herded us out of the soup kitchen as I said, "I mean, *magic*. People don't believe in *magic*. It's like believing in fairies and unicorns and, and, and—"

"And other magical things," Billy finished. I gave him a dark look, but nodded.

Rita folded her arms around herself and peered up at me. "If you'd asked me three months ago I'd have said you were hitting the bottle too hard. But then I got stabbed and should have died, but instead a bunch of cops and ambulance people showed up because somebody who wasn't even there sent them on ahead to save my life. If something like that happens to someone like me, you start to have a little faith in something bigger. I don't know if I believe in magic or miracles all the time. But I believe in you, Detective Walker. I believe in you."

Jeez. I felt like Tinkerbell. My nose stuffed up and my vision got all bleary and for some reason I snuffled a couple times as I patted Rita's shoulder. "Okay. Okay, fine, I guess you told me. All you people are just a lot cooler than I am. So anyway, basically Billy thinks I'm being pulled where I need to go." The very phrase made fishhooks sink into my belly, insistent tug that felt, somehow, like it came from a long way off. I rubbed my stomach and went on. "If he's right, then a murder Friday night and Lynn's death Saturday morning are related, and your missing friends might be, too."

Hope lit Rita's lined features. "So you'll help me look? Even if it's not your case or your jurisdiction?"

I smiled feebly. "No reason to get hung up on technicalities at this late stage of the game." Besides, though I didn't want to say it aloud, exploring the possibility that I was a nexus of some kind was probably kind of important. It might mean those retirement plans to the top of a remote mountain would get moved to sooner rather than later, but it also seemed like if it was an unpleasant reality I was *aware* of, I might be able to mitigate the fallout somehow. "Maybe you could take us down below and we could…"

So we could start hunting for someones or somethings we knew nothing about. That didn't sound like my brightest idea, but Rita clasped her hands together like a kid given a gift, and struck off down the street at a healthy clip. "There are sections of the Underground nobody goes because—"

"They're haunted?" I guessed when she hesitated, and she nodded with embarrassment. "At this point in my life I can safely say less likely things have happened. All right. I'm game for exploring the haunted Underground if you are. Billy?"

"I'm starting to like the idea that your bad guy is in a high-rise instead of mine about him being down in the—"

"Slums," Rita supplied when he broke off, and it was his turn to look abashed. Rita, though, shrugged it off. "It's not like we don't know we're on the fringe, Detective. And I'm sorry about your suit. Most of where we live isn't very clean."

Billy looked down at himself, dismayed. "Maybe I can write off the drycleaning bill."

"Maybe I'll pay for it, in thanks for you trudging around on one of my weird cases."

"I'd be trudging around on it anyway, if it was in our jurisdiction. I'll take you up on that anyway." He followed Rita into an alley where the overwhelming scent of soy sauce and old rice informed us the neighboring building housed a hole-in-the-wall Chinese restaurant. My stomach rumbled despite the hint of decay, but I wasn't quite desperate enough to go Dumpster-diving. Then I wondered if Rita ever had to, and got caught up in a whirlwind of first-world entitlement and guilt that lasted down the length of the alley all the way into a tiny concrete back lot. Boards and fencing made an unfriendly barricade between it and another brick building, but Rita walked up to the fence, twitched aside a section of chain-link laced with green fencing stuff—I didn't know what it was called—and revealed a hole almost big enough to let a rabbit through. "This way."

"Are you serious?" It wasn't even that I objected to crawling into the backsides of buildings. It just didn't look big enough for anybody to fit in. Rita, however, gave me a sour look and crawled into it backward. I exchanged glances with Billy, shrugged, and followed her.

It was bigger than it looked, chain-links willing to flex and let me through. There was maybe four inches' clearance between the fence and the building I clambered into. An enterprising kid might find the hole from the building side, but anybody short of a contortionist would have to come the long way around, down the alley and into the back lot, to actually gain entrance to the Underground. It wasn't bad, as far as secret hideaway doors went. I'd have never noticed it, had Rita not shown me the way.

I backed through a couple feet of wall space before my feet hit dead air. Rita reported, "Ladder," from below me, and I lay on my stomach to kick my feet and find the rungs. The iron gleamed from years of use, reminding me of how many homeless my city held, before I emerged into an un-expectedly well-kept stretch of Underground.

Amber streetlights shone through glass blocks above my head, making streaky shadows on old brick walls. Pipes ran below the blocks, supporting their own miniature ecosys-tems of moss and rust, and even with amber lights, I could see that stretches of the brick ceiling were greened-over with algae or moss, too. The air was fresh, though, the occasional broken block letting in a breeze.

Someone—not the City of Seattle, I was pretty sure—had filled a ten-foot stretch of floor with an elaborate tile mosaic of Persephone entering the underworld. Billy and I both hopped across it, trying not to put our feet down, and Rita took a stiff-brushed broom from the shadows and gave the mosaic a few brisk, efficient sweeps once we'd all moved away.

"There are things like this all over the place down here," she said before I asked. She sounded proprietary and proud, which seemed totally appropriate, and tucked the broom back into its shadowy space while she lectured us. "Artists come down and make them off the tour path. The more fragile ones get destroyed fast, but this and some of the others are really sturdy. The floor's sunk a little, so it's cracked, but we try to keep it clean."

"It's amazing." I studied the mural in its soft light a few more seconds, then looked both ways down the bricked-off city tunnel. It plummeted to my left, eventually heading north toward Pike Place Market, which I thought of as the most visible part of the Underground. It wasn't exactly, but its multiple crooked levels certainly reflected how the city had been rebuilt. I edged that direction.

Rita pointed the other. "There's a lot more Underground this way. Down there is the tourist area, off the Square."

"Oh. Sure." I wrote off trying to be clever and followed the expert. She gave Billy and his suit another apologetic look when she led us through a three-foot-high section of tunnel, but said nothing. We crawled through on hands-and-knees tracks visibly worn into the grime, and came out on the other side with stains I didn't want to think too deeply about.

"Some people are too itchy about tight spaces to go through there," Rita reported when we'd gotten back on our feet. "Makes this a good place to sleep and camp out."

"This" was a stretch of tall walls with distant overhead light grottos, and of broken-into rooms which had once upon a time been storefronts and alleyways. It didn't smell as good here. In fact, it verged on stinking, but it wasn't nice to go into someone's home and comment on the stench, so I kept my mouth shut. Water dripped from an ancient wooden water main, and as Rita led us down the narrow old street, I saw one or two places where somebody had hauled wiring down into the Underground. There might be enough electricity to boil water, and it wasn't cold, which made the stretch of lost city seem pretty habitable.

Most of the people we slipped past were sleeping, though one group was gathered around a small barrel fire set up beneath broken-out glass cubes twenty feet above them. I'd seen steam rising up from grates and manholes dozens of times. It'd never occurred to me that once in a while that steam might be smoke from a fire keeping people warm thirty feet below me. That revelation made the under-city streets seem just a little more lonesome and dangerous.

The suspicious looks we garnered didn't alleviate that feeling, either. Rita's presence kept anybody from getting in our faces, but as we approached the barrel fire, a couple of big guys stood up, bristling with caution. Rita reassured them with conciliatory gestures. "They're friends. They're going to help me look for Rick and Gonzo and the others. Can we borrow a couple flashlights?"

Exasperation slid across one of the men's face, though he dug into his bulky coat and came out with one of the requested lights, then snapped his fingers for somebody else to ante up, too. "Better bring these back. What are you, a goddamned den mother, Rita? Nobody's missing, they just took off…'sides, how're they gonna find somebody you can't? Not like topsiders know the tunnels better than you do."

Rita gave him a perfectly sunny smile. "Magic."

The big guy rolled his eyes in an excellent teenage whatever! approximation and went back to the fire. Rita's comment, though, shook my brain loose enough to hit on the idea of using the Sight, which, aside from making a good lie detector, was also handy for noticing people hidden behind doors and walls.

Just not for noticing people hiding off-property, waiting to do something stupid enough to get shot for.

I dropped my chin to my chest, eyes closed as I worked my way through not berating myself. It didn't seem to matter, though, that I knew very well I'd shoot Patty Raleigh again, and that I'd made the right real-world choice for saving my partner's life. But the memories of that bat swinging toward Billy's head, of my finger squeezing the trigger and of Raleigh collapsing backward in shock, were going to haunt me whether I'd made the right choice or not. I was going to have to live with it, just like I'd had to live with a million other unexpected things over the past fifteen months.

The Sight didn't seem to care much about my little crisis of conscience. It slammed through me again, whiting out everything in my vision. I closed my eyes and reached for Billy's arm, needing something solid to hang on to. I felt him give me a curious look—felt it both from the motion of his body and through a fuchsia flare in the whiteness—but he didn't object. Grateful, I focused on the familiar splash of his aura, waiting for the Sight to calm down.

After about thirty seconds it became clear I was going to be waiting a long, long time. I got sparks of emotional information from the Underground town's denizens, but nothing like the clear readable auras I was accustomed to. At most I could tell that those who were awake and aware were cagey, trusting us about as far as we could be thrown. Not that I needed the Sight to tell me that, but it reinforced a desire to slip by and leave them to their lives. I let my magic fade, normal vision re-establishing itself as I murmured, "Thanks for the flashlights," as sincerely as I could before releasing Billy's arm and heading past the campfire group into the Underground's semi-darkness.

Rita let me take the lead until we were well beyond them, then stepped up again, offering flashlights and a shrug. "I can lead you into some of the more remote parts, if you want. I've been down there already looking for people, but maybe you can see better than I do."

I clicked the flashlight on to make sure it worked, then turned it off again: there were still long stretches of light from the streets above, and I saw no reason to run the battery down. "I might be able to. How far do these old streets go? I remember the tour saying something like sixty blocks burned, but I don't know how big the old blocks were...."

"Farther than I've gone. I haven't been in this part of the city that long. Even we have our territory."

I nodded, though I hadn't quite thought of it that way. I knew I recognized several of the homeless who hung out along the Way, and that I was never surprised when a new face showed up and then disappeared again within a few days. It was a little like prostitutes who worked a specific corner, though I had the good sense not to say that out loud. "Seems like it takes a certain amount of nerve to go exploring down here. I mean, how stable are these old walls and pipes and things?"

"Most of them haven't collapsed in a hundred years. I figure they're not gonna fall on my head today."

"Irrefutable logic." Light from above faded into gloom and first Rita, then Billy and I turned our flashlights on. The bright beams made lost city even less friendly, shedding light where none belonged. Rita gestured us onto hands and knees, flashlights thunking awkwardly as we crawled through a low tunnel. The Underground tour I'd been on had said Seattle's new sidewalks had been built anywhere from three to thirty feet above the old, which I heartily believed as we scrambled up and down steep grades that changed with unexpected rapidity. Rita kept on like she knew where we were going, and after long minutes we came out above a room big enough to be a cave. There was no natural light, but the flashlights picked out a floor a good ten or twelve foot drop from the tunnel mouth. It had seen more than its fair share of subsidence, with water-filled, sandy cracks running along it. Wood and brick pillars supported a ceiling that stretched an easy fifteen feet above us, bent and broken brick suggesting whatever building lay atop it, its weight was too great. Eventually the whole thing would collapse six yards. I wondered if one building falling in would create a cascade effect, reshaping Seattle's skyline once again.

Billy said, "Walker," in an oddly strained voice, and pointed his flashlight across the cavern. I waved my light that way, illuminating another tunnel mouth that had been broken through a building wall rather than having been part of the original street system.

A woman with hip-length golden hair crouched just on this side of that tunnel, hands cupped over a largish pool of water. She turned her head our way, showing long, beautifully symmetrical features, and eyes as gold as mine when I was in the throes of magic usage. They had been brown earlier: that was my first, useless thought.

My second was identical to Mr. Kobe Beef's once he'd determined I wasn't dead. Tia Carley was stark naked, and my tiny little brain couldn't get beyond that fact. She stood up, staring across the distance at us. I had never seen a more athletic, attractive female body in my life: slightly broad shoulders, strong slim biceps, round high breasts and enough taper to her waist that her hips looked lush above long rangy legs. All three of us gaped at her, as unabashed in our staring as she was in her nudity. She remained perfectly still, but even so, she reminded me of the troupe dancers in the midst of the shapeshifting dances. There was something challenging about her, as if she'd been caught, caged, and escaped, and had no intention of ever returning to the cage.

Then her lips peeled back from her teeth in a purely feral threat, and she sprang away from the wellspring in a single lithe bound.

A gold brindle wolf hit the earth when she landed, and disappeared into the Underground's tunnels.

CHAPTER TWENTY-FOUR

Rita made a sound unlike anything I'd ever heard, incredulous dismay mixed with childish excitement and a certain amount of terror. "Was that—did I—did she—?"

"Yeah." I did a 180, flopped on my belly and slithered down the damp cavern wall until I dared drop to the floor. It wasn't that far—maybe three feet, with me all stretched out like that—but I hit with a jolt that knocked my breath loose.

Billy said, "My suit," in resignation, and did the same, then yelled, "Walker, wait up!" as I bolted across the underground room floor. "Rita, you don't have to come with us—"

"Are you kidding?" She tossed her flashlight to Billy—I could tell from the way light splashed over the room—and squirmed down after us. I was just smart enough not to go after Tia without backup, but by the time they got to me

I was dancing with agitation, and immediately forewent smarts to scramble through the beaten-down brick wall, shouting over my shoulder as I lurched down the tunnel.

"Her name's Tia Carley! I saw her at the dance concert, goddamn it, I *healed* her, Billy! She had breast cancer! Shit, I talked to her this afternoon. She was interested in the magic, in shamanism, and damn it, I never even imagined she might be asking because she'd gotten caught up in the same power surge I did last night. Or like Morrison did today. If she got caught like Morrison did, she has no idea what's going on! God, she could've even accidentally killed poor Lynn Schumacher this morning—!"

"If she got caught like Morrison did, how come he hasn't reverted to human? How come she just turned back into a wolf? I don't think she's a victim of anything, Walker. I think she's your killer."

I stopped and flashed my light back to eyeball my partner. "Come on, Billy. I can pop back and forth between shapes. In theory, anyway. Probably. I bet I can. With practice."

"With practice! You just said Morrison was caught. You can't have it both ways, Walker. Either somebody knows what they're doing or they don't."

"So maybe she's—" I couldn't think of what she might be, since I knew she wasn't a shaman, but Billy cut across me, getting straight to the point.

"Somebody who *ripped someone's throat out?*"

I stared at him, and Rita's half-visible shadow behind him suggested, "Let's argue about it somewhere else."

I crawled forward again, light bouncing wildly off the closed-in walls—they were dirt, not brick; someone had dug this space out—and tried to come up with an explanation I liked with regards to Tia. By the time we got free of the tunnel, we were filthy and I was no closer to an answer.

There were, as some small favor, dirty wolf tracks cross-ing the small room we'd entered, which told us which of the two doors—I used the word advisedly—to choose. "Where are we?"

"I don't know. I've never been this far out." Rita looked up anyway, like the ceiling might offer answers. "I think we're getting out of downtown by now. We've come a long ways."

"Then we must be running out of Underground, right? She couldn't have gone far." Determined, I triggered the Sight again, baring my teeth against the now-expected blinding whiteness. It flared without giving me a single hint of the depth of viewpoint I knew it could, like it was unduly impressed with the weight and pressure of earth around us. I wasn't certain, though, if it was the Sight itself at fault or if it was me, this time, since I was trying hard not to think about just how far underground we were. Knowing that, however, and shaking it loose were two entirely different things.

Rita said something, but I stopped where I was, in the middle of the room, suddenly irritated. I had had, even by my standards, a hell of an evening so far. Unlike my usual hellacious nights, though, this one had lined me up with what felt like an atom bomb's worth of fresh power just waiting to be used. Just because my standard operating procedure had always been rushing in where angels feared to tread didn't mean I actually had to do that now. "Billy, I need advice."

He was at the door the tracks led through, scowling down it and clenching his hands like he wished he had his duty weapon with him. He stopped doing both, though, to gawk at me. I couldn't blame him. I didn't remember asking him for advice even once in the whole roller coaster of the past year. I'd barely even asked Coyote for advice, though in my defense, I'd wanted to. He'd just been unavailable for a lot of that time. Which made Billy the better person to ask for advice, probably, since he'd pretty much been around since moment one of Joanne's Shamanic Awakening.

And now that I had his attention I didn't know where to begin. "You know how I told you about my real name?" I finally asked.

His eyebrows elevated, but he nodded and even flickered a smile. "Good thing, too. Caroline Siobhán's a nicer name than Caroline Joanne."

I smiled, too. "Yeah, it is." The Hollidays had nearly named their baby girl after me, which had prompted a confession to the train wreck of a name I never used. That, and they'd gone through a lot, thanks to me, and also I was slowly, cautiously, trying to come clean with the people I was closest to. I'd spent more than a decade holding secrets and damage close to the chest, which was poisonous even for perfectly normal people, and which made a nasty mess of shamanic potential in someone like me. Shedding all the protective layers wasn't easy—in fact, of my friends, Morrison was the only one who knew all the parts of the truth about my history, and that was because he'd gone digging on his own—but I was getting there.

And since shedding was exactly what had happened to me under Rattler's influence tonight, it seemed like this was as good a time as any to start doing crazy things like asking for help and advice. "Earlier, after the truck hit me and my spirit animal put me back together, I had this weird idea. This idea that I'd been...reborn."

Billy, who was no slouch in the detecting department, said, "As Siobhán Walkingstick."

I nodded. "And you saw how wiped out I was. The power got stripped down to a kernel before the troupe danced me up some energy again. Right now I can't See past the end of my nose because every time I try the magic just goes ker-blewy. It's too big. It's—" I waved my hands in the air, not sure what I was trying to express. "More solid? Confident? I don't know. Than it's been. The rebirth, the dance, they *did* something to me."

Billy, strongly, said, "I know exactly what you mean."

Right. Of course he did, and he hadn't even gone through the shedding process I had. He'd just been nailed by what the dance troupe offered. I said, "Right," out loud and itched my fingers through my hair. "So basically I need to know if this is a good time to completely change my modus operandi. If I should make a power circle, sit my ass down in the middle of this room, stop arguing for my own limitations and try to figure out how to make this whole huge-feeling power work for me. I might be able to, I don't know. Map this place out in my head. See—" and I tried to invest the word with a capital S beyond it being the beginning of a sentence "—where Tia went, assuming I can get the god-damned Sight to work right at all. The point is, should I try things I've never tried because I've been too busy busting down doors, metaphorical guns blazing and hoping I don't get my face eaten off?"

"I assume that's the other option here."

"Pretty much."

Billy lost his grip on a solemn expression just briefly, and I tried not to snicker, myself. It was a frustrated sort of laugh-ter, but it was also hard not to appreciate the mucked-up mindset which required asking if getting my face eaten off was perhaps not a good idea.

"How long would the map and search take?"

"I honestly don't know. I don't even know for certain it would work. I mean, it should, if I can control the fricking

Sight. Mapping the layout shouldn't be more than the magical equivalent of clearing all the rooms in a video game until the one big shiny spot left blinking on the screen is the bad guy."

Billy gave me a look which suggested that if he did not have a twelve-year-old son, my analogy would have been utterly meaningless. I shrugged apologetically and went on. "Here's the thing. Conceptually this is new to me, and I don't know how long it would take. Maybe a few seconds. Maybe hours. The problem is I might be all topped up full of shiny strong brand-new ready-to-be-used magic right now, but I haven't tested it yet. I've blacked out Seattle. I've caused earthquakes, for God's sake. If this mapping idea goes wrong, if I pour out too much power down here beneath the city, I'm afraid I could send the whole downtown into Puget Sound."

Billy stared at me a few long seconds, then, in a very steady even voice, said, "Let's bust down some doors and get our faces eaten off."

Tia leaped out of the wrong door and tried to eat our faces off.

She landed on Rita, who was smallest and closest, and who screamed like—well, like she was being crushed by a gigantic wolf. This time I reacted the way I should have when Patty Raleigh came after Billy: shields spun across the room, not just springing up around Rita so Tia's enormous jaws snapped and skidded against them, but then slamming into the wolf, knocking it back. It was the most integrated defense-and-attack I'd ever pulled off, a hint of how my power was going to respond in familiar territory. Premature triumph bloomed in me, though at least for once I appreciated it *was* premature.

Tia whipped around behind the shield, snarling and searching for a way out. There wasn't one: between Raleigh and Morrison in the past thirty-six hours, I at least had the sense to pin the shields up against the wall. "Rita, you okay?"

Her high-pitched, gibbered response indicated I'd asked a stupid question. Billy, though, gave her a brief once-over and reported, "She's all right," which I took to mean she hadn't been bitten or otherwise scathed. I wasn't sure anybody could be mentally all right after that, but one thing at a time. I inched toward the captured wolf, then, in a fit of brilliance, whispered a sword into my hand *before* a crisis demanded I have it.

The blade was a silver rapier, and I did mean silver, as in the precious metal, not just the color, that I'd taken off a god the very first day I'd been a shaman. The weapon had become part of my armament—I'd been taking fencing lessons for the past year so I could use it properly—but nobody in their right mind carried a four-foot-long rapier around Seattle. Most of the time it lived beneath my bed, where despite my utter lack of attention to it, it refused to tarnish. Neither did my necklace tarnish, now that I thought about it, so the maker they had in common had probably done something to the metal.

It was equally likely that its maker had invested it with the willingness to be called across a breach of space, since I didn't think bending space was generally within a shaman's purview. Whether it was my magic or its, though, the sword could be pulled from under my bed and into my hand from a range of up to tens of miles, maybe more, and that let me have it in my repertoire without garnering a reputation as a freak.

Well. Without garnering a reputation as a sword-carrying

freak, anyway. I pointed the thing at the wolf as dramatically as I could, and with my best Errol Flynn sneer, demanded, "Show yourself!"

Wolves perhaps didn't respond well to human language commands. She jumped at me, bounced off the shield and snarled again, showing impressively large canines. Big brave me shrieked like a little girl and cowered back a step before remembering I was the one with the sword, the shields and the human brain. In theory, I had the upper hand. "That's not going to work. Look, I mostly want to know what happened to you. Were you at the dance concert last night? Did you accidentally get transformed during the shapeshifter dances?"

Truthfully, I doubted it. Billy's point about the woman's ability to shift freely made too much sense. Still, there was a passing chance that Tia was a victim, and there was some important law of the land about innocent until proven guilty. Maybe the fact that she remained a wolf now supported that: presumably an in-control human shapeshifter would switch to the form which would permit communication. My sword wavered a bit. I didn't want to stab Tia.

With the unerring sense of a predator recognizing weakness, she leaped again. This time, though, she did transform, lupine body surging to human in a ripple that passed through my shields without a whisper of protest. Rita screamed, but before the leaping woman hit the floor she shifted a second time, front paws catching her weight. She wheeled toward the door she'd come from, and disappeared from sight in an instant.

Rita's scream cut off in astonishment. Billy and I both took a few steps toward the door the wolf had exited through, then stopped, staring at one another. He didn't have to ask: after a few seconds of slow brain-grinding, I said, "God damn it, she's like the goddamned wendigo."

Billy, who hadn't been there for that, only elevated his eyebrows and waited. I transferred my sword to my left hand and rubbed my face until it burned with warmth. "Sort of like the wendigo, anyway. The shields don't work very well on things that are pure or active magic, and the Lower World is all about the magic. Every time the wendigo went there, I lost my grip. And it could slip back and forth without any effort, so basically it was like trying to catch a live fish with bare hands."

"I thought the wendigo was…" Billy trailed off, obviously looking for the right phrasing. "Less human than that."

"Yeah, no, it was. I don't know what she is." I did. I just didn't want to say it, because there was no such thing as a werewolf. Why banshees and thunderbirds and spirit animals were okay and werewolves weren't, I didn't know, but I was determined that there should be no such thing as werewolves. They were too Hollywood, or something. "It's just the principle's the same. The shields don't work well on pure magic, and if shapeshifting between one form and another isn't pure magic, I don't know what is."

Rita, who had a more practical grasp on the situation, said, "Is she going to come back?" which made us all edge into the center of the room, creating a back-to-back triangle. Rita scooped up the flashlight I'd dropped when I'd called the sword and shone her two lights at both doors, then twisted a little to shine one of them at me. "You have a sword."

It was obviously a question. It was equally obvious that an explanation would take all night, so I shrugged. "It's a magic sword."

"People," Rita said, sounding very much like I had not all that long ago, "don't have magic swords."

"They don't shapeshift into wolves, either," I pointed out as nicely as I could. Billy coughed suddenly, and I suspected I'd sounded a lot like he had once upon a time, tolerating my utter refusal to believe what he knew was true. I said, "Sorry," to him, and his cough turned into a guffaw.

"Water under the bridge, Joanie. Water under the bridge. Are we going to stand here all night waiting to see if she comes back?"

It sounded like a good plan to me, but it wasn't actually going to get the job done. "Just give me a minute to at least be damned good and sure she's not lurking around the corner."

"Be my guest."

The Sight flashed on, a burst of white that unexpectedly faded into normality. Well, normality in terms of being able to See beyond the physical walls of the world. I didn't know if it was necessity forcing me to get my act together, or if I was adjusting to the new power level, but either way, the walls around us turned a shadowy gray-green. Most buildings blazed green, a sentry color of certainty in their duty, but these ones were too old and neglected; they'd forgotten their purpose. I felt sorry for them, and like my emotional state affected my magic, white surged up again. I said "Stop that" aloud to myself, and hauled my emotions into as steady a line as I could get them.

The doors on either side of us led into alleys that looped around, explaining how the wolf had come at us so easily from the evidently-wrong direction. Another path led away from that looped hall, and I saw a rush-and-tumble maze of twisty little passages, all alike, leading into stretches of underground that I suddenly, seriously doubted were

Underground at all. "Seattle's not built on a bunch of cave systems, is it?"

"No. It's volcanic sediment and sandstones," Billy said with utter confidence. Rita and I both turned to look at him and he spread his hands. "Robert just did a science fair project on Puget Sound geology. Why?"

I reeled the Sight back in and squinched my face up. "I don't know. Maybe I'm seeing things. It just looks like this direction is riddled with caves and tunnels."

After a long, cautious silence, Billy said, "It was a pretty big earthquake…."

"No. Absolutely not. No fricking way. I do not accept that as a possibility." In order to prevent myself from considering it—because the idea had leaked into my mind, too, and I wanted it far, far away—I took my flashlight from Rita, whispered the sword back to its hiding place beneath my bed and boldly strode through the closest doorway.

Rita, following me, said, "Earthquake?" to Billy in an appropriately hushed voice, but there wasn't anywhere I could escape overhearing her.

"Last July, remember the one that tore up Lake Washington and made Thunderbird Falls? That was Detective Walker."

I muttered, "It was June, and I was having a bad day," and bent forward as the passageway got lower. Rita took a breath like she wanted to ask a dozen questions, but restrained herself as I got down on hands and knees to continue forward. I was certain there was room: Tia, either in human or canine form, had fit through, and I was pretty sure she didn't outweigh me. "Look, I know she isn't right in front of us, but once we get through here I want you to let me take point and you two stay back to back, okay? Rita, are you sure you even want to be here?"

"People have been brought through here recently, Detective. There are heel marks in the dirt, like they were dragged."

I stopped and looked at the dirt under my hands, which was littered with paw prints and, indeed, drag marks. "Please tell me you'd noticed that, Billy."

"Crawling behind two of you who are wiping out the marks? No. Good job, Rita. We owe you one."

"We see a lot more than people think we do," Rita said softly. "Just because you don't see us…"

I said, "Remind me to hire you as my eyes and ears on the street when we get done with this," and Rita breathed a smile behind me.

"Joanne," Melinda Holliday said, loud and clear and *inside my head*, "we have a problem. The police have found Michael."

CHAPTER TWENTY-FIVE

I bucked upright, smashed my head against the low ceiling, howled with outrage and came down again saying, "What the *fuck?*" mostly to the voice inside my head. *"Melinda?"*

"Melinda?" Billy looked around in alarm and I snapped a fist closed like I was snatching the sound from the air.

"Since when is your wife *telepathic,* Billy? Melinda? Melinda!" I finally tried *Melinda?* inside my head, and got startlement back in response. *Melinda, what the* fuck?

Impatience shot through her answer: "For heaven's sake, Joanne, I don't know how long I can maintain this. Wherever you are doesn't have cell reception and this is important. Get somewhere you can call me before they decide to shoot Michael."

I bent double—not that it was far to bend—and beat both fists against the ground, swearing and swearing and swearing. "They found Morrison. I have to go get him."

Rita's protest was as sharp as my own astonishment. "You can't leave! You can't—that thing, it's, it's a, a…"

"I don't have much choice, Rita. We know where Tia is, at least generally. I'll come back for her, but if I don't go get Morrison he's probably going to get killed and—" I broke off, because that sentence finished with *and I would rather let every single person down here die than let that happen.* I wasn't sure it was a lie, but I was very sure it was the wrong thing to say. "Are there other ways in and out of here?"

"Probably, but I don't know! I've never been this far!"

Well, the first tunnel we'd chased our golden goose through had been dug out by hand, not one of the old city streets. I arbitrarily chose to believe that meant it was the main, perhaps the only, access point, and started backing up. "Billy, *shit*, you don't even have your gun, do you?" I knew he didn't, not any more than I had one. Worry was making me ask stupid questions.

"I don't usually bring it to theater performances, no," he said tightly. "What about Melinda?"

"She's fine, she's just *talking in my head*." I was feeling a little over-emphatic, but it was the only way I could keep from shouting everything I said. "Is that normal?"

After a careful pause he said, "No," which suggested to me it wasn't entirely abnormal, either, but I wasn't in the mood to get into it.

"It must have something to do with the dance tonight. Look, if we retreat to the chamber we first saw her in, can you hold the fort until I get back?"

"Me and what army?"

"Ours," Rita offered, sounding determined if not absolutely certain. "Wolves avoid people, right? Normal wolves? So if I go get some of the guys to join us, maybe just having so many people there will keep her trapped."

It was dark and the tunnel was cramped, but Billy and I both turned toward her, lights flashing to illuminate her wide-eyed face. "That," I said in genuine approval, "is a great idea. Thank you, Rita. You're a hell of a woman."

"And you owe me a hell of an explanation." She turned around more easily in the tunnel's confines than either Billy or I could do, and scampered back the way we'd come.

Shamanic powers did not come invested with super-strength, so getting Billy, particularly, out of the chamber we'd first seen the wolf woman in was something of a challenge. Fortunately, I was tall and broad-shouldered, if not superheroic, and once I'd boosted him up he was able to haul me up without much trouble. Rita, who weighed about ninety pounds, was no problem, though it was she who said, "We'll bring a ladder next time."

I let her explain about the golden-furred predator in the tunnels when we got back to the campfire group, and was pleasantly surprised that half a dozen of them agreed, not even grudgingly, to come keep an eye on the chamber. I didn't remember seeing another way out of there, and suggested they didn't even need to go into the chamber itself, but their friend Lynn was dead, others were missing and their attitude had something of a witch hunt to it. I hoped Billy could keep them from going after the wolf, but I had to trust him to it: every minute I stayed below was another minute Morrison could get killed in, and I didn't care how disorganized the homeless mob was when I left them.

It took less time to get back to the mosaic and ladder than it had taken to get away from it. It was one of those fixed truths of the universe: the road back was always shorter, presumably because then I knew where I was going. I scrambled back to the surface and ran for the parking garage, because, like a moron, I had left my phone in Petite. I couldn't re-member the last time I'd run more than a block, much less a whole damned mile. I had an agonizing stitch in my side by the time I collapsed into Petite's bucket seat, lodging dirt and muck in the leather, and frantically dialed Melinda. "Well? Where is he? And how do you even know?"

"I've been listening to Billy's police scanner," she said without the slightest repentance. I wanted to kiss her for the breach of protocol. "He got himself into the Market some-how, Joanne. They're still chasing him around it."

"The Market? What the hell is he doing downtown? And aren't half the internal passages blocked off by gates?" I slammed Petite's door, locking it, and was running again before I'd finished the questions.

Melinda gave a very unladylike snort. "I'm not sure how much locks and gates matter to shapeshifters, Joanne. That would be your area of expertise."

"Like telepathy is yours?" I wanted to keep her on the phone. It was easier to run if I could huff and puff and bellow questions to take my mind off the fact that I was in no condition to sprint around downtown Seattle. I promised myself I would take up jogging Monday morning.

Mel's voice stiffened a little. "It's hardly an area of expertise."

"Oh, come on, Melinda!" I skidded out of the garage, got my feet under me again and headed west on Pine Street as fast as my breathless body could take me. "You're the most understated adept I've met! You've been in a coven, you say you're just a wise woman, I mean come on, what does that mean?" It would have been a more impressive interrogation if I'd gotten the questions out that smoothly, but I was gasp-ing for air about every third word.

Melinda's stuffiness faded into mild amusement. "I told

you covens didn't suit me. I have a certain amount of empathic talent, and the better I know someone, the more attuned I become. A full coven is too large—there are always a few people whose thoughts and ambitions are distasteful, so I decided a long time ago to take my grandmother's path, and remain mostly apart from the magical world. Those who need me, find me."

"And the whole thing tonight? You were talking in my head!" I crashed into a wall, bounced off and hauled ass around the corner toward the Market's main entrance, bellowing, "Detective Joanne Walker, I'm the one here to handle the animal! I repeat, I am in command of this situation, please fall back and report to me!" as I went.

A couple of downtown cops I didn't know appeared, looking somewhere between relieved and outraged. Neither, to my huge relief, had their guns unholstered. Apparently someone had actually listened when I'd demanded the wolf not be shot.

"I take it you're there," Melinda said in my ear. I wheezed, "Yeah," and heard her smile through the phone. "Then go find Michael, Joanne. Certainly that's more important than learning about me and my quiet little magics." She hung up. I bent over, coughing what tasted like iron filaments from my lungs.

One of the cops, bemused, said, "You sure you're in charge?" and I flapped my phone hand at him, patting myself down with the other as I searched for my badge.

Which, of course, I didn't have. I wheezed an obscenity, then waved my phone more urgently. "North Precinct. Detective Joanne Walker. Not on duty, but in charge. Dial Morrison on the phone for confirmation." Morrison obviously wasn't going to answer, but the call would go through to his cell, which identified him as the North Precinct captain. I hoped that would be enough.

The cop took my phone and made the call as I leaned on the building, catching my breath. He looked about fourteen, though he couldn't have been less than twenty-one, only seven years my junior. I hoped he wasn't fresh enough out of the Academy to be determined to do everything absolutely by the book, since Morrison wasn't going to answer. After a few seconds he took a breath like he was about to speak to someone, then let it out as he waited on the brief, clipped message announcing Morrison wasn't available right now. He mouthed, "Not picking up," to me, and said, "This is Officer Donald King with the West Precinct. I was calling to confirm Detective Joanne Walker's jurisdiction in the case of a wolf sighting at Pike Place Market. You can reach me at," and gave a number I promptly forgot. Then he hung up, handed me the phone and said, "It's the biggest damned wolf I've ever seen. It's gotta be four feet tall at the shoulder. You want to be in charge, you got it. What can we do?"

"Point me toward it and whatever you do, just. Don't. Shoot it. In fact, just point me toward it and stay up here to guard the door. Don't let it out, if it runs."

Young Officer King gave me a dubious look, but nodded. "How're you gonna catch it, ma'am? You don't have a tranq gun or a net…."

"Through force of personality." I had my breath back, and pushed off the corrugated steel door I'd been leaning on. "All right. Let me in, let me in, by the hairs, by the hairs on my chinny-chin-chin."

King gave me another uncertain look. "That story didn't end up so well for the wolf, ma'am."

Like I needed a fairy-tale pedant at my back. "Good point. What level's he on?"

"Down next to the comic shop," the other cop said. "Or he was last time we got a look at him. He got backed up against one of the internal gates, so we closed the next one up and called in."

I didn't know how Morrison had gotten that deep into the Market in the first place, but I counted small blessings that he'd gotten stuck, and jogged through the single open door.

SUNDAY, MARCH 19, 1:39 A.M.

Most tourists knew the Market from the ubiquitous fish-monger images: cheerful guys flinging whole fish at one another while maintaining outrageous, loud conversation and flirtations. That was the Market's public face. But in the middle of the night, all that was left of the daytime bustle were concrete floors and the distinct, cold scent of fish. I broke to the left, heading for wood floors and slopes and stairs that offered only emergency lighting and exit signs to see by. In daylight, the Market was quirky, loud, enter-taining and slightly impossible to navigate, since its floors didn't necessarily match up with each other. It was less fun in gloom, though halfway to the comic shop I realized the Sight could take care of that little problem, and braced for brilliance as I kicked it on.

The impossible brightness didn't hit me, this time. I was getting better at tempering the new power. That was good. It showed me warm flashes of human auras that said a couple people slept in shops, which surprised me. The owners had to know about them: homeless people came into the Market to get out of the weather, but I doubted many of them ended up behind the counter in the bead store or under a café table once the businesses closed down for the day. The Market's hours were varied, with restaurants staying open fairly late and farmers opening early, so with restrooms handy and tacit permission from a store owner, it probably wasn't a bad place to flop for a few nights. Certainly safer than being on the street, in a pinch.

Except for the occasional dire-size wolf running around after hours, anyway. The Sight pinpointed Morrison as easily as it had noticed the sleepers: he was one floor below me, and judging from the comparative calm of his aura, no longer terrified. Not happy: there were red spikes through the purple and blue, indicating agitation, but at least he wasn't going every which way with panic. I ran downstairs, trying not to thump too loudly.

Apparently I thumped loudly enough, because instead of a content wolf curled up in a corner with his tail over his nose, which is what I was hoping for, I got a bristly wolf with his back to a corner and his teeth bared. He'd come as far as he could within the Market; there wasn't enough room for him to clear a jump between the gate behind him and the ceiling above it. Of course, I didn't know how he'd gotten through locked front doors, either, so I wasn't absolutely certain the jump was insurmountable. I had the hopeful thought that he'd decided to stop running and wait for me to show up and rescue him, but the snarling muzzle didn't support that theory.

I stopped a good forty feet from him, wondering if making myself smaller would come across as non-threatening or vulnerable to his wolfy mind. Non-threatening was good. Vulnerable, not so much. Instead of trying I said, "Hey, boss," as softly as I could. "It's me, Joanne. Everything's going to be okay, all right? I just really need you to come with me."

I'd read somewhere that dogs had the cognitive power of a two- or three-year-old human child. A two-year-old would almost certainly understand what I'd just said. Whether he'd agree to come along was a whole different matter. That was the price of being two: old enough to comprehend and old enough to be stubborn. Morrison's ears flattened, and I had the distinct impression if he'd understood, he was going to be stubborn. I'd gotten him into this mess. There was probably a certain wisdom in not entirely trusting me to get him out of it, especially since I didn't know how. My best bet was bringing him back to the dance troupe and using the first half of their performance to power his transformation back to humanity. "Snap your teeth once if you understand me."

He growled, which I didn't think was close enough to count. I scowled at him a moment, then sighed and sat down anyway, not caring if my sudden smallness made me vulnerable. I could only think of one way to communicate with him, and trying it while I was on my feet was likely to lead to me falling over. I took one deep breath, and prepared to flee my body.

I should have known it wouldn't be that easy.

Actually the problem was it was way *too* easy. I fled, all right. Under normal circumstances, I'd have fled into some kind of familiar territory, often digging up through the earth to enter Morrison's garden. That was how I saw the human soul: as a garden, with their general mental health reflected in how sparse or lush that garden was. Gary, my septuagenarian best friend, didn't just have a garden: he had a whole jungle, warm and inviting and fantastic to explore. My own, though an awful lot healthier than it had been fifteen months ago, was still pretty spartan, with walls and straight lines and only a few bits where things were starting to get overgrown and develop some personality.

The first time I'd intruded on Morrison's garden, I'd expected it to be tidy and rigid, like mine, which went to show just how well I knew my boss. The psychic reflection of his soul was way toward the Gary end of the spectrum: a mountainous, rugged landscape with vast pollution-free skies and raptors carried on the wind. That was where I expected to end up this time, too.

Instead I shot skyward, fresh new uncontrolled power boosting me to realms I never intended to visit. Air thinned as the sky paled, blue fading until stars sparkled through it. I left behind mountains I'd climbed once, a long time ago: mountains that dwarfed the Himalayas, their sharp peaks stabbing at the cool sky. The sun hung much too far away, so far I doubted I should be able to feel its heat, though the unfamiliar world below me was clearly not frozen.

It was just as clearly not my world. *Things* rode the wind with me, most of them barely held in one shape, like someone had released spirits from their bodies and set them drifting. A few were more real, for lack of a better word: far below me sunlight glittered off gold wings, reminder of the thunderbird I'd once encountered. I triggered the Sight like it might give me binocular vision, but not only was it not designed to do that, it had no effect anyway. I was already viewing everything psychically, and couldn't reach any deeper.

There were lots of places to visit, astrally speaking. Out of all of them, I'd spent the least time here, in the Upper World. In fact, the only other time I'd come here, it had also been an accident. It had been a test, then, though I hadn't known it at the time. I was a little better prepared in terms of knowledge for facing another such test. Sadly, given the events of the evening, I was possibly even less prepared magically, which was saying something.

I was not prepared for a swarm of locusts to buzz out of the pale sky and attack me. Sadly for my dignity, I shut my eyes and screamed like a little girl, flailing in an attempt to get the things off me. Instead they clung with remarkable determination, jillions of little feet sticking to me while I gibbered. I wasn't precisely afraid of bugs, any more than I was *afraid* of mice. But something in my hind brain turned me into a fifties housewife when a mouse skittered across the floor, and apparently swarms of green buzzing bugs did the same thing.

Except the bugs kept buzzing, and I could only keep up the shrieking and squirming for so long before I started feeling like an idiot. Last time an animal had come after me in the Upper World, it had eaten me. The grasshoppers weren't doing that. I pried one eye open to look nervously at them.

They weren't grasshoppers. Lots of them were green, it was true, but the one sitting on my shoulder was a praying mantis, its odd leaflike limbs crooked like Dr. Evil's as it watched me. A shudder started at the bottom of my soul and worked its way up to chill my skin. The mantis lifted its feet delicately and put them back down again as goose bumps disturbed him. Somehow it looked disappointed, which was not an expression I was accustomed to seeing on a bug. I mumbled a sheepish apology, and opened my other eye so I could look at the host of insects swarming me.

They had to number in the hundreds, even thousands. Not all of them were mantises, but enough were: I was pretty sure that many carnivorous bugs could make short order of me if they wanted to. Unlike the thunderbird, though, that didn't seem to be their purpose. They seemed to be waiting on me, which made flailing and shrieking seem even less productive. I pulled my arms in tight, trying not to squish any bugs, and peered at them. Stick bugs, all of them, the sort I'd seen lots of in North Carolina. Those that weren't mantises were my paternal family's namesakes, walking sticks. It would be hypocritical to freak out over a bug I was named after, so I made myself unfold an arm and put a hand out to one of the bigger walking sticks. It walked carefully up my arm, paused at my shoulder to smack the mantis away, then put two of its long spindly legs against my face. I bit back a squeal of panic and stared cross-eyed at the thing.

It stared back. I don't know what I expected from a bug, but that wasn't it. It *should* have been it, since bugs weren't known for their great interspecies communications, but I'd spent a fair amount of time having prolonged discussions with ravens, rattlesnakes, coyotes and occasionally other animals. In my world, a bug that talked to me wouldn't have been all that unusual. But no, it just sat there gazing at me, and finally dropped its feet and walked back down my arm again, leaving me, once more, with the sensation I'd disappointed an insect.

When it reached my fingertips, it jumped off, and the Upper World disappeared from around me.

I was a little surprised to awaken in Morrison's garden. I'd forgotten that's where I'd been headed, before the stick insect interlude. It took a moment to shake off the feeling of hundreds of tiny bug feet crawling all over me, and to take a good look around.

I was in roughly the same place I'd been last time I'd visited his garden: a granite cliff littered with stubborn trees and a vista that overlooked half the world. Precarious for me, perhaps, but it was an easily defensible spot. Morrison could effectively shove an unwanted visitor off the cliff, if he had to protect the core of what he was. The whole garden was wild country, the sort that could kill somebody anyway, if they weren't careful, and the fact that it reflected Morrison's soul said a lot about his confidence and competence.

It was also perfect territory for a wolf, but I doubted Morrison would be shapeshifted here. If he was, the situation was a whole lot worse than I thought, and my half-baked ideas of bringing him back to the dance troupe were going to require a great deal more baking, and probably Coyote's guidance as well. My Coyote, Little Coyote, not the desert-stalking archetype. I didn't want to bother *him* for any reason, not if I could avoid it.

Nor did I want to start bellowing for my boss. That seemed inexcusably rude, as if barging into his garden wasn't already. So I stood there, watching an eagle on an updraft, until I got the spine-itchy feeling of someone looking at me. I turned around.

Morrison sat a few yards away, a magnificent silver wolf with blue eyes and an expression very like Morrison-the-man could wear: one that said, somewhat impatiently, *What are you doing here, Walker?*

"What I'm not doing is having yet another silent conversation with an animal. Come on, Morrison. I know this place, right here, and if I know it, you can't be so far gone as to be stuck as a wolf in your own garden. I'm sure it's very sexy and all, but I need to talk t—"

He shivered into human form somewhere far too close to the beginning of my last sentence, and remained where he was, with the exact same expression he'd had as a wolf. Except now he was--well.

At least he was dressed. Or at least mostly dressed, which he wouldn't be if he'd shifted back to human in the real world. He was in jeans, which Morrison almost never wore, and a snug tanktop-style undershirt. No shoes. No socks.

No *shirt* over the tanktop, and for some reason the tank was about eight hundred times more provocative than being totally shirtless would have been. It was the whole promise of something more, I guessed, but damn, it worked. A year ago I'd thought he was a little soft around the middle. The softness had disappeared over the course of the past twelve months, but the tanktop provided an opportunity to appreciate just how not-soft he was. Really clean solid muscular arms looped around his knees. Broad smooth shoulders with the shadow of a tattoo on one, though I couldn't see what it was. The idea of Morrison having a tattoo at all cranked my brain around a few times and set it on a bewildered spin cycle. It was not, however, my brain which was doing most of the assessment of a half-dressed Morrison, so I didn't really miss it as I licked my lips and kept right on gawking.

After a while he arched one eyebrow, which reminded me he was quite aware of my staring. I cleared my throat, wondering why on God's little green earth I ever opted to use a word like *sexy* in relation to my boss within his hearing, and then wondering if that word choice had precipitated his clothing decisions on a subliminal level. It took another long moment or three to get past that idea and finally croak, "Hi."

"Last time," Morrison said, "you said this always works in fairy tales. Which one are we in now, Walker? Beauty and the Beast?"

"I hope not. It took more than a kiss to break that spell." Once more, I wished I'd shut up ahead of time.

Because it was Morrison's garden, he was suddenly no longer in front of me. I spun to find him farther away than he'd been, sitting on a picnic table that hadn't been there before, with a knife and some kind of wood carving in his hands. Morrison. Half dressed, wielding a knife, creating art. And here I thought he'd cornered the market on sexy before. I went back to staring at him wordlessly, aware that my heartbeat had accelerated and my cheeks were growing steadily warmer. The tattoo was still a shadow, distance obscuring it. I really, really wanted to know what it was, but my scratchy voice said, "I didn't know you sculpted," instead of asking.

"My dad taught me." That was clearly as much information as he intended to divulge. I took a couple tentative steps toward him and said, "We have a problem."

"Yeah, Walker, I know. I chose Beauty and the Beast over Sleeping Beauty for a reason. What are you going to do about it?"

He was a lot tetchier than he'd been last time I was here. I no doubt deserved it, but it made me feel small and unhappy anyway, and I offered my explanation to the ground, instead of him. "I can try changing you back right now. I'm pretty sure I've got the raw power."

"But."

I looked up, more determined to face that tone than I was inclined to slink away. "But it's really raw right now. Like I blacked out Seattle raw."

Morrison sighed, though his attention was all for the carving. Quick knife strokes pared away the wood, small muscle movements in his arms smooth and distracting as it took on a shape I couldn't recognize from the distance. "And the other choice?"

"You stay a wolf in the real world until I can get you back to the dance troupe, where they can do the transformative dances and I can get Coyote to help me focus so I'm sure nothing will go wrong when you change. The only risk there is you staying more in wolf-brain than I wish you would, but I'm kind of hoping me coming in here to talk to you will wake your human mind up more. The shock of shifting without warning can make somebody go all animal, but you're obviously still in here."

"And how do I retain my own mind when we leave here?"

"I don't know. Focus on me. I'm a constant, I'll be right there."

"You're a constant something, all right." Morrison stood up unexpectedly and I fumbled the catch when he tossed the carving to me.

It was a jeans-and-sweater–clad woman with short-cropped hair and the most delicate slice of a scar marring her right cheek. I jerked my gaze to Morrison, but he was already gone.

In another moment, so was I.

CHAPTER TWENTY-SIX

Morrison was standing over me when I opened my eyes. Looming, actually. Officer King's estimation of Morrison's wolfy self's size had been off, but not much. He was a good three and a half feet at the shoulder, bigger than a Great Dane, and broader in the chest than any canine I'd ever laid eyes on. I hadn't really had time to appreciate that when I'd been wrestling with him in the theater. I wasn't strictly sure I wanted to be appreciating it now, since I had the very clear impression he could crush my skull in his jaws pretty much on a whim. All in all, I preferred the partially dressed man, not that I would ever, ever say that aloud.

Fortunately, he couldn't read my mind, and since he hadn't crushed my skull, I offered a tentative, "Hey, boss. This mean you're in there?" which got me a steely-eyed glare I interpreted as an affirmative. My shoulders slumped and I rocked forward until my hair brushed his fur, which made both of us startle. "Sorry. All right, look, let's get you out of here. There are a couple cops up above. Try not to scare them." I got to my feet. Morrison's head came up to the bottom of my ribs. I resisted the urge to curl my fingers in his ruff and tried very hard to act like I was just walking out of the marketplace with my boss at my side.

It worked all the way up to the point we were actually walking *out*, when King and his partner both said "Jesus *Christ!*" and other high-voiced panicked exclamations of that nature. Morrison, human brain in control or not, growled, and I raised my hands, getting between him and the officers. "It's okay. It's okay. He's…" I was going to get in so much trouble for this. "He's tame. He just got loose tonight and has been a little freaked out."

"He should try being me!"

"I don't think that would make either of you happy. Look, thanks for calling me in." Never mind that they hadn't. Maybe they wouldn't notice. "I'll let citywide Dispatch and Animal Control know that the wolf has been contained. No more high alert for tonight."

King blew out a long breath. "Hope not. It's been a crazy day. You heard about the murder just up the street this morning, right?"

I very much didn't want his thoughts going that direction, not when Lynn Schumacher's death had all the earmarks of a dog attack. "It's the full moon coming on, is all. Everybody's a little crazy around the full moon. C'mon, fella." I clicked my tongue at Morrison, whose expression told me I would die soon and painfully, but he trotted along beside me as I hurried up the street, leaving the two young officers behind. As soon as we were out of earshot I muttered, "Sorry," then called Dispatch as promised. Morrison watched the whole thing, then gave a great huff that I anthropomorphized as relief. Although maybe it wasn't anthropomorphizing if he was actually a human. Dictionary definitions weren't meant to encompass my life. Either way, I made the tactical error of reaching out to rub his head as if he *was* a dog, and discovered that wolves could move very, very fast when they wanted to. My wrist looked astonishingly small and delicate in his mouth. I swallowed and Morrison let me go, but with a dire look which indicated next time he'd probably chomp my arm off.

My vague intentions of bringing him into the Underground evaporated. "Let's get you someplace safe."

He whuffed, and I picked up the pace, heading for the parking garage. I didn't want to think about his big hoary claws scraping up Petite's black leather seats, but he stepped into the car with unexpected delicacy, as if the same thought had occurred to him. For a man who considered my relationship with my car to be pathological, I thought that was very considerate. I leaned past him, locked the door, said, "Stay," and hopped back out of the driver's side to lock the door behind me. Shapechanged boss or not, there was an I-hated-to-say-it werewolf down below, and half a dozen totally ordinary people standing between it and another potential early-morning murder. Morrison was going to have to wait.

I'd made it forty feet when I heard the distinctive sound of Petite's door slamming again. I turned to find Morrison with an absolutely filthy look which obviously said, *You didn't think I was smart enough to open a goddamned car door, Walker?* A few long loping steps brought him to my side, his expression still infuriated, and I stared between him and the car. "Did you lock her?"

He bared his teeth at me. Of course he hadn't. Petite

required thumbs to lock from the outside. Chastised and grumpy, I skulked back to Petite to lock her up safely once more.

If I thought sections of the Underground smelled, my opinion held nothing on Morrison's: he sneezed violently for a full sixty yards, and came through the worst bit looking like it was all somehow my fault. I said, "You could've stayed in Petite," which was petty, true, and got me another dirty look. I'd had no idea dogs were so good at looking disgusted without also being threatening.

Most of Rita's friends had evidently joined her. The remaining two or three were sacked out near the fire and didn't notice me sneaking by with a giant white wolf on my heels. He and I crept through the tunnel leading to the wolf-woman chamber, and I waved Billy down. He swung up the ladder—one of those chain and metal jobbies they recommended for second-floor fire escapes in private homes—and came nose to nose with Morrison.

Neither, to their credit, yelped, but it looked like a near thing on both parts. Billy's eyes bugged and I raised a defensive hand. "He wouldn't stay in the car. I don't know how I'm going to explain him to them."

"…as a police tracking dog…?" Billy suggested weakly. "A police tracking dog the size of Godzilla? Jesus, Joanne, look at him!"

"I know. I guess mass doesn't convert away to make normal-size fauna. Do you think they'd buy it?"

"I think it doesn't matter anyway. How do you plan to get him down there?" Billy pointed to the twelve-foot drop to the chamber floor, a factor I hadn't previously considered.

Morrison growled and edged forward, ears back, to peer over the tunnel's edge. Then his massive shoulders rolled, a *no problem* shrug if I'd ever seen one, and he surged forward, clearing Billy's head easily and landing three-quarters of the way across the chamber with little more than a grunt.

It was enough to garner attention, and nobody else was as manly as Billy had been: half a dozen homeless guys *did* shriek, piercing squeals that echoed off the ceiling. Billy swore and jumped to the chamber floor, trying to break up their vocal panic with his own deep assurances: "Police dog, here to help us track. I know he's huge, but he's not aggressive. Just don't get in his face."

"Doesn't look like a fuckin' *dog* to me," somebody snarled. I saw tension ripple down Morrison's spine before he looked over his shoulder and gave me another *this is your fault* glare. I didn't think that was quite fair, since I'd told him to stay in the car. On the other hand, if he had, I'd have never seen my shapeshifted boss heave a mighty sigh, lie down, and roll over on his back to loll about and invite belly scratches. Ginormous or not, with his tongue hanging out and his spine all a-wriggle against the floor, he didn't look even slightly dangerous, and the wolf aspects seemed much less dramatic.

I slithered down the rope ladder, scraping my hands and stomach in my hurry, and scurried over to rub Morrison's tummy to prove it was safe to do so. He was going to kill me. Oh, God, he was going to kill me, bring me back and kill me again, even if he had to spend a million years learning magic just so he could do it. And if he didn't, I might do it myself, because I was pretty sure I deserved to be killed repeatedly for getting either of us into this situation.

The snarly guy muttered, "I'll be damned," and Rita snuck over to scratch Morrison's chest tentatively. He tolerated it for a good ten seconds from both of us, then flipped over again and stayed down, chin on his paws in what I assumed was his best attempt at non-threatening behavior.

Probably everybody else interpreted the furious glare he fixed on me as attentive-waiting-for-commands behavior.

"All right," Billy said. "We've got our crew in place now. Thanks for helping me hold down the fort. It's best if you head back to your fire now. Wolves won't generally approach a group of humans or fire, not that we expect this one to get past us. Watch yourselves, though."

A few of them started to protest. Morrison sat up. Suddenly none of them wanted to hang around anymore, and there was a rush for the ladder, which, after some debate, they left in place. Thoughtful of them. Within about two minutes, Rita, Billy, Morrison and I were the only ones left, and Rita was staring hard at my boss. "He's the same size that woman is."

"Bigger," I said ill-advisedly. "Probably has forty pounds on her."

She swung around to glare at me, though she pointed an accusing finger at Morrison simultaneously. "Is he like her? A werewolf?"

Morrison turned his head so slowly I hardly saw him move, but I certainly felt the incredulous weight of his expression. "This is why I didn't want you to come along," I said to him. "I didn't want to explain everything right now. And no," I said to Rita. "He's just a victim of me screwing up. Werewolves don't exist and even if they did, every piece of folklore I know says they're bound by the phases of the moon."

"Which is full tonight," Billy said. I wanted to kick him. "And if that woman wasn't a werewolf," he continued, "what was she?"

"Well, whatever she is, Morrison's not, okay? She could shift back and forth and he can't." They were right. Tia was a werewolf. And she was probably the dance theater killer, because if legend was right and werewolves were tied to phases of the moon, she probably had some kind of major power suck going down around the full moon, and I was pretty damned certain the murder's timing wasn't coincidental. Moreover, tonight, *Sunday* night, not Saturday which I suspected Billy had meant, was the actual full moon, which probably meant if we didn't stop the bitch—no pun intended—she'd attack the dancers one more time.

I did not want to fight a werewolf. It was up there with zombies. Traditional creatures of the night were just not my thing, damn it, not that anybody had asked me what my thing was. I said, "Shit," under my breath, and more clearly said, "Rita, this is probably a good time for you to cut loose, too. If she's a werewolf, hell, I don't know what happens if you get bitten by a real werewolf, but it can't be good."

"No," Rita said in a small voice. "I got you into this. I'd like to see it through."

"You…" Had gotten me into it, actually, what with giving me the dance concert tickets in the first place, but even so, I shook my head. "This is what I do, Rita. It's my job."

"You're a police officer," she said incredulously. "Werewolves aren't your job."

I pinched the bridge of my nose. "My duties encompass a lot more than your average cop's. Trust me. This is what I do. You didn't get me into anything I wouldn't have ended up in one way or another."

Morrison cocked his head, curious motion, but Rita remained unconvinced. "I'd still like to help if I can."

Feeling completely absurd, I said, "Morrison?"

He looked between us, then pulled his lips back from his teeth, indicating what he thought of the idea. Billy snorted and Rita scowled, obviously afraid we were making fun of her. Feeling even more absurd, I said, "Rita, this is our boss. Captain Morrison of the Seattle Police Department. I sort of have to do what he wants in this situation."

"...your boss is a werewolf?"

I was going to personally hunt down and bludgeon whoever it was who was responsible for werewolf legends. Never mind that it would no doubt require time travel and knowledge of languages which had long since slipped out of human memory. It would be worth it. While I worked up a response that wasn't "Arrrrgh!" Morrison got up, walked to Rita and sat down in front of her. He was nearly as tall as she was, which made making eye contact easy before he slowly, deliberately, swung his head back and forth in an emphatic *no*.

"Holy shit, he understood me! You understood me?"

Morrison nodded this time, big heavy bob of his head. Rita squeaked, "You're a cop? You're a *captain?*" and he nodded each time, showing infinitely more patience than I would have expected. Rita goggled at him, then at me, then wrenched her jaw up and said, much more quietly, "Do I really have to leave? It's my friends who are missing."

Morrison put his head to one side, sympathy in the motion, but nodded again, then gave me a gimlet stare. I stepped up, knowing exactly what he wanted me to say. "A few months ago a civilian got invo—" No. That was wrong. I backed up and started again. "I got a civilian involved in one of my cases, and she nearly got killed. Pulling that kind of stunt again will lose me my job. She volunteered, too," I said to Rita's unspoken protest. "But from where I'm sitting, where the captain's sitting, that doesn't make a lot of differ-ence. You understand?"

She wasn't a big woman, but she got smaller, shoulders

curving in and head lowering. "I understand. You'll find them, though, right? You'll all come back?"

"We'll do our best. And Rita? Thank you for bringing us down here. I know that made you nervous. You've been a lot of help."

She gave me a wavering smile, not one of the ones that took years off her age. "You're welcome." She looked at Morrison a moment, shrugged and said, "Nice to meet you, Captain," in a voice that suggested she'd probably lost her mind, but at this point was just going with it.

Morrison lifted his right front paw, quite solemnly, in an offer to shake. Rita's expression transformed, laughter running through her, and she shook his paw before climbing the rope ladder with more lightness than I'd expected twenty seconds earlier.

"Well," I said when she was gone. "Anybody bring any silver bullets?"

Billy and Morrison turned identical glowers of exasperation on me and, chastised once more, I led the way through the tunnels in search of a werewolf.

The Sight hadn't burned out my visual receptors or my brain when I'd used it in the Market, so I was cautiously willing to press it ahead of where we crawled and walked, hoping I'd get some sense of what lay ahead. Mostly I got a sense of open spaces beneath the city that I was sure no geological survey could be aware of. Or maybe all earth was riddled with pockets of emptiness and tunnels that sometimes went nowhere and sometimes connected; I had no idea. Unless given some kind of extenuating reason not to, like a sinkhole suddenly opening up, I tended to think of ground as solid. Still, apparently Robert Holliday's science report hadn't mentioned anything about tunnel-riddled bedrock beneath Seattle, so the fact we were working our way through non-old-city tunnels boded peculiar, if not ill. "Hey, Morrison, can you smell anything down here that isn't us?"

I peered over my shoulder as I asked, and got his nose-wrinkled expression of distaste in exchange. I took that as a yes. "Anything female?"

Morrison stopped dead in the middle of the tunnel, giving me an excellent wolfish glare. Billy backpedaled, trying not to trip over him as I spread my hands in self-defense. "What? Are you telling me you don't know what girls smell like?"

His nose wrinkled again, this time so delicately it looked like deliberate refrain from commentary on the smell of one particular girl, i.e., me. I turned back to the path, muttering, "I had no idea dogs were so expressive," and actually felt the snap of his teeth as he just narrowly missed biting me on the ass. I bet anything that meant "Wolves aren't dogs."

Evidently I'd put an idea in his head, though, because he pushed past me, head extended long and low as he scented the air. His ruff fluffed up and he glanced at me, then paced forward just slowly enough that we could keep up. I ducked through stretches of tunnel that Morrison fit through more tidily, Billy a few steps behind me, and we caught up to our boss at the mouth to a narrow natural cave dripping with water.

The brindle wolf stood at its far end, one paw lifted in a classic attentive pose. Morrison stood in exactly the same position, neither of them looking certain as to what to do next. I felt like a wildlife photographer who'd accidentally come across the shot of a lifetime, gold wolf and silver examining one another in a primal size-up. Then Tia wagged her tail in a blatantly come-hither sweep and leaped into the darkness at the cavern's far end.

Morrison *whurrfed,* a noise that was nothing at all like a human response to anything, and my stomach turned to lead. "Oh my God, Morrison, don't you dare."

He *whurrfed* again, then darted forward at a pace we measly humans couldn't hope to match, disappearing after the werewolf.

CHAPTER TWENTY-SEVEN

"Why..." Billy's voice sounded dreadfully thin and hollow, like he knew the answer to the question he was trying to ask, but hoped against hope I might have a response he liked better. "Why would he do that...?"

"It could be that he can keep up and we can't, so he's forging on ahead to keep tabs on her." It was the most harmless explanation I could come up with.

Sadly, Billy didn't believe it any more than I did. "You have to go after them before—before something awful happens."

I was pretty sure "something awful" loosely translated as "before Morrison bangs a she-wolf," but I wasn't nearly man enough to say it aloud, either. I just stood there, arrested by the potential horror of the situation unfolding somewhere ahead of us. Billy nudged me and I flinched. "I can't just leave you here. And I'm not even sure I can shift without..."

I waved a hand, attempting to encompass vague but terrible things with the gesture.

"Joanne," Billy said, firmly, "if you don't haul ass after them and stop Morrison from mating with a werewolf, obliterating Seattle with too much magic use is going to look like the preferable alternative once he's human again."

He was right, but I shook my head and jolted into a jog. "No, not unless I have no choice. We can catch up. How does this crap end up happening? I'm trying, Billy, I'm really trying to get things right, and my best efforts still end up with Morrison chasing a piece of ta—"

Billy burst out laughing and I threw a smirk over my shoulder at him as we ran for the far end of the cavern.

Nearly an hour later we'd squeezed through more tight spaces, damp stone and slippery earth than I'd imagined could exist. There were spurs going off all over the place, some too narrow to fit through, others far more wide and inviting than the areas we'd squished through. If it weren't for the paw prints leading us, we'd have been hopelessly lost, and as it was I had no concept at all of how far we'd come. Billy, behind me, panted as heavily as I did, which made me feel equal parts better and horribly guilty. We'd sloped down through most of our travels, and however deep we were, it was warm enough to be this side of muggy, and I wished I'd left my sweater behind. Not enough to take it off: it cushioned me against the rock spurs and the occasional fall, and didn't tear as easily as Billy's magnificent, ruined suit. I was going to have to learn to sew to make him a new one.

"Do you even know what direction we're headed?" he asked for the third or fourth time.

I bared my teeth at the darkness beyond the flashlight's reach, and said, patiently, "Not really, no. All I know is these

aren't natural caves and tunnels." I'd said that as many times
as he'd asked, but the repetition was almost better than the
silence. There was nothing quite like a zillion tons of earth
pressing down to give a girl a proper sense of mortality. And
that was from someone who'd been stabbed, hanged, skew-
ered and squished enough to make Jean Grey look like a
piker.

Of course, answering made me dwell on the aforemen-
tioned unnaturalness. It was increasingly clear to my damaged Sight that the areas we squeezed through were new
formations. Concerningly familiar silvers and blues ran
through them, mostly in vertical spikes, like someone had
taken a giant wedge and hammered it into the earth, then
rucked it back and forth a couple times to open spaces where
there hadn't been any before. There were other colors, too,
colors I recognized as remnants from the coven I'd worked
with briefly. Mostly, though, the lingering impression was
of me. One Joanne Walker, shaman extraordinaire, who had
rearranged Seattle's topography most of a year ago, apparently far more thoroughly than I'd realized.

Since the city hadn't collapsed in a giant sinkhole, I wasn't
too worried about the modifications to its underpinnings.
What I *was* concerned with was why anyone would bother
going this deep into the altered earth. I couldn't come up
with any reasons I liked, since an hour's fast walk through
muck and stone was a bit much for privacy's sake. Of course,
it probably wouldn't take a four-legged wolf nearly that long,
which thought I didn't much care for, either. Morrison could
get in a lot of trouble in an hour. I tested my magic again,
nervously, and felt it still sparking like a volcano waiting to
go off. Volcanoes under Seattle would be bad.

Billy said, "Hold up," all of a sudden, and I stopped dead,
clicking my flashlight off, as if its light made us vulnerable.

He flashed his own at me, somehow indicating irritation with the motion, but said nothing, and after a couple seconds I heard what had stopped him: water dripping.

More to the point, water *echoing*, like it had lots of room around it when it plopped to the ground. Below that, there was a dull rumble that reminded me of heavy machinery working in the distance. Frankly, if somebody had heavy machinery down here, I was going to be really irritated, because it meant there was a much more accessible way into the warm earth-scented burrows we'd made our way through. Then again, the temperature hadn't changed at all, so probably nobody up ahead of us had a Caterpillar making a nice smooth grade to the surface.

Billy tapped my shoulder. I turned and he put his finger over his lips, then gestured me forward before turning his own flashlight off. I put my hand on his chest, holding him in place until my eyes gradually picked up hints of light from well in front of us. I crept forward, hearing Billy's occasional breath that let me know he was still with me, and after a long few minutes in the dark, we edged our way into the mouth of an underground cavern.

About a million things were wrong with it. First, it existed at all. I didn't think that was good. It was of respectable size—I probably couldn't throw a baseball well enough to hit the far wall—and it seemed to me like somebody should have noticed a hole this big beneath Seattle. I was sure people came out with ultrasound machines to look for stuff just like this, but nobody'd ever mentioned it, not even after the earthquake. I tried, briefly, to remember the guy's name who'd found me in the earthquake's aftermath. He'd been a geologist. I bet he'd be plenty interested in an enormous, roughly circular pit somewhere under the city.

The second and larger thing wrong was that even with

the knotted-down Sight I was using, the whole place was
sheeted with magic. It imbued the walls and flowed out of
them, drizzling to the floor and wafting like fog across the
damp stone. Even the water condensed and dripping from
the ceiling was filled with power. Droplets and tiny streams
glowed in a not-even-slightly natural way, even given that
water, the stuff of life, tended to be rather radiant in the
Sight.

This was supercharged, radioactive-bright water, except
without the hideous dangerous auras I'd imagine actual ra-
dioactivity gave off. The point was, water, stone, the world
in general, wasn't normally so magic-laden that it looked
like a touch would explode it.

Which probably explained why my geologist pal hadn't
found the place. It seemed very possible the whole extensive
underground network was sufficiently power-ridden that
it actually didn't exist within the mundane world. It was
like somebody had opened pockets of another plane into the
Middle World.

That somebody, of course, was me. Unfortunately, that
was pretty much exactly what I'd done with the coven:
ripped a hole between my world and the Lower World, letting demons flood through and wreak a bit of havoc. I knew
it'd left scars—and a waterfall—on Seattle's surface, and all
of a sudden I was quite sure of just how far we'd traveled.
I sank back half a foot and breathed, "I think we're under
Thunderbird Falls," to Billy.

I was getting really good at reading people's unspoken
commentary. The look Billy gave me very clearly said *does
that really fucking* matter *right now?* I shrugged and went back
to studying the Things That Were Wrong, going so far as
to shut the Sight down briefly so I saw only the normal
world.

There were flickering torches set high in the stone. Their smoke wafted up, trapped by water-dripping limestone, and never managed to make an escape: even knowing they were there, I could barely catch the scent of flame and smoke. Their light reflected off damp walls and a low shallow pool at the cavern's far side, giving the whole place an otherworldly glimmer even without the Sight.

It was, however, just slightly possible that the otherworldly aura was dramatically enhanced by a thirty-foot-tall wicker man in the cave's center.

He—and it was alarmingly clear it was a he—was raw and fresh-looking, as though the trees used to weave him had only recently been stripped and woven together. He was strong, though: his architect had done a good job supporting his thick, stubby arms. I could tell because cages dangled from the ends of each, like thief cages of old hung at crossroads to warn travelers that the locals meant business when it came to crime.

Except they weren't peopled with thieves. Both of them had a single person in them, wearing the sort of eclectic, cobbled-together outfits Rita wore. Her missing compatriots, squished into short uncomfortable wicker coops. Nor were they the only two: the wicker man's sturdy legs each contained another person, as did his torso. His head looked large enough to hold a sixth person, but it was empty, and I wondered if Lynn Schumacher had been intended for that spot.

Worse, I wondered if Morrison would take his place.

There was no immediate sign of my wayward boss, but we were too low to see beyond piles of shredded wood that lay around the wicker man's feet. I didn't like that pile. It suggested bonfires, and I had the vague, uncomfortable idea that wicker men often came to fiery endings. I was not about to watch one wicker man and five real men burn to death, regardless of what else happened. My overenthusiastic magic would have to come to heel, or I would—

Distressingly, the only way I could think to finish that idea was *or I would risk knocking a hole through to the world above*, which would have been just fine if I wasn't really quite sure we were beneath Lake Washington. I mean, yes, that would be better than exploding a hole in downtown Seattle, but in terms of a dramatic rescue it would be an utter failure. I didn't want to save these guys from burning to death only to drown them.

Images of shielding them all in bubbles and letting them bob to the surface came to mind, complete with *pop-pop-popping* sound effects. Great. I had a backup plan, in case everything went stupidly, spectacularly wrong. Too bad I didn't have a decent primary plan.

Billy elbowed me and nodded toward the firewood ring just as movement caught my eye, too. Tia paced out of the ring like Lady Godiva sans the horse. A moment later Morrison, still very much a wolf, trotted after her, his head nearly level with her ribs. There were worse places for it to be level with, all things considered. Billy widened his eyes at me and I shrugged, as wide-eyed as he was. I didn't know what had been going on behind the wooden ring. I was pretty sure I didn't want to know. I had a horrible feeling that at some point, I'd find out.

The idea made me exhale just a little too loudly. Morrison's ears cocked and he looked my way, but Tia didn't. Apparently werewolves didn't retain canine senses in human form. I filed that away under "Thank God for small favors" and stayed where I was, stomach clenched as Morrison gave me a long, steady look to make it clear he knew I was there.

A flicker of hope danced through me. Maybe he *had* chased Tia in order to keep an eye on her. Maybe it hadn't just been wolfy instinct out to get him—and eventually me—into trouble.

Nah. Nothing was ever that easy. I almost smiled, and Morrison caught up to Tia with a couple of loping steps, evidently uninterested in Billy and me. Billy performed a soundless collapse of relief which would have done Charlie Chaplin proud. I wanted to follow suit, but I remained as I was, tense and wide-eyed, for just a few seconds longer while I tried like hell to make out what was supposed to happen in this underground cavern.

A sacrifice, obviously: people didn't go around randomly constructing wicker men in magic-born, power-filled chambers and then stuffing the wicker men full of expendables just for the fun of it. But if there were werewolf gods, I knew nothing about them, including why they might want sacrifices, or whether this might be an annual thing or just a special occasion.

A penny dropped, quick twist of certainty at the back of my mind: it was a special occasion. The same special occasion which prompted the ghost dance killing. The moon was full, or would be tonight, and the equinox was only another day away. It still wasn't a perfect alignment like it had been the year before for the banshee murders, but it was close enough.

The only question was, close enough for *what*. Not that it mattered, particularly: it wasn't very likely Tia would sit down, explain it all and make such sense that I'd say, "Oh, well, okay, go ahead then, light 'em up." A burble of relief slipped through me. I was a full day ahead of schedule, with the full moon not being until tonight. Between being here early and having stopped another ghost dance murder, for once I had the upper hand. Particularly since Morrison hadn't informed his new lady love that we were there. All I had to do was tiptoe up and bash her unconscious without being noticed, and we could get all our answers later.

It sounded like a respectable Plan A. I very cautiously triggered the tamped-down Sight again, hoping it wouldn't blast my eyeballs out. It merely filtered on, the way it was supposed to. Pleased, I tapped Billy's shoulder and went into a complicated mime routine trying to explain what I intended to do. After about thirty seconds of playing peekaboo, which completely failed to get across the idea of "I'm going to wrap myself in an invisibility cloak," he rolled his eyes, mouthed, "Just do it," and hunched back down to await my antics.

If the Sight could knock me senseless for a couple minutes, I could hardly imagine how badly something that inherently screwed with the laws of physics might end up if I wasn't careful. I delved into my magic more delicately than I'd ever done, trying not to do more than scrape enough off its surface to bend light around myself. Even those tiny scrapes left bright silver-white marks, like I was coming dangerously close to unleashing power I was totally unprepared to deal with. If I had to do anything fast while we were down here, that Plan B with the bubble shields might well come in necessary.

Gradually I felt like I'd succeeded, but one of the problems with this trick was I could still see myself. In fact, I was pretty sure it violated laws of physics all over the place, since I could also see *out* of my invisibility cloak, which technically I shouldn't be able to do. Magic, however, wasn't physics. I tapped Billy's shoulder again and he flinched, suggesting he couldn't see me. Satisfied, I crept forward, flashlight knotted in my hand like the bludgeoning tool it was shortly to be used as.

Morrison and Tia had gone halfway around the wicker man, Tia stopping every few feet to examine something. I paused where she had, trying to see what she'd seen, but gave it up after a couple of attempts and edged around the circle as quickly and quietly as I could, until I was opposite Billy and only a few yards from my furry boss and his golden-haired girlfriend.

Tia scruffed the top of Morrison's head and said something inaudible to him. He lay down immediately, chin on his paws, but his whole body quivered like a dog who wasn't at all sure he wanted to do as he was told. I wondered abruptly who was the boss in a wolf pack, the alpha male or the alpha female. In an awful lot of pack structures, the males were there for protection and breeding, and the females ruled the roost. Morrison looked very much like his roost was being ruled. Tia crouched to scruff him again and he lay flatter, ears and tail full of displeased body language, but Tia ignored him as she laid a hand on the wooden ring she'd built.

Fire exploded everywhere.

CHAPTER TWENTY-EIGHT

I hit the nearest cave wall with my spine and slithered down whimpering with pain and confusion. The wicker man's firewood ring was fully ablaze, pouring off heat that turned dampness on walls to steam, and though the wicker man himself wasn't yet on fire, his occupants were shrieking bloody, terrified murder. That seemed perfectly reasonable, and any second now I was going to extricate my backbone from stone and leap forth to rescue them. Any second now. Honest.

Rather than engaging in that activity, though, my brain insisted on whirring around the idea that setting the wicker man alight now, before the fullest moon, made no sense. There were five human beings in that thing. Just the right number for points of a pentagram, if that sort of thing was important, though if the poor bastard in the torso had been in the head I'd have thought it more likely to be relevant.

On the other hand, the torso was probably sturdier. A sufficiently motivated kidnap victim might be able to wrench the head off. Or maybe Lynn really had been intended to fill that last space, and the guy in the torso represented heart's blood. Given what had happened to Naomi's heart, that didn't seem impossible, either.

This was a lousy time to hypothesize. I tried straightening up and discovered part of the reason I'd been sitting there was for the second time that night, moving hurt like hell. The healing magic within me was going gangbusters again, and I kind of didn't want to know just how much damage I'd sustained bashing into the rough cave walls.

I could almost hear Coyote's scolding: "If you would remember your shields, Joanne, this kind of thing wouldn't happen." I nodded obediently, trying to make a note. Mental shields were all well and good, but when someone had been put on a warrior's path, she probably ought to make a habit of permanent physical shields as well. I promised myself I'd get on that as soon as I could walk again. A deep breath made my back crack, and I thought maybe I had another thirty seconds or a minute before I trusted all my parts to properly do their thing.

Thirty seconds was a long time in terms of dry wood and smoke inhalation. Teeth gritted, I shoved myself upward. Black swam through my vision and I clenched my eyes shut, determined not to pass out. I was not going to let people die because of a measly cracked spine.

Tia Carley put her hand around my throat and strong-armed me up the wall.

Her eyes were fire-gold, like she drew on magic to have the strength to hold me there. Like the flames behind her fed her, for that matter: she was beautiful in their light.

Dangerous, bonkers and scary, but beautiful. I clawed my hands around her wrist, trying to loosen her fingers, but she squeezed a bit harder, making it difficult to get purchase.

"Shaman. Healer. You're even better than the dancers. That was you there tonight, wasn't it? Shielding them? I *tried*," she said with a note of petulancy. "I tried to scoop your magic last night after you healed me."

Ah. That had been the nosing-about I'd felt. It hadn't felt like an attack, but perhaps she'd been being careful. Or maybe my shields had been well in place for once. If I had a time machine I'd go back and check, but I didn't, so I just hung there on the wall clawing at her wrist while she added, "Breast cancer," incredulously. "What kind of bullshit is that? I'm barely even human, and you waltz up and tell me I'm going to die of breast cancer? That I've got a predisposition for it? That bitch queen screwed us even more than I knew."

I said, "Bitch queen?" except with her hand crushing my larynx, it came out a lot more like "Kakghk agggh?" Pain erupted in my stomach, the familiar feel of fishhooks hauling me somewhere else. I wished they'd haul me out from Tia's grasp, but they weren't nearly that accommodating. They didn't really have to be, though: she'd grabbed me too high, under the jawbone, which meant I wasn't going to choke out anytime soon. I only needed another ten seconds or so to get my spine in alignment and then I was going to kick her naked pansy ass from here to eternity.

"Doesn't matter. I've got you now. I won't need the dancers tomorrow."

Goddamn it. Three nights of power. Three nights of ghost dances. Three nights of sacrifices. I'd prevented Winona's death earlier, which was probably why the wicker man's denizens were getting toasty tonight. They'd almost certainly been intended for tomorrow night's party. But I'd shown up on the scene, so Tia was improvising, and damned if she wasn't doing it well.

I stiff-handed her in the throat.

It wasn't what I wanted to do. I really wanted to kick her in the gut so hard she'd fly back and land in her own bonfire, but I didn't have room to pull my legs up that far. Besides, it would've been telegraphed, whereas unwrapping one hand from the grip at my throat and jabbing the eighteen inches to *her* throat took almost no effort.

Her grip weakened satisfyingly and she dropped me. I fell to my hands and toes and sprang forward, tackling her. I had two inches and at least twenty pounds on her. One solid slam against stone and a fist to her jaw should have been all it took.

Except instead of landing on top of a wheezing, gasping woman, I landed on top of a snarling, snapping wolf, and the fist I was driving toward its face suddenly looked very small and vulnerable in comparison to all those teeth. I pulled the punch and got a paw across my face for my troubles. My glasses went flying and pain erupted where claws scored their mark. Half a second later we'd both twisted and flung ourselves aside to land on our feet, Tia on all fours, me on just the two. I couldn't see well out of my left eye, puffy flesh and tears already marring my vision. Aggravatingly, that was the eye I had better vision in, so although I was by no means debilitated, Tia's edges were a little softer than I might have liked. It didn't matter. If I could see well enough to drive without my glasses, I could certainly see well enough to beat a werewolf into next week without them.

She leaped at me and I ducked into the attack, shouldering up to catch her chest and use her own momentum against her. She went a lot farther than either of us expected, hitting the ground with a yelp that turned to furious growling. I spun, ready to catch her the same way again, but she darted around me and came in for my hamstrings, moving faster than I'd known wolves could do. I jammed my hips forward, narrowly keeping my legs out of her teeth, and it struck me, a little belatedly, that an unarmed human versus a wolf was probably shit out of luck.

I reached for my sword, and got a shock when it refused to come at my call.

Tia circled around and flattened me in the moment I stood there dumbstruck, her full weight bearing down as she drove her teeth at my throat. Smacking my head against stone was a sufficient wake-up call to get me in action again, though my brain was a static mess of bewilderment. Fighting, though, wasn't necessarily a brainy thing to do. I grabbed two fistfuls of Tia's ruff and kicked her in the belly, using leg strength to throw her over my head. I caught a glimpse of a magnificent aerial twist and she landed on her feet, facing me but still skidding backward from momentum. It gave me enough time to roll to my own feet and try again to call my sword to me.

I got a sensation of magnets interacting: magics rejecting each other, rebounding when they tried to meet. Then Tia had her feet under her again and was charging forward. I threw myself sideways, landing alarmingly near the bonfire. It was picking up serious heat, now that I noticed it: all the cave's dampness had been sucked away and the close quarters were making air thin and dry. I doubted Tia had considered that when she chose the cavern as her magical roasting pit. Her captives were screaming and coughing, and frustration tore through me. Short of bringing down the ceiling, I didn't know how to magically put a fire out, and any experimentation would give Tia more than enough opportunity to chew me into little bits. It had to be one crisis at a time, but I didn't see how I was going to get everybody out of there alive, that way. Not without throwing myself wholesale into a magic whose topped-up, shiny new strength didn't yet have any grasp on consequences or limitations.

Tia came at me again, and the time for debate ended. I whispered, *Rattler, help?*, and when Tia hit me, it was a coyote she rolled backward over the broad stone floor.

There was something to be said for the element of surprise. She had, perfectly reasonably, expected to smash into a six-foot-tall, hundred-and-sixty-five-pound woman. The same amount of coyote was a whole different mouthful, pretty much literally: her teeth snapped on where my throat should have been, but I'd changed shape so radically she caught air half a foot from my skull instead. Almost without losing momentum, she jumped away again, then spun back to gape at me, an expression as comical on a wolf as it was on a human. Then she fell back a few more steps, hackles rising warily.

Part of my brain—the part that was pure coyote, I imagined—informed me that wolves were bigger and stronger than coyotes. That they were a higher-apex predator, and that I shouldn't mess with one. But that part didn't take into account the magic at work with both of us. Tia was broader than I, musculature heavier and more compact. I was rangier, longer-legged and therefore theoretically faster. She no doubt had far more experience fighting in canine form, but I outweighed her any day of the week and twice on Sundays. Even my canine mind was starting to think it looked like a fair fight, and I could almost see Tia's own wolf-brain calculating just what the hell its odds were against a coyote bigger than itself. Feeling confident, I took a step forward.

And tangled myself in my jeans. Tia's lips pulled back from her teeth in a distinctly wolfish grin. She charged as I scrambled and kicked my way free of the pants. My sweater and T-shirt were a constrictive mess, but they were also a barrier: I crashed to the side and her teeth snagged in knitted cotton, tearing it but not me. She turned again, snarling, and this time I deliberately let her grab a mouthful of sweater, then used her ferocious, angry tugging to help me back out of it. The T-shirt loosened instantly, no longer as twisted around my body, and I chalked it up to good enough as I swung to face my opponent.

My vision erupted. Every flicker of movement suddenly caught my attention: Tia, minutely shifting her weight as she tried to decide whether to press the attack. That was fine. That was detail I wanted.

Flame darting in and out of existence was *not* detail I wanted. Every lick that reached for the wicker man or the ceiling caught my attention, dragging it away from the imminent assault. Trickles of water I'd thought steamed away glittered at the cave's top edges, tiny droplets forming beautiful, shining, distracting jewels. Terrified men scrabbled and reached out of the wicker man, trying to escape somehow; acting like prey animals, making me want to pounce and bite and tear. Bits of branch fell away inside the fire ring, their disintegration to charcoal and ash vivid and compelling. Smoke roiled up, fascinating in its curls. *Everything* demanded my full regard, and my brain shrieked, trying to process the overload of motion surrounding me.

I collapsed, paws over my eyes, and howled a miserable cry against stone. It echoed, rebounded and came back to me as the cries of frightened humans; as the snap and bite of flame in the air; as the hiss of steam and the drip of water. Tia's breath, far too quiet for any reasonable chance at being heard, scraped at my ears with its harshness, and the clack of her claws against stone sounded like apocalyptic drums, pounding in the end of the world.

And her *smell*. Not human, not animal, but something in between. Not even like Morrison, whose scent leaped to my attention over the fire and smoke and steam. Somehow he had been one thing, man and man-scented, and now was the other, wolf and wolf-scented, but Tia was neither and both. Transforming would never change her scent: she would always smell half-wild, musky, carnivore, to a nose sensitive enough to catch it. I didn't know how I'd missed it at the theater, it was so obvious to me now. Everything, *everything* was obvious, so obvious as to pound me down, a sensory overload I was totally unprepared to deal with. Exploding the amulet, being bowled over by too-vivid Sight; those things had warned me about the price of untempered magic, but this was a thousand times worse. This was the world hammering into me, taking full advantage of the enhanced senses a coyote had over a human.

For one brief, horrifying moment I wondered just how badly I could have damaged the world around me if I'd tried an external magic rather than one as internal as shapeshifting, and then the world, in the form of Tia Carley's lupine self, came up and laid the smacketh down.

I was already on the floor, flat as I could get, as if spreading myself thin might reduce the raging strength of sensory attack. She landed on me with a crunch, and to my eternal gratitude, it appeared my sense of touch hadn't been blown beyond the edge of coping. Possibly being hit by a semi and then thrown into a wall had already pushed it beyond its ability to respond any further, but I didn't care. At least there was one aspect of a too-loud, too-vivid, too-smelly world I wasn't entirely inundated by. Heartened by that one small gift, I surged upward, shaking Tia off before she got her teeth into me. Teeth, ugh: I bet my sense of taste had been upgraded, too, and I gagged on the memory of the theater door handle.

The world seemed a little less overpowering once I was back on my feet. I shook myself, then let out what was meant to be a barbaric shout, something to expel excess energy from within me. It came out a series of tripping howls and yips, not very barbaric at all, though it was plenty wild, and to my huge relief, it did batter down some of the extreme-sports levels of attention I was paying to everything.

And like it had physical presence, it dampened some of the fire. Inside a breath or two, the air was cooler, smelling less of flame and smoke and more of terrified, unwashed humans. I sneezed, made a mental note to apologize to Morrison for laughing at him when we'd walked through the stinky sections of Underground, and staggered in a clumsy line, trying to shake off the last of the blowout's after-effects.

Clearly they'd only affected me. My head was still ringing when Tia slammed into me from the side, knocking us both into sooty but not-flaming firewood. I caught a glimpse of one of the caged men above me, his expression twisted with bewildered relief: whatever was going on, he wasn't going to roast to death in the next three minutes, which made his life a whole lot better than it had been thirty seconds ago.

Which made *my* life seem a whole lot better than it had thirty seconds ago. I twisted under Tia, got my teeth dangerously closer to her jaws, and then for the first time in my life, found myself in the middle of a dogfight.

I'd seen them, of course. Usually just brief spates, two animals suddenly making themselves a single roiling ball of teeth and claws and snarls. Nobody in their right mind

wanted to get in the middle of that: it was obviously dangerous, and a fire hose seemed like the best way to break it up.

From inside, a fire hose seemed like the best way to break
it up. I had no idea how to win this fight, but I didn't have
to: my coyote brain knew exactly what to do in a tussle with
another dog. Tia moved one way; I was there to meet her.
I jerked another direction; she was there to stop me. Claws
and teeth flashed, striking scores. Fur flew, and the animalistic scent/taste of her blood settled in my teeth. We smashed
into the wicker man's foot, a fact I knew only because the
guy inside it screamed.

Tia, infuriated, broke from me to go after him. I jumped
after her, astonished at how far I could move in a single leap,
and bore her to the ground with my superior weight. She
flipped on her back before I could get my teeth into her
neck, and we were at it again, muzzles in each other's faces,
canines slashing and trying to hit vulnerable territory.

Then as fast as we'd come together, we broke apart again,
both of us circling and snarling, waiting for another moment
to attack. My lungs burned with effort and every nerve in
my body was ratcheted up as I slunk around, head lowered,
ears back, teeth bared.

It felt fantastic. It felt brutal, ugly, dangerous, *alive,* and I
didn't know if it was the animal or the human in me that
loved it. I feared it was the human: animals didn't fight for
fun, not like this. They fought for dominance or survival. I
didn't think they walked away from fights triumphant, not
the way people did, and I didn't know if the warrior's path
I was on meant if it was okay to revel in warfare while in
animal form.

Tia came at me one last time, and it ceased to matter.

CHAPTER TWENTY-NINE

Smoke and flame and blood: those were the scents in Tia's fur and in the whole of the cavern. I had no time to look, but I thought the reprieve was over. Whatever my little magic overload had done, it hadn't put all the fire out, and it was picking up speed again. I had to quit screwing around, for all that torn fur and blurred vision and general heaving and panting suggested I hadn't been screwing around at all. Part of me screamed to finish it, to end the battle in as brutal and final a manner as necessary.

But I was a human in coyote's clothing, and like it or not, Tia was at least partially human under her own lupine coat. Decent humans did not go around killing one another. But we weren't exactly in the right physical forms to sit down and discuss the matter, and I seriously doubted Tia would shift back to her beautiful naked human self if I went that route. In her shoes—or paws—I'd just jump on me and rip my throat out. Which, as far as I could tell, pretty much left me with the option to do unto her before she did unto me.

I'd already shot somebody this week. I was not delighted with the prospect of causing grievous physical harm, by which I meant almost certain death, to a second party inside forty-eight hours.

Knowing I would lose time and ground, knowing I would almost certainly regret it, I went within and whispered, *Rattler? Raven? Guide me?*

We ssstrike, Rattler replied instantly. He was a white streak against blackness in my mind, barely there, as if he, no more than I, hadn't yet fully recovered from the blast at the theater. But he was confident in his response, which was more than I could claim. *We hunt, we shift, we heal. Life is sssacred, shaman. Yours no lessss than othersss.* Theirsss *no lessss than othersss,* and I knew he meant the men trapped in the wicker man above me. *You did not ssstart this battle,* he told me. *There isss no shame in finishing it.*

Good enough, from a predator. I repeated *Raven?,* and my other guide soared out of darkness, power flexing with each beat of his wings.

It shed light on a field of war. There was nothing familiar about it, none of the tanks or guns or trenches from the past century or more of warfare. Instead, a few surviving horses picked their way across bloody, mashed-down grass, and whickered in distress at the bloody short swords and leather armor that lay on and around innumerable human bodies.

Ravens by their dozens dropped to those bodies and sank talons into dead flesh, then rose again with souls clawed in their feet. They winged into the sky as if burdened by the weights they carried, and one by one winked out, carrying the dead into another world. They returned as rapidly as they'd left, falling to earth again and again, ferrying mortal souls into and through the Dead Zone to whatever lay beyond.

And when their duties were done, when no more souls were left to draw from one world to the next, they quite horribly landed on the bodies and began to gobble the choicest bits: eyes, torn bellies, tongues from open, once-screaming mouths.

I gagged and clenched my eyes shut against the vision, which was remarkably ineffective against something playing in my mind. Raven swept his wings again and wiped away the images, then gave me a beady look from first one eye, then the other. I swallowed bile and said *Yeah,* hoarsely, which I thought was a pretty good trick for a non-vocalized response. *I think I get it. Death's part of the cycle, right? If that's what it takes…?*

He gave a satisfied *quark!* and both my spirit animals disappeared to leave me bowled over and rolling through firewood with Tia Carley's teeth snapping at my throat.

I'd clearly missed a couple rounds while I was talking to my guides. We'd scattered from the wicker man and knocked embers and brush over half the cave. I smelled burned fur, and it wasn't all Tia: coyote fur somehow had its own special stink when it burned, distinct and separate from toasted wolf. There was more blood than there'd been, too, some of it tinged with my scent, some of it with Tia's. I hurt in new places all over my body.

I had spent a lot of time hurting in new places the last several hours, and it was starting to piss me off. I writhed under Tia's weight, flinging her away, and charged after her single-mindedly, leaping the fire ring again to put us right back under the wicker man. She'd started this fight, what with murdering Naomi Allison and probably Lynn Schumacher,

never mind the more literal attack just a few minutes ago.
She'd started it, but I was by God going to finish it.

With that thought, I let most of my rational mind go.

I'd been right. My longer legs and rangier form gave me
a speed advantage, once I gave in to the coyote form. Tia
rushed me and I spun to the side, cornered on one foot, and
tore flesh from her haunch as she crashed by me. Her yelp
was pure soprano pain and fury, but when she came back at
me, I was already gone.

Gone *up*, in a leap very much like the one I'd performed
outside the theater when people'd started screaming. Coyotes were springy like Tiggers, a great mass of potential able
to leap straight up and dive forward to catch a rabbit. Or in
this case, a wolf: I landed on Tia's hindquarters. She collapsed under my weight, which probably wouldn't happen
with a normal wolf and coyote, and in her surprise, flipped
over to engage in another whirlwind struggle of tooth and
claw. But I already had the upper hand, and no compunction
against using my greater weight to keep her pinned.

Panic soured her scent as I crawled up her body, and her
struggles altered from attacking to escaping. Her back claws
raked my stomach and I snarled with pain, but disembowel-
ing me would take more time than she had. There was one
thing she could do to—if not win, then at least not perma-
nently lose—this fight, and she was much too deep in wolf-
mind to think of shifting shape.

Grim and determined, I sank my teeth into her throat and
held on.

Blood, salty, tangy, sweet, flooded my tongue. I wanted
to be all coyote, all predator, all beast, so that all the blood
meant to me was survival. I couldn't divorce myself that far:
I knew all too well that it meant Tia was dying, too. She'd

murdered at least two people. In a dog-eat-dog world, that certainly meant she deserved what was coming to her.

But coyotes weren't dogs.

I eased off just a fraction, certain Tia had already lost enough blood to reduce her aggressiveness. I was right: she flinched and gave me a wild stare, scrabbled a little, then lay still, gold eyes wide on mine. Her breathing was fractured, blood pumping into my mouth with each gasp. It drooled out again past my teeth and gums, taste growing more bitter. More like death, I thought, and in weariness, released her.

She surged once, trying to regain her feet. I put my—paw; it was still a paw—out, placing it over the bleeding holes in her throat, and let my shoulders sink. Whispered, *Rattler,* one last time, and dreamed myself human again.

Blinding power deluged me, this time ripping away all the rich, overwhelming senses of the coyote form. It was as debilitating to be human as it had been to be a coyote: suddenly I was blind, physically weak, unable to scent, barely able to hear. Nearby fire was hotter against my mostly-bare skin than it had been against fur, the air drier and less comfortable to breathe, but I could hardly smell the flame. I wanted to cry, bereft of the animalistic world, but instead I leaned forward, numb human senses all I had at my disposal, and risked calling the healing magic that was my birthright.

It responded: that was never the fear. It responded brilliantly, an outpouring of strength more significant than I'd ever commanded. I clenched a fist over Tia's throat, throttling my own magic back to something more manageable: I had no desire to repeat the cancer incident. Just like always, I still needed control, not raw power.

The fire ring, battered and broken as it was, was a place of ritual. Condemnable ritual, maybe, but ritual. I extended my other hand toward its boundaries and split my concentration: one part of me holding Tia in stasis a few seconds, not yet healing her, and the other part lighting up a power circle in what had, moments earlier, been a sacrificial monument.

The cave itself responded, magic flowing from its walls into the floor and then upward around the circle I created. Feeling like I hadn't spoken in years, I said, "Raven," out loud.

He dropped from the ceiling, a sketch of light and wings, to land by Tia's head. A look of unmistakable greed crossed his birdy face, and I chuckled despite myself. "No. Her pretty gold eyes aren't for you to eat. I'll bring you shiny food later, Raven. Right now she's dying and I need you to help me walk the line and bring her back."

The bird tucked his beak into his ruff and gave me a disbelieving stare. I said, "I know," very quietly. "You gave me the all-clear. The warrior's path permits her death. Maybe it even encourages it. But it's not what I want, Raven. I don't mind being a fighter. I can kill, if I have to. But I don't have to this time. I'm going to find another way. Will you help me?"

Raven *klok*ed as softly as I'd spoken, then sprang up and beat wing around the circle, stopping four times to crash his wings against it. Cardinal directions, I expected; power criss-crossed me as he smacked the final line into place, and I felt something uncoil within me. Rattler unwound from my abdomen, a thing of light and lines just as Raven was, and inclined his head to me, as if respecting the choice I'd made. He stretched out along Tia like he'd done to me earlier on the street, then hissed once in anticipation. It had only been seconds, but it felt like I had been holding back power forever when I finally released it, trusting Raven and Rattler to be my tempering.

The healing itself was easy, with two spirit guides and the untapped magic pounding through me. Rattler's first gift had been the sloughing away of all my time-consuming visualizations, all my vehicle metaphors and layering processes that had let me heal before he came to me. Both patient and healer only needed the right mindset, the acceptance of the basic shamanic belief that life was change, and change could be effected instantaneously. I *knew* it could be done, and it was easier on a canine mind, even one burying a human mind within it, than it would have been on a conscious human. Inside one breath she was bleeding out from the throat; inside the next, she was listless from blood loss, but whole. Even burned patches of fur were restored, and all the smaller wounds from our fight disappeared.

Awakening outrage lit Tia's eyes and she writhed under my hand, which still lay tight against her throat. I shook my head, denying her escape. Pinning her down not just with my weight, but with sheets of silver-blue magic. Contempt flashed across her face, expressed by a curled-back lip that exposed her canines. I felt a surge of power as she attempted to transform from wolf to human shape.

It should have worked. Hours earlier, it had: I'd been unable to hold her behind shields in the moment of transformation, one magic canceling the other out. But I had Rattler with me now, and he lay coiled around Tia like she was his own oversize stuffed animal. Her shifting powers were inherent, as much a part of her as her nose, but Rattler was a master of shapechanging, as would be any creature which shed its skin. Between his will and mine, she would remain in wolf form until I chose otherwise.

And choose I did. My magic already lay in her flesh, from the wild and exhausting battle against cancer all the way to the healing I'd just performed. I let it sink deeper, searching inside for the gift, or the curse, that made her what she was.

Werewolf, no question about it; the word itself was a point of pride to her. A point of vulnerability, too: it meant so much that it offered me a path into a deep part of her soul, a place I had no business going.

I went.

A man-made stone hill of ridiculous height swelled up before me, then faded again, leaving behind a vaguely recognizable afterimage: steep sides, a broad flat top and greenery below; one hill built on another. Then it was gone entirely, a midnight garden growing around me. Ancient woods with massive, wide-spread trees and thin undergrowth littered a rolling landscape, forty shades of green. But something unhealthy discolored its beauty. Darkness turned greens to ichory black and throttled the life from the great trees. I'd never entered a garden that felt rotten to—or from—the core; even my own Spartan internal world was only that, not spoiled. I turned cautiously, wishing I had my sword in hand, but tight-woven shields would have to do.

A cave mouth, alarmingly familiar, lay to my left. Last time I'd seen it, a rockslide had been pulled into it, blocking it. Now, though, it was open to the world, and a mewling black beast crawled from it as I watched. It was followed by two more, all of them nasty little things covered in slime, though they rolled and rubbed themselves in dry moss until the goop came off. They got bigger as they rolled, shedding the worst of their ugliness and taking on a more common-place form: wolves, born from the bowels of the earth. They paced toward me without seeing me, growing larger with each step, until they were in front of me, and abruptly, all at once, threw off their lupine bodies to become women every bit as striking as Tia Carley was.

I shot a compulsive glance at the night sky. The moon was quartered, just enough to spill light through the wide-spaced trees. Not, certainly, the full moon werewolves were legendarily bound to.

The three women leaped into canine form again, leaving one another behind. I followed one, inhumanly quick on my feet as I often was in gardens; no need to change form here, for which I was grateful. My quarry stopped often, becoming human, seducing and killing men—always men, never women—and moving on. Time and again she met with her sisters, all of them vicious with killing pleasure, and as weeks rolled into years it because obvious these beasts were by no means tied to the moon. Their power came from somewhere else: from the cave they'd crawled from, and from the being who lay somewhere within it. A banshee had called him the Master, and what little I knew about him said that if werewolves were his creatures, the world would be a better place if they were eradicated.

Time, as if in response to my thought, warped forward. The three wolf sisters came together and faced a woman with light-colored hair. She was unarmed and unafraid, waiting on three killers beneath the light of what was now a full moon, and when they were within a dozen feet of her, she knelt and put her hands in the earth.

Shockingly, I recognized the gesture. I'd used it myself, calling up a power circle to contain a wendigo only a few months earlier. Magic sprang up for her as it had done for me, flares bringing my attention to a huge circle of standing stones so distant from us and from one another that I'd never have noticed them without the magic suddenly flowing through them.

I didn't understand a word of the language she shouted in, but I didn't need to: its effects were vivid and obvious. The wolf sisters collapsed in on themselves, writhing, howling, twisting as their very bodies were reshaped. As the magic inside them was countermanded by someone else, their master howled up out of the darkness to object. The fair-haired woman slapped his presence away as if he was nothing more than an annoying bug. The moon rose and set and rose again as the woman worked her magic, and on the final night, the third night of the full moon, she left the sisters beaten and battered, but not dead. Come morning, they staggered to their feet and tested their shapeshifting skills, and found themselves as werewolves of legend were: bound to human form all but three nights of the month.

Cursed to human form: that was the word Tia had used. The fair-haired woman had cursed them to near-mortality, and in doing so used more magic than I'd ever seen anyone do. My stomach lurched, pulling me toward that show of power, and for the first time in my life I actually wanted to follow. To find out who she was, and to study with her, learning what more I might be able to do.

I would, I promised myself. Very soon, I would. But time twisted again, dragging me out of the midnight garden I thought represented the past, and thrust me into a spiky angry garden I was reasonably certain represented Tia's current situation. Thorns dragged at me, prickling protests that told me what she'd been trying to do, though having touched on the Master's presence in a world gone away, I almost knew already.

So much power necessary to break the fair-haired woman's spell. The troupe with their transformative dances, with the enormous gathering of healing magic meant for so many people, offered her almost the only chance she would ever have to break the magic binding her to a mostly-mortal life. She was sick, from her ancestors' points of view; all the werewolves through history were, tied as they'd been to the moon. Only healing magic could cure that. Three nights of the dancers' power sucked up might have been enough to counter the ancient magic. Failing that, having discovered *me*, my own talent might be enough to rip apart a spell set millennia ago.

And only the death of innocents could feed the Master, who was weak. I'd interrupted his feeding a year ago; my own mother had done the same, almost thirty years prior to that. He had to be starving by now, but a wicker man full of people who'd done nothing to deserve death might have offered him enough appetizer to lend Tia's desperate transformative magic a little strength. It would certainly endear her to him, so if he should ever loosen himself from the rubble holding him down, he might turn some aspect of his power to freeing her from the constraints her kind had been put under centuries ago. As far as hedging bets went, it was a good call.

Except I wasn't going to let her do it. Not on any level, not tonight, not ever. I reached for Rattler, feeling his comforting presence, and turned my attention to Tia.

Judge, jury, executioner. That was the role I'd seen Big Coyote in, in his white-hot desert. I played the same one now, without compunction. I knew now what the anomaly I'd seen in her DNA was. Not the cancer which had attacked her, but a twist of genetics that made her other than human. I *unwound* that spur, unthreaded it and filed it down with a rattlesnake's rattler made raspy, made it smooth and even, nothing unusual about it. It felt almost gentle, the push of magic that slowly altered the wolf under my hands into a woman again, but I wasn't kidding myself. There was nothing gentle or kind about what I was doing. It was ruthless and brutal and I had no doubt at all Tia would probably rather die than be changed the way I was changing her.

That would have to be her choice, though. I wasn't going to make it for her.

I finally sat back, letting go the magic that pinned her down as I let go the healing—if I could call it that—magic as well. Tia's eyes opened and I saw—only saw, didn't feel—her reach for the shapeshifting magic; saw her try to become what she'd been, a massive, dangerous beast who preyed on those weaker than herself.

Saw her try, and saw her fail, the magic no longer hers to command. No longer an active part of her, though I wasn't really certain I'd stripped it away entirely; I wasn't sure that could be done. But it would take years at best for her to find it again, and I thought a lifetime might not be enough.

Her screams tore at my skin as I got up to find my clothes.

CHAPTER THIRTY

The cavern, which I had by and large failed to pay any attention to, was filled with enough smoke to provide me some degree of modesty. Not that I knew where Billy or Morrison were, and not, at the moment, that I particularly cared if everybody got an eyeful of Mostly Naked Joanne. I found my shredded sweater and nearly gave up on even trying to wear it, but shapeshifting, it turned out, didn't heal all wounds, and I was too tired and much too dull-witted to heal myself right then. I stripped my T-shirt off, wrapped it around the worst of my injuries, discarded another blown-out bra and yanked my sweater on. It wasn't quite as revealing as nudity, so I called it good and shoved around for my jeans.

They were in wretched condition, torn up from Morrison's antics at the theater, and then from me shifting in them again. But, like the sweater, they were slightly better than parading around naked. My shoes, at least, were unscathed, and I found the copper bracelet Dad had given me, though my glasses had disappeared entirely. Still, once dressed, I was afforded some degree of decency, which was about as much as I could ask for. Only then did I look around, trying to think what else needed to be done, now that the werewolf was neutralized.

It took a moment to realize there was no more fire. Smoke, yes, lots of it, but the fire itself had blown out. Not because of lack of oxygen, though given the cave's dimensions and the fire's size, that would've been my first guess. The way I wasn't lying on the floor choking for air, however, suggested something else had happened, and it seemed likely the something had been me. Even the wholly internal magic of shapeshifting had whooshed enough power over the room to almost obliterate the flames once. For all I knew, building my power circle—which still shimmered around the cave—had sucked up the fire's energy and converted it to something less harmful. Maybe Billy had a better idea of what had happened, or maybe I could reconstruct it once I sat down to clear my head. Either way, it fell under yet another thing I didn't have to worry about at that red-hot second, which was all that really mattered.

The wicker man was next. I sluffed back toward him with half-formed intentions of pulling his branches apart by hand if necessary, and arrived at one of his hollow thighs to find it unoccupied. That made no sense, so I went to the next one, which was empty, too. Not burned, not full of dead men, just a bit broken apart and empty. So, when I tilted my head back, were the cages and the wicker man's torso. I couldn't wrap my mind around that, but Tia was still screaming, which gave me something else to do. I crossed to her, crouched, and said, very gently, "If you don't shut up I'm going to disconnect your vocal cords, Tia."

My magic gave a disapproving thump that turned the world white with its emphaticness, but Tia didn't know that. When my vision cleared again she was enraged but silent. I patted her cheek and stood up, knowing I was a world-class asshole and absolutely, utterly unable to give a shit.

Billy, from about a million miles away, said, "Joanne?"

I turned around, waving my hands in the air to clear smoke, and the world began to resolve in a manner which made sense again. My partner was mooshed up against the boundary of my power circle, wolfy Morrison on one side of him and five goggle-eyed homeless guys on his other side. I should have known he'd deal with the rescue while I dealt with the werewolf. That was just basically the kind of person Billy was.

"We're stuck," Billy said cautiously. "Something's holding us in."

"That'd be me." I was a little afraid to bring the power circle down. I'd leeched magic from the very walls of the cavern to build it, and I was uncomfortably aware that the cave was a magical creation itself. I wasn't sure what would happen if I dissolved the circle, particularly with the way my power was exploding in and out. In theory, the circle's magic would just melt back from whence it came, but theory wasn't working out so well for me right now.

"I'm going to shield you," I said after a minute. "I think the shield will let you walk through the power circle unscathed. Then just get out of here, okay? I'll be right behind you."

Nobody on earth would believe that line, including my partner. He gave me a very hard look, but nodded. I pulled up my favorite pearlescent Star Trek style shield idea and wrapped all seven of them in it, whispering encouragement to the circle that while it was a keep-things-in circle, my magic could and should be let out. Then I nodded at Billy, who edged forward, rolling the shield with him. It bumped against the circle, which hesitated, sighed, and let him out. The five guys he'd rescued hurried after him.

Morrison, damn his wolf eyes, stayed. The shield popped around him as the others got farther away, and he just sat there, waiting, his expression patient.

"I can't change you back while we're down here, Morrison. I mean, I think right now I could, but you'd be naked."

His ears flattened and he looked at himself in such a Morrison-the-man way that I surprised myself with a laugh. "It's a long walk home, naked. You might as well go with them. Get Billy to drive home…" Not that Billy could, because he'd come downtown in Petite with me, and I was still in the round room beneath the lake with no absolute sure method of escape. "Okay, get Billy to call Gar…*shit*."

Morrison's tongue lolled out of his mouth, wolfish amusement, and he lay down where he was, obviously and irritatingly content to wait on me and whatever final dramatics I had up my sleeve. I groaned and finally turned back to Tia. "Well, what am I going to do with you."

Her face contorted in a furious sneer. "Kill me."

"Mmm. No. I'd have done that already if I was going to. Look, boss. For once I've actually caught the killer alive and well. I bet we can even get her up on kidnapping charges. Those guys Billy's helping sure saw her face. I don't see how we're going to make Naomi's and Lynn's murder charges stick, but we can probably manage attempted murder for what happened down here. The forensics team is going to hate this. Is it even our jurisdiction?" I was talking to hear myself, because Morrison couldn't answer and I didn't want Tia to. In fact, what I wanted was to keep talking until I was certain Billy and the men whose names I didn't know had gotten far enough away that I was sure bringing down the power circle couldn't hurt them.

That, however, had seemed like a better plan before Morrison decided to stick around. I was willing to risk my own neck, and even willing to risk Tia's, since I didn't like her very much, but Morrison was a different kettle of fish. Or pack of wolves. Something animal analogy, anyway. And I'd obviously run out of words, so I sighed, knelt at Tia's side and said, "C'mere, boss. I need you right beside me if this goes pear-shaped."

He got up, trotted over and lay back down again. I put one hand in his ruff and took Tia's hand with the other, building a shield around all three of us. A visible one, for once: I wanted Morrison to understand why he shouldn't go dashing off, and for him to be able to see the limits of where he could dash to if he was seized by an irresistible urge to do so. Though, really, that sounded much more like something I'd do than Morrison.

"This, Joanne," I said under my breath, "is procrastinating."

Very cautiously, I powered down the circle.

An unkindness of ravens exploded within the confines of my skull.

It wasn't my Raven: these were three, and they beat wing around a tall, slender, dark-haired woman who stood with her back to me. She wore midnight-blue robes: certainly nothing modern, which left her arms bare. *Strong* arms, both biceps banded with knotwork tattoos defining a curve of muscle that said whoever she was, she'd spent a lot of time at hard physical activity. A silver link circlet glittered against her hair, and when she turned toward me, I recognized it with a shock: it was my necklace, triskelions breaking apart silver tubes, with a delicate four-spoked power circle as its pendent/centerpiece.

And it was seated above a face which flashed from fresh-faced maiden to grim warrior to death's skull, each one glaring at me in expectant challenge.

The incessant fishhook tug in my belly turned to a fist, knotted around me and *yanked*.

CHAPTER THIRTY-ONE

SUNDAY, MARCH 19, 3:38 A.M.

I had to move. Fumbling around with my power, trying to find the most tentative, safe way to get Morrison, Tia and me out of there, was no longer an option, not with claws hauling me out of the chamber, out of the Underground, out of every last excuse I'd ever made up. I bent and scooped Tia into a fireman's carry, not sure how I'd get her through tight tunnels that way but damned certain I was not going to flop her gorgeous naked self over Morrison's furry back. She bellowed an objection that went abruptly silent when Morrison snapped his teeth half an inch from her nose.

Ravens kept beating at the inside of my head, making my vision flash white and overwhelming, but power called like to like, and we slipped through the circle I'd raised without it objecting. I kept my own shield up, but put Tia down to walk on her own, sandwiched between Morrison in the lead and me behind her. She tried once to bolt, and bounced off the shield so hard I expected to hear a clang. Morrison made a very human sound of amusement as she staggered back into line, and she didn't try that again. I let the circle fade once we were back in man-made territory, and all three of us stopped, hairs lifting on napes as the walls around us shuddered and rumbled. I felt the cavern—not exactly collapsing. Disappearing. Refilling, like the bits of world that had been taken away were finally returning. I wondered if Thunderbird Falls would still be there when we got out.

Rita waited for us in the stretch of Underground we'd paused in to borrow flashlights and recruit a small homeless army. Relief and joy already permeated her aura, but it redoubled when we appeared, and she dashed forward to hug me, despite my burden and my torn-up clothes. "Detective Holliday brought the guys topside so he could call an ambulance for them. He said he'd wait for you. Thank you, Detective Walker. Thank you so much. You—" Her voice went ragged and her hands fluttered, trying to make up for words that meant too much to speak.

I'd gotten pretty good at nonverbal communication lately, though, and interpreted the fluttering as "You came through for us against the odds." Trusting that was close enough to right, I pulled a little grin up for her. "You're welcome. And please, call me Joanne. I should be on a first-name basis with my streetwise eyes, right?"

That wonderful smile of hers lit up again. "Joanne."

Tia snarled, "Please. Can we just arrest me so I don't have to listen to this sentimental shit?"

I was happy enough to oblige. Rita led us back to the Persephone gate, more for the company than the necessity, and when we crawled out into a Seattle back lot, Billy was waiting for us. Alone: he had the good sense to be alone, which meant not having to explain the hundred-and-ninety-pound wolf who scrabbled out behind Rita. He put Tia in cuffs, and I went to get Petite while Morrison waited in the alley.

There was something appealing about having a giant silver wolf climb into Petite's limited back seat and stretch out. Not quite as appealing as a tuxedo-clad Morrison in the front seat would've been, but still, somehow it went straight to the emo twelve-year-old girl inside me. "It's about four in the morning," I said to his reflection in the rearview mirror. "I don't really want to wake the dance troupe up. I can bring you home and try shifting you back myself, or we can wait until a more reasonable hour and go see them then. Which do you want to do?"

Improved non-verbal communications or not, I'd clearly offered too many choices to a creature who couldn't actually talk. Morrison glowered at me in the mirror until I sighed. "Sorry. Home?"

He lay down, which I took as a yes, and drove us to his house, where, with an expression of great regret, Morrison nosed out a spare key—under a rock by the door, yes, but by the back door, and it proved to open a shed in the backyard rather than the house. The house key was in a small nail-filled box in a larger toolbox. I wisely did not say, "Christ, Morrison, any thief would just break a window anyway," and let us in the back door.

Morrison left me in the kitchen, his toenails clicking until he reached carpeted floors. Nosy and curious, I followed him as far as the living room before realizing he was going to a bedroom. I wobbled in place, curiosity warring with bravery, but being a chickenshit won out. It didn't matter: a few seconds later he emerged again, dragging a blanket which he managed to fling over himself quite tidily before looking at me with a certain amount of flat expectation.

"Ah. I take it we're not waiting on the dance troupe, then."

He cocked his head, conveying "No shit," although that wasn't a phrase I remembered Morrison using. Feeling a bit random, I said, "I need some of your ties," and went to get a handful, my shyness at entering his bedroom completely evaporated. He didn't stop me. He just watched, not growing even one whit more incredulous as I made a circle around him with the ties. Dogs did baffled very well, so I translated his unchanging expression as my behavior being par for the course. "Salt would probably make a fine circle barrier, too," I muttered in unasked-for explanation. "But it'd be a bitch to get out of the carpet, and the ties are invested with a sense of you as a man. Just don't cross out of the circle, okay?" I stepped within it myself, then lit it up with power: keep-things-in, keep-things-out. "Rattler?"

"She isss busssy today," my spirit guide responded in amusement. "Sso much help nessssesssssary." He was a thing of light and lines, but Morrison nearly startled out of his skin, suddenly on all fours with snapping teeth bared. I put a hand on his big furry shoulder, less surprised than I should have been that Rattler had appeared visibly to my boss. I'd called him up by name, out loud: that had to signify quite a lot to him, in terms of what I trusted Morrison with.

"It's been a rough day. I'll bring you gifts, don't worry." Raven liked shiny food. Rattler was more fond of, well. Snake food. Rats and rabbits. I wished he'd develop a taste for Pop-Tarts, but it didn't seem likely, so the pet store on the Way had been getting my business recently. They had pre-frozen snake food available, and Rattler, thank heavens, didn't seem to care if it was fresh or frozen. I didn't quite get how spirit animals managed to eat, or at least partake of, physical food anyway, but the arrangement was satisfactory on all sides, so I didn't worry about it too much. Either way, Rattler gave a satisfied hiss and wound his barely-corporeal self toward Morrison.

Who sat, ears flat against his head as he gave me a credible wolfy scowl, and then lay down with the air of one who would have words with me when this was over. Well, I needed to have words with him, too, and he probably wouldn't like them, so that was fine. My stomach jolted, fresh reminder of the insistent tugging within, and I knelt between my boss and my spirit animal, one hand extended toward each.

Even with all the fresh newborn Siobhán Walkingstick power flaring through me, it would have been easier with the dance troupe and their focused, deliberate shifting magic. It wasn't difficult to envision Morrison as a man—God knew I could call up his image in an instant, usually when I didn't want to—but pouring him from the wolf mold into the man mold simply took a long time. Rattler's presence was a calming thrum at the back of my mind, promising that caution was wise and the attempt would be effective for all its ponderousness. Morrison, unaware of that surety, lay there patiently, blue gaze never straying from my face as he slipped toward human. There were a handful of moments when he looked like a Hollywood special effect, flawlessly blurred between man and wolf, before very suddenly he was himself again.

I had never had occasion to greet someone who had spent several hours as a wild animal thanks to my screw-ups. I was still trying to figure out what to say when he got up, remarkably dignified for a man draped in a blanket, and went to find clothes.

Saved from having to address the topic of his shapeshifting, I mumbled, "I need to borrow your phone," to his retreating back, and did so without actually getting permission. He came back in jeans and a tank top like the one he'd worn in his garden just as I was hanging up. My brain slipped a notch and I stared at him in drawn-out silence, wondering just what that choice of wardrobe meant. Maybe everything. Maybe nothing. After a good solid minute of us both just standing there looking at one another, I decided somebody had better say *something*.

"I need some time off," was unquestionably the wrong thing to say, but my mouth said it anyway. Morrison's expression darkened and I pinched the bridge of my nose. "What I really mean is—"

"You don't have any time off, Walker."

Contrary to the end, I said, "Yeah, I do, a couple weeks. I still get my vacation, don't I? Even if—"

"Fine. Take it. Get out of my hair." He brushed by me, scowling, and went into the kitchen, where he began making a pot of coffee. If he was anyone else, I'd say he began slamming things around to make a pot of coffee, actually, but that would be far too emotional and temperamental for my boss.

I stomped after him. "Captain, listen to me. I—"

He growled, "I thought I said you could have your time off. What the hell do you need now?" in a credible wolf imitation.

I stuck my jaw out and stared at the ceiling, willing patience into my voice before I dared look at him again. "I don't know how long I'm going to be gone."

His nostrils flared. I mashed my lips together, glaring as he snapped, "Your mother dying again?"

I was going to kill him. That was new. Usually I figured

he was going to kill me. I snapped, "No, but maybe she's sending me messages from beyond the veil. You know. The usual," right back.

Flippancy was the wrong approach. Morrison started yelling. Overall, he probably had every right to: he'd had something of a bad night, and it could all be laid at my feet. I, however, just kept talking beneath the shouting. It wasn't that I had any expectation that he'd hear me. It just helped me not listen, which I didn't want to do. Eventually my explanation ran out, but Morrison's head of steam didn't. I sighed and said, "Captain," to no avail. After a few more seconds, I tried, "Boss?" but that went over like a raindrop in a thunderstorm, too, so I moved on to, "Morrison!"

It was like talking into outer space. His outrage swallowed anything I had to say, but if I waited for him to wind down on his own, I'd still be there an hour after I was supposed to be at the airport. I put my shoulders back, drew a deep breath and bellowed, *"Michael!"*

The silence that followed was so complete the coffee pot's sudden burble sounded like a jet engine exploding. Morrison gaped, florid color fading.

"What do you suppose we would do," I said conversationally, "if we ever had sex? I mean, what would we call each other? Captain and Walker? Morrison and Detective? Or would we just find excuses to not call each other anything?"

Morrison's eyes bugged. I couldn't decide if I wanted to shut up or if I was enjoying the left field my brain had gone out to. I hadn't been previously aware that I'd spent subconscious time on this subject, but given the way I was running off at the mouth, it seemed I had. "It's not that Michael isn't a nice name," I went on blithely. "It's just that you look like you're having an apoplectic fit at being called by it, and I can only remember you calling me by my given name once."

"*Siobhán.*"

The world went out from under my feet. When you live in the altered state of reality I'd gotten used to, that sort of phrase was dangerous to use, because it could be literally true. In this case, I was pretty sure it wasn't, but it sure felt like it. My knees went weak, my vision tunneled, and I felt all floaty, like Wile E. Coyote right before he noticed the road had been painted over thin air. I had to try twice to wet my lips, because someone'd taken sandpaper to my throat. "…I meant Joanne."

A very faint light of triumph glittered in Morrison's eyes, and the brief smile he offered made my stomach turn into a round stone of alarm before it sank toward my still-floaty feet. I could feel the color Morrison had lost starting to flood my own face, and now I wished very much that I'd shut up a long time ago. Possibly years ago. Morrison left the counter to come stand toe to toe with me. I had shoes on and he was in stocking feet, so I had a slight height advantage, but I seemed to have forgotten how to breathe. Morrison didn't appear to be having that problem. I thought it was probably a bad sign for the home team that the competition was still breathing when all signs pointed toward me being dead. On the other hand, dead had to be better than standing there in Morrison's kitchen working up to enough heat for self-immolation.

"Overlooking," Morrison said from about three inches away, and so quietly a fly on the wall wouldn't be able to hear a thing, "the sheer inappropriateness of this conversation, I try to leave work at work as much as possible. I prefer to be called Michael in bed. Was there another point to this discussion, Detective Walker?"

I couldn't blush any harder, but there was one worse thing I could do. My eyes betrayed me, filling with stinging tears. I told myself it was embarrassment, which was true, and that it wasn't gut-wrenching disappointment at the rebuke ending in my formal title instead of my name, which was so patently untrue I didn't think anybody in the entire universe would believe it. I rolled my jaw forward until the joint hurt, trying to counter emotional pain with the much, much less agonizing sensation of physical pain, and averted my gaze.

That was a mistake. Moving my eyes made the tears spill over. I bit my tongue until I tasted blood instead of letting myself lift a hand to wipe them away. Maybe Morrison wouldn't notice, if I didn't draw attention to them. Maybe a meteor would smash through the ceiling and end my humiliation, too. I wasn't counting on either.

My throat was so tight that the words I forced out actually hurt, thin scrapings in the air. "I'm sure there's paperwork I could fill out for a sabbatical or a leave of absence, but any way you look at it I effectively took one of those eighteen months ago when my mother died, so I figure I'm probably screwed in that department." The unfortunate choice of words hit me a little too late, but since ritual suicide sounded like a better option than trying to correct myself, I just kept talking. "I've got to go to Ireland. I don't know how long I'm going to be gone, and I don't even know what I'm going to be like when or if I come back. So what I'm really trying to say, Captain, is that you win. You win. I quit."

"Well, thank goddamned God," Morrison said, and took my face in both hands to guide me into a kiss.

On a list of Things Joanne Was Expecting, that one hadn't even been penciled in. In the unlikely event it had, I would have imagined it as the possessive, frustrated kiss that impatient film noir heroes give the aggravating women of their dreams.

Morrison kissed me like he was apologizing for making me cry. Thumbs on my cheeks, brushing tears away over the thin scar, and he traced that scar like it meant I was fragile. His mouth was warm and soft and tasted a little bit like coffee, but once I'd noticed those things I didn't seem to be able to quantify anything anymore, and besides, the floor had fallen out from under my feet again. I really thought I might be floating, so wrapping my legs around his waist seemed like a very sensible thing to do.

One or the other of us ran out of air before I got that far, though, and we broke apart, me with an astonished gasp and Morrison with that glimmer of satisfaction in his eyes again. I wet my lips two or three times and searched for something more intelligent to say than, "Buh," and Morrison's grin turned first sly, then slightly embarrassed. The embarrassment gave me something to hang my hat on, and I squeaked, "Speaking of sheer inappropriateness?"

"I'm—"

I clapped my hand over his mouth. "I swear to God, Morrison, if you say *I'm sorry* I will break your nose." I thought I was more likely to knee him in the crotch, but men never think that threat is funny. Broken noses, funny. Bruised dangly bits, not funny. Morrison's eyes crinkled a little and he took my hand away from his mouth to reveal a crooked smile.

See?

The smile fell away, though, and he put his thumb into the palm of my hand. I curled my fingers around it, like we were about to begin waltzing. "I don't want you to quit, Joanie."

"Don't." My voice shot up to a strangled register and I forced it back down. "Don't you even dare start calling me Joanie now, Morrison. That is not fair." My hand had tightened around his, hard enough to make my fingers ache. "Really? You mean that?"

Morrison pulled his lips back from his teeth, brief expression of frustration. "Yeah, I do. You're turning into a decent cop, Walker. I never thought I'd say it, but you're doing a good job."

A knot I hadn't known was there suddenly unraveled in my heart, sending sprays of light along a vision of a cracked windshield that flashed before my eyes. I could all but hear the glass crackling and fusing back together, sunshine heating it into something strong and whole again. When the flare of brilliance faded, there was still a vicious shatter-spot in the windshield, a hole punched almost all the way through, with spiderwebs of dark, injured glass radiating out from it.

But for the first time since I'd seen that windshield when I lay dying in a garden of my own mind, there was more whole glass than damaged. I laughed, a surprised little sound, and put my forehead against Morrison's shoulder like it was the natural thing to do. "Thanks, Captain. Thank you. That means more to me than I know how to tell you."

"You're still quitting, aren't you."

I nodded against his shoulder and he put his mouth against my hair. "Thank goddamned God," he said again. "I should've said resignation accepted before I kissed you."

"I'll consider not suing."

He chuckled and tightened his hand around mine. "We need to talk, Walker."

I backed up enough to give him a sloppy half smile. "About the elephant in the room, sir?"

Morrison looked pained. "Considering how long it took to get you to start calling me sir, I hate to think how long it's going to take to get you to stop. Yeah," he said more quietly and more seriously. "About the elephant in the room. We've been dancing around it a long damned time."

"Yeah. We have been. Well. I knew I had been." I let out another breath of laughter and closed my eyes a moment. "No wonder you were so pissed off about Mark Bragg. That makes me feel better. Shit, Captain. It's always been you. Didn't you know that?" I didn't know why he should have. It took me ages to figure it out.

"No." He shrugged, small motion. "I didn't. Between Ed Johnson and you taking the promotion to detective, and your damned mentor—"

"Coyote," I said softly. "Yeah, that was...but no. That's not going to work for me. There's...too much give, there."

Morrison spread his hand without letting go of mine. "And that cab driver of yours—"

"*Gary?*" I flung my hands up and stepped back, laughter mixed with outrage. "What is it with everybody thinking I've got something going on with Gary? He's seventy-four years old! He could be my grandfather! I love him, but come on! God! If I had half the sex life you people think I do, I'd—I'd get laid a lot more." Oh, yes, that was me, mistress of witty repartee.

Morrison's voice dropped about two octaves. "If you'd like to write a letter of resignation, that's a topic I'd like to address in some detail."

A blush that started somewhere around my navel—or possibly several inches lower—crept up to my cheeks. I covered my face with my hands, feeling like a glowbug, and sighed. "I can write the letter, but this conversation and...everything else…is going to have to wait. I've got to go to the airport. My flight is in two hours."

"What?" Good humor drained out of Morrison's expression, leaving something more vulnerable and bereft than I'd expected. Regret lanced through me and I bit my bottom lip.

"I'm leaving. When I said I had to go to Ireland, I meant right now. I've got this sick knot in my stomach yanking me that way. I've got to go. I need you to go see Jim Littlefoot this afternoon and tell the troupe they're safe now, okay? Please. I would, but—"

He ignored the request, which I knew didn't mean he hadn't heard it, or that he wouldn't do it. What he said, though, in a low voice, was, "You have a real knack for running away from things, Walker."

A whole new kind of pain replaced regret: anger, sharpened with the discomfort of knowing how right my boss—former boss—was. "I know. I know, and that's why I've got to go. There are things there I've been running away from a lot longer than I've been running from this." I made a little circle with my hand, encompassing the both of us. "I'll come back, Michael. I just don't know when."

"If you don't," Morrison said in a low rumble, "I'm coming after you, Walker."

I managed a quick smile. "I'm counting on it, sir."

Morrison reached up to brush his thumb over the scar on my cheek again, then let his hand drop as he nodded toward the door. "All right. Go. Get out of here. I don't want to see you again until you've got this thing settled." Familiar gruffness filled his voice, but for once I wasn't fooled. I stepped forward to steal one brief, hard kiss, then bolted for the door before I could say anything to mess the moment up.

Two minutes later I was on the road, my heart still

hammering until it made my stomach sick. I had to get to Ireland because of the pull I'd felt, because of the women I'd seen in my visions, and because of one other thing I hadn't told Morrison. Something I was going to need help with, help that neither he nor anybody else I knew could provide.

Help finding a cure, because I'd been bitten by a werewolf.

★ ★ ★ ★ ★

Tune in next time for
RAVEN CALLS
Book Seven of THE WALKER PAPERS

Acknowledgments

My editor Mary-Theresa Hussey, to whom SPIRIT DANCES is dedicated, deserves a particular shout-out this time around. I made Matrice crazy by sending her the final scene in this book years before the rest of it was written, and she's been waiting for it ever since. I hope it was worth the wait. :) (*Editor's note: Yes! Finally! And where's the next one?!*)

The rest of the usual suspects know who you are: the Word Warriors, who helped me get this book finished with literally days to spare before my son was born, Jennifer Jackson, Agent Extraordinaire, Paul "Beta-Reader" Knappenberger, and my husband, Ted, without whom I wouldn't be doing any of this. You're all my heroes.

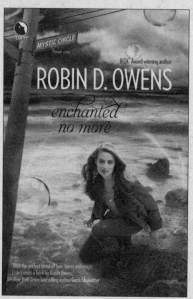

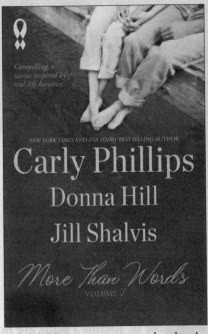

THIS NEXT CASE
IS *WAY* OUT OF HER JURISDICTION....

From acclaimed author
C. E. MURPHY

Seattle police detective
Joanne Walker started the
year mostly dead, and she's
ending it trying not to be
consumed by evil. She's
proven she can handle the

ller?

e,

Trou
abou
to th

c
s
al

A

!